SPARK SOLO

SPARK SOLO

CARRIE J EVANS

Published by Iristotle.
www.iristotle.com
First Iristotle printing: 2024

IRISTOTLE and Iristotle logo are registered trademarks of Iristotle Holdings LLC

ISBN: 979-8-9887066-0-1 (Hardcover)

ISBN: 979-8-9887066-1-8 (Paperback)

ISBN: 979-8-9887066-2-5 (Digital)

ISBN: 979-8-9887066-3-2 (Audio)

Cover design by Carrie J. Evans

LCCN: 2023917002

Published in the United Stated of America
10 9 8 7 6 5 4 3 2 1

This book is for my mothers:

*For my biological mother, D, who gave me a
strong emotional and educational foundation
and taught me how to have lifelong friendships.*

*For my godmother, B, who taught
me how to show up as a human and a young woman.*

*For my Aunt Q who is constantly teaching
me to listen to and live by my knowing.*

*For my Aunt A who has taught me to live
with kindness, gratitude and style.*

*It's also for my friends, Belinda, Reiko, Jennifer,
Adrienne, and David, who patiently supported
me throughout the process of writing this book.*

And for my dear friend Tracy.

1

―――――――

BLIND DATE
FRIDAY, AUGUST 4

IT WAS FRIDAY EVENING, and I'd finally settled into my house. It was a wonderful space with four bedrooms. I was pretty sure I had the intended living room set up as my den and the intended den set up as my office. I chose warm colors, creams and rusts, for the common areas and cool blues for the bedrooms. Except for the kitchen where the floor was tiled, the floors were a lightly stained hardwood. The furniture throughout was rustic wood. I was going for warm, cozy, and functional. For the first time in a long time, I felt like I could relax and be at peace.

That evening, I was going on a blind date with Michael, the brother of my best friend Arielle, or Ari, as she preferred to be called. They are twins who were both put up for adoption and had recently become acquainted. After a conversation with her adoptive mother, in which Ari found out he existed, she became obsessed with finding him. Two months before, she'd succeeded. They were born here in LA. Michael was happy to make contact with her. Two weeks after that, she'd flown out from New York, where she lived, to meet him in person in LA. Together, they located their birth records and spent a few days getting to know each other. I didn't get to meet him then because I was in New York directing a shoot. Ari met his adoptive family. She thought his mother and brother were kind and impressive. I think he hung out with her once after that in

1

New York. Ari really liked Michael. She said he was charming and genuinely seemed to like women.

My legal separation from my legitimately angry husband, Greg, had been made official a few days before, and I'd filed to convert it to a divorce earlier that day. My primary goal was to get Greg to agree to a settlement that wouldn't dismantle everything I'd built and get it finalized. To achieve that, I had to lie low, avoid arguments with him, and give him time to accept that our marriage was over.

Ari wanted me to celebrate that milestone by getting back on the market. Being on the market was the last thing on my list. I just wanted to spend some time being by myself. I needed to find friends and build up my support network. That was my second goal. However, all the way from New York, she'd set up this date with her brother—drinks, dinner, and dancing—despite my goals and without my permission. She said that Michael and I had that "dance thing" in common. He was a professional, the principal male dancer for the Torus Contemporary Ballet Company, which was based in LA.

I'd diffuse things immediately by saying we should aim at being friends. Maybe I'd at least get someone I could talk technique with out of this. One thing was certain: if he was doing this for her, he was kind and patient.

I dressed in jeans, a simple but artsy designer shirt, and some strappy but comfortable sandals, in case things went well and we ended up dancing. I was playing it sexy in an understated way.

My doorbell rang, and I opened the door. *Okay. Okay.* The pictures Ari sent me were all headshots. I knew he had a pretty face, but I wasn't properly prepared for the whole package. He was gorgeous. He was tall, maybe six feet four inches, slim, and muscular—dancer muscular—well-defined but not bulky. I consciously suppressed a deep inhale, smiled politely, and casually looked directly into his eyes so that my gawking remained my secret. "Hello, Michael."

"Nice to meet you, Sammi," he said as he offered his hand.

I put my hand in his. He had long graceful fingers, and his grip was firm but gentle. "Same. Come in for a moment. I'll get my purse." I stepped aside, motioning for him to enter.

"Of course." He gave my hand a gentle squeeze before letting it go and walking into my house.

He was wearing jeans and a nice shirt with a stylish pair of loafers. I really appreciated the way he was working his jeans. *Man.* The place where his obliques met his hip bones was probably too much to handle. I could see he had a tattoo on each arm, but I couldn't tell of what because his sleeves were hiding most of them. It made me wonder how he looked shirtless. I lifted my eyes to the level of his as he turned around, then glanced away, as our eyes made contact again, to close the door. "I don't know if you've realized it yet, but your sister is a piece of work."

He chuckled. "I'm starting to understand that."

"What did she tell you about me?"

"Not much. She said that she has known you her whole life and that you're her best friend. And we have that 'dance thing' in common. What did she say about me?"

"About the same. She's still getting to know you. So far, you seem pretty nice. And we have the 'dance thing' in common." He smiled and I returned it. He did seem nice. After a beat, I said, "I know that Ari planned this evening as a date and placed us in it, but I don't want to go that route. Given that she's my best friend and you're her recently located, long-lost brother, I'd really like us to be friends. So can we just hang out and get to know each other on that level, okay?" *I delivered that pretty well.*

He half smiled, pursed his lips, and tilted his head slightly. "Okay." He had nice lips, and I was pretty sure he was laughing at me.

I needed a moment to get a little perspective. "I'm gonna use the ladies' room, then I'll be ready to go. Make yourself at home. There's sparkling water in the fridge."

"Okay. Thanks."

Once in the bathroom, I looked at myself in the mirror. It had been a minute since I'd been in the game. I liked the game, and I still had it. I adjusted my hair. I was wearing it out, a kinky-curly mane. I decided on red lipstick instead of nude. I hadn't prepared to deal with a pretty boy ego. I don't know why I didn't anticipate he'd be fine. He looked like what I'd expect Ari's brother would look like. He had creamy high yellow skin, big brown eyes, and dark brown, almost black, mixed kid hair, just like Ari. His hair wasn't as curly as hers though. They both had nice, perfectly rounded noses with beautifully shaped lips and high cheekbones, like people from West Africa. And his body was banging. I wondered if he'd put all his eggs in the "I'm hot as hell" bucket. Well, my bet was he was either incapable of having an actual conversation or his ego was the size of Everest. Whichever, at that moment, I was about the fishing, not the catching. I needed to get out of the net I was in. I had no intention of getting into another one anytime soon.

Maybe I could screw him before we settled into the friendship phase. My bet was that he was a player, which would make him the perfect prospect for a casual encounter. I located the condoms I'd bought for just such an opportunity. I put them in my purse, just in case. *Shit.* It hit me that I was horny. I hadn't had a thought like that in a good while. I needed to slow my roll—but I was bringing the condoms. I took a deep breath. I knew how to deal with pretty boys.

"Would you like to use the facilities?" Yep, he was sexy.

"Nope. I'm good." He had his back to me, so I could really take him in.

"We're ready to go then. Do you know where any of the places where Ari booked us are?"

He turned to face me. "Yeah. They're not too far from where I live. Ari asked me for options."

Hmmm. Well, he'd probably just rattled them off from in his head. "I'll drive my car, so if things go really wrong—"

He choked down a laugh as he interrupted me. "I think we'll be okay. I'll drive. No matter what happens, I'm sure I'll be fine with bringing you home."

"Are you laughing at me?"

"I am." He grinned. He stepped aside and motioned toward the door. "After you."

I didn't expect him to be honest. I didn't know what to say and found myself grinning too. I shook my head and headed for the door.

He was driving a BMW 4 Series coupe.

"So you like cars?" What I really wanted to ask was how he was driving this car on a dancer's salary.

He responded, "Some of them," as we got in.

As he was driving to Ari's first place, he asked, "Are you from here?"

"No. I'm from Atlanta. After college, I met a boy and decided to stay with him out here in California."

"And that didn't work out?"

"Nope. But I like California. So, for now, I'm staying. How about you?"

"I grew up here. I've traveled some but have never had the urge to move anywhere else."

"Did you go to college?"

"Yep. Caltech." He smiled and glanced at me. He arched one of his eyebrows.

"Really?"

"I studied chemistry." He was still smiling, pleased with himself.

He had a brain to go with his beauty. And he'd used it. *Okay.* "So how did you end up dancing professionally?"

"Dancing was always my passion. I got an opportunity to audition. I was accepted and have never looked back. What did you study in college?"

"Engineering undergrad. Fine arts masters."

"Where?"

"Georgia Tech then NYU."

He nodded in assessment. "So what're you doing now?"

"Directing and producing. Mostly film. Some television."

"So where does dance come in?"

"I used dance to keep me sane and focused. It was my escape in college and how I got the energy to get through school."

He nodded. "So on some level, you're a geek?"

"Yes, pot." I smiled and wondered if my humor would make sense to him.

He chuckled out loud and responded, "Okay, kettle." He was just as corny as I was.

We walked into the cheese and wine shop where Ari had booked us for drinks and chose a flight of wine and cheese. The conversation flowed easily.

"Since Ari and you went to all the trouble to arrange this elaborate date, I think we should toast the occasion that prompted it."

"Which is?" he asked.

"Ari didn't tell you anything? Really?"

"No. She asked me if I was free on Friday. When I said yes, she asked me if I'd take you out." He half smiled. "She said I could consider it a mercy date." He quickly covered his mouth.

I narrowed my eyes and gave him the finger.

He held up his hands and said, "I'm kidding. I'm kidding."

I stayed silent for a moment to let the discomfort hang a little. Then I said, "We're celebrating the fact that I filed for divorce today. This 'mercy date' is her attempt to get me back on the market." I raised my glass. "Here's to letting bygones be bygones."

We clinked glasses.

"So this is the same guy that you stayed out here to be with?"

"Yep." I pursed my lips and stared at my hands. I felt a little sad about things not working out with Greg, but more than that, I was really going to miss spending time with his family, especially his mother and her sister. I guess it was obvious because Michael looked at a loss as to how to respond. I put the focus on him. "So are you dating? Are you serious about anyone?"

"No." One word; then he fell silent.

I coaxed him. "So have you had any serious relationships? Or do you just play the field?"

He took a deep breath, as if considering. Then he said, "A bit of both, actually," and stopped talking again.

I hunched my shoulders and shook my head. "And?"

He looked at me as if he'd just realized something. He was trying not to smile. "I was in a really serious relationship my last two years in college. When I decided to dance professionally instead of pursuing a career in science, she ended it. She said she needed someone with a real career. Since then, I've been playing the field for the most part. I was with another person for a year or so, but that was never gonna work out."

"So two years, huh?"

"Yeah. You?"

"Nothing really serious until I got married. We were together a little over two years, married one and a half of them." I paused. He was sexy. Given that he'd given himself the space in this culture to dance ballet, I wondered where he was on the sexual spectrum. The question "Do you date men?" came out unfiltered.

He smiled slightly again. "No, I date only women." He gave me a pensive look. "Why did you ask that question now? It's a little forward."

I hunched my shoulders. "You're male and a dancer in a contemporary ballet company. I figured it would be a question you get all the time. It's commonplace in the dance community."

"True." He shook his head and laughed a little.

"What's so funny?"

He gave me a quick glance. "There was a time when I would've kicked your ass for asking me that question." He chuckled.

"Why? There's nothing wrong with being gay or bisexual."

"I agree. However, when you're a straight, adolescent male who's trying to establish his sexuality, you defend it in the most demonstrative way you can: by kicking the ass of the questioner and then taking his girl."

I was sure that being a beautiful male had made it that much worse. "So it happened often?"

"Yeah. I kicked a lot of asses."

We drifted into easy conversation and realized we were running late for Ari's next destination.

By the end of dinner, we were having fun. When the check came, I reached for it, saying, "Let me get this. You've been so gracious to go through with this 'mercy date' situation that your sister put you in."

"No, it's fine. I've got it."

I shook my head. "Come on, now."

He paused and took in the fact that I was serious. "Fair enough. Let's split it."

"Okay."

"Okay."

As we got into his car, he asked, "Are you up for dancing? Or do you want this 'mercy date' to be over?"

I chuckled. He was asking me if I wanted to stop staring at him —if I wanted to forgo a chance to feel him up on the dance floor. I was cool. So I said, "I love to dance. I'm always up for dancing. That's not logically a question, as far as I'm concerned."

He smiled. "I can relate. I know of a really good dance party that's happening tonight. It's hip-hop. Are you okay with that?"

I shook my head. "I don't see how that's a question either?"

He smiled. "Good." After a breath, he said, "The dance party is on me." He glanced at me to see my reaction.

I shook my head and tried to think of something witty to say.

When he could wait no longer, he said, "I can get us in free." He was proud of that corny-ass response and went into an all-out fit of laughter and posturing. It was obvious he felt as comfortable as I did.

I kept shaking my head and took it in. *Yes*, I thought, *at the very least, I'll get a friend out of this.*

As WE EXITED the coat check, which I insisted he pay for, and walked into the main area of the club, it was clear that we were on his playground. Given the looks I was getting from other women, I didn't think he usually arrived with a date. I was careful to give him space —enough so that most of the women didn't see me as an obstacle. It wasn't a "date-date" after all. It made me wonder if he had a reputation for callousness. At one point, we got separated when one of his fans swooped in. Clearly, he could have gotten laid that night whether I chose to jump him or not. He didn't even have to ask. I hung back a bit to take in the spectacle. When he realized I was no longer by his side, he looked around and spotted me behind him. He hunched his shoulders and gave me a confused look, motioning for me to join him, which earned me some sharp stares.

When I caught up to him, he asked, "Do you still want to dance? Why did you stop walking with me?" He was so used to that treatment that he was oblivious.

Yes. Definitely a player. I chuckled and said, "I got cut off by one of your fans. So I decided to enjoy the show."

He pursed his lips and smiled. Then he nodded his head and said, "Come on; let's dance."

He could move. We went at it step for step, song after song. It was timeless. He was fun to dance with. He wasn't clingy and domineering like some men. He didn't have a need to direct my movements. We made contact, but it wasn't inappropriately intimate. Dancing together was even easier than conversation. I was thinking,

Oh, shit, because I was really turned on. He was kind and silly—and intelligent. Up to that point, it seemed that he had his ego in check. He was good at the game.

Two hours after we hit the dance floor, we were both drenched. He said, "Let's get something to drink. What would you like?"

"A Syrah if they have it." The thought, *Can I trust him not to put something in my drink?* flitted across my mind. He was Ari's brother, and he seemed to value that relationship. So I pushed it aside.

"Cool, I'll get it. Sit here. This is my favorite spot to watch the crowd from." He looked at his phone as he walked away. I wondered who was trying to get in touch with him.

I looked at my phone, which had buzzed a few times in the past two hours. There were texts from Sylvia, my mom. As usual, she'd written essays I'd have to read later. I was sure she just wanted to know where things stood. I responded in a quick text. "The separation is official. Divorce papers are filed. I'm out having fun. Talk to you tomorrow. Love."

When he came back, I asked, "Were the drinks free too, or do you need help covering them?"

He narrowed his eyes and gave me the finger.

It was all I could do not to say, *With pleasure.* But I was cool. So I just laughed and imitated the posturing he did earlier.

He narrowed his eyes a bit more and focused on the glasses of wine.

I asked, "What's up?"

"I don't know which is mine and which is yours. Do you mind if I taste both of them?"

"No. Go ahead."

He tasted one and then the other. He set a glass in front of me. "This one is yours." He kept looking at it.

"You're not sure, are you?"

He laughed and shook his head. "Nope. Not at all."

"Let me try. Do you mind?

"Of course not."

I tasted both. I gave him a serious look. "You got it backward. This one is definitely yours." I switched glasses.

He smiled. "I'm positive that you're wrong." He tasted and switched them again. We played that game a few more times. Ultimately, we ended up sharing the two glasses of wine and giggling until we settled into a comfortable silence.

A slow song came on. He offered his hand and said, "May I?"

I put my hand in his and followed him to the dance floor. Finally, I got to touch him. I put my hands on his shoulders, and he rested his on my lower back. All the muscles in his shoulders were clearly articulated. The slow set lasted awhile, and we relaxed into each other a bit. My cheek was resting just above his defined, but not overly developed, chest, and I felt comfortable putting my hands just above his hips. He had that wonderfully sexy furrow between his hip bones and obliques. Soon, I was thinking about the dimples in his lower back and the goody trail on his sculpted abdomen. I shook my head to bring myself back to reality. I was glad he couldn't see my face.

He said, "I'm hungry. Would you be up for grabbing something to eat?"

"Sure."

"Good, let's go." He took my hand and led me from the dance floor. He glanced back. "I think you're beautiful, by the way." He kissed my knuckles.

I was sure he'd made that move a thousand times. He was good. I had no complaints as I followed him out of the club like all of those who had gone before me. "Thank you. I feel the same about you." I knew he was smiling, but he'd earned it. I was right. He was the perfect person to sleep with casually. Maybe I could end up with a friend and a fuck buddy.

WE FINISHED our snack and leaned on the side of his car to look at the moon and the ocean. While holding my hand, he said, "I guess I should take you home now. Did you have fun?"

"Yes, you?" I was a little tired, but I was having fun.

"Me too. This is the best 'mercy date' I've ever had."

In response, I pushed him playfully. He pulled me into his arms, looking shocked by his own reaction. We both stood there, wrapped in each other's arms, motionless. I wasn't sure who moved first, but we kissed. A short, sweet, chaste kiss. He closed his eyes and shook his head. I cleared my throat.

He stepped back. "We should go."

"Yes."

We got into his car. He took my hand, kissing my knuckles absentmindedly, and said, "I like the way you dance. I want to do this again soon."

I followed suit by taking his other hand. "I'd like that." I kissed his knuckles softly.

Then we were exchanging tender kisses that deepened ever so slowly. When we came up for air, I wasn't sure how we'd ended up kissing so deeply. I lost myself in his kisses. I couldn't remember the last time that happened. I felt an intense connection between us. I wasn't sure why, but I asked, "You live near here, don't you?"

He looked at me for a moment. "Yeah." He released my hand and pulled out of the parking spot. The next thing I knew, we were parked in what I assumed was his driveway.

"This is not what I meant," I said.

"I know. Do you want me to take you home?"

"No."

"Good." He got out of the car. I sat there, motionless. Suddenly, I wasn't sure if I could fuck him casually. He opened the car door for me, and I followed him into his house. "Do you want something to drink or anything?" he asked.

His den was a nice size. His furniture was all dark leather and wood, the floor darkly stained wood. He had interesting artwork on the walls, and everything was nice. It was worn in, like he had used the room. It felt like a home.

I wandered over to his fireplace and gazed at the picture above the mantle. When I turned around, he was right in front of me. He was as smooth as he was pretty. I'd have to play this game carefully so we could stay friends. I reached out and gently brushed his top lip with my thumbs. I softly kissed him there. He responded by placing his hands on the sides of my face and tenderly kissing my bottom lip. He deepened the kiss, his tongue dancing with mine, and he stepped forward to pin me between him and the fireplace. I caressed his shoulders and took in how well-defined his muscles were: traps, pecs, the ripples of his abdomen. I followed the line of his pants across his lower abdomen, across the furrow between his obliques and hip bones. I skimmed my hands down to the bottom of his butt. As I raised them, I grabbed on. He responded by pushing his hips forward and firmly pressing his erection into my abdomen. I moaned into his kiss. He paused and smiled on my mouth. As I tried to catch my breath, he trailed tender kisses over to my ear and along my jawline. His hands moved across my collarbones and down to my breasts. I felt him smile on my neck before skimming his hands down my abdomen and pausing on my hips. He slipped his fingers under the hem of my shirt.

Leaning back so he could look in my eyes, he asked, "May I?"

I looked at him incredulously. "No, I'm standing here grabbing your ass and grinding on you because I want to go home."

He looked at me and didn't move.

I took a deep breath and shook my head. "Yes, you may."

He chuckled and bit my jaw as he lifted my shirt and unfastened my bra. As he skimmed my nipples with his thumbs, he parted my lips with his tongue and caressed my tongue softly in the same rhythm. I grabbed his tongue with my teeth, lifted my leg up around his hip, and pushed my hips into his as I pulled him toward me. After tilting his head back and moaning loudly, he lowered his head and took my left nipple into his mouth. He intensified the gentle caress of my right nipple into a rolling pinch and matched that touch with his tongue and teeth on my left nipple. I leaned my head back and enjoyed the sensation. I thought to myself, *Okay. So I am doing this.* I took a deep breath, and my insides clenched. "Shit, Michael." I breathed as I erupted into an orgasm. He stood up, and I hugged him to steady myself as the world went out of focus for a few seconds.

When I opened my eyes, he said, "You're very responsive" and kissed my forehead. He leaned back and took the button to my jeans in his hands. "May I?"

I gathered my thoughts and tried to catch my breath. I'd never come like that before. *Okay. Okay. What was I trying to think about? Oh, yeah. We need to talk before we go all the way.* "When's the last time you were tested?"

"Two weeks ago. All clear. I haven't been with anyone since then. You?"

"A while ago. I was faithful to my soon-to-be ex-husband. We haven't been physical for a long time."

He kissed my nose. "So you're a little horny, then." He glanced down at his hands, which were resting on the button of my jeans. "May I?"

Right. He knew he was doing wrong. I shook my head. I wanted to say, *Obviously, I'm not enjoying myself, so I want to go home,* but I remained silent and narrowed my eyes at him.

He smiled, kissed my forehead, and said, "I need your permission."

Fucker. I gave in. "You may."

He chuckled. "Are you sure?"

I shook my head and gave him the finger.

With that, he smiled triumphantly. "With pleasure."

He unbuttoned and unzipped my pants and pulled my pants and panties down in one fluid motion. He had to stop when he got to my ankles because I still had on my sandals. I laughed as he fumbled to unfasten them. As he stood, he lifted me so I was sitting on his mantle. Instinctively, I started to close my legs, but he caught them, placed them over his shoulders, and pushed them further apart.

"Man," he said as he looked at my most private part. He caressed the full length of my sex. He opened me and moaned as he slipped his thumb inside of me. He kissed my belly button and started a trail of kisses toward my clitoris. He planted a tender kiss and blew. "Are you really sure?"

I sent daggers from my eyes.

"Understood." He started a slow, sweet caress with his tongue. As I mounted, he slipped two fingers inside of me to caress my G-spot.

I don't think I've ever had both types of orgasms at once. My body erupted into the powerful waves of a spasm. A strange sounding, "Arrgh," was all I could say. He stood and passionately kissed me. I opened to the full force of his offering.

"Wrap your legs around me." I complied and he picked me up. I was still in the throes of my double orgasm. I didn't open my eyes to see where we were going. He sat me down on his bed and said,

"You don't need this," as he removed my shirt and bra. I still hadn't opened my eyes. He stepped away.

Once I was feeling a little more grounded, I looked to see where he'd gone. He'd already taken off his shirt and shoes and was in the process of removing his pants and boxer briefs. Full-frontal Michael. He had amazing legs, and his feet were calloused but beautiful. His toes were made for sucking. And then, there was the jewel. As if he could hear my thoughts, he started to stroke himself as he sauntered back over to me. He still hadn't given me a reason to guard against him. The possibilities were overwhelming. He kneeled between my legs and stopped stroking himself only long enough to push my legs further apart as he moved forward.

"Are you on the pill?"

"Yes."

"Do you want to use a condom? It would shield some of the intimacy." He leaned forward and kissed my chin.

I was surprised by the question. "You feel it too?"

"Yes."

"I don't think it would be much of a shield."

"Me neither." As he kissed me tenderly, he eased into me. His breath caught.

The pressure of him was intense. He picked me up a little to move us to the middle of the bed and laid me back. With his eyes on mine, he eased out of me and back in a few times. When I relaxed a bit, he pulled my left leg up around his hip. He slipped in a bit deeper and I gasped. Reflexively, my hands moved to his hips.

"Are you okay?" He paused.

"Yes, just, it's been a while."

"Okay. Just relax and enjoy this." He kissed my nose.

He positioned himself on top of me, making full contact with my body but holding his own weight. Ripples ran through my body, and I moaned a little. Then, as commanded, I relaxed and let my body respond in a sensual but metered way appropriate for a casual encounter. He let out a hiss and added a swivel to the in and out motion, a slow, gentle waltz rhythm. He was pulling me back toward orgasm ever so slowly. His eyes were barely open, and he was growling deep in his throat. I didn't know how much more I could take, and that sound tipped me over. He came with me—loudly.

"Shit." He collapsed, giving me his full weight. He was heavier than he looked. When our breathing returned to normal, he eased out of me.

I gasped again.

"Are you okay?" he asked again, raising his eyebrows.

"Yeah. I'm just ..."

"... really sensitive," he finished my sentence.

"Yeah, right now." I was slowly slipping into my postcoital coma.

"Will you stay with me tonight?"

"You mean the rest of the morning. It's at least 4 a.m. Yeah," I whispered. It wasn't like I was about to get up. I didn't have the energy to shake my head.

"Good. That was amazing."

"Hey."

"What?"

"You didn't ask permission."

"Oh, shit. You're right." He chuckled. "May I?"

"Maybe."

"Okay, let me know when you're sure." He snuggled up behind me and kissed my ear as I drifted off.

I woke up to the sun shining brightly on my face. Michael had wrapped his body around me from behind, one of his legs threaded through mine. We hadn't moved much since I'd fallen asleep. His scent. His embrace. I liked it. I was going to have to work harder than I anticipated to keep this casual. Then again, given the reactions I'd observed at the club the prior night, he was a player, which meant I could just be cool and let his game run its course.

2

MORNING

SATURDAY, AUGUST 5

As I opened my eyes, he leaned down to kiss the corner of my mouth. He was smooth, really smooth.

"Good morning." He trailed his hand down my arm and entwined our fingers. "How did you sleep?"

"Really well. You?" I shifted a little so I could look at him easily, becoming aware he had a raging erection. It was pushing against my thighs. It seemed he'd been waiting for me to wake up.

His hips pushed forward reflexively in response to my movement. He closed his eyes for a second, and a smile flitted across his lips. He kissed my nose. "Me too. Last night was amazing, really intense." He shifted his gaze from our entwined fingers to my eyes. He was being sincere. I could feel it, and it caught me off guard.

"Yes. It was." I looked at him, trying to comprehend how ... close, connected, intimate? I couldn't find right word, but I felt it, despite my intentions. It didn't make sense. I couldn't think of anything else to say, so I looked at our hands.

"Breakfast?" He leaned his forehead against the side of my head.

I looked back into his eyes. I stretched up and kissed his bottom lip.

His jewel pulsed between my thighs, and he rolled his eyes. "Ignore him. He does this in the morning. He's especially excited that you're here."

I chuckled. "Me personally, or women in general?" I squirmed a little and squeezed my thighs together around him.

His hips pushed forward again, and he purred a little as our nether regions slipped past each other. "He definitely likes women in general. But he has taken a particularly special liking to you."

"So you're saying it's personal?"

"It's definitely personal." He leaned over and kissed me, playfully caressing my lips and the tip of my tongue with his tongue.

I smiled as I responded to the movement of his tongue with my own. He deepened the kiss. His hips pushed forward, and he was inside of me, all of him at once.

I gasped. "Oh, hi."

At the same time, he hissed and squeezed his eyes. He looked at me and released an aspirated "Ah …" He inhaled but said nothing else. I was pretty sure he was caught off guard as well.

My insides pulsed in response to his presence.

He shook his head and growled a little. Then he kissed my shoulder and positioned us so we were both on our knees. It felt like we were in a field. Our bodies flowed together. Our movements were more urgent and forceful than before. Within a few minutes, I was screaming his name.

He came a minute or so after I did. When he'd caught his breath, he cleared his throat and said, "As I was asking, before my friend so rudely interrupted me, will you have breakfast with me?"

"No, Michael. I want you to take me home immediately."

"That's happened before. It's not wholly impossible." He looked serious.

"Yes, I'll have breakfast with you."

"Good. Let's take a shower." He smiled and I got the sense he had something up his sleeve; but I let it go.

He'd jumped me twice. I was going to get my revenge in the shower. I followed him through the bathroom door. Thankfully, it was just as clean as his bedroom, because I really needed to pee. I made a beeline for the toilet. I wondered if he cleaned his home himself. Then I noticed he was staring at me incredulously. "What?"

"You're peeing in front of me."

I looked at him like he was an idiot. "Okay. You know people, men and women, pee. Right? And we both know that you're intimately familiar with female anatomy in general and mine specifically. You can't be surprised that I pee. So I don't see your point."

He shook his head and pointed his finger at me as he turned to switch on the shower. I thought he'd enjoyed my response. After I was done, I followed him in. He handed me some rose-scented shower gel, and I raised my eyebrow.

"It was on sale." To him, it was just soap. The scent was irrelevant.

We joked while we bathed, and we kept our hands to ourselves. I thought we were both trying to process the intensity of last night. It was good, easy, disarming.

I turned to face him, and he was looking at me pensively. He said, "I like hanging out with you. You have a good sense of humor."

I went up on my tiptoes and just barely kissed his lips. I leaned back before he could kiss me back and kept doing that until he stopped trying. Then I pulled his top lip gently with my teeth while tracing my tongue across it quickly. He didn't move that time. So I did the same thing, but slower, with his bottom lip. I smiled against his mouth. "Just take it, okay?" I said. I placed his hands on the ledge in the shower that was behind him.

"Okay." He relaxed against the ledge. His jewel made it clear this was working for him.

"Good." I tilted his head so I could reach his earlobe. I French-kissed it for a second and trailed love bites down to where his collarbones met in the front. At the same time, I was caressing both of his nipples with a featherlight touch. He inhaled deeply, pulled me toward him, and pushed his erection against my abdomen. I kissed his Adam's apple and put his hands back on the ledge, pushing his body back until he relaxed again. As he did, he moaned. Then I sucked, nipped, and kissed his right nipple while using my left hand to alternate softly grazing and pinching the left one. I rubbed my right hand down his ass to the back of his right thigh and pulled it forward so I could straddle it and use my sex to caress it slowly in a circular motion.

He hissed and flexed his pelvis forward reflexively. He uttered some muddled word. I looked down and saw that he was starting to come a little. So I broke contact and slightly pushed him against the ledge. With my lips our only point of contact, I kissed his breastbone until his breathing equalized some. I looked up at him. He made eye contact. I kissed him softly on his lips and then went down on him, no holds barred.

"Fuck," he grunted as he came forcefully in my mouth. Before I knew it, he'd folded me into a warm embrace. He was kissing me and purring as he rocked me. Once he'd regained his equilibrium, he stepped back and rubbed his thumb across my top lip with a thoughtful expression on his face. "Let's get dressed or we won't ever get breakfast."

"Okay." I kissed his shoulder.

We stepped out of the shower, and he wrapped me in a towel and grabbed one for himself. Back in his bedroom, we realized that half of my clothes were in the living room. "I'll get them." He headed out of the bedroom door.

As he rounded the corner, I heard him say, "Why are you here, man?"

What? I thought he said he didn't do men. I crept around the corner to spy. He was still putting on his towel, so this must've been someone he was familiar with. When I got to the end of the hall, the guy was holding my jeans. He was tall and muscular like Michael. His muscles were denser and shorter from lifting weights though. His skin was toffee, and he had brown eyes. His hair and beard were the same length, just past morning shadow. He was attractive too.

"So do these belong to your blind date, or did you bring someone else home?"

"Goodbye." Michael picked up my underwear and grabbed for my jeans.

"So it's blind date girl. Ari's friend, right?" The guy stepped out of Michael's reach. They'd played that game before. I was right. I could relax and let his game run its course. I didn't have to worry about him getting too serious.

"Damn it." Michael reached and missed again.

The guy looked at the label inside my jeans. "She's a little out of your league, ain't she, bro?" Okay. Hopefully, that was his brother. The guy stepped back again. "So her pants are out here, but yours aren't. You went down on her!" It was an accusation. "Wait. You like her."

"Fuck you, man. Out!" That time, he got the jeans. He pushed the guy back through the front door and locked all the locks.

He turned to head back to the bedroom and saw me. "Sorry about that. That was my brother, Alex. The concept of boundaries is lost on him." He kissed my forehead. "Here are the rest of your clothes."

"So I take it you two are close?"

"Yeah." He shook his head and rolled his eyes. "There are moments when he's much, much closer than I want him to be."

I smiled to myself. I could relate. There were times when Ari was in my business when I didn't want her to be—I wouldn't give that up for the world, and I had a feeling he wouldn't either.

ON THE WAY to wherever we were going to have breakfast, he glanced at me. "Do you want to run by your place and change clothes?"

I responded in the affirmative and quickly changed into a casual but stylish outfit along the same line as his.

When we were on our way again, I asked, "So where are we going?"

He grinned. "A favorite spot of mine." He was holding something back. I gave in and played along.

A few minutes later, we pulled into the driveway of a house. He'd been really kind so far, so I tried to stay relaxed. With an enormous smile on his face, he jumped out of the car fast. When I got out, he took my hand and kissed my knuckles. He unlocked the door, and as we entered the kitchen, a beautiful older woman turned around and smiled broadly as soon as she saw him. Her coloring and features were similar to his brother's. I assumed she was his mother.

"Morning, Mikey." She hugged him warmly and kissed him on the forehead.

He returned her hug and stepped back and gestured toward me. "Mom, this is Sammi. She's Ari's best friend."

She offered her hand. "Oh, it's really nice to meet you. I take it the date went well last night." The coolness of her response let me know she was used to this.

"Yes, it did," I responded, and tried to suppress my blush.

To me, he said, "This is my mom, Helen Shelly."

He'd totally blindsided me. But I was cool. "It's really nice to meet you too, Mrs. Shelly." I took her hand and squeezed it gently.

"Helen," she said as she returned my gentle squeeze.

"So. Breakfast?" Michael chimed, quite pleased with himself.

She asked, "What do you want to make?"

He responded, "I'm hungry as hell. Definitely pancakes. Do you have any of that bacon I like?"

She took bacon, eggs, and milk out of the fridge. She looked at me. "Would you like some coffee?"

I responded, "Actually, I prefer tea … if it's not too much trouble."

She pointed to the pantry behind me. "The tea is in there. Take whatever flavor you like. The cups are in the cabinet over there."

Michael filled the kettle and put it on the stove to boil. Then he started working on making the pancakes.

She had my favorite flavor, a minty, orange mix.

She looked up. "That's my favorite."

"Mine too." I smiled. "Can I help?"

"No," they said at the same time. Michael added, "Just sit back and relax."

She asked, "How did you and Ari meet?"

"We went to school together. We met in first grade and have been best friends since day one."

"That's how it was with Mikey and Alex. They were brothers the moment they met each other."

"How old were they?" I asked, looking at Helen.

Michael answered, "We were three."

Helen added, "… and a half."

"One of mom's work colleagues was my foster parent. They came over so we could play together."

His mom said, "When we got ready to leave, Mikey assumed he was coming with us. He stole my heart."

"I'm her favorite. She loves me more than Alex and Trina," Michael said, grinning broadly.

Before I could ask, Helen shook her head and said, "Trina is my daughter, Alex and Mikey's younger sister. She's going to college in Chicago."

Together, they whipped up a full monty breakfast. We settled into a silly, easy conversation and got well acquainted as we ate. She talked about being a psychiatrist. I talked about being a filmmaker and how dance was the way I stayed sane. Michael talked about choosing to dance and all the fighting that resulted from that choice. He complained rehearsals weren't going well in his dance company because the choreographer couldn't make up his mind. I also learned he had a modeling contract that had been renewed and was more lucrative. He was planning to go to New York for a shoot within the next few weeks. I told them funny stories about Ari and me. They told me a few funny family stories. I liked Michael and his mom. When we finished eating, they let me help clear the table and put the dishes in the dishwasher.

I looked at my phone. It was 1:30 p.m. *Ah, man.* "Michael, I have a meeting at three. I need to get going."

"Okay. I'll take you home."

I offered Helen my hand. "It was really nice to meet you. Breakfast was a lot of fun."

She gave me a warm hug. "Come back anytime. I'm really glad Mikey brought you over." She gave Michael a hug and told him to call her before next Saturday.

As we pulled out of the driveway, I said, "Thanks for the heads-up. I can't believe you took me to your mom's house with absolutely no warning. I'm glad that I'd had a shower and got fresh clothes." I paused. "Your mom is really nice."

"She liked you. She's not always so open."

"Was that a test?"

"Nope. I knew she'd like you." He looked at me. "I like you too."

I glanced over at him. His game was silky smooth, but I wasn't in high school. "Yeah, I like you too. Last night was really intense. And then you introduced me to your mom? What was that about? You need to take a step back and slow down ... I'm not divorced yet."

"I agree. My mom and I usually have breakfast on Saturday morning. I was going over there, regardless."

"So that's how you exit from your Friday night stands?"

He shook his head. "When it ends in a stand, seven times out of ten, I don't stay the night. So no." He gave me an amused glance.

"And the other three times?"

He smiled. "It depends on how things are going and my mood." He lifted his eyebrow.

"Okay." I gave in.

"If you ask the question, I'll answer it."

Sucker. I just narrowed my eyes.

He grinned. "I bring women over to eat breakfast with my mom often enough that it's not a big deal, not an indication that I'm getting really serious or anything. My relationship with my mom is really relaxed. She's chill."

"So you do it frequently?"

He shook his head no. "Maybe once or thrice a year."

"For her approval?"

He shook his head again. "More for her reaction. I can't imagine her giving approval. Or disapproval."

"Do you only take the ones you like? Or is this one of your moves?"

"As a move, I'm not sure how it would be helpful." He looked at me. "Regarding how I feel about the woman, it's a mix. Sometimes, it's a woman I like, sometimes, it's because I need to see her 'you gotta be fucking kidding me look' before I do something stupid, and sometimes, it's because she wouldn't believe me otherwise. I'm really close to my mom. She sees my life as it's happening."

"Is it always so evident that you've just spent the night?"

He looked at me like I was stupid and smirked. "Well ... yeah."

I put my hands over my face. I wasn't in high school, but I hadn't ever just rolled up on someone's mom like that.

"Okay. So my mom knows that people have sex. Given that she has given birth to two kids, it's clear that she's intimately familiar with it. She knows I have sex. She knows I like sex. Given that I'm twenty-eight, she's certainly not going to be surprised that I just had sex. I don't see why that should be embarrassing."

I didn't move my hands.

"She always made us feel that it's just a natural part of life. It's not a big deal to me."

He was quite the player, I thought. "What effect do you expect for breakfast with your mom to have on the woman in question?"

"Given that we've already had sex by the time that we get to breakfast, I don't see what you mean."

"Come on, Michael. You live in this culture. Though it's commonplace for you and Helen, you know that it means something significant for a guy to take a girl home. Do you do it to disarm people?"

"How do you mean?"

I gave him a disbelieving look. "For the ones that you like, if they're not savvy, it can give them a sense of false security. You could use that as leverage to get away with stuff down the road. Don't pretend that you haven't considered it."

He took a moment to consider what I'd said. "I hadn't thought of using it as leverage, actually. I don't play games, Sammi. Playing games makes things really messy. I find that you can get what you want with a lot less headache if you're just straightforward." He looked at me.

"So why did you take me to your mom's house?"

"I already answered that question. Because I like you, and I knew my mom would like you." He gave me a sideways glance. "And I didn't want our date to end. In this case, I hope the effect is that you like me too." He kissed my knuckles and half smiled, obviously pleased with his response.

I wasn't done with the topic. "You do know that it's odd for you to introduce someone to your mother so quickly, right?"

He tilted his head and lifted his eyebrows slightly. In a thoughtful tone, he said, "Not to me. Like I said, we're close. I don't think of it that way. I have to go with what feels natural to me. At the end of the day, that's all I've got."

"Well, I guess I can't argue with that." He seemed to have some depth. I gave him that.

Back at my place, he walked me to my front door. We hugged each other. I tiptoed up and kissed his cheek. "Let's give each other a few days to let the dust settle."

He kissed my forehead. "Okay, I'll call you tomorrow." Before I could say anything else, he left.

My mom had called twice that day and texted a few times. My mother was a judge. She was poised, mentally tough, and thorough to a fault. She had to be to succeed as a Black female judge in the South. She applied those skills to all aspects of her life. And mine. She wanted to interrogate me to assess how things had gone the day before. I called her before she went insane.

She answered on the first ring. "Hello, I was starting to worry."

"You know better, Mom. How are you?"

"I'm fine. So how did it go yesterday?"

"Not much to report. Greg's lawyer acknowledged my petition for separation with my lawyer on Wednesday, and I filed to convert it to a divorce yesterday. I signed the papers, and Grant took them." I settled into my favorite chair.

"Well, everything's in order then. Grant's one of the best." I'd let her choose my lawyer, Grant, to avoid intense scrutiny of every aspect of my divorce.

"I'm so happy you're ending things with that Greg. You deserve so much more than he'll ever be able to give."

"I know, Mom."

"You know, not all men cheat like him and your father. Promise me you'll keep trying, sweetheart."

My father was a whore too. That was the reason my mom ended their relationship. My relationship with my father ended when I overheard him calling me a blank—as in a blank bullet—while he was talking to one of his friends. They were talking about how procreation only counted when it resulted in the birth of sons. I understood in that moment my father didn't truly respect me. He saw me as lesser because I was female; he felt I would never make an impact. So I divorced him too. Our relationship, if you could call an association with a person who doesn't respect you that, ended that day. As soon as I was old enough, I changed my last name to my mother's maiden name. Years later, my mother was still concerned about how that had affected me.

"I promise. That's not my focus right now though."

"Okay. You're right." She took a breath. "You're calling back late in the day. Did you party all night?"

"Yes, Mom, I did. I danced all night."

"Did you go out by yourself?" She was trying to be sly by asking the question backward.

I gave her a general answer. "No. I was with friends."

"Good. I'm glad to know that you're making friends, having fun again. I was worried about you."

"I'm fine, Mom. I need to prepare for a conference call for work. I'll call you later."

"Okay. Love you now."

"Love you too, Mom."

I looked down and saw a text from Ari. "Call me."

It was only 2 p.m., and it was a conference call. I had time. So I called her back.

"You fucked my brother," she said for hello.

"Why would you assume that?"

"You're just now calling me at two on the afternoon after the date. So you two hit it off really well."

"Yeah. You could say. Why didn't you warn me that he's gorgeous?"

"I said he's handsome. I showed you pictures. You have access to the internet—you could've looked him up. So … can he fuck, or is he an F-16?"

"He definitely doesn't fuck like he's sixteen. It's clear that he likes girl parts, and he's very, very skilled at pleasuring them. He seems to enjoy pleasuring them. You don't get the feeling that he's doing what he thinks he should so that he can get on to getting himself off. You know how most men rut when they fuck?"

"Yeah."

"He doesn't do that. He's all light and integrated and agile. He wields it like it's a wand, a magical wand."

Ari squealed. "Okay, stop. That's too much information."

"I'm just answering your question."

"He's my brother. A simple 'he fucks well' is enough. I'm glad that you had fun. I'm glad you went out and got laid. It's been way too long since being with a guy was about having fun for you."

"Yes. I definitely had a good time. It's pretty obvious that he gets laid whenever he wants. Women literally throw themselves at him. I expected him to be much more superficial than he's been so far."

"I'm just getting to know him too. But he seems pretty grounded."

I looked up and nodded. "Yeah. Well …"

"What?"

I laughed. "He took me to have breakfast with his mom this morning."

"What?"

"Right! Now check this. In his book, it was just breakfast. Apparently, he does it often enough that his mom finds it normal too."

"That must've been interesting."

I huffed. "What? Rolling out of bed and then rolling up to his mom's house after the first date? Yeah, it was. She took it in her stride. She's used to it."

"Hmm. It was obvious when I was there that they have a really close relationship. How was he otherwise?"

"He's intelligent and silly. Really silly. He has a good sense of humor. He seems like one of the good guys." I smiled, remembering the night before.

"So … you like him."

"Yes, I do. He plays the game well. He's smooth and charming. I expected to have at least two reasons to write him off by now. I have none."

"Coming from you, that's a compliment. *Wow.*"

"Yeah. But we both know that, at some point, he'll come up with something. They always do. Speaking of, I'm still married to Greg. I need to get out of the mess I'm in before I start something new. So it doesn't matter anyway."

"That's true but my takeaway here is that he made you think about starting something new." She sounded pleased with her decision to set up the date.

"So he did. Like I said, he plays the game well. Ultimately, I think he'll be a good person to have recreational sex with. Speaking of sex, where do things stand with Matt?"

She responded, "You inspired me. I broke up with him last night. It was time. I'd been putting it off."

"Any prospects?"

"I'll be working on that tonight. I'm going dancing with the girls."

"I wish I were there." I really missed being in New York.

"I'll do a few shakes for you."

"Thank you. Hugs to everyone. Let me jump on this call."

"Bye."

I WAS glad that Ari had set up that date. For a while, my life had been about finding resolutions. Hanging out with Michael rekindled the sense that I could move toward something. It was nice to be back in the game.

As I was getting into bed that night, he sent me a text. "Sleep well :-)."

I responded, "Sleep well :-)."

I drifted off with a smile on my face. I woke up feeling energized and decided to go to a 1 p.m. Acroyoga class.

3

ACRO

SUNDAY, AUGUST 6

As I was finishing up my breakfast, my phone rang. Michael's name appeared on the screen. He was playing hard.

I answered, "Hello."

"Good morning. How are you?"

"Well, and you?" This was the second day in a row he'd said good morning to me. I liked it. I was grinning. *Yep.* I was going to have to work to keep my guard up.

"I'm okay. How was your meeting?"

"It was fine. We set the production schedule for the commercial we're working on."

"Did you leave some time for us to hang out in a few days after the dust settles?" He sounded somewhat sarcastic.

"Actually, no." I let him hang for a moment.

"Why not?" He sounded confused.

"Because, in a few days, I'll still be in Vancouver filming."

He sighed, realizing I was playing with him. "So when do you get back?"

"Friday evening. We could hang out then," I said, giving him some hope.

He huffed. "When do you leave?"

"Tomorrow morning."

"Are you busy today?"

"I'm going to an Acroyoga class. And packing."

"Well, I vote we let the dust settle while you're out of town. Can I join you for the Acroyoga class?"

"Um." I paused and tried to think of a reason why not. Nothing came. He'd turned the tables. "Okay." I went with it.

"Cool. What time?"

"One o'clock."

"Where's the class?"

"Not too far from where I live."

"Okay. I'll see you in an hour or so." He hung up.

So I was about to spend an hour and a half basically feeling this man up. Then I realized I'd just invited him into the space where I relaxed. What if he made it another one of his playgrounds? I took a shower to clear my head.

Truthfully, I didn't want to avoid seeing him. After today, I'd be away for almost a week. This could be fine. I just needed to make sure that he respected the fact that this was one of my safe places.

An hour later, he was knocking on my door, wearing gray straight leg warm-up pants that stopped just below the knee and a black tank top. The sleeveless shirt accentuated the shape of his arms and shoulders. It also showed off his tattoos, one at the top of each arm, of muscular male characters. They were slightly abstract and perfectly placed. *Likey, likey.*

"Hey." I stepped back to let him in. The rear view was as nice as I'd remembered it.

As he walked in, he took my hand that wasn't touching the door and kissed my knuckles. "Hey." He held on to my hand as I closed the door. When I turned toward him, he asked, "Have you eaten? I'm starving. I have to eat before we go to this class."

"Yeah, I already ate, but there's a place right next to the studio that makes really good omelets."

"That works."

"Do you have a mat?"

He shook his head no.

"I'll lend you one of mine. I hate slippery mats." I grabbed the mats and my car keys. I also grabbed the beach throw that was on the table by the door, just in case.

When we got outside, his car was parked neatly right behind mine. He said, "Umm, yeah. You're blocked in by me. I'll drive."

I wondered if he was trying to avoid my driving or my Mini Cooper. As he drove to the restaurant, I asked, "Are your tattoos symbolic of something, or do you just like the way they look?"

He responded, "They're a very stylized version of the Nio, guardians of the Buddha. Depending on how you look at it, they symbolize life, the beginning and the end. To me, they symbolize balanced masculinity, something I strive for."

I asked, "Are you into Buddhism?"

"No. I like these symbols and what they mean to me."

"I like them. They're really done well."

"Thank you."

"Are they ever a problem when you dance and model?"

He shook his head. "Not usually. I work with a modern ballet company. They don't care. If they don't want to see them when I'm modeling, they cover them up."

Once we arrived, we were seated, and he placed his order. I ordered two of their hot healing tonics, one for me and one for him. As soon as they brought the appetizers, he dug in. He really was hungry. I decided to bring up my Acroyoga issue. "Have you ever done Acroyoga before?"

"Yeah, two or three times. I do stunts like that for a living, so I'm not really drawn to it to relax or have fun." He was chowing down.

Good. It was a nonissue. "So is this a mercy hang?" I turned up one corner of my mouth.

"No, I have a sense of how you move. I think I'm gonna have fun." He met my gaze and held it, suppressing a smile. He was up to something.

I chuckled. He was really disarming. I shook my head and looked away.

"What's up?" He cocked his head to the side.

I looked at him to make sure he was really listening to me. "I'm still married. I'm not ready to start something new. I want to make sure you understand that. I don't want you to think that I'm leading you on."

"I understand." He smiled thoughtfully. "Are you still hoping to get back with your husband? Are you still in love with him? What's his name?"

"His name is Greg. Greg Albert. And no, I'm not hoping to work it out with him. I've never really been in love with him."

He was taken off guard by my response. He narrowed his eyes and opened his mouth like he was about to say something. Then his expression changed, and he asked, "Greg Albert? You mean boy band Greg Albert?"

"Yep. That one." I took a deep breath and closed my eyes. "It's a really big mess, and I'm not sure how long it's gonna take for me to get out of it."

"I'll bet. Did you feel connected to him? Do you still feel connected to him?"

"Yeah, I did love him, but I don't feel like his partner anymore. I haven't seen him in two months."

"How long have you felt like it's over?"

"For at least four months."

"So you've had some time to process it. You just haven't finished making it official."

"Yep." Being divorced from Greg almost felt like a pipe dream at that point. And I definitely hadn't considered a new relationship at all. I had no parameters for that.

"You filed for divorce, and then you celebrated it. It doesn't dominate your thinking. I think it's more behind you than you realize."

"True. But I don't know what I want. I don't want to bring you into my confusion."

"Okay. Thanks for being upfront about where you stand. Don't overthink it. Look, are you having fun?"

"Yeah. It's just ... well ... sex between us is intense. That may be my fault. I'm not sure I remember how to date anymore in terms of intensity." I was thinking about the connection I felt with him, but I didn't say it.

He tilted his head thoughtfully. "You're worried that you're in the habit of relationship sex. I get it. I've been there. You're not gonna work through that by thinking about it. If you're gonna move forward and start dating, the only question at this stage is, are you having fun?"

I nodded my head. "Yes."

"Me too. That's why I'm here. We've had one date. I don't know where this is gonna lead, and I don't have any expectations. I'm just trying to stay open and let it be what it will. Relax. Enjoy it. Let it be."

"Okay. I'll try. Eat your omelet before it gets cold."

He inhaled the omelet. I pushed the tonic toward him. He sniffed it suspiciously. "The omelet was really good. What's this?" He took a sip. "I like it."

"One of their secret healing tonics." I smiled. "Thank you. At the very least, I hope that we can be friends."

"Me too."

"Just so you know, the class that we're going to is more about Thai body massage than stunts, by the way."

He looked indifferent.

As we walked into the studio, heads turned. Meagan was at the front desk. I swiped my card and stepped aside so she could give Michael one of their sign-up forms and I could enjoy the entertainment. On cue, she gawked.

She regained her composure. As she handed Michael the forms, she said, "Mr. Shelly, I really enjoyed your performances last season. My favorite piece was 'Iconic.'"

Michael glanced at her quickly, said, "Thank you," then focused on the forms.

Meagan continued, "Let me know if you need any help with the forms."

He responded, "I've got it," without looking up.

She kept going. "So what brings you to the studio today?"

He met her gaze, then politely said, "My date," as he glanced at me.

I had my elbow up on the counter with my chin resting on my palm, clearly enjoying the show.

He narrowed his eyes at me and took my hand. As we turned into the classroom, he whispered, "You know you're wrong."

I placed our mats and, with a look of innocence and confusion, said, "What are you talking about?"

Before he could respond to me, the teacher, Laura, stepped up to introduce herself and flirt. He turned toward her to be polite and let her finish her performance. Behind him, I snorted a stifled chuckle. He put one of his hands behind his back and gave me the finger.

Once everyone had a partner, class started. First, the pairs massaged each other's hands and feet in tandem. He had good hands. When I started to massage the space in between the bones that made up the ball of his foot, he stopped massaging my foot, closed his eyes, and grunted softly, "That's the spot. Yeah. Right there." He kissed the top of my foot, then resumed his massage.

When it was time for the main part of class, flying Thai body massage, he set himself up to base first.

I said, "Oh, no you don't. You're not that slick. I'm basing first so that I don't have to work after I get my massage. That way, I can be completely relaxed when I leave."

I set myself up to base him by lying on my back and putting my feet up in the air with my legs together so that I was shaped like the letter *L*. He leaned the tops of his thighs into my feet and gracefully let himself tip over so that his chest and belly were touching the front of my legs and his legs were perpendicular to his body with his feet in the air. He kept the weight in his legs, so it was easy for me to hold him. I could tell he wasn't used to being lifted because I had to peel his hands off the floor to get his full weight. I jiggled my feet a little to help him to relax and trust me. Following Laura's instructions, I massaged and stretched his back and arms. He smiled and purred as I did to let me know that he really enjoyed it. We switched. He kneaded my muscles with the same intensity and care that I did his.

As we were rolling up the mats to leave, he said, "Thank you. I needed that."

"I'm glad you liked it. Would you come to another class?" I was slightly worried again.

He took the mats and walked toward the door. "With you, yeah. Your massages are actually helpful. There's nothing so irritating as going to get a massage and having it feel like the person's just putting lotion on you."

"Yeah, I know what you mean."

"I don't see why we would, though. That class was pretty straightforward. I'm sure we could replicate it on our own easily."

I almost said, *I'm sure there are some tricks we haven't learned.* But it was better to leave well enough alone. As he threw the mats on the back seat of his car, I asked, "Do you have plans for the rest of the afternoon? Would you like to relax on the beach for a little while?"

He smiled. "Yeah, I'd like that. Give me a minute to ditch Alex."

He took out his phone to call his brother, and I stepped away to get my beach throw from his car. I heard him say, "Tell her something came up and I couldn't make it today," as I returned. They exchanged a few more lines of banter before he hung up.

I said, "If you are expected elsewhere, that's fine. I won't feel offended."

"I've ditched Alex. It's all good." The way he half smiled afterward let me know he was happy with his decision.

I accepted his choice by offering him my hand. He took it. We grabbed some smoothies and walked down to the beach.

Once we got situated, he said, "So you've had dance training?"

"Yeah, I grew up dancing. Then I studied in New York for a few years after college."

"Really?"

I turned to look at him. He was staring at the ocean. "I got a chance to audition at a good dance school. I got in."

"Hmm." He was reassessing me while continuing to look at the ocean. "Did you try to pursue it as a career?"

"No. I love moving deeply, extremely, but I don't have a need to perform."

"Do you still take dance classes?"

"Yeah."

"Then you should come take a class with me." He closed his eyes and lifted his face to the sun.

"I'm not at your level, Michael. At most, I can handle an intermediate class right now."

"That would work. I know a really good teacher. We'll go when you get back." He smiled, turned to look at me and kissed my nose.

I kissed his chin. "What would you have done with a degree in chemistry?"

"I don't know ... work for a company making chemicals." He kissed my cheek.

"Would you have enjoyed that?" I kissed his nose.

He brushed his lips across mine. "Probably not. Definitely not as much as I enjoy dancing." He softly kissed my lips.

I rubbed my nose against his. "Was chemistry something that you always knew you wanted to do?" I kissed him back with just a bit more intensity.

"More like it was something I was always good at." He rubbed his forehead on mine and smiled. He was waiting for my next question.

I returned his smile. "Why not chemical engineering?" I asked, kissing his cheek.

He laughed. "I made that career choice when I was a very wise seventeen-year-old boy." He touched his lips to mine.

I gazed into his eyes and enjoyed the feel of his lips. I opened my mouth a little. He mirrored my movement to keep our lips in contact, and we held that position, just looking at each other for a while. Finally, I smiled and skimmed my teeth across his bottom lip. "So you liked chemistry?" I didn't know if it had ever been so easy to get to know someone.

He smiled back. "Yeah, especially when it involved rapid oxidation."

I was so attracted to him. "What is it with male humans and fire?"

"Watching stuff burn is very, very satisfying. You should try it sometime." He skimmed my lips with his tongue.

I met his tongue with mine. We played for a moment; then he deepened the kiss.

"Would you make a different choice today?" I leaned my forehead to his and closed my eyes. I was so turned on. I was glad the state of my nether regions was my secret.

"I don't know. Maybe comp sci." He paused. "Are you making fun of me, Sammi?"

I shook my head without breaking contact with him. "Uh-uh. It's just an honest question. I'm genuinely curious." *Note to self, he's sensitive.*

"Your turn. Would you have liked working as an engineer?"

"I don't think so, but that was never my plan," I replied as I kissed his chin.

"What was your plan?"

"My pl—"

He kissed me before I could get the second word out. He smiled. "Say that again. I didn't get that."

"Filmmaking was always the plan."

He leaned back a little and gave me a confused look. "So why did you go to engineering school?"

"Because I like math and science, and because I thought I'd be a technical producer and do special effects."

"Hmm." He trailed kisses along my jaw. "So what happened?"

I leaned my head back to give him access to my neck. "I found out that I enjoy directing and some of the nontechnical aspects of production in film school." He was still kissing my neck. My whole body was tingling. It felt new and familiar at the same time. Mostly to maintain control of myself, I took his chin and guided his face back to mine. We hovered within millimeters of each other.

He whispered, "So your plan also changed along the way."

"Yep."

We kissed each other softly and sweetly. It slowly grew in intensity. After ten minutes or so, he took my hand and put it under his shirt so I was touching his erection through his pants.

I smiled on his mouth. "I don't think this is appropriate."

He smiled back. "I want to go back to your place."

"When?" I toyed.

He moved my hand down his erection.

"Why?"

He moved my hand back up to the original place and bit my bottom lip.

"Okay," I said, kissing his nose.

He broke physical contact and leaned back on his arms, bent his knees a little, and leaned his head back. Then he took a deep breath and closed his eyes.

Okay. "What are you doing?"

"I'm thinking about my mom. Give me a few minutes," he answered without opening his eyes. "It would be inappropriate for me to stand up right now." He smirked.

I laughed out loud, and he gave me the finger.

I tried to grab it so I could tease him, but he balled his hand into a fist before I could. I decided to throw away our trash to give him some space.

BY THE TIME we got the door closed at my house, we were both undressed. I led him to my favorite reading chair. It was leather and slightly oversized, perfect for curling up with a book and some tea. I spread the throw across it so we wouldn't stick to the leather and pushed him down into the chair and straddled him. He hadn't quite regained his erection. So I sat with my sex on his and resumed the kissing game. When he was ready, I took him inside of me. He held my hips and moved me up and down. That wasn't how I wanted to move at all. I let him do it a few times, then stopped him by taking his hands from my hips. I sat all the way down and became motionless. Then I took the middle finger of both of his hands and said, "These have been very active today." I took one into my mouth and sucked it hard and circled it with my tongue before doing the same to the other. When he got used to the pattern, I squeezed his penis hard with muscles in my pelvic floor, then rippled the squeeze up my abdomen. I wasn't typically inspired to move like that when I was just having sex casually. Something about him was messing with my boundaries.

He squirmed and moaned a little. Then he relaxed back to take in the sensation.

I repeated that movement a few times and undulated my pelvis gently.

He inhaled sharply and matched my movement. He pressed his hand against my abdomen, which intensified the sensation.

As we mounted together, the urgency and speed of our movements increased. He came first, hard and loud. A few strokes later, I followed. I relaxed into my blissful place to enjoy the aftershocks of my orgasm.

"Are you going to sleep again?" He was fidgeting underneath me.

"I'm not done with my orgasm. Shh."

He chuckled. After about ten seconds, he said, "But ..."

I sat up and looked at him incredulously.

He laughed. "I was just gonna suggest that maybe we both could nap comfortably if we lie down."

I kept looking at him.

He swallowed and said, "You know, on a bed."

I pointed. "My bedroom is through that door, up the stairs. It's the door at the end of the hallway. You can carry me." I repositioned myself so that he could easily pick me up and relaxed again.

"Carry you?" he tried to protest.

"Yes. All you did was sit here. I did all the work. Then you interrupted my aftershocks." I put my head on his shoulder.

He opened his mouth to say something, but instead, shook his head. "Okay." It almost sounded like a question.

He stood up with me in his arms and took me to my bedroom. We lay in silence, absent-mindedly playing handsy, lost in our own thoughts.

After a while, I shifted to look at him. We were lying on our sides, facing each other.

"You know, you're right. You're in the habit of relationship sex." He kissed my forehead. "Since I like you, I'm gonna give you a lesson on the difference between relationship sex and dating sex."

"You'd do that for me?" I gasped.

"Yep." He took a long, deep breath. "But only because I like you."

"You're too kind."

"True. For my own good, even." He smiled. "I'm gonna show you some of the things that you've done that are totally inappropriate for dating sex." With a stoic expression, he leaned over and French-kissed me urgently. "That kiss, for example, is appropriate for dating." Then he leaned forward and barely kissed my lips. "That one, on the other hand, is not. And neither is this one." He softly pulled my top lip with his teeth and traced it with his tongue.

"I'm not sure I understand. Can you show me again?"

"Yes. But only once. So pay attention." He repeated the kisses.

"I think I see the difference."

"Good." He leaned forward and barely grazed my top lip with his tongue.

"Now, for proper nipple protocol. While this touch is acceptable for dating ..." He rolled one of my nipples between his thumb and index finger. "You could even add a kiss like this." He sucked my other nipple firmly and squeezed it with his lips. "However, touching a nipple like this while dating is wholly inappropriate." He tried to emulate the way I was grazing his nipple in the shower.

I lifted his chin so I could look into his eyes. "Would you be referring to this one?" I started grazing and pinching one of his nipples with my fingers.

He leaned his forehead to mine. "*Hmmm.* Yeah, that one."

"So this is not appropriate either?" I added licking and nipping his other nipple to the mix.

He inhaled deeply and purred, "No. Not at all."

I kissed his nipple and stilled my hand. "Okay, I understand."

He smiled. "Good." He grazed my top lip again. "Moving on." He pushed my shoulder so I was lying on my back and pulled my leg closest to him over his hips. He inserted two fingers into me and moved them in and out, gently but urgently. "This is appropriate for dating sex." He continued for a minute or so. "But you wouldn't do this." He added a circular motion to the in and out movement of his fingers and circled my clitoris with his thumb.

I moaned and matched his rhythm with my pelvis.

"And you absolutely wouldn't do this," he added, kissing my lips, one, then the other. "Or this." He sucked my earlobe and trailed kisses down my neck and back to my mouth. He continued as my body tensed around his fingers.

It only took a few minutes for him to bring me to orgasm. He withdrew his fingers but continued to kiss me until I regained my equilibrium.

When I opened my eyes, he said, "Did you get that?"

I pulled his face to mine and kissed him softly. "Got it."

"Good. Moving on." He rolled on top of me and pushed himself deep inside of me. He held his own weight, swiveling his hips as he eased in and out at an easy tempo. "Now, while this would be appropriate for relationship sex, you'd never do it while dating. I'll continue for just a little while so that you fully understand the movement."

"You're so kind." I panted.

"I know." He continued until I started to quicken. Then he stilled himself. "I think you understand." He moved in and out, no swivel. Full strokes at an urgent pace. "This is how you fuck while dating."

I moaned into a rolling orgasm. He rode me through it. As my focus cleared, he came strongly and silently.

When he'd landed, he said, "Finally, this is a definite no-no for dating. Especially after sex." He kissed me tenderly and pulled me close. After a few minutes, he asked, "Did you get all of that?"

I hunched my shoulders. "I may need a recap. I think I missed a few details."

He laughed. "That lesson was free. You have to pay for the next one." He kissed my forehead. "And you're gonna have to wait because I'm hungry."

"Me too. I think we should go out."

"Agreed."

We went to a noodle shop. I earned another finger for giggling as our waitress eyed him down and tried to chat him up while he was trying to give his order. She almost completely forgot to take mine.

"It's not right how much you enjoy my pain." He sipped his tea.

"Don't front. You know you like the attention."

"There was a time when I was younger when that was true. But in time, it got old."

"But you don't have to work to get laid."

"I do to get laid well." He smirked.

"You didn't work to get laid by me."

"Yeah, I did. Everything has its price. When I was in high school and everything was about looks, I was living the dream. But now, I find that the first thing that women who have their shit together do is write me off. They assume that I'm dumb and shallow. And flippant. It's an uphill battle to get them to see beyond my physical appearance. Some people can't see me as a person because of it. They seem to relate to me as a trophy or something."

I just looked at him. He was so much more grounded than I thought he'd be when I met him. It was disarming.

He waited a moment and said, "Go ahead. Deny that you wrote me off."

"Okay. You have a point."

He grinned. "Like I said." He was pleased with himself. "What time's your flight in the morning?"

"Seven."

"Let me stay with you tonight. I'll drive you to the airport in the morning."

My first thought was I should say no. But I was having fun, and he understood we were not starting a relationship. My heart was still safe. My wards, the protections I had around it, were mostly functioning, and I felt mostly clearheaded. So I said, "Okay."

4

———

ARI

FRIDAY, AUGUST 11

THE REST of the evening was fun and easy. He watched me pack, and we watched a classic sci-fi movie. I was impressed he'd seen it before. I struck up a deeply geeky conversation about cycles and the fact that rhythm seemed to be a basic truth that was reflected through everything: dance, the periodic table, the seasons, the cosmos. He followed my lead effortlessly. We talked geek for hours before going to sleep. I hadn't done that since I left undergrad. It was nice. Really nice.

He dropped me off at the airport the next morning. I got on the plane thinking about how much I'd enjoyed hanging out with him the day before. I was glad to be going into a week of hard work in a different city. I could come up for air and fortify my wards. I wondered what he was going to do to mess things up.

The week went by quickly. My days were so packed that my texts were few and far between. Michael and I established a pattern of checking in every evening. He talked about his rehearsals and how Alex got on his nerves. He listened attentively when I talked about the shoot and all the personalities involved. We got along well. I got my head clear about the fact that I wasn't interested in starting something new. I also talked to Ari a few times. I gave her my flight details, as usual, and told her that Michael was going to pick me up on Friday. She was pleased she'd introduced us.

TO MY SURPRISE, my excitement stirred as I entered the baggage claim area where we'd agreed to meet. When I caught sight of him, I gasped a little. He was working a pair of jeans and a T-shirt. He had that male *V* thing mastered. His hips ... just tall and lean and muscular and graceful. All two hundred pounds of him. *Yum.* I watched the women ogle him while he ignored them for a moment before I stepped into his line of sight with a smirk on my face. He could tell that I was basking in his "pain." As I neared him, he hugged me and leaned in to give me truly sweet kiss. It was like he was absorbed in that moment. That was new. The world disappeared for a second. He'd caught me off guard.

With his arms wrapped around me, he said, "Hey, beautiful."

I hugged him back. "Hey, Michael. It's good to see you."

He kissed my forehead.

"Is it good to see me too?" I turned to see Ari with a big smile on her face.

"Ari?" we said at the same time. We were both surprised to see her.

"In the flesh." She included herself in our embrace. "I know what we're doing tonight," she said with a devious look on her face. "It involves dinner and dancing."

Michael exhaled slowly and closed his eyes. I was pretty sure that meant he was irritated.

I laughed and hugged my friend tightly. "I've missed you, girl."

She hugged me back. "Me too. Are you waiting for luggage?"

"Nope."

"Cool," she said. "Let's go."

Michael put his arm around my waist and gestured to Ari. "After you." His tone was slightly dry.

Ari chuckled. "I don't know where your car is, Mike."

He inhaled and widened his eyes. "Come on."

By the time we pulled into my driveway, Ari had made dinner reservations for us at her favorite restaurant and downloaded our tickets to the dance party we were going to. As she walked through the door, she said, "I'm going to my room. I need to change. Mike, let's drive your car tonight. I want to ride in something more luxurious than the Mini Cooper. Too bad we can't all fit into Spencer." She headed off down the hall. Before she turned into her room, she yelled, "Oh, and Mike, I want to go to breakfast at Helen's in the morning."

I looked at Michael. "Are you okay?"

He crinkled his brow and narrowed his eyes. "Yeah. Spencer?"

"My Ferrari."

"You have a Ferrari?"

I nodded. "A Spider."

He looked surprised.

"What? I like cars."

He was reassessing me. And the house. After a moment, he said, "Well, this is going to be an adventure."

"We're going to have a lot of fun. I need to change, and I want to take a quick shower."

He picked up my bag and gestured for me to lead him to my bedroom. Once we got there, he sat on my bed and took out his phone. I picked out one of my dressy minidresses and a pair of knee-high Roman sandals to wear.

Michael asked, "Did you know that Ari was coming?"

"No." I headed into my bathroom.

He got up and followed me in. No hesitation. While I undressed, he asked, "How did she know when and where to meet us?"

"We always give each other our flight info when we're traveling. I told her that I was meeting you in baggage claim."

"I see." He took a deep breath, like he was trying to calm himself.

"Are you angry at Ari?"

"Honestly, I find her demanding, a bit selfish, and rude. She just co-opted our evening without even asking if we had plans or if we wanted to join her."

"Lighten up."

He threw his head back and huffed, pissed.

"She's just trying to surprise us with a visit."

"She didn't try to compromise with us. She just made plans to her liking. And she's bossy. I don't know why you're not irritated."

"You're taking her actions and words the exact opposite of the way she means them. Relax a bit, and you'll notice that she's toying with you."

He massaged his forehead. "I don't know. Maybe."

He walked over to the commode and started to pee.

I looked at him in disbelief and horror to see if I could break his mood.

He smiled wryly and said, "What ... you do know that people pee, right?"

I flashed the finger at him and jumped in the shower. He hung out and chatted with me and played with his phone while I got dressed and put on my makeup. When I was done, we headed back downstairs. Ari was wearing a minidress too. He looked back at me like he'd just realized I was wearing one. He raised his eyebrows, closed his eyes, and put his hand on his forehead as if he had a headache.

"What?" Ari and I said at the same time.

He answered, "Nothing. You two are stunning." Then he focused on Ari. "Should I call one of my friends to be your date?"

Ari responded, "Nope, I want to hang out with just the two of you."

He responded, "Okay, let's get going 'cause I have to stop by my place to change."

On the way over to Michael's, the conversation was awkward. Michael was genuinely irritated by Ari. He was taking her wit way too seriously. Ari and I waited in his living room while he changed.

She squinted at me and asked, "Was it my imagination, or did he follow you to your room while you showered and changed?"

"Right. No. That was reality."

"Was he trying to get busy?" She slanted her head in anticipation of me answering yes.

"Not in the least. He was chatting and playing with his phone the whole time."

"Okay. He's really relaxed around you. It's been what? A week?"

"Elapsed time. We really only spent two days together. I agree. It's really easy for us to be around each other." I exhaled slowly.

"Have you guys talked about it?"

I nodded. "Yes. I told him that I don't want to start anything new. He said that he understands."

"Well, as long as you're having fun. You deserve this."

Michael came back into the living room. He'd changed into some black dropped-crotch, straight leg pants that pooled at his ankles, and a beautifully painted long black shirt with muscle sleeves. The painting on the T-shirt and his tattoos complemented each other nicely. He slipped on a jacket that matched the pants. It was a thigh-length Japanese-influenced blazer. He had style. He looked at Ari and gestured toward what he was wearing. "Do you approve?"

Ari looked at him, meeting his gaze, and with a bossy, irritated tone, said, "Turn around."

Michael narrowed his eyes and complied.

Ari hunched her shoulders. "That'll do."

Michael chuckled. "Glad Her Majesty is pleased."

He gave us both a once-over. To Ari he said, "Are you sure you don't want a date? You two look really beautiful. I'm not sure I'll be able to guard both of you by myself." He pulled me toward him and put his arm around me.

Ari responded, "I'm sure." I could tell she was pleasantly surprised by his sweetness.

Michael hugged me a little and grinned at Ari. With a smirk on his face, he pointed her toward the door. "So out." He threw his knapsack over his shoulder.

Ari smirked and headed for the door. We followed her out.

As we were starting the drive to the restaurant, Michael asked Ari, "So what do you have planned for after we are done with breakfast tomorrow?"

She glanced at me as she responded with the same attitude she'd been giving him since we met at the airport. "I will tell you that when I feel it's appropriate." She shrugged her shoulders to me slightly. She was wondering if he was finally catching on to the fact that she was being playful.

Consciously or unconsciously, Michael mirrored Ari's expression. "Aw, come on. You can do better than that. Surely, you didn't fly all the way out here with a half-baked plan for the weekend."

Michael was starting to understand where she was coming from, and it was game on. Ari dawned a look of sheer joy. "When I informed you of the plan for this evening, you got all flustered,

Mike. I don't want to overwhelm you again. Let's stick with what you can handle."

Except for the fact that Ari's voice wasn't deep like Michael's, the timing and tone in which they spoke were exactly the same. They had found their rhythm and settled into a witty banter. I was glad she'd found him. It was wonderful to witness. Dinner was delicious and filled with jokes and laughter.

As we walked up to the entrance of the venue, Michael looked at Ari and said, "Ari, this is a very pretentious crowd. Are you sure you really want to go to this party?"

Ari responded, "Nope. I'm auditioning the event producers to host an event for the firm that I work for. They're gonna give us VIP treatment, so take advantage of it. Hopefully, the music is good enough for us to get our groove on."

After we'd made our way through the entrance and they'd taken our coats, we stepped into the atrium. It was beautifully decorated in an art deco motif with dramatic LED lighting. Collectively, we paused to look around and take it all in. A brisk movement caught my eye. There was a gorgeous woman, maybe ten or fifteen years our senior, blazing a trail toward Michael. With her dark curly hair and olive skin, she looked Italian. He was looking up as she approached from his side, so he didn't see her. I took a step back. I was already giggling to myself. She grabbed his ass with one hand and ran the other hand across his chest as she stepped in front of him so he could see her.

Michael didn't jump. Recognition registered immediately, and he grabbed both of her hands and brought them together in front of her, saying, "Hello, Maria. How are you?"

"I'm very well, darling." She stepped back, freed her hands, then opened her arms in a grand gesture. She looked Michael up and down. "You look absolutely fabulous!" She stepped forward and, in the same movement, reached for his junk.

Reflexively, he pulled his hips back and leaned forward. Maria tried to kiss him on the lips. Michael just evaded it by turning his head. She got his cheek instead. He grabbed both of her hands again. "Maria, stop."

Maria responded, "Oh, Mike. You're always so coy. We really must have dinner sometime."

He answered, "We're not having dinner, Maria." He still had hold of her hands.

Ari, standing a foot or so to Michael's right, had turned to watch the interaction.

Maria shook her head and caught sight of Ari. Then, shamelessly looking back and forth between them, she compared their features. After a moment or so, she said, "Mike! Is this your sister? You two look so much alike. She's gorgeous."

To Ari, Maria said, "You're beautiful, darling. Have you considered modeling?" Maria wrung her hands free of Michael's and stepped back. "You two could do shoots together. Yes. It would be phenomenal. Absolutely phenomenal!"

Someone else captured Maria's attention. She looked at Michael and said, "Do bring her in, Mike. Love you, darling." She blew him a kiss and scuttled off.

Michael took a deep breath, and Ari and I burst out laughing.

Someone took my hand. I turned to see it was the concierge. As he placed it on his elbow, he cleared his throat and said, "Please allow me to show you to your table" to the three of us. To me, he said, "I have to say, you look absolutely ravishing tonight, milady." He showed us to our table, then kissed my hand and bowed away.

The event coordinator was waiting for Ari when we got there. She had samples of their cocktails and hors d'oeuvres on the table. I ended up sitting between Ari and Michael on the same side of the table. The coordinator told Ari a little about each hors d'oeuvre that had been served and about alternatives. As she walked away, Ari and I both looked at Michael.

Though we'd just had dinner a short while ago, he somehow had room to enjoy the hors d'oeuvres. He answered the questions that were looming. "That was Maria Leone. She owns the modeling agency that I work for. Yes, she's always like that."

Ari asked, "Have you had sex with her?" She was trying to shock Michael.

He shook his head no without looking up from the second plate of hors d'oeuvres.

Ari asked, "Would you?"

This time, he looked up, chewing. He shook his head again. "Uh-uh." He licked some sauce off his thumb. "I don't shit where I eat."

Ari was still looking for buttons. "If you didn't work for her, would you?"

Michael took a sip of one of the sample cocktails, then met Ari's gaze. "Yep."

Ari was surprised. "Really?"

"Yes. Without hesitation. I hear she knows how to have a good time." He kept her gaze.

She just looked at him incredulously, like she was trying to figure out what to say.

Michael half grinned. "It's no secret that I'm a whore. So why not?" He moved on to the next plate of hors d'oeuvres.

Ari asked, "Do you feel harassed by her?"

Michael responded, "Somewhat objectified, yes. Harassed, no. Offended, no."

"Why not?"

"Well, when you're modeling, objectification comes with the territory. I'm being a specimen, so I deal with it. She makes it clear the offer is on the table, and it doesn't matter to her whether you take it or not. It's not a power play. Work is not at stake. Also, she watches out for all of her models, all of her employees. She goes the extra mile to help people when she doesn't have to. So I don't feel harassed. And I don't feel offended because, on some level, I think she does it to toughen people up. I believe she's just playing."

Ari was processing Michael's answer. I thought he had her on her back foot. She changed the subject. "How tall are you?"

Michael responded, "Six four."

"Isn't that tall for a male model?"

"It depends on the designer."

After a moment, Ari stood. "Well, I'm gonna go dance." She trotted off.

Michael watched her step onto the dance floor as two guys stepped up to join her. He looked at me. "She's a character."

"Yep, I think it may be genetic."

He took my hand and kissed my knuckles. "The music isn't bad. Want to dance?"

I stood up. "I do."

We headed for the dance floor. The mix was quite eclectic. We had fun trying to remember the right dance for each song that was played. After a while, Michael looked toward our table and muttered, "Dammit" under his breath. Before I could see what he was looking at, he was in front of me, leading me by the hand back to our table. When we got there, I saw Ari was talking to a blond cutie with shoulder-length hair. He was sitting to her left. And they were enthralled and giggling. Michael offered me the chair one seat away from Ari's right. He was menacingly calm. It was unnerving. He took the seat just to Ari's right. His hips were a little forward, and he was leaning back in the chair, wide legged, pressing his fingertips together in his lap. His foot was resting on the back of Ari's chair. Aside from the daggers coming from his eyes, he looked like he was relaxing. He was gazing intently at the guy who was talking to Ari.

After a minute or so, the guy felt Michael's gaze and looked at him. He recognized Michael immediately and dawned an "oh shit" look. Unnerved, he said, "Hey. Mike. Man."

Michael didn't move or speak. He maintained a dagger-like gaze. Ari looked at Mike and was stunned into silence and stillness like me.

The guy looked from Michael to Ari and back a few times. "Um. This is your sister? Yeah, I should go." He stood up and started walking. Michael stood and followed him … all the way to the exit.

Ari and I looked at each other in shock. As we watched, Michael made his way back to our table. Ari whispered, "His name was Lucas."

Michael hailed the waiter as he sat down. He was completely relaxed again. He looked at us. "Sorry about that. That guy is an asshole. He's a fucking grifter."

Ari was still processing *angry* Michael. "Okay."

Michael looked at Ari. "And no. That wasn't about cock-blocking. Are you sure you don't want a date?"

I asked, "What did he do?"

Ari said, "No, I don't want a date."

The waiter came and brought a flight of white wines and more hors d'oeuvres. Michael took a sip and said, "You don't want to know."

I could tell that I should leave it alone.

We stayed for a few more hours, sampling and dancing.

WHEN WE GOT BACK to my place, Michael grabbed his knapsack and followed us to the door. In tandem, we looked at the knapsack, then at him.

He said, "What? It's almost two in the morning. If we're going to my mom's for breakfast, I'm not driving all the way back home." He raised his eyebrows and waited.

I smiled at him and kissed him on his cheek. His game was good. "You're welcome to stay, Michael." I chuckled to myself that he'd assumed as much.

Ari looked at us and raised her eyebrows, shook her head, and sighed.

I unlocked the door. Once I was inside, I reached down to take off my knee-high Roman sandals.

Michael was suddenly on his knees in front of me. "Let me do that. I've been wanting to take these apart all evening." He started to undo the buckles in the front.

I stopped him. "Don't undo the buckles. They unzip in the back."

"Really? Ah. Cool." He unzipped both and slipped them off my feet. He stood and asked, "So am I sleeping with you or in a guest room?" He was smirking.

I narrowed my eyes and said, "A guest room."

"That's what I thought." He leaned in and gave me one of those tender, present kisses. He looked back at Ari.

Ari looked at me, then at Michael. Her expression said, *Alrighty, then*. She said, "I guess that's my cue. Good night, you guys."

I gave her a hug and walked up to my bedroom. Michael gave her a hug too. I left them chatting and went straight to my bathroom to take off my makeup. As I walked back into my bedroom from the bathroom, Michael walked in and closed the door. He'd already taken off his shirt and was stepping out of his pants. He threw his clothes and knapsack on the chair near the door. All he was wearing was a pair of boxer briefs. *Yum.* I paused a moment to enjoy that sight. Then I reached back to unzip my dress.

"Let me help you with that," he said. He stepped behind me, unzipped the dress, and undid my bra. He helped me out of both and tossed them on the chair with his clothes. He turned me around, and, with his hands on either side of my face, kissed me slowly and deeply. His tongue touched mine softly. I reached up to his face with my hands and reciprocated his tenderness. We kissed for a few minutes. He smiled on my lips and said, "I missed you, beautiful."

I was thinking, *Fuck, I really like this man.* I asked him, "Did you sleep with anyone else while I was away?"

He shook his head. "Uh-uh. Did you?"

I answered, "No."

"Good."

I wanted to make sure he realized I wasn't expecting to settle into a relationship with him. "You know that I'm not expecting you to date me exclusively, right? You can sleep with other people."

He looked at me like he was assessing my mental stability. "I know. It's my body, so it's my choice. Right?"

I didn't know that would be a touchy subject. I looked at him like he was a little crazy too. "Absolutely."

He half smiled. "Now that we're clear about that." He kissed me more passionately than before. He let his hands slide down from my face to my breasts, where he paused for a second to caress my nipples with his thumbs. He skimmed the backs of his nails down my rib cage and around my waist and slipped his hands into my panties to caress my ass. Pulling me closer, he pressed his erection into my abdomen. He broke off the kiss and said, "I want to taste you," and picked me up. As he laid me down on my back, he slipped off my panties. He kissed me once more on my lips and trailed kisses down my body as he pushed my legs open. When he reached my clitoris, he kissed it and leaned back a little to look at my vagina full-on. He spread it open with his fingers and ran his nose the full length of my vulva and inhaled deeply. He peeked up to look into my eyes. "I like your scent." He licked my full length before concentrating solely on my clitoris.

I moaned and said, "Oh, Michael."

He brushed my opening lightly and smiled against my sex. "You're ready."

I felt him kick off his briefs. He rubbed my body with both of his hands, over my abdomen, my breasts, my armpits, and my arms, to clasp my hands in his. Keeping our hands together, he positioned our arms so they were on either side of my head and he could support his weight on his elbows. He parted my lips with his tongue and pressed himself into me in the same fluid motion. I groaned loudly. He kept his pelvis still for a minute and continued to kiss me until he felt me relax around him. Lifting his head, he undulated his pelvis—full, hard strokes at a steady, intense pace. His eyes were closed, and he was losing himself in me. I was pretty sure I heard myself growling. He had me pinned so I couldn't move, but my body *needed* to move. So I wrapped my legs around his and pulled him just a little closer so I could use his legs as leverage. I pulled him in deeper, gasping a little and moving with him. He opened his eyes and said something I couldn't understand. I felt a ripple go through his body. He tried to pull out and stop the motion so he wouldn't come, but I held him inside me with my legs and kept moving. He lost it. He didn't make a sound, but his body spasmed through his orgasm, almost violently. Just as his orgasm started to ease, mine began. He kept the rhythm until my orgasm waned. Without disengaging our sacred connection, he shifted us so I was lying on top of him. I was dazed. We gazed at each other and shared a tender kiss. He squeezed me a little. As I dosed off, my thoughts drifted to the truth that my connection to Michael wasn't as casual as I intended it to be. I was going to have to figure out a way to pump the brakes.

I woke up to an alarm going off. Michael turned it off and said, "We need to get up in a little while. It's already nine thirty."

I responded by covering my head with the sheet.

5

ARI, MICHAEL, HELEN
SATURDAY, AUGUST 12

I HEARD a knock at the door, followed by it opening and Ari saying, "It's time for you guys to get up. I'm hungry. I'm ready for breakfast."

Michael yelled, "Out!" and hurled a pillow at her. I realized we were still connected. My body clenched in response, and his body responded in kind. I uncovered my head and reached up to kiss him. Our bodies made tender but passionate love to each other. We were both spent when we finished. Our connection was palpable, and the intensity of it overwhelmed me. We looked at each other in silence for a few minutes.

I pushed away from him and said, "We should go."

He replied, "Yeah."

I got out of bed and took his hand, leading him to the shower. We showered quickly, only exchanging soft kisses. We didn't speak. He put on warm-up pants, a T-shirt, and sneakers from his knapsack. I dressed similarly. I hung up my dress and gave him hangers for his suit, opening the door to go downstairs.

He stopped me, saying, "Hey, do you have any leave-in conditioner?"

"Yeah, but I don't think you need it."

"Where is it?"

I led him into my bathroom and handed it to him.

He rubbed a good bit of into his hair. He looked at me and said,

"Now my hair will still be wet when we get to my mom's house, and it'll be crystal clear that you've just had your way with me." He chuckled and kissed the corner of my mouth. A thought ran across his face as he brushed my cheek with his thumb. "Are you sure you don't want Greg back?"

Where is that coming from? "I'm sure that I don't want him back. Why?"

He kissed my bottom lip. "When he comes to his senses, he's gonna want to come back."

"What makes you say that?"

He chuckled. "Call it male intuition. Let's go."

When we got downstairs, Ari sensed the connection between us immediately. She looked at both of us in turn and said, "Okay. You two might need to slow down. She needs to finalize her divorce …"

Michael took my hand and kissed my knuckles. "Yeah. I got that memo." He looked at me and added, "We're just hanging out, enjoying it as it comes." He was consciously working on my wards.

I looked at him and said, "You're right, Ari." I was way off course from where I'd intended.

She pulled us into a group hug, then took a deep breath. "Let's go. I'm hungry as hell." She looked at me and said, "Can you make my favorite breakfast and some of those little rolls? I've been craving them."

"Yeah. I already have everything I need here."

I threw everything in a bag, and we headed out.

WHEN WE WALKED into Helen's kitchen, she wasn't there. Ari walked toward the table on the far side of the room. Michael ushered me toward the kitchen island. Together, we started taking everything out of the bag.

Helen walked in. She saw Ari first. "Ari! It's good to see you again, sweetheart. What brings you to LA?" She gave her a warm hug.

Ari responded, "Work. And I miss my best friend," she glanced at Michael and waited a second, "and my brother."

"Well, I'm glad you and Mikey are getting to know each other."

Then she saw me. She said my name sweetly. "Sammi. Good morning, dear. We had so much fun last weekend. I'm happy to see you again." She gave me a warm hug too.

I hugged her back. "Good morning. We did have fun."

She walked over to her son. "Hi, Mikey." She kissed him on the cheek and stepped back and crinkled her brow. "It's not good to walk around with your hair soaking wet."

Michael put on his most innocent face. "I know, Mom," he said, then cut his eyes toward me.

In spite of myself, I blushed with embarrassment, turned away, and started separating the food.

I thought that Helen swatted Michael playfully before asking, "What's all this?" gesturing at the food on her island.

Michael responded, "Sammi's going to cook Ari's favorite breakfast for us."

Helen started to protest.

I said, "Please let me do this. It'll be my pleasure."

Michael, with a sarcastic glance at Ari, added, "Besides, it's what Ari wants. And that's all we've been doing since she got here yesterday, what Ari wants."

Ari narrowed her eyes. There was a slight smirk on her lips. I knew what she wanted to say.

Ari and Helen sat at the kitchen table, and Michael volunteered to be my assistant. He was quite adept in the kitchen. Helen had taught him well. We sliced and served pears and peaches with fresh cream to snack on while we prepared the rest. Within thirty minutes, breakfast was ready. We served spicy sausage with warm applesauce and hominy grits. Ari's favorite rolls were actually miniature buttermilk biscuits. Everyone was pleased.

As I got up to clear the table, I finished off the last bit of cream. Ari motioned to me that there was some at the corner of my mouth. Before I could reach for a napkin, Michael took my chin and tilted my head so he could kiss it off. He tenderly kissed my top lip, followed by my bottom lip, and then settled into one of his sweet and present kisses. The world slipped away, and I was swept into his affection. After a few seconds, he smiled against my lips and kissed my top lip again. Slipping away from me, he took the dishes from my hands and walked toward the dishwasher. I landed back in the world to the realization that Helen and Ari had witnessed our kiss. Again, as if I were twelve, I was embarrassed. I didn't know where to look, so I turned toward the stove and busied myself with clearing the pans.

Conversation was easy. Ari retold some of the stories I'd told last week from her perspective. We talked about politics and how to save the world. She made me do some of the silly dances from our youth, and we laughed at Michael when he didn't quite get one of them. The morning passed quickly.

By NOON, we were back at my house. Ari made her way to the kitchen, and Michael came in to get his suit and knapsack from my bedroom. I followed him.

Once we were inside, I hugged him. "I had fun last night and today. Thank you."

He smiled warmly and hugged me back. "Me too. Thank you. I'm gonna leave so that you guys can have some time. Let me know if you want to do something later."

"Okay."

"I'll say goodbye to Ari."

Without thinking, I reached up and took his face in my hands and kissed him sweetly.

"See you later." He took his things and left the room.

I took a deep breath and sat on my bed, placing my head in my hands.

When Ari walked in a few minutes later, I was still sitting there, lost in thought.

She said, "Wow," as she sat down next to me. "You guys have an intensity."

I shook my head. "Ya think?"

"Thought you two would hit it off. I didn't expect it to be this well."

I looked up at her. "It's so easy. There are moments when I want to let my guard down and give in to the myth of the fairy-tale relationship. *Relationship!* That's the exact opposite of what I'm trying to do right now."

"I know. You were just looking …"

I glared at her.

"Okay, I was just looking for someone you could date."

"I wasn't ready to start dating."

"Then you fucked him."

"Pheromones. Hormones. I thought he'd be the perfect person to fuck casually. I expected him to be shallow. Do you think he's gonna be shallow soon?" I put my hand on my forehead.

"The way he kissed you at Helen's … umm, no. It's obvious that women and sex are easy to come by for him. He's already in your pants, and it's clear that you like him. I don't see a reason for him to kiss you like that in front of his mom unless he really likes you too. I think he was just being in the moment."

"Yeah. Well, he's made all these moves a million times. And though he hasn't given me any of the typical pretty boy bullshit yet, I'm sure that it's only a matter of time."

"Maybe. Have you talked to him about slowing things down?"

"I've done my best to make it clear that there's nothing to slow down. I didn't intend to start something new right now. I told him that. He said he got the memo."

"He did say that," she replied slowly.

"He keeps catching me off guard. He's fucking up my wards, and he knows it!" I exclaimed.

"Maybe you should change your tactic."

"What do you mean?"

After thinking for a minute, she replied, "Acknowledge that you guys are starting something and agree to take it really slow."

"So you think that I'm doomed."

"It's obvious to me that you guys are into each other."

I paused to try to organize my thoughts. "The connection's just there, and it's so strong. It feels like any action, no matter how small, just makes it more apparent. Kinda like we're finding out about something that already exists."

"I can see that."

I shook my head. "I'm way off the rails. I have to get this back on track. I have two goals: get divorced and spend some time just being single."

She laughed. "I know you choose to be with people that you

don't think will follow through. I don't think that's gonna work the way you want it this time."

"You're such a romantic. And you're right. Most of my relationships, even my marriage to Greg, have been calculated risks. I've always kept my heartstrings under control. Maybe my algorithm let me down. Then again, maybe it's only a matter of time. After all, Michael's a very pretty boy."

"Maybe you're right. Maybe not. I don't know. Either way, you can't limit your future based on the actions of jackasses from your past or what you've seen. There will come a time when you have to stop guarding your heart."

It wasn't that time. "Well, that was just our third date, Ari. There've been no declarations."

"Talk to him about taking it slow when you think it's a good time."

I hugged her. "Okay. I prefer the 'We aren't starting anything' approach. How long are you staying?"

"I'm catching the red-eye back tomorrow night."

"Let's take a quick nap, and then I'll take you to that gallery that I told you about."

"Sounds good."

I lay back on my bed. "You and Michael should hang out later without me tagging along. I can do a little work. I need to prep for editing the footage we shot in Vancouver."

As she left my bedroom, Ari said, "We'll see."

After our naps, Ari, the financier, looked over my books and made some recommendations. Then we got cute, and I took her to a gallery I liked. She fell in love with a painting that had an interesting 3D effect. We decided to grab some food and relax on the beach for a little while.

When we were on our way back home, Michael called me. I answered the phone on the speaker system in my Mini Cooper. "Hey, there. Ari and I are in the car. You're on speaker."

"Hey. What are you guys up to? What are you doing this evening?"

I thought back to the conversation Ari and I had held earlier. "I have to be ready to edit the footage on Monday. If I work this evening, I can relax and hang with you guys tomorrow. So I'm gonna stay in."

"I'm gonna hang with a few of my friends tonight. I was hoping to introduce both of you to them. Do you really have to work?"

I gave the steering wheel a white-knuckled squeeze. "Yes, I really have to work." I glanced at Ari for support.

She piped in, "I don't have to work, and I don't want to sit at her house while she does. So I'm game. What do I need to wear?"

Michael responded, "Casual. No jeans. No sneakers."

"Sounds good. Just so you know, we're riding in Spencer tonight, and I'm driving."

Michael sighed. I could almost feel him rolling his eyes. "Okay, Ari. Come over to my place. We're gonna hang here for a minute and then start cruising, okay?"

Ari responded, "See you soon."

Michael said to me, "I wish you were coming too. Don't work too hard. I'll see you tomorrow, right?"

"I wish I didn't have to work. Yes, I'll see you tomorrow."

"Okay. I'll talk to you later."

Ari and I responded, "Bye," and I hung up the phone.

Ari looked at me. "What do you have for me to wear?"

I shook my head. "That depends. Do you want to go easy on them, or do you want to make a statement?"

"I try not to do easy."

"Okay. I have the perfect linen shorts suit with a sexy camisole."

When we got back to my place, I helped Ari perfect the outfit. She was visibly excited, and I was glad they'd have some time. I checked in with my mom, then settled into my work.

6

———————

BEACH HOUSE
SUNDAY, AUGUST 13

AT AROUND 1 A.M., Ari called. I answered, "Hello."

"Hey, how's it going?" She'd been having fun. I could hear it in her voice.

"Really well. I got a lot more done than I thought I would. Sounds like you're having a great time." I smiled.

"Soooo much fun! I wish you'd come. I really like Mike's friends."

"Next time."

"Most likely, I won't be in LA. It would've been perfect if we'd met them at the same time."

"Hmmm." I thought it was best like it was.

"Can we go to the beach house? Please, please, please. It would be amazing to spend the day chilling there tomorrow. We could drive up tonight and wake up there in the morning. I'll take my stuff so that I can go straight to the airport from there."

"Okay. That would be relaxing."

"Great. Can Mike come too?"

"So you're really liking your brother?" I was smiling broadly.

"Yeah, I am."

"Of course, he can come with us."

"Okay. We'll be there in the next hour." She hung up. That's why I loved Ari.

THEY ARRIVED about ten minutes after I finished working. Michael had followed Ari in his car and was visibly exhausted. Ari was happy and excited. She was talking a million miles an hour, telling me about their evening.

Michael moved around her so he was standing next to me, and we were both looking at her. After a moment, he took a deep breath. He reached out and put his left hand over her mouth and said to her, "Ari. Relax. Breathe." He looked at me, and with his right hand, he tilted my chin up and gave me a tender kiss. "She's been going on like this ever since we left the hang forty-five minutes ago. Is this normal?" He feigned a look of concern.

I laughed.

Michael had to snatch his hand back when Ari tried to bite it. He looked at her. "And she's feral." He chuckled.

Ari narrowed her eyes at Michael and looked at me. "Well, I hope you're ready to go." She was chastising me for laughing, which made it worse. "It'll only take a second for me to get my bag." She turned and walked off toward her room.

Still laughing, I responded, "I'm ready. My bag is by the door."

I looked at Michael. "So you guys had a good time?"

"Yeah, we did." He leaned on the table by the door, smiling.

True to her word, Ari was back in just a moment. "Okay, let's go."

We followed her outside. She went to the trunk of his car and put her hand out. "I'll drive." Michael looked at me, squinted his eyes, and slightly shook his head. He handed her the keys and got into the back seat of his own car. He dosed off immediately.

We put our bags in the trunk and were off. Ari started from the beginning and tried to recreate all the funny moments that had happened during their evening.

When she took a breath, I said, "Tell me about his friends."

"Well, it's true what they say about birds of a feather. All of his male friends are really handsome." She paused and nodded to add emphasis. "The girls are really attractive too, but their attractiveness is beside the point. The point is, they're all very intelligent, and they seem to have a real bond, like with our friends. They've been hanging out for a while, at least since college."

"Who was your favorite?"

She angled her head and crinkled her brow slightly. "Wow, I don't know. They're all so different. Paulo's really cute and sweet. And he's a big, silly flirt. Vic is witty and charismatic, very good looking and very smooth. I think they both do something with software. Chris doesn't say much, but when he speaks, he's always on point. His eyes are green and brown, really beautiful. Alex, Mike's brother, is quite handsome too."

"Yeah, I saw him briefly on the morning after our first date. What do Chris and Alex do?"

"Chris has an MBA. Alex is a photographer."

"Alex must be really good if he can make a living at it. Are they a homogenous group?"

She shook her head. "Not at all. They're very eclectic, like our friends. I think Paulo is Brazilian. He's got big brown curly hair and brown eyes. Racially, he's ambiguous to me, but I think white Americans perceive him as white. He's a little taller than Mike and leaner. Vic is Chinese. He wears his hair long. He's tall too. Chris is Black, from the islands."

"What about the girls?"

She smiled, which meant she liked them. "Alicia is pretty and smart. She has a strong personality and a way with words. I wouldn't want to cross her. She's from Colombia. I think she's a lawyer. Jilly, the other girl, is a white American. She's finishing up a PhD in physics, I think. She was kinda quiet. I got the sense it was because she was tired."

"Hmmm." I looked at Michael. He was sleeping soundly in the back seat.

"What?"

"I'm glad that you guys spent the evening together."

It had been a good visit for them. They were much more relaxed around each other. Even with the stop to pick up groceries, the drive only took an hour.

When we got there, Michael was still asleep. So Ari and I took all the bags in.

Michael realized we'd reached our destination and made his

way into the house before I went out to get him. He made a beeline for me. He put his arms around me and rested his forehead on mine with his eyes closed.

The tenderness of his gesture disarmed me. I took his hand, and the whole time I was leading him to my bedroom, I was thinking about how he kept slipping around all my defenses. Without pausing, he stripped down to his briefs, kissed my forehead, and collapsed in bed.

I went back downstairs to help put away the groceries and make sure Ari had everything she needed.

Ari yawned. "I'm tired."

"You should be. You had a big evening. I'm glad that you followed your intuition and looked for him. It seems like you guys are getting closer. That makes me happy." I gave her a hug.

She hugged me back. "Does it make you as happy as when he—?"

I smacked her on the head, playfully, before she could finish the sentence. "Good night."

"Good night."

Michael was out cold when I climbed into bed.

WHEN I WOKE UP, the sun hadn't quite cleared the horizon, but Michael wasn't in bed. I got up and brushed my teeth. The first person I found was Ari. She was fast asleep in the screened-in portion of the deck just off the den. Michael was on the floor, quietly stretching on the side of the deck adjacent to the kitchen. I made myself a cup of tea.

He was massaging his foot. I decided that the least intimate place for me to sit was behind him. "Good morning. You're up early. Did you sleep okay?"

He leaned back into me. "Like a stone. Good morning." He knew what he was doing. I had to give it to him—that was a good response. *Okay. Maybe facing him would've been better.*

I started to crawl around him. The next thing I knew, I was in his arms, and he was kissing me tenderly, passionately. He pulled me into the moment. In the same rhythm, I kissed him slowly, tenderly, deeply, really enjoying the feel of his lips and tongue.

He purred. "Ummm."

When the kiss ended, I fought for my equilibrium and reached for his foot. "Let me. What's bothering you?"

"My feet always get tight."

"I get that." The muscles in his calves were clear and distinct. His feet and toes were long and graceful. "It helps if you relax the calf muscle first." I kneaded the back of his calf.

He winced. "Aaahhh, that's just stuck."

Ari stirred.

I let go of his calf and mimed, "Shhh." I stood up and motioned for him to follow me. We went back to my bedroom. I started to fill the jacuzzi on the adjacent deck. I chose the rose-scented bath oil because it was the same scent as his soap. I let him smell it before putting some in the tub. I meant it as a joke, but he didn't catch the reference. While the bath filled, we took a quick shower. Once it was full, I positioned him so the jets were hitting his spine and then started working on his calf again. I asked, "Was your brother there last night?"

"Alex? Yeah. He came by for a little while." He rolled his eyes.

"Did you have a good time? How was it having Ari there?"

"If you'd come, you'd know."

I narrowed my eyes at him.

He chuckled. "Yeah, I had a good time. We always laugh a lot. Ari fit right in."

"Had Alex met Ari before?"

He nodded. "Mm-hmm. He met her the first time she came out."

"What does he think about her?"

"He'd only met her that once. His response to what I've said about her is that she seems really cool. Did you not come because you think it's too soon to meet my friends?"

"Some. And I wanted to give you and Ari time."

He hunched his shoulders, smiled, and shook his head a little. "Okay." He leaned back. "Other than Ari, you haven't mentioned any of your friends. Is it because you think it's too soon for that too?"

I chuckled. "No, it's because I haven't had a chance. This is only the fourth time that we're hanging out, Michael. Most of my friends are in Atlanta and New York. One of my friends from home lives out here too, but we don't get to spend much time together. Up until I decided to leave him, I let Greg be my focus out here. I've only made one or two new connections."

"Do you typically lose yourself in relationships?"

"No, that's not it either." I wasn't ready to tell him that story. I paused to figure out what to say. "Greg had just had that really bad accident, and I focused on helping him recover." I switched calves.

Michael squirmed. "This one's really tight. I twisted my ankle, and I think there's still scar tissue."

"Okay, relax. I'll be gentle." I lightened the pressure so he could relax.

"Do you have any siblings?"

I shook my head. "No."

"Where's your mom?"

"In Atlanta."

"Are you close to her?"

"She's not privy to all of the intimate details of my life like your mom, but yeah."

"Hmm." He closed his eyes. He only grunted occasionally as I finished the second calf and both of his feet.

When I started to rock his ankle gently, his eyes popped open. He said, "We'll be friends forever. That feels soooo good."

He was definitely charming. I kissed the ball of his foot and rocked the other ankle.

"Thank you. That's better."

"I'm glad." I was still holding his foot in my lap and started playing with his toes, feeling pretty turned on.

"Did I speak too soon? I thought you were done."

"Not quite." I sucked his second toe.

He met my gaze and waited for whatever was coming next.

I sucked the next toe.

"That feels surprisingly good."

I played with his toes for a few more minutes. Then I moved close to him, between his legs, taking care to spread them wide as I approached. I anchored myself with my hands on his thighs and softly touched my mouth to his and parted his lips with my tongue.

I kissed him with purpose, swirling my tongue against his. He responded by putting his hands on the sides of my face and sucking a little, as if he were pulling my kiss into himself. I leaned my hips against his thighs and stroked his erection up against my abdomen, one hand after the other. His pelvis flexed reflexively in rhythm with my hands.

After a moment, he pulled away from the kiss and stilled my hands. Looking into my eyes, he said, "I don't want to come like this."

"Okay." I stood up, took his hand, and stepped out of the jacuzzi. I led him over to a lounge chair, grabbing two towels on the way. I covered the lounge chair with one of the towels so it would be soft and comfortable against his skin. I motioned for him to sit down, following him onto the chair, quickly pushing him back and straddling him before he could settle. Before he could get situated, I took him inside of me.

He hissed in surprise. He put his hands on my hips and lifted me slightly to get comfortable. Then he let me settle back down on him. We both groaned a little.

He waited to see what I was going to do.

I remained perfectly still … and struggled to keep a straight face.

He narrowed his eyes in confusion.

"You're the leader in this lounge chair game. Do you want me to go round and round or up and down?"

He smiled and whispered, "Fuck." He pulled my face to his and kissed me deeply. Then he pushed me back a little and kissed each of my nipples in turn. He lay back and flexed his pelvis. "Round and round."

I moaned a little. "Okay. Round and round is not strictly legal for dating sex, but since I like you, I'll give you a taste."

"You're so kind. I like you too."

I made tiny circles with my pelvis. He inhaled and settled back to enjoy. When he started to move with me, I made the circle bigger and added a slight undulation. He moaned and put his hands on my hips. He was about to come. He ran his right hand up my body and inserted his thumb into my mouth. I sucked on it and ran my tongue around it. Almost immediately, he removed it and circled my clitoris with it. After a few minutes, I surrendered to a chaotic orgasm, and Michael surrendered with one of his own.

We relaxed and curled around each other. The sun was just above the horizon. We enjoyed the view and the sound of the ocean for a little while.

Michael said, "I'm really hungry. Let's eat breakfast."

When we got to the kitchen, it was 8:30 a.m., and Ari was still sleeping. We had Greek yogurt and granola, and I made a big smoothie batch with fresh fruit and spinach.

Before Michael could ask why I'd made so much, Ari came around the corner. She walked straight to the blender and poured what I'd left into a big glass, taking a gulp. Looking at us, she said, "Good morning." She began looking around the kitchen like she'd lost something.

Michael replied, "Good morning, Ari."

I pointed toward the yogurt and granola on the kitchen table.

Ari sat down and dug in.

I asked her, "How'd you sleep?"

"I love to wake up here, basically on the beach. I don't think I turned over. Have you guys been down to the ocean yet?" She was inhaling the yogurt and granola.

I said, "You must be starving."

"Yeah, I'm really hungry." She looked at Michael. "Did we have dinner last night?"

He nodded. "You ate twice and had dessert."

She looked back at her food. "It must be all the laughing. I feel like I haven't eaten in two days." To Michael, she said, "Thanks for introducing me to your friends. I had so much fun."

Michael smiled. "Yeah, it was a good time. I'll be in New York in a few weeks. You can reciprocate."

"Okay."

Michael and I leaned against the kitchen island and watched in awe as Ari downed the remainder of the yogurt and granola.

As she got up to put her bowl in the sink, I said, "This weekend is the first time I've spent time around you two since you met. To me, you guys are starting to feel like siblings. It's really nice to observe."

Michael nodded. "I don't know. I had my doubts, but now she *may* be growing on me."

Ari gave him a measured look. She wasn't quite awake enough for a quick comeback, but the wheels were turning.

Michael smiled at her mockingly; it had the desired effect.

I chuckled. "I have a million questions."

He responded, "Shoot."

I asked, "You have your birth certificates, right? Are you interested in looking up your birth parents?"

Michael responded first. "Since I can remember, my answer was no. I feel that I found my true mom. Now that I'm an adult, and I've met Ari, and I know that our birth mom was alone and eighteen when we were born, part of me wants to reach out to let her know that we found each other and that we're okay."

Ari answered pensively, "I hadn't thought of it that way. 'Til now, I was okay letting her choice stand. I just felt that Mike and I didn't get to choose whether we knew each other. That didn't seem fair. I could imagine reaching out to her."

I asked, "Which one of you was born first?"

Michael responded, "That … is … obvious. One of us is aggressive and demanding. The other is laid-back and patient."

Ari playfully shoved Michael.

I stepped out of the way.

Michael absorbed her shove. He grabbed her wrists with his right hand and maneuvered her into a headlock under his left arm. Once he'd secured her, he transferred her wrists to his left hand. Then he stood there and chuckled while she tried to free herself. He added, "And ever a gentleman."

When it was clear that she couldn't wriggle free, Ari looked up at Michael.

Michael responded by tapping her on the forehead every few seconds, laughing.

Ari glanced at me. "Are you just gonna stand there grinning, or are you going to help me?"

She was my best friend, so I had to help her. I stepped in and tickled Michael's rib cage, causing him to let go of Ari and grab my hands. Then Ari tickled him too. After a minute or two, all three of us were on the floor and Michael was crying uncle. We sat on the floor laughing for a while.

I asked, "Did you wrestle with your other sister?"

"Trina? No. Trina's eight years younger than Alex and me. She was always too little to wrestle."

I said, "But you wrestled with Alex."

"Daily."

Ari asked, "Why do you think it appropriate to wrestle with me?"

Michael responded, "Because it's so much fun." He tickled her rib cage, and I tried to help her by tickling him. He quickly pinned her with his legs and grabbed me before I could move away. He somehow managed to pin me with his upper body and one of his arms. With his free arm, he alternately tickled both of us. I could get a counter tickle in now and then, but it wasn't enough to free us. When it was clear Michael wasn't going to get tired, both Ari and I tapped out. Michael quickly moved out of reach, and he performed a victory dance, complete with a song.

After breakfast, we went for a dip in the ocean and played frisbee. Then we came back to the deck and chilled on the lounge chairs. Ari and Michael dozed off. I read a little, then dozed off too. We woke up around lunchtime and chowed down on cheese, salad, prosciutto, and fruit. We played at the beach for another hour or so. As we settled around the table to finish up the food we'd brought, Michael's phone rang.

He answered it without leaving the table. When he was done, he said, "Our artistic director just broke his foot. He has a workshop in Phoenix this week, so I'm going to do it for him. I leave in the morning." He looked at me. "We'll be apart for three days. Can we stay together tonight?" He took my hand and kissed my knuckles.

The fact that he posed the question like that made two things clear: first, he'd gotten my memo about slowing down and not spending too much time with each other, and second, he was pushing the boundaries by suggesting we spend a third night together. I looked at Ari for strength.

She shrugged.

I looked at Michael and closed my eyes for a second. I willed myself to say no, but nothing happened.

Michael asked, "What is it?"

I looked at Ari again and replied, "She's my best friend, and you're her brother. We have to be so careful, Michael."

He kissed my hand again. "We're adults. As long as we're honest and kind to each other, everything will be okay."

I pursed my lips. "Until you have a family with someone else and there's a celebration at your house—and I can't come because we've fucked each other."

They looked at each other, surprised.

Ari held up a hand to Michael and said to him, "I've got this." To me, she said, "If that's what the future holds, you already have that problem. At least two of the women that we ran into last night had slept with Mike. Now they're his friends." Then she smirked and said, "Look, by his own admission, Mike is promiscuous. A future partner will have a hell of a time trying to avoid everyone he's ever fucked. So that won't be a problem."

Michael looked at her in disbelief. He was trying to figure out how he ended up under the bus. Within seconds of looking at Ari, his disbelief melted into an eye roll and an ill-suppressed smile.

It made sense though. I responded, "Two very good points, Ari. Thank you." I avoided eye contact with Michael and kept a serious, straight face.

He inhaled deeply to regain his composure and asked, "Are you two done?" The quiver of his lips undermined his efforts to look and sound serious.

We both nodded yes. Ari lost control and giggled first.

"Good, so let's make a plan." He broke into a smile, completely failing at keeping a straight face.

Ari wasn't helpful. I agreed to let him stay and be his airport buddy. I'd have to repair my wards while he was gone.

I HAD A FEW GOOD, productive days. Michael and I exchanged a few texts during the day and checked in at night before bed. Talking to and playing with him added a levity to my life that I hadn't had in a long time. In spite of trying to reason to the contrary, I found myself looking forward to picking him up at the airport.

7

ALEX

WEDNESDAY, AUGUST 16

It was 6:20 p.m. when I arrived at the airport, and his flight had already landed. I spotted him leaning against the counter of a kiosk that was closed, waiting. I decided to sneak up on him from the side and give him the Maria treatment. I was approaching from his left side. As soon as I could touch him, I grabbed his left butt cheek with my right hand and ran my left hand across his chest.

He didn't miss a beat. He reached around my waist with his left arm and pulled me around to face him. With his right hand, he moved my left hand to his other butt cheek. He hugged me warmly and kissed me presently. "Hello, beautiful."

I responded, "It's good to see you."

"It truly is." He gave me a little squeeze. "It's clear that you intend to have your way with me. Before I can allow myself to be alone with you and fully at your mercy, I need to deliver this cake to my mom." He nodded toward the box sitting on the counter next to him. "It's from one of her good friends who lives in Phoenix. I'll be murdered if she doesn't get it tonight."

"Okay." I handed him his car keys and led him to his car.

Helen pulled into her driveway a moment after we did. We followed her into her house, with Michael carrying the cake. She insisted we stay and have a piece, and we talked about our weeks so far.

I imitated Michael crying uncle when Ari and I tickled him at the beach house.

When I was done, he said, "Finish the story. State what happened next."

When I pretended not to know what he was talking about, he told the story himself while tickling me. We were all laughing in that way that made the back of our ears hurt.

The kitchen door opened, and Alex, who had come by Michael's the morning after our first date, walked in saying hello. Michael, Helen, and I responded in kind.

To Alex, Michael said, "This is Sammi, Ari's best friend." He gestured toward me. To me he said, "This is my brother, Alex."

Alex extended his hand. "Nice to meet you, Sammi."

I shook his hand and said, "Same here."

Alex crinkled his brow and narrowed his eyes as he let go of my hand. It was an odd response.

He caught them up about his week without looking my way again.

I started to feel uncomfortable, but I tried to ignore him and act normally.

When Alex got up to get himself a piece of cake, I excused myself to use the restroom. Maybe he wanted to say something to Michael and Helen privately. I took my time to give them space. When I came out of the bathroom, Alex was in the hallway. I assumed he wanted to use it too.

I said, "I'm sorry. I didn't know you were waiting."

He replied, "Cut the act. I recognize you."

"I don't know what you're talking about."

"Please. Cut the bullshit. I saw you with Pete at that estate party. I know you're one of his whores."

My mind raced. Could he seriously be talking about the party that derailed my life?

"So now you remember." He stepped closer to me, then leaned down and whispered, "Walk away from my brother."

I tried to take a step back and found the wall. *Fuck.* "I never whored for Pete."

"You're lying. I saw you with my own eyes."

Michael came around the corner. "What's going on?"

Alex answered, "She's one of Pete's whores, man. I'm asking her to leave us alone."

I said, "I never wh—"

Alex put his hand on the wall next to my head and leaned in. "Quiet. Your charade's up. No one's interested in your lies."

Michael shouted, "What the hell is wrong with you, Alex?" He spun Alex around so he was no longer blocking me and pushed him into the wall. The whole hallway shook. "Sammi is not a whore, Alex. Of that, I'm sure."

Alex responded, "She is a whore, Mike! I saw her at one of Pete's parties. And now you brought her to our mother's house! I'm sure half of Los Angeles has fucked her since then."

I went into doubt about everything I thought I knew about what happened when I went to that party with Pete. I didn't remember Alex. I became afraid that Pete might not have been the only person I had sex with that night.

"More than half of Los Angeles has fucked you, Alex. A lot of people go to Pete's parties. Pete is a low-life and a criminal. I told you to stay the fuck away from him, time and again. What's going on, Alex? I can tell when you're hiding something. What have *you* done?"

It felt like it was only Pete. Evidence supported that conclusion. Maybe the drugs affected me more than I realized. Did I miss something? I was leaning against the wall for support. The hallway shook again, and my focus shifted to Michael and Alex. They shouldn't be fighting. I reached toward Michael and tried to push him away from Alex. "Please don't. I just want to go home."

Helen put her hand on my shoulder. She pulled me away from Michael and Alex, a look of concern on her face.

Alex took my plea as confirmation, and he said, "See, I told you. She's a whore, man."

Michael slammed Alex into the wall. "What have you done, Alex? What are you hiding?"

"Beating my ass won't make her any less of a whore, Mike."

Michael forced Alex into the wall again. They started to tussle and almost knocked over one of Helen's vases.

With a stern, menacing tone that was just below normal conversation volume, Helen said, "Have you lost your ever-loving minds? You're inside my house."

They disengaged immediately.

Helen touched Michael's shoulder. "Take her home, Mikey. She's clearly shaken."

Alex opened his mouth to say something, and Helen said, "Don't you say another word, Alex, or I'll slap the shit out of you myself." He closed his mouth.

Michael embraced me. He held my head against his chest. "Are you okay?"

I didn't realize I was trembling until Michael touched me. I whispered, "Yes. I'm fine." I looked at Helen. I said, "I never—"

She put her hand on my shoulder again and interrupted me. "I know."

Michael walked me toward the door. I let him support me and tried to relax.

Michael paused. He said, "We're not done, Alex."

He took me outside and helped me into his car, and we rode to my house in silence. I kept replaying that evening at Pete's in my mind. When he parked in my driveway, all I could think about was how I wanted to escape. *If I'd stayed focused on my goals, this wouldn't have happened. I need to end this now and get back on track.*

I swallowed and said, "I'm not a whore, Michael."

He turned my head so I made eye contact with him. "I know that, Sammi."

"I don't think we should see each other again. I don't want you to fight with your brother over me. I don't want to bring tension to your family."

He shook his head as if he were shaking off my words. "What happened?"

I felt like he deserved the truth. "I met Pete in New York. He was charismatic and kind, very much a gentleman. We talked on the phone a few times a week for four or five months. I went out with him five or six times in New York. He didn't even try to kiss me. He invited me to come to a party out here after I finished a shoot. I accepted."

I closed my eyes for a second to actually remember Pete. I hadn't thought about him in a good while. I thought of Pete as a WASP. He was average looking. His charisma was his draw. In hindsight, I could see that he had this air of normalcy around him he'd used to slip beneath my guard. "The party was part of a weekend affair at a luxurious estate. I arrived on a Thursday and planned to leave the following Sunday. I was so excited. The party that Alex is talking about happened on the interim Saturday. It was huge and full of celebrities. Pete took it as an opportunity to try and impress me with all the famous people that knew him. I met Greg that evening. When Pete got bored with hanging out with the celebrities, he suggested that we move on to the more exclusive part of the party. We decided to make out instead. I remember going into a den with him. We were the only people in there. I remember starting to make out with him. A while later, I woke up on a loveseat in that same room. Pete was gone, but I wasn't alone. There were other people in the room. They were having sex. I could feel that I'd had sex. That was when I realized he'd drugged me."

Michael slammed the stirring wheel. "So Pete raped you. Why didn't you go to the police?" His brow furrowed deeply, his jaw clenched, and I could see the veins at his temples.

I closed my eyes. "Because I consented to having sex with him, Michael. To a lot of people, that means that he had the right to do whatever he wanted to me."

"That's bullshit. Did you consent to being drugged?"

"No, I didn't. You're right. He raped me. Based on Alex's response to seeing me, maybe he let other people rape me too." A shiver ran up my spine. I had no idea how to process the information Alex had just given me.

"Until now, you were sure it was only Pete, weren't you?"

I nodded. "That's how it felt."

"I think you should trust yourself, Sammi. All Alex really said was that he saw you."

I nodded again. He was right.

It was time to course correct. "I had an amazing few weeks, Michael, really amazing. I really like you. But I'm gonna end this now." I kissed him on the cheek and got out of the car.

I'd only taken a few steps when he pulled me into his arms. "You put Pete and his shit behind you. From what I've seen, you didn't let it make you bitter or closed. You're a really strong person, Sammi. I want to give us a chance." He kissed my hair.

Shit. He was acting like he really cared. Working through my rape with him seemed like too much to ask. We were just hooking up casually, not trying to start a relationship. I tried to step back, but he only loosened his embrace a little. "Michael, you don't deserve to have to deal with my drama. I have no idea who I had sex with that night."

"You mean who raped you." His brow crinkled with anger. "Two things. I'm not walking away from you because of this. And I can't remember everybody I've fucked either. I always had a choice in the matter." He kissed my nose.

I said, "Michael, I'm still married to Greg." I needed to refocus.

He responded, "Your relationship with Greg is over, except for the paperwork."

Outside wasn't the place for what was becoming a discussion. "Let's go inside where we can talk."

We went inside and sat down on a couch. Despite my best efforts, I was still trembling a little. Michael's brow was still deeply furrowed as he pulled me close.

I took a deep breath. "Be logical, Michael. You've only known me for two weeks. This association is not worth creating a rift between you and your brother."

"I disagree."

"Two weeks, Michael."

"I know you feel our connection. How many times have you felt something like this?"

I just looked at him. I couldn't contradict his point.

He continued, "Either way, Alex and I have some shit to work through now. And what's happening between you and me is not the cause."

"I'm so sorry." Tears came. I couldn't fight them.

He squeezed me to him.

I realized I wasn't going to win that argument that night. I tried another approach. "Okay. I need some time to process this information." I suppressed a shiver.

"Okay. I need to be here for you tonight."

"Okay." I gave in to his embrace. The last time someone held me like that was in high school. It was my grandfather. Michael's stomach growled, and that made me smile. "You're hungry. I'll make dinner."

He responded, "Are you sure? We can go out … or order in."

"I'd planned to make dinner for us, and I don't really want to go out now."

"Let me help."

We got up and walked into the kitchen. I pointed to the wine on the counter. "Your contribution will be to pour us wine and keep our glasses full. This meal has some complexity." I looked at him to catch his reaction.

He reached for the wine and narrowed his eyes. "Oh, I have skills. Is there a salad? I'll make that."

I pursed my lips and shook my head. "Hmmm. I don't know."

He smiled and poured our wine. As he handed me my glass, he said, "Whatever. What's the recipe?"

"We're having a salad made of cucumber, tomatoes, green cabbage, and onions topped with a dill and vinegar dressing."

"That sounds good." He helped me set everything out.

I smiled. "You're sure you up to this?" I handed him a bowl, a knife, and a cutting board.

I had the salmon marinating, and I'd already prepped the string beans. So all that was left was to cook them. I put the salmon in the oven and turned on the rice maker, then relaxed to take a few sips of wine while I watched him make the salad. He made a beautiful salad and mixed in the perfect amount of dill for the dressing. The salad was ready. The salmon was about half done. He watched me sauté the string beans. Before we sat down, I put our dessert, guava turnovers, in the oven. We sat down at the island in the kitchen, and he chowed down. He was still eating when I got up to whip fresh cream to go with our turnovers. I was surprised I'd made more dinner than he could eat.

"I'm so sorry about this, Michael."

He put his hand on the side of my face. "This is just the most recent of many times that Alex and I have argued about Pete. Alex became friends with that asshole when we were in high school. Around junior year, Pete got tangled up with some dark characters who were trafficking sex, drugs, you name it. I was pretty sure that

Alex would end up in jail if he continued to hang out with Pete. It's like Alex can't tell the difference between right and wrong when he's around Pete." He paused, lost in some remembrance, then shook it off. "We had some pretty bad fights about him back then. Based on what Pete did to you, I think I actually underestimated how low he could go." He brushed his thumb across my cheek and kissed my lips lightly. "I'm sorry that Pete hurt you." He leaned his forehead against mine and closed his eyes. "Now Alex needs to come clean about what exactly he's hiding. It's true that this has come up in the context of what happened to you, but it's not because of you. The Pete issue between me and Alex is all Alex's fault." He opened his eyes and kissed me again.

I hid my face in his chest. "I don't think I can face your mom again. I'm so embarrassed."

He lifted my face and waited until I made eye contact. "There's no reason for you to be embarrassed. It wasn't your fault. Mom isn't holding it against you. She's worried about you."

I closed my eyes, and another shiver ran through me. "I've got to find my equilibrium about what happened with Pete again."

"How did you do it before?"

"Before, I worked through the fact that, despite me having consented to have sex with him, Pete drugged me. I had a really good therapist who taught me how to let my feelings come as they will and how to deal with them. She also gave me exercises to keep me from thinking about it incessantly. Some of it was my grandfather who told me that if an event is messed up, it's going to be messed up, no matter how long you talk about it. He said to talk about it only long enough to get clear about it, and then move on to the real work of choosing whether or not you're going to let the actions of assholes add limits to your life."

"I like your grandfather."

"Yeah. Grandfather was very special. And I was lucky that Pete didn't beat me up or brutalize me. He was wily enough to make me think I had a choice. Mostly, I had to break the inclination to think about it constantly. And I studied *Wu Mei Pai*, Ng Mui style martial arts from this incredible woman and healer from China, Dr. Maggie, to get a sense of physical safety. And truth be told, she's the person who put Greg back together."

He was pensive. "Does Ari know about all of this?"

"Yes. I can't imagine a better friend. I can't imagine my life without her." Tears escaped my eyes.

Michael kissed them away.

"You don't deserve all the drama that comes with my exes in your life. You just don't."

"Whether or not I want to deal with your demons is my choice. Believe me, I have my own demons." He paused and said, "Put yourself in my shoes. If you knew that Ari was involved with some really shady people in the past, and then you found out that they'd hurt me, would you willingly turn your back on me?"

When I looked at him, I really saw him, his soul, for the first time. Everything was right there in his eyes. He was truly kind and loving. He had a beautiful spirit. And he cared about me. He'd touched my heart. I loved him. *Fuck.* I whispered, "No."

"So stop trying to get me to do that." He kissed my forehead and leaned his forehead against mine. "Okay?"

"Okay." I gave in, took the turnovers out of the oven, and offered him one.

"Good." He dug in. "What is this?"

His enthusiasm made me smile. "A guava turnover."

"This is *delicious.*"

I watched him enjoy two of them. The evening had taken its toll on me. "I need a shower. I'm exhausted."

"Okay." He cleared our plates and cleaned all the dishes we'd dirtied making dinner. He led me through the den, where he picked up his bag, and up to my bedroom. Once we were there, he kissed me gently on my cheek and sat down on one of the chairs.

I showered as quickly as I could. I was stunned by Alex and by how I felt about Michael, but mostly, I just wanted to lie down. When I came out of the bathroom, he was standing by the window.

He walked over to me and hugged me tightly, then motioned toward my bed. He pulled back the covers. "Lie down." I complied. He pulled the covers over me and tucked me in. "Relax. I'm gonna take a shower too." He walked into my bathroom.

"Okay." His mood had shifted. He was tense, almost angry. I guessed the situation was also overwhelming for him.

When he was done showering, he came back into my room

wearing a T-shirt and boxer briefs. He seemed more relaxed. He turned off the light and settled into one of the chairs.

"Michael."

"Yes?"

"There's no reason for you to sleep in that chair."

"Are you sure? That was some pretty heavy stuff that came up tonight."

"I'm sure. I'm not in that situation anymore. You're not one of them."

He crawled into bed with me. "I want to hold you tonight."

"Okay." I snuggled against his chest.

He embraced me warmly. I dozed off, listening to his heartbeat and breathing.

MY THOUGHTS WERE RACING when I woke up. It was before daybreak. A dream in which it wasn't just Pete was lingering in my mind. I was still questioning my memory of the experience and slipping into a thought loop. I needed to stop that.

When I regained consciousness that night after Pete had drugged me, my first thought was to leave as quickly as possible. I had been unconscious for a few hours, and the party had petered out; on my way back to my room to get my things, I only saw one other person who was awake. While I was making my escape, I came across what must've been the security room. The door was slightly open, and there was no one in there. There were closed circuit TVs connected to cameras throughout the estate; it looked like they were recording everything that happened at those parties. Since the party was over for that night, whoever had been manning the room must have left. They were making what looked like sets of copies on thumb drives that were neatly dated and labeled. The room wasn't really organized other than the sets of thumb drives. I was pretty sure they wouldn't notice. So I took a set for myself. When I got home, I found the footage of the time that I was with Pete in that room. I didn't have to wonder what he'd done to me.

As part of my therapy, I wrote my memories and my feelings

about the experience down. I decided that reading my journal and watching the video again would calm my mind.

Michael was still holding me. He was fast asleep. It took me a few minutes to wiggle out of his embrace without waking him up. I went to my office and fired up my old computer. My memories were in line with my journals.

I took the thumb drive with the video on it out of my safe. I knew it like the back of my hand. I queued it to five minutes before Pete and I entered the room. I watched as Pete and I started to make out. I watched myself losing consciousness. I watched Pete make sure that I was unconscious. I watched Pete rape me. I watched him cover me up and leave the room. I watched as I slept. No one touched me. There was sex happening all around me, but no one even paid attention to me. Some people watched a guy with thick, shoulder-length locks that covered his face have sex with two women. I watched myself wake up and leave that room. I pulled the video cursor back to the beginning of my rape. I'd seen that video a thousand times. I wasn't the only one raped that night. I didn't need to watch the rest of it.

I was awake from then on. I didn't have sex with anyone else. My memory, my journal, and the tapes matched each other. Though Alex said that he saw me at that party, I didn't see him, and I didn't see him in the video. I still had no idea what he was reacting to.

8

───────────

POST-TRAUMA
THURSDAY, AUGUST 17

I WENT TO THE KITCHEN, made some tea, and grabbed a breakfast bar. The sun was rising as I curled up in my favorite chair in the den and surrendered to my feelings.

The thing that scared me the most came up first. My wards had failed completely. I'd fallen for Michael, and I was vulnerable to him. I didn't want to be vulnerable. What was I … in high school? Maybe I was infatuated. No, that wasn't it. The way I felt wasn't about sex either. It was about his presence and his kindness, and how easy and fun it was to be around him. I tried a different angle. Maybe I wasn't in love with him. Maybe I just loved him like a dear friend. Nope. That didn't work either. I hadn't managed my heart well. Two weeks later, like I was sixteen, I was in love with him. It felt good, but it was too fast. And I knew better than to think it was going to last. He was going to roll through me like a steam engine. There was nothing I could do about it at that point except accept it and move on.

Then there were all my feelings around being raped. I let them wash over me. Seeing Pete check to see if I was still conscious erased any doubt that he'd drugged me on purpose. I'd gone over my interactions with him a thousand times trying to find warning signs I'd missed—reaching for responsibility and, perhaps, self-blame. My tears came. I had to tread those thoughts carefully. Pete was a master con artist. There weren't any signs. Despite my vigilance, I'd

85

made a mistake and I'd trusted him. My whole body shook. I sat with the feelings and experienced them. After a while, the thought, *You're not there now*, surfaced. *You got out and you're safe* surfaced. Then I remembered my choice. He couldn't have my power. I breathed into that feeling for a few minutes.

I wondered what dating would be like in the future. Greg and I had hung out for almost a year and a half before we started dating. Michael was my first real date since Pete raped me—it wasn't a natural date because Ari had orchestrated it.

Michael. Alex. Michael was so angry at Alex last night, so certain he was hiding something. He was right; they had their own history with Pete that had nothing to do with me, but I couldn't see how I was going to be around Alex without there being tension.

I heard Michael stirring. I got up and quickly returned to my office and put my computer away. I walked back into the kitchen and rinsed my face in the sink. He walked into the kitchen just as I finished drying it with a paper towel.

"You've been crying. Are you okay?" He came over and hugged me.

"Yes. I'm okay."

He stepped back and tilted my head so he could see my face. He was looking into my eyes. "Are you sure?"

"I'm sure."

He looked worried.

I had to be honest so he could feel grounded through this. "You're right. I've been crying. Remember, I told you I try to feel my feelings as they come."

He nodded.

"Well, that's what I was doing. They'll come in waves for a few days, and then they'll subside. I've been through this before."

"I haven't. Are you being straight with me? Are you really okay?"

I hugged him. "Yes, I'm safe, and I'm okay."

He looked at me like he was trying to decide if he could believe me. "Okay. Are you going in to work today? Do you want me to stay with you?"

"I'm working here, at home, this morning and going in this afternoon. We're presenting the commercials that I've been working on.

It's the final step for this project, and no, I don't want you to follow me around while I work." I smiled.

He almost smiled. "Okay." He paused. "I know you want to limit the time that we spend together so that we don't move too fast, but I need to know that you're okay. I want to be with you for the next two nights. Please."

His eyes. What could I say? "Okay." I changed the subject. "Would you like an omelet?"

"Yeah, that would be good." He was watching me like a hawk.

I met his gaze and shared my strength with him. "Michael, I recovered from the actual event to the point that you didn't even suspect that it ever happened. I hadn't thought about what happened in at least a year. Last night, Alex made me wonder if the situation was worse than I thought. I put that to rest by looking at my journal this morning. Pete is the only person who raped me that night. This is overwhelming, but it'll pass. Trust me."

That seemed to land. "Okay." He nodded, mostly to himself. "Okay." He opened the coffee maker. "Do you want some coffee?"

"Sure." I made a small omelet for me and a huge one for him.

True to form, he ate like it had been days since his last meal.

I asked, "What do you want to do tonight?"

He answered, "Let's stay at my place. Come over after you're done with work, and we'll figure out what to do about dinner."

"Okay. Are you going to work?"

"Yeah."

"Would you like to take the leftovers from dinner last night for lunch?"

He smiled broadly. "Yes, that would be great."

I cleared our plates and packed his lunch while he put on some jeans and a fresh T-shirt. As he was leaving, he stopped to give me a warm hug.

I leaned back to make eye contact. "Thank you for being here, Michael." I kissed him with all the gratitude and passion that I wasn't ready to voice.

He returned the kiss cautiously at first and relaxed into a more passionate response. He smiled on my lips. "You're welcome."

Without separating from him, I said, "See you this evening."

He maintained contact and said, "Okay."

We hugged for a short while more. Then he turned and walked out.

As I closed the door behind him, I said, "I'll let you know when I'm on my way."

I leaned on the door, wondering if I would ever escape the drama that happened when I met Pete. Time would tell. I went to my office with the intent of looking over the presentation that we were going to make this afternoon. As I sat down, my phone rang. It was Ari. I was sure Michael had called her.

Ari opened with, "Do you need me to come out there?"

"No. Michael's pretty intent on hovering. I don't know if I could withstand both of you hovering at the same time."

"Okay. Mike said he spent the night."

"He was a perfect gentleman, Ari. He tried to sleep in a chair. I had to ask him to sleep with me. He held me close all night. He didn't try to get busy. He took good care of me."

"Good. How much did you tell him?"

"I told him the truth."

"About everything? Including what you did to Pete's car?"

She was referring to the fact that, in a moment of rage, I'd tampered with Pete's car before I left the estate to get back at him. I didn't think the car would make it out of the driveway, but somehow, it did. And Greg was driving it instead of Pete. I'd caused Greg's accident. After the accident, Pete sent me a text to let me know he knew I'd tampered with his car. That was why I didn't press charges. There were only three people who knew: Pete, Greg, and Ari. I intended for it to stay that way.

"No, no. I stayed focused on that night." I recounted what I'd told him. Then I added, "I didn't tell him about the night before. I didn't tell him about the thumb drive."

"Did he ask why you hadn't pressed charges?"

"Yeah, I said it was because I'd consented."

She understood. "So Alex was there. Michael thinks he's hiding something."

"They've known Pete since high school. Go figure."

"I know, right."

I exhaled. "I don't know what Alex is hiding. I went over my journal and looked at the video this morning. Pete was the only person who touched me. I didn't see Alex at that party. I didn't see him in the video either."

"You looked at the video? Again? Are you sure you're alright?"

"Yeah. You know how my brain works."

"You tortured yourself with that video."

"It was the only way I could find my way to a sense of peace. I wasn't torturing myself. I was looking that monster in the face so that it no longer had any power over me. I know that video by heart. I can replay it in my mind. Alex made me wonder if I had missed something. Watching it this morning stopped me from second-guessing myself."

"Okay. Well, I guess that makes sense. So you're okay?"

"Alex stunned me. I'm better now. I'm worried about Michael, though. He seems a little freaked out."

Ari responded, "He's definitely concerned."

"He's also really angry at Alex. He lost his temper and stopped just short of hitting him."

"That's not your fault, Sammi. Alex brought that on himself."

"I know." I paused.

Ari asked, "What's up?"

I whispered, "I'm in love with Michael, Ari. I feel like a teenager. I couldn't help it. If you could've seen his eyes … He's a good person, and he really cares about me."

She chuckled. "I saw that coming, and I know what you mean. I've seen him look at you. You don't choose who you love. It just happens, and he does care. Go with it, girl. I think it'll be alright. Did you tell him?"

"No." I took a deep breath. "Just want the drama to end, Ari. I can't believe that this Pete stuff has come up again now."

"Yeah. It's a lot. It'll end. You're gonna get through this."

"Yes. Tell Michael that so he can relax."

"I will. I gotta go, but I'll check in tonight."

"Okay. Love you."

"Love you too." She hung up.

Talking to Ari always made me feel better. I reviewed the presentation. It was in good shape. I decided to go in to work early because I didn't want the opportunity to worry about how I'd fallen for Michael.

When I got to work, I shared the presentation with my colleagues for last-minute comments and inputs. We ended up having a great discussion about the effect of media on culture. We came up with some great ideas for future projects. When we broke for lunch at 1 p.m., I texted Michael, "I'm still okay. How are you?"

He texted back, "I'm good. Even better now."

Fifteen minutes later, I got a picture of him eating the lunch I'd made for him. He had such a beautiful smile. I sent a picture of me blowing him a kiss.

The presentation started at 2:30 p.m. It went well. We ended up brainstorming about possibilities for future ads.

ALL IN ALL, I had a good day. I was busy and didn't have time to think of Pete or Alex except for fleeting thoughts. It was 5:30 p.m., and I was sitting in my office preparing to leave work when Ari called.

I answered, "Hey, I'm fine."

She responded, "I know you're fine. I have a confession."

"What did you do?"

She whispered contritely, "I accidentally told Mike that Pete raped you more than once."

"You just came out and said that?"

"No. He asked me were you saying that you didn't remember Alex to protect his relationship with Alex, and I responded that you don't remember the rapes."

"Damn. How did he take it?"

She answered, "He has quite a temper."

"That he does."

"I'm sorry, Sammi."

"I know you didn't do it on purpose, Ari. I'll be honest with him. Thanks for the heads-up."

"Let me know how it goes."

"I will." I hung up and took a deep breath. It was surreal that I was processing this with Michael two weeks after meeting him. I texted Michael, "I'm done for the day. Is it too early for me to come over to your place?"

He texted back, "No. I'll leave work now. See you soon."

He was waiting for me in his driveway when I pulled up, and he smiled when he saw me. That was a good sign. He wasn't as freaked out as he was when I'd last seen him. As soon as we got inside his place, he kissed me. It was tender and present and passionate. I let the world and all the drama fade.

I snapped back to reality when I heard a man clear his throat and say, "You know, you're only about fifty feet from the bedroom."

Michael let out an exasperated breath and responded, "Maybe we aren't planning on using the bedroom, Paulo. Why are you here?" So this was a friend of his. People were comfortable walking in on him.

Paulo, who was still closing the front door, smirked then locked it after himself. He had deeply tanned skin with big, curly brown hair. His eyes were medium brown. He was taller and not as muscular as Michael. While eyeing me up and down, he answered, "I was in the neighborhood. I'm here to eat dinner." He bowed and took my hand, saying, "Surely, you're an angel come to Earth, my dear. My name is Paulo, Paulo Buarque. I'm very pleased to meet you. You are?" He was smart enough not to say a name, knowing Michael was a player.

I responded, "Sammi."

Paulo looked at Michael and said, "You wholly failed to describe her beauty, Mike. I see why you were holding out on introducing her to us." To me, he said, "He's a little intimidated by me. He's afraid of the competition."

Michael shook his head and said to me, "Paulo and I grew up together. Given how he just barged in, you can tell he's like a brother to me, and as you can see, he's basically insane."

Paulo scrunched his face and shook his head. He glanced back toward the door. "I thought you drove a Ferrari."

I responded, "I have a Ferrari, but I don't drive it every day."

He sized me up for a moment, then asked, "So what are we having for dinner?"

Michael was speechless. I liked their banter. I looked at Paulo and said, "I don't know, Paulo. What do you have a taste for?"

Paulo responded, "You're the angel here, my dear. Your desire is my command."

I answered, "You're quite handsome and charming, Paulo. I understand why Michael's intimidated. I have a taste for something spicy." Michael was shaking his head and choking back a laugh. Paulo was actually stunning.

Paulo replied, "I just bought some steaks. Mike can make us steak with peppercorn sauce."

I laughed. "I'd like that very much, Paulo. Thank you." We looked at Michael.

Paulo added, "You heard the lady. Get to it."

He tried to look displeased. "Whatever."

Paulo handed him the bag he'd set on the table near the door.

Without looking in the bag, Michael said, "So you came over for me to cook your steaks?"

Paulo responded, "No, I came over and brought you some really good steaks for dinner."

We followed Michael into the kitchen area and sat down at the kitchen island to watch him cook. He seasoned the steaks. Then he used a slicer to slice potatoes into chips. He mixed oil and salt in a big bowl and positioned three cookie sheets on the counter. With a dubious look, he said to Paulo, "Can you manage to coat these potatoes with oil and lay them out on the cookie sheets?" He looked at me, pointed to the refrigerator, and, with a mostly straight face, said, "Can you handle making us a salad?" Then he poured himself a glass of wine and leaned back to chill and watch Paulo.

Paulo said, "He can be so rude. We're his guests. He's making us work, and he hasn't offered us any wine."

They made me laugh. Ari was right—Michael's friends were a lot of fun. I started working on my assigned task.

Michael said, "Come on, man."

I turned in time to see Paulo lay a potato slice on one of the cookie sheets. Michael dumped all the potatoes into the oil and salt and motioned for Paulo to mix them. Apparently, he'd been dipping them and laying them out one at a time. Paulo did as he was shown, then started laying them out one by one again. Michael shook his head and laughed. "Really, Paulo?" Michael grabbed a handful of potatoes and showed him how to spread them onto the cookie sheets. I laughed out loud.

Once Paulo got the potatoes in the oven, Michael sautéed the steaks and made the peppercorn sauce.

Paulo muttered something to Michael's back, then looked at me and asked, "Would you like some wine?"

I responded, "Why yes, I would."

Without looking at us, Michael said, "Since you guys are chilling, you can put the silverware and salad on the island."

Paulo motioned for me to take a seat. He set the salad and silverware on the island and handed me a glass of wine. Michael plated our steaks and potatoes. We started in on a really good meal.

Paulo said, "What've you been beating this time, man?" Michael's knuckles were red and a little swollen. I hadn't noticed before. This situation was affecting him more than he was letting on.

Without looking up from his food, Michael responded, "I spent the morning at the sparring gym." He was underplaying it.

"Hmmm." Without pausing, Paulo added, "You remember that time we snuck out to that party in San Diego when we were in high school?"

I guessed it wasn't unusual for Michael to beat on things.

Michael laughed. "Yeah, we took my mom's car, and it wouldn't start when we were ready to come back."

Paulo snickered. "Because it was out of gas."

Michael finished, "We were begging to get in trouble."

They settled into a playful banter. When I could, I sided with Paulo. We finished dinner.

I asked Paulo, "What would you like for dessert?"

Paulo responded, "Based on what I saw when I walked in, you guys already have plans for dessert. I know how not to overstay my welcome. I want a plate to go, Mike." Paulo got up and cleared the table.

Michael nodded.

Paulo looked at me and said, "Oh, yeah. We're celebrating our friend Alicia's birthday tomorrow at seven. You're cordially invited." He looked at Michael. "Later, man."

Michael handed him the plate he'd requested. "Bye, Paulo." Michael followed Paulo to the front door and locked it behind him. I followed him. When he turned around, I was standing right in front of him.

I said, "What was it that you were saying when we were so rudely interrupted?"

He smiled. "I can't remember. Do you know the subject?"

I put my arms around him. "It had to do with this."

He looked confused. "I still can't remember."

I tilted his head and started to trail little kisses across his lips.

He responded, "Ah, yes. Now I remember." He kissed me passionately that time, but he didn't take the next step. Instead, he let the kiss resolve. He said, "You seem like you had a good day."

I stepped back so I could see his eyes. They were filled with tenderness. "I did have a good day." I looked at his hands. The situation was clearly traumatic to him. "Are you okay, Michael?"

He huffed. "I was pissed, extremely pissed, earlier. I went to the gym and got it out of my system. I'm okay now." His eyes were overflowing with concern and anger.

I said, "Ari told me that she slipped up."

"He raped you more than once, Sammi." He furrowed his brow and narrowed his eyes in anger. "Can you tell me what happened?"

I looked down to clear my thoughts.

"You don't have to. I understand if it's too much."

It was way too soon for us to be dealing with this, but dealing with it, we were. I looked at him again. The truth. "On the night before that big party I told you about yesterday, only a handful of people were at the estate. As far as I know, Alex wasn't one of them. Pete and I had sex in the room I was staying in—we had separate rooms. I remember starting to have sex with him but not how it ended. Everything seemed normal afterward. Nothing was out of place in the room. The way he was acting was normal; he was holding me when I woke up. I'd just finished a real difficult shoot and was exhausted. I decided I must've passed out because I was tired, or maybe I'd had too much to drink. In that moment, that conclusion made sense. The thought that he'd drugged me didn't cross my mind. Looking back, I feel like an idiot."

He pulled me close and muttered, "Fuck" through gritted teeth.

I took a deep breath and grounded myself in the moment. "It's in the past, Michael. Only you and I are here right now, and we've only been kind to each other."

"I know. You're right. I guess I need a little more time to process it. I just want to make sure that you're okay."

He'd only been dealing with my drama for about forty-eight hours. I could give him time to process it some. I changed the subject. "I like Paulo. And you don't have to feel obligated to take me to Alicia's dinner tomorrow."

Michael relaxed a little. "He liked you too. And I don't. You, however, are obligated to show up at Alicia's party tomorrow. If you choose not to go, you'll have to explain your 'settling dust' thing to him. I'm not taking the blame for you not being there."

I smiled. "Okay. Do I need to bring a gift?"

"No. Dinner is the gift."

It was 8:30 p.m., and I knew what we weren't going to do. I said, "It's too early for bed. Do you want to come scouting for film sites with me?"

He responded, "Sure. What time do you have to be at work tomorrow?"

"I don't have to work tomorrow. I'm in between projects right now."

He asked, "For how long?"

"At least a week. Maybe two."

"I have to go to New York next week for a shoot. Come with me. Ari wants to see you."

They'd discussed it. I hadn't considered they'd gang up on me. "Maybe."

"We don't have to stay together. You can stay with Ari. I can stay in a hotel."

I gave him a little more hope. "Okay, I'll think about it. What time do you have to be at work tomorrow?"

"Eight."

"Let's walk. We won't stay out too long."

We left his house and walked toward the closest main street. I watched him, trying to assess his mood. I wanted to ask him a question, but I didn't want to upset him.

He stopped walking and looked at me. "What?"

I decided to go for it. "Did you talk to Alex?"

"No. He's not communicating with me. He hasn't responded to

my calls or my texts. I apologize for his behavior last night. You didn't deserve that."

"It wasn't your action, but thank you." We continued walking.

"Don't worry about Alex and me. We'll be fine. Focus on taking care of yourself."

I wanted to say I could do both, but I could tell it wouldn't be constructive. "I am. I trust myself, my experience of that night. I don't know what Alex is reacting to. Maybe Pete usually brings call girls to parties with him."

His brow crinkled. "With Pete, anything is possible." He seemed pissed again.

I said, "Hey, look at me." I kissed him. "Those steaks were delicious. You and Paulo together are hilarious."

He kissed my forehead and hugged me. "I'm okay, Sammi." He put his arm around me.

We walked and consciously chatted idly while looking at houses, corners, restaurants, and stores in his neighborhood. We went back to his place and, like the night before, took separate showers. I fell asleep in his arms.

I woke up at 9:30 a.m. Though Michael had left for work almost two hours before, his scent lingered on his pillow. I basked in it while I planned my day.

9

ALICIA'S PARTY
FRIDAY, AUGUST 18

IF I WAS REALLY GOING to take a dance class with him, I needed to work on my technique, my strength, and my endurance. I'd go to Amanda's studio. Amanda Turner was a few years older than me. She'd studied at the same ballet school I did when I was a teenager in Atlanta. She was my ballet big sister, my mentor, and she had become my friend. She grew up in LA and had been back for about five years. I took most of my dance classes and did most of my workouts at her studio. It would be good to see her today.

When I sat up, I saw that Michael had left me a note and the keys to his place.

Good Morning Sammi. X.

I hope you slept well. I made you breakfast. The hot water, tea, and granola are sitting on the island in the kitchen. The fruit and yogurt are in the fridge.

Call me if you need me. I'll come back home. Text me to let me know that you're okay.

Mike

He was still worried. I had to figure out how to help him through this. I started by texting him. "Morning Michael. I'm just now waking up. I slept really well. I'm okay. Much better than yesterday so don't worry. Thank you for breakfast. I'll check in later. X." I sat there and thought about what else to say to him. A few minutes later, he responded with a smiley face, which probably meant he was busy.

I got up and got dressed. When I got to the kitchen, I saw that Michael had made a presentation of my breakfast. The place that he set even included a cloth napkin. My heart was putty in his hands. I texted him, "Breakfast is beautiful." He didn't respond. I ate and got on my way. I had to go home and change before I went to the studio.

I ARRIVED two hours before the 1 p.m. class, so I had time to stretch and check in with Amanda, the only person other than Greg who I knew when I came out here. I started coming to her studio after he recovered. Our relationships were our go-to conversations. She was in the studio alone, standing behind the reception desk, looking at the computer, when I walked in. The way she held herself because she was a dancer, the set of her neck and shoulders, added a sense of regality to her thick head of naturally red hair.

Without looking up, she said, "Hey, how goes it?"

I responded, "Good. You?"

"How long has it been since you were last here?"

"About three weeks."

"Seems like longer."

"Nope."

She asked, "So where do things stand with the Greg thing?"

"The separation's legal, and I've filed to convert it into a divorce."

"Are you ever going to tell me what happened between you and Greg? Because of the accident, things always had a certain intensity, but there was a time when he worshiped and adored you." Greg's celebrity sometimes made people idealize my marriage to him.

The short answer to that question was no. But I had to tell her something to put the subject to rest. "He never worshiped or adored me enough not to cheat on me. You know that. Sometimes loving a person and being dedicated to and honest with them isn't enough to make things work out."

She shook her head regretfully. "Hmmm. I get that." She finished whatever she was working on and looked at me. "You look good, really good. You're glowing. What haven't you told me?"

I diverted, "How was that date you had planned the last time I was here?"

"He was a nice guy. Conversation was okay. Dinner was really good. Dancing." She made a scream face. "There was no spark. Done. Back to you."

I shook my head. "What do you mean?"

"Uh-uh. Who are you dating? What's his name?"

I suppressed a smile. "Is it really that obvious?"

"To me it is. I'm listening."

"Michael Shelly."

She smiled too. "He grew up to be quite the specimen. How long?"

"Yeah, he's gorgeous. For just a few weeks."

"He's hard to pin down. How's that going?"

"I expected him to be shallow, but so far, it's been really nice."

She nodded. "Mm-hmm. Yeah, I bet." She paused. "I was thinking of introducing you to him. I thought you two might hit it off."

"If he's hard to pin down, why would you introduce me to him?"

"Because he's a good person. I've never seen him be cruel. He's not a player. I mean, he doesn't play games. The face he presents is true. He tells you what he's up for up front. Women get frustrated with him when they want more than he's offered. They always hope he'll change his mind. I know that you know better."

I used to. I'm not so sure anymore. I asked, "How do you know him?"

"I studied at the same dance school as he did when we were kids. I was a teacher's helper. I ran into him when I moved back out here. He rolls through the studio and causes a lot of commotion from time to time. How did you meet him?"

"He's Ari's twin brother."

"Ari Campbell?"

"Yeah. She found out she had a twin about three months ago and looked him up. She conned him into taking me out on a blind date."

"Wow, that was some blind date." She closed her eyes. "I knew that she made me think of someone. How could I not have made that connection?"

"It's really unbelievable when you see them together."

She looked at me again. "You really like him, don't you?"

"I do. It's not good to fall for guys like him."

"Yeah, they can be flighty sometimes. But you never know. Either way, enjoy it while it lasts."

"He wants us to take a ballet class together. I have to work up to that."

She nodded aggressively. "True. He's a really good dancer. Have you seen him perform?"

"No, not yet." I didn't know if I could take seeing him perform.

My phone buzzed. It was a text from Michael. "And so are you. X." It was quickly followed by another text. "How's it going?"

I responded, "I'm fine. I'm hanging out with Amanda Turner at her studio. I'm gonna take a class. She says hello."

He responded, "Tell her I said hi too. See you in a few hours. Call me if you need me. X."

Amanda chuckled. "He's really got you going."

I rolled my eyes and shook my head. "He told me to tell you hello."

She laughed again. "Mm-hmm."

I hit her playfully. "You're worse than Ari." I started walking toward the dressing room. "I'm going to get changed and stretch before class."

"Mm-hmm."

I TOOK THE CLASS, then worked out on the machines in the studio until about 4:30 p.m.

Michael texted, "I'm done. Where are you?"

I responded, "I'm about to leave Amanda's studio."

He texted back, "Stay there. I'm close by. I'm hungry. I want to get something to eat."

I responded, "Aren't we going to dinner in a little while?"

He texted back, "They're getting started at six thirty. There's no telling when we'll eat. See you soon."

Michael was talking to Amanda and a few other people when I came out of the dressing room. It was especially nice that a few of the young male students were among that group. The boys were hanging on to Michael's every word. One of them had even adopted his stance. Michael had his back to me. Inspired by the conversation I had with Amanda earlier, I took a moment to admire him. His hair was wet, and his curls were slowly freeing themselves from the weight of the water. He was wearing a sleeveless T-shirt with large openings for the arms, a pair of skinny jeans, and some slip-ons. The T-shirt hung to about an inch below his hips. It accentuated the musculature of his shoulders and back and the narrowness of his hips. With those lean, strong thighs and perfectly defined calf muscles, he definitely had the legs to work those jeans. The slip-ons showed off his sexy, suckable toes. It was funny how his physical beauty that loomed so large when I first met him a few weeks ago had been dwarfed by his presence and kindness. I'd forgotten to ogle him like I should.

When I broke out of my reverie, I realized Amanda was watching me check him out. He turned his head to follow her gaze. He excused himself from the conversation and reached his hand out for me. His knuckles were bruised from yesterday's bout at the sparring gym. As I was walking across the room to take his hand, one of the modern teachers walked out of a classroom and stopped short when she saw him. She quickly regained her composure and mumbled an awkward hello, followed by a knowing glance at a woman in the group of people he and Amanda were talking to. I guessed these were two of those frustrated women Amanda was talking about.

He took my hand and kissed it when I got to him. He tilted my head up to meet his gaze with his other hand and whispered, "How are you?"

I whispered back, "Fine."

He searched my eyes for evidence it was true. When he was satisfied it was, he said, "Good," and gave me a quick and tender kiss. "Are you ready?"

"Yeah, let's say goodbye to Amanda." I knew she was watching us like a hawk.

"Okay."

Hand in hand, we turned toward where Amanda was standing a few feet away.

She broke away from the group. "You guys heading out?"

I responded, "Yeah."

She looked at Michael and at me. "Mm-hmm. You two should come and take one of my classes."

Michael nodded. "We will. Maybe sometime in the next few weeks."

She said, "I'm holding you to it."

Michael let go of my hand to give her a hug and walked over to the front door.

Glancing at me, Amanda responded, "I think you really got him going too."

I responded, "He's been really kind. I'll see you later."

She said, "Mm-hmm. Okay."

I FOLLOWED Michael out of the door. I expected us to pick up something quick. Instead, he chose to eat in and did so at a normal pace. Only then did we go to his place so I could drop off my Mini Cooper and change. Michael insisted I take my time. At about 6:45 p.m., his phone buzzed. It was a text from Paulo listing the things he wanted Michael to pick up on his way over. He chuckled. He said that text was the signal it was time to go. Paulo didn't live far from Michael. We stopped by three stores on the way over.

When we walked in, at least seven people were there already. Paulo said to Michael, "Thanks, man. Alicia's about five minutes away. Alex should be here in a little while."

The thought of Alex showing up filled me with angst. It dawned on me then that these weren't just Michael's friends. These were Alex's friends too. I wondered if anyone had warned him I'd be here. Since Paulo had invited me yesterday, I was an unexpected last-minute addition.

Looking at me, Paulo said, "I'm glad you came." He gave the bag I was carrying to Michael and took my arm. "Let me introduce you to everyone." He led me into the kitchen where a few people were helping him finish preparing and cleared his throat. "Everyone, this is the elusive Sammi that we've been hearing about."

I smiled and said, "Hello."

Paulo pointed to each person. "This is Jilly, Vic, and Chris. Mike, Alex, and I went to high school with Alicia and Chris. Vic and Jilly went to Caltech with Mike and me." Ari had described everyone very well.

Michael came over and joined the circle by hugging me from behind.

I said, "It's nice to meet you all. I've heard good things. Ari couldn't stop talking about you guys. What can I do to help?"

Paulo was looking at Michael. To me, he said, "Set out the cutlery and glassware please." We broke the circle and got busy with our tasks.

A few minutes after we had everything set, Alicia walked in with really handsome guy in tow. We all wished her a happy birthday and settled into the wonderful Brazilian meal that Paulo had a hand in making. If I hadn't seen it for myself, I wouldn't have believed that Michael had eaten dinner earlier. We started out talking about politics and the state of the world. Then the conversation turned to taking a group vacation to escape it all. A few moments later, my cell phone buzzed. It was Ari.

I excused myself and went into the kitchen to answer. "Hey, girl. How's it going?"

She responded, "I'm fine. How are you? Was today better than yesterday?"

Was today better than yesterday? She's been talking to Michael. "Tell Michael I'm fine. I'm at a party for Alicia with Michael and his crew."

She laughed. "Got it. I wish I were there!"

"Me too. Alex is on his way. I hope he doesn't have another outburst."

"Has Mike talked to him? Are you okay to deal with him?"

I responded, "I don't think so. I can handle it."

"How is Mike? Is he still freaked out?" He was working his way into her heart too.

"Michael's hands are all bruised. He spent yesterday morning beating things at a sparring gym because he was so angry. Yes, he's still freaked out. I'm worried about him."

She replied, "Well, I'm glad you guys are coming to New York. We can work through this together."

You guys? "I haven't decided whether I'm coming yet. We've been together since he got back. I think a little space would be a good idea."

"Yeah, but what do you really want to do?"

"Not helpful."

"I'm just keeping it real." She paused. "I really want you to come to New York. *Please.*"

"I'll think about it."

"You don't have to stay with him while you're here."

I exhaled. "I'll think about it."

"Michael's coming to New York in less than forty-eight hours. Make up your mind by tomorrow. Let me know how things go with Alex tonight. Try not to worry about it."

"Okay. Love you."

"Love you. Bye." She hung up.

Alex was sitting at the table when I walked back into the main room. I gathered my calm and thought of Michael and Ari working together to make sure I went to New York with him and let a smile come to my face. I avoided eye contact with Alex and took my seat next to Michael. Being around his friends had really helped Michael relax. He was leaning way back in his chair. He rested his arm on the back of my chair and absentmindedly caressed my shoulder with his hand. Paulo and Alicia were doing most of the talking, so I focused back and forth between them. At some point, Alicia stopped talking in mid-sentence to look at Jilly. We all followed suit. Then we all followed Jilly's gaze to Alex.

He was staring, more like glaring, at me. Since I'd only seen him once before, I didn't really have a point of reference, but Alex looked tired and possibly high. My presence was clearly bringing up something unpleasant about that night at Pete's for him. I felt Michael shift in his seat. Alex shifted his focus to Michael, and I did too. Michael was looking back at Alex with an icy gaze. My heart sank. Discord between the two of them was the last thing I wanted to happen. I had a feeling Alex needed the support of his friends and his brother more than usual right then. After a minute or so of them glaring at each other, Alex violently pushed back in his chair, stood up, and stormed out of Paulo's house. My bet was that no one had warned him that I'd be there—in his safe space with his friends. I didn't feel good about that.

Paulo watched Alex leave. Then he looked at Michael and asked, "What? Is he in love with her too?"

I was shocked that Paulo said that out loud in front of their closest friends. I looked at my hands and tried not to blush. I hoped that Michael didn't feel cornered.

Michael huffed and said, "Yeah, something like that." Then he squeezed my shoulder so that I looked at him. He searched my eyes to see if I was okay.

I smiled slightly to give him a yes.

He kissed the side of my mouth. He turned back to Alicia and restarted the conversation where she'd left off. The core group of them seemed unaffected by Alex's behavior. I guessed that Michael and Alex fought in front of them from time to time. It took the rest of us a little while to recover.

Michael and I left the party an hour or so later. On the way to his house, I wanted to talk about Alex, but I wasn't sure that was wise. I decided to talk about Alicia and Paulo. "Was that guy Alicia's boyfriend?"

"Jason? I think so. Why?"

"He didn't seem too comfortable with the way that Alicia and Paulo interact with each other. Have Alicia and Paulo ever dated?"

He smirked. "No. They don't seem to notice that they come across as attracted to each other."

"Have you ever asked him about it?"

"He says it's not like that. She's like his sister."

"Maybe they don't want to risk their friendship."

He asked, "How would they be risking their friendship?" He turned into his driveway.

"It's not always easy to be friends after being lovers, especially when new partners come along."

He rolled his eyes. "We aren't in high school. We're adults. We all have histories." He got out of the car and went inside.

As we walked into his place, he said, "You can jump in the shower first if you want to."

I didn't want to shower separately. I responded, "No, you go ahead. I'm going to check in with my mom for a minute."

"Okay." He walked off toward his bedroom.

I waited until I heard him turn on the water, then undressed in his bedroom and joined him in the shower. He had his back to me. I put my arms around him and kissed him between his shoulder blades.

He turned around and stepped back so that we could share the stream. "Hey."

I put my hands on the sides of his face and kissed his top lip and then his bottom lip.

He put his hands on the sides of my face and kissed me passionately, and I responded in kind. He let the kiss resolve and said, "I'll wash your back." He put shower gel in his hands while I turned my back to him. He massaged my neck and shoulders with the lather. His hands were strong, sure, and gentle. He meticulously worked his way down my back. It felt amazing. The tension from the past day or so washed away. When he reached my waist, I turned around to face him. Without hesitation, he continued to wash me. Everywhere. When he was done with my feet, he stood, put the shower gel in my hand, and said, "Your turn." He turned his back to me.

I washed him like he'd washed me. When I was done, I kissed him passionately. He returned the kiss as I caressed his penis.

He broke the kiss, removed my hands, kissed them, and said, "Let's go to bed."

I responded, "Okay."

He wrapped me in a towel and got one for himself. I followed him into his bedroom. I watched him dry off and put on a pair of boxer briefs. I didn't know what to do. So I just stood there with the towel around me.

He looked at me. "Do you have something to sleep in?"

"No." *My plan was to get laid.*

"Here." He tossed me one of his T-shirts.

"Thanks," I said, putting it on.

He got into bed and motioned for me to join him. I crawled in and faced him. He put his arms around me, and I looked into his eyes, trying to figure out what he was thinking. He returned my gaze and stroked my cheek.

I asked, "Has finding out what happened made it so that you're no longer sexually attracted to me?"

He looked at me like I was straight stupid. "No. Why would you say that?"

"Because we haven't had sex since you found out."

"We haven't had sex since Alex cornered you the day before yesterday. You need time to process that. And then tonight, he acted like a complete asshole. I apologize for his behavior. I'm sorry, Sammi." There was a mixture of rage and concern in his eyes.

"Thank you." I touched his cheek. "Alex looked really bad to me tonight. Have you spoken to him?"

He closed his eyes. "I've reached out. He's still not communicating with me."

"Well, he seems pretty shaken up. I think he needs you and your friends right now."

"He's obviously talking to our friends, at least a little bit. I can't make him talk to me. Mom was able to schedule breakfast with him tomorrow. I'll try to talk to him then." He shook his head. "You were really shaken up."

I took a deep breath. "I was shaken up. You're right. But the past two days have been good. Even tonight at Paulo's, I was fine. You've taken good care of me. That stuff hasn't been at the forefront of my thoughts." I paused and approached things more directly. "Michael, I have to deal with what happened, and, as you choose, you do too. Don't let it affect how we express with each other. Don't bring it to bed with us."

He narrowed his eyes. "Are you sure?"

"Absolutely. All of that stuff had already happened the first time we made love. The only difference between now and then is that you know about it and Alex freaked out. I enjoyed making love with you then, and, given the chance, I'd enjoy making love with you now. Please don't let some assholes who are not here keep us from being us with each other. Please don't let Alex freaking out keep us from being us."

He stared into my eyes. "So you're not doing this because you think it's what I want."

"No. This is all about what I want."

"So you're just thinking about yourself." He almost smiled.

I kissed his forehead and hugged him. "Yes, I'm really selfish." I looked into his eyes until I could see that he was starting to relax into our connection. I kissed him, then bit his top lip. I leaned back to gauge his response.

He met my gaze, then moaned as he pressed his growing erection into my thigh. Keeping his eyes on mine, he helped me out of his T-shirt and kissed me. His passion was there. His abandon wasn't. He started to caress my breast carefully, tenderly, and reestablished eye contact. I closed my eyes for a second and let my body squirm in response to his touch. He almost smiled again. Without breaking eye contact, he kissed and nibbled my breasts. I moaned as a ripple ran through my body. He trailed his hand down my abdomen, pulled my leg around his hip, and softly caressed my clitoris.

Looking intently into his eyes, I let out a voiceless, "Ahh." My hips matched his rhythm. His hips pushed forward reflexively, and he stopped kissing my breast. He put his nose to mine so he could look more directly into my eyes and slipped his fingers inside of me. Involuntarily, my eyes closed, and I felt myself spasm around them.

He said, "You're sure." It was more of a confirmation to himself than a question to me.

I answered anyway. "I am."

He rolled me onto my back and, ever so gently, eased into me without breaking our gaze. He paused until he was sure. Then he made slow, tender love to me. It was the concern and caring in his eyes that tipped me over. He smiled as I came and released into a controlled orgasm of his own. I hugged him tightly. He hadn't quite made his way back yet.

When his orgasm waned, as if he seriously didn't know what the answer would be, he asked, "Are you okay?"

I kissed him tenderly and looked into his eyes, stroked his cheek, and smiled. "I'm more than okay."

He smiled back. "Okay." He relaxed into my embrace and drifted off to sleep.

So much for hooking up with him casually. The situation with Alex had intensified our connection. Both of us were completely off course.

10

RECOVERY

SATURDAY, AUGUST 19

WHEN I WOKE up the next morning, Michael was still asleep in my arms. I stayed still and enjoyed the rhythm of his breathing. He woke up a little while later. I kissed his forehead as he opened his eyes.

He closed them again. "Hey."

"Hey."

He propped himself up on his elbow so he could look at me, searching my eyes for a moment, and said, "You're okay."

I smiled. "I am."

He smiled back. "Was last night okay for you?"

I nodded. "Mmm, it was nice."

"Just nice?" He tilted his head slightly and squinted his eyes.

"Yeah, just nice, but only because you were so restrained. You were tender and loving, and that was wonderful—but you weren't in your flow last night. It felt like you were afraid that I was going to break. The assholes were still in bed with us."

"I just wanted to make sure that you felt safe and that you really wanted it."

I looked at him to make sure I had his attention. "I am safe, Michael. I'm with you." I kissed his forehead.

He hugged me.

I tilted my head so I could see his eyes. "I promise you that I'll never lie about wanting sex with you. Understand?"

"Understood." He gave me a quick kiss.

"Good, because I want you to make love to me. Just you. No assholes allowed."

He relaxed some. Something in his eyes told me he was finally hearing me. "I can do that."

I leaned in and kissed him deeply. Just as we were getting into our flow, his alarm went off. It was 9 a.m. He reached across me to turn it off.

I said, "If you have somewhere you need to get to, I can take a raincheck. I don't want to make you late."

"I'm going over to my mom's. If I'm late, it won't be a problem. I'll just tell her that you wouldn't let me get out of bed until you had your way with me."

I tried to stifle a blush. I didn't know why I found that so embarrassing.

He chuckled. "Now, where were we?"

I got comfortable on my back and clasped my hands behind my head. "You had just promised to make love to me." I puckered my lips for a kiss.

He caressed my lips with his index finger. "So you want me to do all the work." He kissed my cheek.

"No, I'll be working on receiving."

"You mean just lying there." He kissed my nose.

"Receiving."

"While I work really hard." He kissed the other cheek.

"I'm very demanding."

"That you are." He stroked my cheek and planted three soft kisses on my lips. "So you're committed to being completely passive and not helping at all?"

I inclined my head. "Mostly."

"Okay, just getting clear about where I stand." He gave me one of his passionate, present kisses. His body set a rhythm. In a fluid motion, he transferred the kiss from my mouth to my clitoris. I hissed his name. He kissed me there until I started to slip toward orgasm. He transferred the kiss back to my mouth, hooking my knees with his elbows on the way. He fell into me. I closed my eyes and moaned loudly. His hips gently kept the established rhythm.

When I opened my eyes, he said, "Let me know if this is too

much." He positioned me so that my knees were on his shoulders and my pelvis was tilted up to receive. His rhythm became more urgent, and he added a swivel to his stroke. Using his shoulders for leverage, I let my body wind like it wanted to. He laughed out loud and lost himself. We came undone together. It was a good while before we landed.

I said, "That was nice."

He laughed and hugged me. "No, that was absolutely inappropriate for dating sex."

"You're not so good at dating sex."

"I blame that on you. You make inappropriate demands on me."

"And you bear no responsibility?"

"None. I'm innocent."

"Okay, while we're talking about how inappropriate I am, I've decided to go to New York with you. And we can stay together."

He smiled broadly. "What about the dust?"

"The dust has a mind of its own. It doesn't seem to want to settle."

His phone buzzed. It was a text from Helen.

He said, "Now that you're done with me, I need to leave. Mom and I are going to talk to Alex later on. She wants to talk to me first."

"Try to make sure that he's alright, Michael."

He pondered what I said for a moment. "Okay."

We rinsed off and got dressed quickly.

As we were about to get into our cars, I hugged him and said, "Call me later to let me know how it went with Alex and to make plans for New York."

"Ari and I made a tentative plan in case you said yes. She got you a ticket. Call her to work out the details." He got in his car and pulled off before I could say anything. They'd been plotting behind my back.

I WAS GOING to my Acroyoga class and was hungry. I decided to go to the restaurant that I'd taken Michael to a few weeks ago.

I called Ari before I went in. She answered, "Hey, girl. What's up?"

"Rumor has it that I already have a ticket to New York."

"You were taking too long to make up your mind. I got you a ticket with my miles. You're welcome. You're coming, right?" I could tell she was beaming.

I huffed. "I decided to come about an hour ago."

She laughed. "I bet you did. So it's good I got the ticket."

"Whatever, Ari. You know it's wrong to go behind my back like that, right?"

"You've done it for me. More than once. Just say, 'Thank you, Ari. I love you.'"

She was right. I had and I'd do it again. I rolled my eyes before I gave in. "Thank you, Ari. I love you. You happy?"

"For now."

"So what are my travel plans?"

"You guys are leaving LA tomorrow morning at nine. You'll arrive in New York at around four. You're going back to LA next Friday evening. Mike's booked in a hotel in Midtown from Sunday through Tuesday. He'll stay with me Wednesday and Thursday nights. You can stay with me or him, wherever you want."

"Why are we coming back on Friday? Why don't we stay the weekend?"

"I don't know. Mike mentioned a party or something. Ask him."

I said, "Okay. I think it would be good for the three of us to have dinner. You can help me to talk Michael through all of this drama. I know it's short notice, but I want to have dinner with our girls. You can host. I'll buy the food. We'll have takeout and see what comes up after that."

"Sounds good. What happened with Alex?"

"Ah, man. Not much. He glared at me and then stormed out. He was intoxicated, and he looked terrible. Michael was furious with him. I find the discord between him and Michael, and the fact that Alex didn't stay with his friends, hard to take."

Ari responded, "None of that is your fault."

"Yet, none of it would've happened if I hadn't been there. Michael and Helen are meeting with Alex now. I hope they can work through this at least a little bit."

"I hope so too. I agree with you. It'll be good for the three of us to have dinner tomorrow. I'll make a reservation. Try not to take on what's going on between Alex and Mike."

"I'll try not to."

She said, "It's a thing you cannot change."

That truth made me feel better instantly. She knew all my triggers. "I needed to hear that. Thank you. I'm going to my class. I want to grab a bite to eat first. I'll see you tomorrow."

"Okay, bye."

I had a leisurely breakfast, during which I realized that my cycle had started. This would make New York interesting. I didn't understand why everything felt so intimate to me when it came to Michael. I'd had other lovers.

I checked in with my mom to let her know I was going to New York. I got the throw out of my trunk and went to hang on the beach until it was time for class.

The Acroyoga class was a good follow-up to yesterday's workout. It was about 2:30 p.m. when I was done stretching and chatting after class.

I texted Michael to see if he was still with Alex. "Are you still with your mom and Alex?"

He texted back, "No, I'm at Paulo's."

I had a million questions, so I called him.

He answered on the first ring, "Hey."

I asked, "How did it go? Is Alex okay?"

He was silent for a minute or so. *Not a good sign.* He answered, "It didn't really go at all. I don't know much more about what's going on with him than I did before we talked. He pissed me off. So I left. He stayed. It's clear that he's upset about something, but I don't know what."

Michael still being pissed at Alex wasn't what I'd hoped for. "Like I've said, it's clear that he really needs his friends right now. And his brother. Try not to be so angry with him—"

He interrupted me. "I *am* angry with him, Sammi. I can tell that he's hiding something. I have a feeling that he did something really fucked up—"

"Whatever happened, based on the way he looked last night, my sense is that it's really bothering him. He needs support to get through it."

He was quiet again. "When I'm calm, I agree with you. He's with mom now. I came over to Paulo's to ask him to keep an eye on Alex. Alex isn't communicating with me. So there's not much more I can do." He changed the subject. "Did you and Ari finalize plans for New York?"

He was with Paulo. I'd have to wait to ask what more he found out. "Yes, Ari told me the plans that you two made. You, Ari, and I'll have dinner tomorrow night. I'll stay at Ari's on Sunday night. On Monday evening, I'm having dinner with my girls. I'll stay at Ari's on Monday night. There's no telling how late we'll finish." *And that way we can have some space from each other.*

"Sounds good. We'll stay at your place tonight and leave from there to go to the airport in the morning."

I looked at my phone. He was countering with a way for us to stay together. He thought he was smart. I knew that his plan was the easiest way to proceed, and I couldn't think of a good comeback. I rolled my eyes. I couldn't be totally agreeable either. "Whatever, Michael. I'll see you tonight."

He laughed at me. "I'm looking forward to it."

I squinted, touching my head. "Bye, Michael."

"Bye, Sammi." He was still laughing. *Sucker.*

I had to figure out what to do with the rest of my day. It was moments like this when I really missed my friends in New York. I was happy to be going there the following morning. I needed to cultivate the connections that I'd made here in LA. So I texted Amanda to see what she was doing. She was going to a music festival. She invited me to tag along, and I took her up on the offer.

Just after 9 p.m., I got a text from Michael. "What are you up to?"

I responded, "I'm hanging out with Amanda. We're listening to music. What are you up to?"

"Just hanging out with my crew at the pub. Do you want to meet up?"

I texted back, "Let's just meet at my house. I'm going home soon. I'm tired and I haven't packed yet."

"Okay X."

By 10 p.m., I was so tired that I couldn't keep my eyes open. The past few days had worn me out. I went home and packed. After I stuffed the last thing in my carry-on, I decided to chill for a minute before taking it downstairs.

THE DOORBELL WOKE ME UP. I was still sitting on the floor next to my bag, with my head resting on the ottoman in my bedroom. It was 11:30 p.m. which meant I'd been sleeping in that position for at least an hour. The doorbell rang again, and my phone rang. It was Michael.

I answered, "Hey. I'm coming."

He responded, "Okay."

I hung up, and without becoming fully conscious, made my way downstairs to let him in.

When I opened the door, he said, "I woke you up. I'm sorry."

"No. It's good you did. I fell asleep in an awkward position on the floor after I finished packing."

He locked the door and put an arm around me. "Let's tuck you in properly."

I rested my head on his shoulder and let him lead me back to my bedroom. He helped me undress, and I crawled into bed.

11

NEW YORK BOUND
SUNDAY, AUGUST 20

I woke up to the alarm on Michael's phone. He was sharing my pillow and my side of the bed with me. I had to crawl over him and to the far side of the bed to get to it. He didn't stir at all. It was 5:30 a.m. We needed to be at the airport by seven. We had to rush.

I shook Michael. "Hey, wake up."

Nothing.

I shook him harder. "Come on. Get up. We have to go."

He put his hands over his eyes and grunted. He opened his eyes as he slid his hands down his face. When his eyes finally focused, he smiled. "Morning, beautiful." He ensnared me in a hug and rolled onto me, planting kisses along my jaw. His beard was unusually scruffy, and he smelled like alcohol. He must've had a lot to drink the night before.

I grabbed the sides of his head and pushed him away from my neck. "Whoa, whoa, whoa. We've gotta get up. We're running late."

He looked at me like I was speaking a language he'd never heard. It seemed he was still a little drunk.

I slid out from underneath him and sat up. "We have a flight to catch. We're going to New York. Come on." I stood up and pulled his arm.

He covered his eyes again with his free hand. "Right. Shit." He let me help him stand up as he leaned on me and held his head like it was hurting.

"We have to take a shower." I led him into the bathroom and gave him something for his headache. I showered and then showered him while he continued to cradle his head. I dried us off. Luckily, I had clean underwear, socks, and a T-shirt for him from when he'd stayed over before. He slowly dressed himself. I helped with the button on his jeans and his belt. Pushing him toward the front door, I ran into the kitchen to make an energy drink with electrolytes for him and grabbed some extra packets for the trip.

The car pulled up as soon as we got to the door. I was glad I'd reserved it the day before. I opened the door and nudged him toward it with our carry-ons in tow. He was still barefoot, but I'd deal with that on the way to the airport. He was in the back seat of the car with his head back and eyes closed by the time I locked the door and made it there myself. I handed him the energy drink, which he downed in three swallows. Then I handed him his socks and sneakers. After a minute, he opened his eyes and put them on.

He was mostly awake, and the airport wasn't crowded. So we made good time getting to the gate. We walked straight onto the plane. As we settled into our seats, it was clear that the painkillers and electrolytes had taken effect. He took my hand and kissed it. With his other hand, he turned my face to his. After looking deeply into my eyes, he stroked my cheek and kissed me on the corner of my mouth. He settled into a comfortable position and closed his eyes again. I napped on and off during the flight.

He didn't wake until we were landing. Stretching and putting his arms around me with his forehead against mine, he said, "I'm sorry I was so hungover. Thanks for taking care of me." I opened my mouth to respond, but he gave me one of his sweet and present kisses before I could say anything.

ARI WAS WAITING for us when we walked into the lobby of the hotel where Michael was staying. She gave me a warm hug. We said, "I'm so glad to see you" at the same time. Then she gave Michael a hug. It was clear their relationship was deepening. Michael walked away to check in.

Ari said, "I made dinner reservations for seven, and it's only five now. So we can take our time getting there. Looks like things are going really well between you guys."

I glanced at Michael. "We've coupled, haven't we?"

She winced, as if she didn't want to say it out loud. "You really have."

I covered my face.

She laughed. "Sammi's got a boyfriend. Sammi's got a boyfriend." She was chanting it like we were in kindergarten.

I pushed her. "Stop. He's not my boyfriend." We both giggled.

Michael walked up. "What's the plan?"

I responded, "Our dinner reservations aren't until seven. The three of us need to talk. I'd prefer to have that conversation in private in your room and then go out to dinner."

Michael said, "That's fine. But I need a snack." He handed me one of the keys to his room.

Ari said, "Oh, yeah. These are for you to use while you're here." She gave Michael the keys to her brownstone.

He responded, "Thanks, Ari."

That reminded me that I still had the keys to his place. I started fishing around in my purse for them as we all walked over to the concierge to order room service. Michael ordered a huge cold cut sandwich. Ari and I ordered bottled water and tea. We were in the elevator when I found them.

I gave Michael his keys back. "I've been meaning to return these since Friday."

He opened his mouth like he was about to say something. He stopped. Then he said, "Thanks."

After we'd made ourselves comfortable in his suite, Ari started the conversation. "You guys have had a challenging few days."

I responded, "Yeah, just when I thought it was safe to have a normal life, my past reared its ugly head. It's been hard on Michael. He's been on edge ever since Alex lost it."

Michael opened his mouth. I think he wanted to deny it, but he couldn't.

I looked at him. "I'm sorry that you found out what happened to me like you did, and so soon. I would've waited a good while after we decided to be in a committed relationship to tell you about that." I looked at Ari. "Knowing has put stress on the way that he relates to me. He's not as relaxed and carefree as he was before. He's constantly guarding and checking to make sure I'm not falling apart now. He's been pretty freaked out."

Michael said, "You're right. It did freak me out. I still can't believe Alex pounced on you like that. And it's really fucked up that Pete drugged and raped you."

Ari said, "It's a lot to deal with."

Michael nodded. "It is. Over the past few days, Sammi's taken care of me much more than I've taken care of her. I was really worried about her at first, but I believe that she's okay now. I have a better sense of how strong she is."

Someone knocked on the door, and we paused to receive room service. Michael started in on his sandwich as soon as the waiter served it to him.

When the waiter left, Ari continued, "You're right. She is really strong, and she's had time, counseling, and lots of support."

I said, "You shouldn't have to deal with this, Michael."

He responded, "You say that like you're guilty of something. You realize that none of it was your fault?"

I answered, "I'm worried about you." I showed Ari the fading bruises on his hands. "These were a lot worse when he first made them. Yesterday, he talked to Alex, and yesterday evening, he went out and got wasted. He was hungover enough this morning that I was afraid I wasn't going to be able to get us to the airport in time for our flight. He couldn't even shower by himself."

Ari looked at Michael. "What happened with Alex yesterday? Why'd you get wasted? And what's with the beard? It's not trimmed or anything. I've never seen you so unkempt."

Michael stuffed the last piece of his sandwich into his mouth. He stood up and let out a big exhale. "They asked me to let my beard grow for the shoot. They'll do whatever they have planned with it tomorrow. I was hungover because I didn't drink enough water. I was mostly sober when I got to Sammi's house last night. The conversation with Alex didn't go well. I don't know much more about what he did than before Mom and I talked to him. He did say that he saw Sammi unconscious and that the only person he saw touching her was Pete."

"He corroborated my story."

Michael nodded yes.

I asked, "Did he say why he thought I was working for Pete?"

"He thinks that the only reason a woman would've been in that room was because she was working."

Ari asked, "Did he say anything else?"

"He keeps asking what Sammi accused him of."

I said, "So you still don't know what's got him so upset."

Michael responded dryly, "He's hiding something, and based on the way he's acting, whatever it is must be really bad."

He sat down again and raked his hands through his hair. He looked at me intensely for a minute and offered me his hand. I put my hand in his, and he wrapped both of his hands around mine and said, "As you know, Alex isn't communicating with me right now. I reached out to Paulo and Alicia and asked them to talk to him. Apparently, I get a particular look on my face when I'm pissed at Pete because Paulo guessed that whatever Alex and I are fighting about is connected to Pete. Once Paulo mentioned Pete, Alicia inferred that you were drugged and raped. She has a friend who went on a date with Pete and also ended up drugged and raped. I didn't volunteer anything. They don't have any details." His eyes had gone cold.

I could tell his temper was raging. I rubbed the side of his face and kissed his cheek to soothe him. I would've never told Paulo and Alicia about what Pete did to me. But given the situation with Alex, I didn't think there was a way to avoid it. I preferred that they knew a summary of the truth to them thinking I'd worked for Pete. On some level, I was relieved to know I wasn't the only one he'd tricked. But the idea that Pete had put other people through his shit sent a shiver through me.

In a flash, Michael reached out and lifted me onto his lap. He wrapped his arms around me and buried his face in my breastbone. I felt him trembling. I couldn't tell if it was anger or if he was crying.

Ari and I exchanged a look. I hugged him back. We waited a while as he stayed like that.

Ari asked, "What's going on, Mike?"

He loosened his hug and sat back in the chair. His eyes were glassy, but there were no tears falling. I could see all his concern and anger and disappointment in them. He whispered, "I'm worried that he raped someone. Though she can't bring herself to say it, mom's afraid of the same thing. My mom's terrified for him, and that scares me. I don't even know how to process this possibility from my brother."

I said, "Believe in him, Michael. Let him know that he has the benefit of your doubt. And be there for him."

Ari kneeled beside the chair and put an arm around him.

He returned the gesture and said, "Thanks, Ari." He looked at me, said, "Thanks, Sammi," and kissed me tenderly. Then he looked at Ari.

Ari quipped, "What? I'm not going to kiss you."

He half smiled, amused.

Ari continued, "Seriously, this will all work out. Hang in there." Her stomach growled. "I'm starving; let's go get some dinner."

We consciously chose lighter conversation during dinner. Michael said his days would start at 5 a.m. and end ten to twelve hours later on the two days of the shoot. We agreed that we wouldn't see him again until Tuesday evening when the shoot was over.

***

It was after 10 p.m. when we got back to Michael's hotel. The first person we saw was Maria, the owner of the modeling agency he worked for. She noticed us immediately and made a beeline toward us. Michael positioned me in front of him with his arm around me.

Maria walked up and said, "Good evening, Mike. How are you?"

He responded, "I'm well and you?"

She answered, "Fine, fine. Is your suite sufficient?"

"Yes, yes. It's very nice. Thank you."

She put her fingertips on my chin and moved my face from side to side so she could observe it. "She's lovely, Mike. Quite lovely."

I looked at Ari, and we stifled a giggle.

Michael removed her fingers from my chin. "Why are you here, Maria?"

Maria looked at Ari. Without looking back at Michael, she answered, "Rumor has it that Noelle's off the wagon. If she's high, the success of this shoot will fall entirely on your shoulders. So you'll need to be compensated at double your rate. Since I had to change my schedule and come to New York to deal with this, I'll also need to be better compensated." She looked at Michael. "I'm here to make sure we both get what we deserve." She was all business. I saw the protectiveness and respect that Michael mentioned before. She turned and motioned to a young man with a camera bag. As he approached, she said, "Filipe, do you remember that I told you that Mike has a sister? Well, here she is. Photographing the two of them for our campaign would be perfect, don't you think? In fact, I could see the ad with all three of them." She stepped back to get a better vantage point.

It was clear that Filipe and Michael knew each other. Filipe smirked at Michael and sarcastically responded, "That would be absolutely phenomenal, Maria."

Maria caught his tone and swatted him. "Whatever, Filipe." She turned and walked away. Over her shoulder she said, "I'm serious about that, Mike. See you here in the lobby at 5 a.m."

Michael just shook his head.

Ari said, "Well, I wouldn't want to cross her."

Just then, a group of models exited the hotel bar. The women were tall and skinny. The men were taller than male models usually were, Michael's height, with a lean muscularity similar to Michael's.

I nudged Ari and nodded in their direction.

She said, "Damn, are you all having a party or a dinner or something for this shoot, Mike? If so, I need to be invited." She'd made eye contact with one or two of them.

One of the female models tried to make eye contact with Michael, but he didn't seem to notice. He responded, "Most of these boys aren't able to converse at the level you're accustomed to, Ari."

"Yeah, well, I can converse with the ones who can. And a man can always exercise his right to be silent. I don't need them to say much."

He responded with an appalled, "Ari!"

She answered, "Cut the shit, Mike. You know exactly where I'm coming from." Ari had worked her magic. Two of the men started walking toward us. The women waved hello to Michael and walked the other way. I was sure they were scoping out prospects too.

The men both kissed Ari's hand when they got to us and said hello to me politely. Michael still had me in the shield position with his arm around me, so I got no flirt. They spoke to Michael who introduced them as Dezeri and Karin. Dezeri had beautiful deep chocolate skin and playful eyes with soft, round African features. I was pretty sure he was from Nigeria. Karin was Indian. He had creamy brown skin, loose, curly locks that fell to his shoulders, and a smile that betrayed his kindness. Maria had good taste in men. Ari was in full swing and soon gave me her "give me space to work my magic" look.

I disengaged myself as Michael's shield and took his hand. "Come on. Let's go get my bag." I started walking before he could protest.

He looked back at Ari, then at me. "So that's how you two bring it?"

I smiled. "Only when the tide is high." We got on the elevator.

When we got to his suite, I pulled my carry-on to the door, turned, and hugged him warmly. "You're a good person, Michael. I really like you."

He put his forehead to mine. "You're a good person, Sammi. I really like you too."

I took my time and let the depth of my feelings pour through my slow, soulful kiss. It took him a moment to understand the rhythm of it. When he did, he freely and openly received the reverence and gratitude I was offering.

When the kiss resolved, he asked, "Are you sure you want to leave?"

I answered, "No, but I'm sure that I need to rescue Dezeri and Karin from your sister."

He opened the door. "Get out of here, then. Before I try to convince you otherwise."

"Good night." I walked out.

"I'll talk to you tomorrow."

"Have a good shoot."

"I'll try."

I turned for the elevator and heard him close his door.

I walked up to Ari, Dezeri, and Karin.

Dezeri asked, "So what are you ladies doing with the rest of your evening?"

I chuckled. *Not that.* "I've had a long week. I really want to get to a place where I can catch up with my friend here and get some rest."

They stood up. Karin said, "It was a pleasure to meet you, Ari. I hope I get to see you again."

Dezeri took my carry-on. "We'll help you ladies get a cab."

The cabs were lined up outside the hotel. Karin opened the car door, and Dezeri put my carry-on in the trunk.

As the car pulled off, Ari said, "Which one …?"

"They work with Michael, Ari. They're off-limits."

She looked back in the direction we came from. "Yeah, you're right. It's too bad, really. Dezeri is supporting himself in grad school with the proceeds from modeling. He's quite intelligent. Karin is trying to figure out how to forge his own path instead of taking over his father's business."

"If you really want to date one of them, fine. I'm just saying you're not in Vegas. Are you working tomorrow?"

She answered, "No."

"Good. Let's have breakfast at the diner in the morning."

The conversation died down. Ari woke me up when we got to her brownstone in Brooklyn.

"Wow," I said. "I dozed hard. I missed half of the ride here."

"You seem tired. Go to bed when we get inside. We'll catch up in the morning."

I walked into Ari's brownstone, went to my room, and went to sleep.

12

———

MY GIRLS

MONDAY, AUGUST 21

I woke up at 8:30 a.m. Michael had sent me a text wishing me a great day at 5 a.m. I texted him back and wished him the same. I treated myself to a long, luxurious shower with plenty of pampering afterward. I hadn't spoken to my mom in a few days, so I called to let her know I was in New York. Ari was dressed, and it looked like she had been working for a few hours when I walked into her office. She lived and breathed finance.

"I thought you said you weren't working today?" I asked.

Ari responded, "I didn't plan to. I woke up early and decided not to waste the time. I've put in half a day. That gives me back half a day to spend with you guys." She was focused on her laptop.

"You work too much, Ari."

"I have to stay at the top of the game." She closed the laptop and leaned back in her chair.

"You seemed really interested in Dezeri and Karin. Does that mean that you're getting over Matt?"

"I am over Matt. I really want a connection worth investing in."

"That's not easy to find."

"No, it isn't. So you're finally giving in to being with Michael?" She smiled.

I let out a sigh. "Resisting it didn't keep me from falling in love with him. It's all too fast, and the timing's wrong though. I wanted some time to just be with me once I got free from Greg." I paused to

126

collect my thoughts. "All the drama derailed my intention to keep it casual and just intensified the primal connection that we have. We've spent considerably more time together during the last few days than we would've under normal circumstances."

"He's really being there for you, isn't he?"

"Yes, he is. Your brother's a really good person, Ari. I think this situation is hard on him." I rested my chin on my hand.

"I think he's a good person too. You're taking good care of him. He seems to find comfort in your presence. You guys will get through it." She was such a believer.

"I don't know. We'll see."

"I'm really happy that you guys hit it off. I like you two as a couple. I hope it works out."

"If my past doesn't mess it up and he doesn't do something fucked up, maybe it will."

Her face lit up. "Would that be a droplet of optimism I hear? You're really in love."

"Don't talk about it too much. I'll freak out." I laughed.

"Speaking of the past, any progress on the divorce?" she asked in a low voice.

"Just an acknowledgment from his lawyer to mine that he received the papers."

"So you haven't seen him?"

I shook my head. "Or heard from him."

"Wow. How long?" she asked in shock.

"About three months now."

"He hasn't restricted your access to any of his accounts?"

I shook my head. "He knows that he'd be broke if we weren't managing his money."

"He hasn't contested the money that's in the joint accounts?"

"No," I answered.

"Since you don't want half, have you decided how much you are going to ask for as part of the settlement?"

"Some percentage of what we've earned for him. I didn't marry him for his money."

She prodded, "How much?"

"I just want to have enough to continue to do my art without worrying. Maybe I'll ask for a fourth of what's in the joint accounts.

And my house, the beach house, and the brownstone here in New York. I don't want to dismantle all the work that we've done. We've built a really good portfolio."

She looked at me like I was stupid.

"A third?" My voice cracked.

She asked, "What about the amount that you kept him from squandering?"

"I can't quantify that, Ari."

She responded, "I can. And I have." She opened a spreadsheet on her laptop and put it up on the big screen in her office so I could see it too. "I found the analysis we did when you realized how fast he was burning through money."

"I forgot about that."

She pursed her lips. "Well, I didn't. Based on his burn rate, he had, at most, a few years' worth of funds left. He related to his bank account like an ATM. Remember now?"

"Yes."

"Uh-huh. And remember how you decided to invest in a series of deals that made him wealthy. Thanks solely to you, he now has a well-managed portfolio."

"Only because of your financial genius."

She responded, "We got really lucky on a few of those investments. I feel like you're totally discounting the financial contribution you made. You didn't enter that marriage broke and without means, Sammi. You were having great success at establishing your career, which you put on hold. And since we were already building your portfolio, you had a significant amount of capital for your age." She waited to see how I would respond.

I hunched my shoulders. She was correct. I was discounting my financial contribution.

"You put in your whole savings and borrowed a little to make the minimum on the first deal."

"Yeah, but 90 percent of it was his money."

"Exactly 84.526 percent. And all of the initiative was yours. Without you and your connections, there would be nothing to discuss now. What's more, you've left it all on the table, Sammi. All of the money you invested, all of your money, is in those joint accounts. All of the funds that you've used for yourself and to buy your house, the beach house, and the brownstone are less than half of the percentage that you initially invested."

"I don't know."

Ari countered, "I do. Given that he'd have nothing, and your investments are his only real source of income, you deserve at least half of what he's worth. And I mean half of his full estate, not just the joint accounts. Even if you take half of his estate, he's better off than he was."

"What about what I did? He could've died in that car accident. What about all the pain he endured?"

"What about all the shit that he's done to you? You made a mistake. It happened one time. He's consciously cheated on you and been an asshole to you over and over again by throwing his fucking tantrums."

"I'll think about it. Let's change the subject and go get breakfast. I'm hungry."

She stood up and walked toward the door of her office. "How long do you have to wait before you start negotiating the settlement?"

I followed. "I don't know. I'll ask my lawyer when I get back to LA."

"Have you given your lawyer all of the financial records?"

"Not yet."

She gave me a stern look. "You need to. I'll work up a detailed report that's easy to follow. I'll be a witness if you need it." She put on shoes and opened the front door.

I responded, "Alright, alright. I'll give him your report as soon as I get back to LA. I promise." I put my shoes on too and walked through the door.

"And you'll let them give you half."

I closed my eyes. "I'll let them give me half of what's in the joint accounts."

"If you were male, there would be no discussion. You would have no doubt that you earned it. You would feel entitled to half of the estate or more." She walked toward the diner.

I followed. Compliance was the only thing that would work when Ari knew she was right. "You're right, Ari."

"After breakfast, let's go check out a property."

"No more than two."

We entered the diner, and I ordered my favorite breakfast sandwich. Ari got an omelet. We lingered there for a few hours. Then she took me to explore two Brooklyn neighborhoods in varying states of redevelopment. By 2 p.m., she needed a nap.

I passed the afternoon brainstorming and getting my head around upcoming projects.

I DECIDED we were going to have Jamaican food for dinner. Ari was still sleeping when I went out to pick it up. The aroma woke her up. I was in the process of setting the table with place settings, wine, and flowers when she walked into the kitchen. She took one of the plates, filled it with food, and started eating before I could finish. With such short notice, the only people who could make it were Kumiko, a friend of mine from grad school at NYU, and Val, an ex-roommate of ours who went to grad school at Columbia with Ari. They arrived at the same time, a few minutes after Ari started eating. I'd just finished opening the wine and putting it on ice. Before I could get the food into serving bowls to present it, Kumiko and Val had made their plates and joined Ari at the table.

Val said dryly, "You're not really planning on dirtying all those bowls, are you?"

Ari matched her tone. "Why don't you just sit down and eat?"

I gave up and joined them at the table. The food was great. We started talking after we all had our second helping.

Kumiko said, "First things first. Ari says you're dating Michael. How's that going?"

Val asked, "Michael?"

Kumiko crossed her arms and leaned back in her seat. "Ari's brother. I'm listening."

"I'd say it's going well." I tried to look nonchalant.

Kumiko asked, "Have you slept with him yet?"

Val looked confused. "I thought you were still married to Greg."

I answered, "I filed for divorce."

Val responded, "I can't imagine why a woman in their right

mind would ever leave Greg. He's the perfect man as far I'm concerned."

I gave Kumiko an appalled look. "That's personal."

Kumiko responded to Val, "You haven't seen Michael."

Ari answered, "She slept with him on the first date."

I gave Ari a dirty look.

Ari mouthed back, "Whatever."

Val said, "Greg has so much going for him: looks, talent, wealth." She was terminally infatuated with him.

Ari and I exchanged a knowing glance about the person who Greg really was.

Kumiko patted my hand. "Well, I understand how that could happen. So is he an F16?"

I answered Kumiko, "No, Michael is definitely not an F16."

Val shook her head. "I can't believe you're cheating on Greg."

Kumiko said, "Elaborate."

I told Val, "We're legally separated."

Ari said, "Don't elaborate. He's my brother."

"Let me get this straight; you're willingly breaking up with Greg? That makes no sense to me. He's such a dream," Val said, exasperated.

Ari said, "It makes perfect sense to me. It's long overdue."

I responded to Val, "At this point, it doesn't really feel like leaving Greg. We haven't been together in a meaningful way in a long time."

Val responded, "You're married to him."

"Legally, but not emotionally." I took a breath. "This isn't really about me and Greg, Val. It's about you and Robbie. Greg and Robbie are guys who put it right on the table; they can't be caught. You can't have a relationship with them because they're not emotionally available. Period. If you're a woman, the best you can hope for is someone to have sex with when they're not out fucking someone else. And the lack of emotional availability is totally reflected in the sex. It's not personal or intimate. It's just physical."

Ari looked at Val. "Listen. Matt is a guy who can't be caught. Our sex is just physical. But I get my kicks. Every time. I haven't made any commitments to him. And I'm not being faithful to him, hoping he's going to change his tune."

I looked at Val too. "Listen to Ari's point; what doesn't make sense is to think you're ever going to end up with a real partner who's present for you in a meaningful way. It's best to just take his word for it and move on. You've been waiting for him to change his behavior for a year now. You're wasting your time."

Kumiko huffed. "Let's talk about Michael. Is he available?"

I answered, "So far, Michael's been available. He's a present and extremely generous lover."

I asked Kumiko, "So how's Luke?"

Kumiko answered, "Luke is sweet and kind, and he loves me. He's not selfish sexually, but he's just not a very physical person. He'll never be more than a F18. I feel guilty, but sometimes, I want to be with someone who'll work me over. Do you think that I'm wrong to want that?"

I answered, "Are you wrong to want to be satisfied sexually? No."

Kumiko asked, "Do you think that I should leave him?"

"I can't answer that. Everyone has to find the balance of physical and emotional that works for them." I looked at Val. "If you can make a relationship work with a purely physical connection, own it and go for it." I looked back at Kumiko. "If you can make a relationship work on a purely emotional connection, own it and go for it."

Kumiko looked down. "I do love Luke. But ..." She hunched her shoulders.

Ari responded, "You're a dancer, Kumiko. Luke doesn't move unless he has to. Your respective relationships to the physical body are exactly the opposite. The fact that he's not satisfying your needs doesn't make him wrong. You two just don't match in that category. There's probably someone out there for whom he's the ultimate lover. And you can love him as a friend. He doesn't have to be your lover to have a meaningful place in your life."

I said, "You've got to decide where you stand and be real about it. And trust that it's for the best."

Ari raised her glass. "Here's to keeping it real."

We all toasted.

Kumiko asked, "Would you be willing to share Michael?"

I laughed. "Michael would probably be pissed if I suggested it. Greg, on the other hand, would be flattered."

We moved on to talking about work and what we wanted to cultivate in our careers, which segued into a discussion about the state of the world and how to make it better. A few hours and a few bottles of wine passed. We were giggling about funny things that had happened to us over the years when my phone buzzed.

It was a text from Michael. "Where are you?"

I responded, "I'm at Ari's."

He replied, "You said that we could stay together. I'm holding you to that. I'm on my way. See you shortly. X."

I showed my phone to Ari.

She held up her hands and laughed.

I texted him back, "Okay."

Val asked, "What's going on?"

Ari responded, "Mike's on his way." She smirked.

I shot daggers from my eyes toward Ari.

The doorbell to her brownstone rang. I could hear Michael working on the locks. Ari chuckled. "He's holding you to that, without any doubt. He must've been a few blocks away." Ari got up to help him.

She opened the door, and Michael walked in with his carry-on in tow. He was wearing a sleeveless version of one of those clingy shirts that men work out in, with shorts and sneakers, looking like the ultimate athlete. His hair had been cut masterfully. Even though it was still damp, you could see how it was designed to accentuate the shape of his face. They had trimmed his three-day-old beard to highlight his cheekbones and lips. The girls fell silent. Ari rolled her eyes.

Michael hugged Ari. "Hey, sis." He waited for her to lock the door and followed her into the part of the room where we were sitting. He stood behind my seat and kissed my forehead as a hello.

Ari said, "Mike, you met Kumiko when you visited me the last time; she studied dance with Sammi. This is Val. Val went to grad school with me."

Val and Kumiko both nodded and remained silent.

Michael smiled. "It's good to see you again, Kumiko. It's nice to meet you, Val. I have no intention of imposing on your get-together. I've had a day from hell, and I've come to crash. I'm exhausted, and I hope you don't find it rude that I do that now. Have a good rest of the evening." He took a few steps toward the staircase, then held out his hand for me to join him. I could see the stress in his eyes.

I got up and took his hand.

He whispered, "I want to sleep where you're sleeping."

I led him to my room.

He followed me in and closed the door. When I turned to face him, he hugged me and put his forehead against mine. He said, "Now that you know that I've had a hard day, you want to hold me tight and kiss me deeply."

I rubbed his cheek. I whispered, "Yes, I do." I pulled him close and kissed him as sweetly and as deeply as I could. He purred softly with the pleasure of receiving.

As the kiss resolved, he rocked me in our embrace and said, "Thank you. I needed that more than you know."

"What happened?"

He shook his head. "As Maria predicted, Noelle was high as a kite. The photos are designed to be suggestive. It seems she has no idea what's real and what's for the shoot. She's concluded that she and I are in a relationship. When I left the hotel, she was standing outside my room, yelling that she couldn't understand why I wouldn't let her in. Her manager was trying desperately to get her back to her own room. Given that she's addicted, she'll be high all day tomorrow too. I wanted to come to be in our space to recover and prepare."

"I think you need another kiss." I kissed him sweetly and deeply again.

His jewel stirred. He laughed. "Obviously, you've helped me get my mind off the challenges of today." He stroked my cheek and kissed me again, tenderly. "Get back to your friends before you get carried away. I'm going to crash."

"Do you want a glass of wine or something?"

"No, I just want to fall asleep where you're going to sleep." He stepped back and took off his shirt and shorts in the same motion. I watched as he dropped them in a pile on the floor.

I picked them up and put them on a chair. When I looked at him again, he was already making himself comfortable in my bed. I leaned over and kissed him on his forehead.

He smiled and said, "Good night," before closing his eyes.

As I walked back into the room, the conversation halted, and Val and Kumiko stared at me expectantly. I shrugged and said, "He came to crash. He's going to sleep."

Kumiko said, "And you let him? I'm sorry, Ari, but he's sexy as fuck. I didn't expect to see you again tonight."

Ari laughed. "They also bathe each other in nonsexual situations."

"Thanks for oversharing, Ari."

Kumiko asked, "How long have you two been together?"

Val held up her hands in confusion. "So you're officially a couple with Michael, and you're still married to Greg?"

I looked at Kumiko. "We've been going out for a few weeks." To Val, I said, "I'm legally separated from Greg. Michael and I aren't a couple. We're just dating."

Kumiko responded, "You act like a couple."

Ari said, "They are a couple. She's in denial."

I answered, "We haven't made any declarations or commitments."

Kumiko responded, "Well, I want to date like that."

Ari held up her glass and said, "As do we all."

They were right. He was the kind of man we all dreamed of. I said, "Yeah, I fear I'll never recover from him."

Kumiko raised her glass. "Here's to you never having to."

I touched my glass to hers. "Thank you."

Kumiko responded, "You can still elaborate."

Ari said, "Not with me sitting here."

Val looked toward the staircase. "He's really attractive."

The rest of us burst into laughter. Somehow, we ended up talking for a few more hours. Kumiko talked about how the documentary she was working on was helping her to come to terms with the challenges of respecting traditional Japanese culture for your elders while being wholly American in terms of your experience. We listened to Val and Ari commiserate about being minority women in finance, Val from the Latina perspective and Ari from the Black perspective. It was funny how, when you were with good friends, conversation flowed. At 1 a.m., we called it.

I asked, "Do they still play live music at that little club in the Village?"

Val said, "Yes, on Wednesday through Saturday."

I said, "Let's go there on Wednesday. It shouldn't be too crowded. I need to get my groove on. Let folks know."

Ari said, "That'll be fun. I haven't been there in a few months."

We said our goodbyes, and Val and Kumiko left.

Ari said, "Tonight, I'm exhausted."

I responded, "You should be. Go to bed. I'll clean up."

She hugged me. "I'm glad that you are here."

"Me too."

She headed upstairs to her bedroom, while I cleaned the kitchen and took the garbage outside. Then I went upstairs to take a shower. Michael was sleeping soundly when I got into bed. He didn't stir at all.

I woke up at 10 a.m. Ari and Michael had been gone for hours. I took my time getting dressed and spent my day running errands and meeting with people to talk about two projects I was anxious to be a part of.

One of the projects was a series about a young woman entrepreneur navigating a world of men with humor and skill. It wouldn't start production until early next year. I had been hired as the director, and I liked the way it was written. I wanted to make sure I had some authority to implement my vision for it. So I made the meeting about me signing on as an executive producer as well. I was happy with my role as the producer for the other project, an independent film with a three-week shoot that was set to start in two weeks. So that meeting was short and sweet.

My errands, which were quick meetings about maintaining my network in New York, were scattered all over town. So they took me the entire afternoon.

13

ERRANDS
TUESDAY, AUGUST 22

Just after 3 p.m., Michael texted me. "I just finished. Do you want to meet up?"

I called him. "I do, but I need another two hours."

"Okay, I'll meet you at Ari's. What was that you guys had for dinner last night? It smelled delicious."

"Jamaican food."

"Is it the restaurant in Ari's neighborhood?"

"Yes."

He said, "Text me the name and what to order. I want what you guys had last night."

"Okay."

"Should I get enough for you and Ari?"

I answered, "Yes, that would be nice. Let Ari know that you're doing that so that she doesn't pick up something on her way home."

"Okay."

"I'll see you in a little while." I smiled to myself. He was truly kind.

"Okay."

I hung up and texted him the link to the restaurant and a list of what to order. I had one more errand for my project. I checked to make sure a few of my favorite shops were still open. Finally, I stopped by the grocery store.

It was 6:15 p.m. when I walked into Ari's brownstone. Michael's shoes were at the door, and the smell of the food filled the air. I could tell Ari wasn't home yet because her slippers were by the door. There was quite a bit of food on the kitchen island and a few bottles of wine, but Michael wasn't in the kitchen. It was quiet, so most likely, he was asleep. I put up the food I'd bought and went upstairs to find him.

When I tipped into my room, he was lying across my bed, fully dressed, with his eyes closed. They opened a few seconds later. He said, "Hey," and opened his arms for me to join him on the bed.

I crawled into his arms. "I'm sorry I woke you."

"I wasn't sleeping. I heard you when you came in. How has your day been so far?"

"Productive. I got some things done for my next project. How was yours?"

"Long. Better than yesterday, but still trying. Noelle was driving her manager crazy when I left the studio. I'm sure they're spinning up into party mode by now at the hotel. We can go back later if you want, but I needed to get away from it for a while."

"You shaved your beard."

"Yeah, I don't want a beard right now." He rested his head against mine.

"Did you eat?"

"Yes, that food was amazing. I'm going to eat there every day 'til we go back to LA. It was good to see you hanging out with your friends. You guys had fun?"

I smiled. "That's an understatement. We talked and laughed until 1 a.m."

We looked at each other in silence for a few minutes. I marveled at the intensity of the connection we shared. It felt like it just was. It was here before we knew it existed, and it would be here no matter what we did. I marveled at the depth in his eyes. I could stare into them forever. Like the first time we kissed, I wasn't sure who moved first. I was just suddenly aware we were kissing slowly and tenderly with presence and adoration. The world fell away. I don't know how long it lasted. When it resolved, we both laughed. I wanted to tell him I loved him, but it was just too soon. No other words fit.

Then our passion rose. We kissed again, but this time, the kiss was jagged and fiery. For a while, there was only the kiss. Then our bodies moved together. It was only when he unbuttoned my jeans and slipped his hand into my pants that I came to my senses.

I stopped his hand. I was panting. "Michael, we can't."

He rolled back, concerned. He was panting too. "Is something wrong? Are you okay?"

I answered quickly, "Nothing's wrong. I'm fine. It's just ..." Words escaped me. I felt like a silly sixteen-year-old.

He relaxed some and looked at me intensely while he waited for me to finish the sentence.

"I-I-I'm ..." I was tongue-tied.

He squinted his eyes. "You're not going to say we can't have sex because you're menstruating? Are you?"

My words came back. "How do you know I'm on my cycle?"

He wrinkled his brow and looked around like he was trying to make sense of the question. "Because we had sex on Saturday when it was starting?" He stated it like a question and bit his lip to suppress a smile.

I said, "And you didn't say anything?"

He laughed outright. "No, I figured since it's your body, you knew. I also assumed that it wasn't the first time, so you knew how to handle it." He was enjoying himself.

I felt silly. I covered my face and rolled away from him.

He stopped laughing. He rolled me back to face him and peeled my hands away from my face. "What's this really about?"

"Our connection is so intense, so intimate for me. I just ..." I didn't know how to finish that sentence.

"You're trying to maintain some boundaries. Sex while you're on your cycle feels too intimate right now. I get that." He kissed each of my hands in turn.

"Thank you."

He asked, "When's your last day?"

"Tomorrow."

He said, "We don't have to have intercourse. We could just make out." He buttoned my jeans.

"Okay."

He pulled me close. He started the fiery kiss, and we moved together again. After a few moments, he asked, "Can I touch you?"

I covered my eyes. I hoped he didn't think I was toying with him.

He continued, "Not to have intercourse. I just want to see you come."

"Michael …"

"It's too much?"

I nodded.

He said, "Okay," and hugged me in closer and kissed my forehead.

An involuntary pulse ran through my body. His body responded in kind, and we were moving again.

He asked, "You feel that, right?"

"Yes."

Abruptly, he disengaged and got out of bed. He pulled me into a standing position after him. "Let's go downstairs. There's only one way things are going to end if we stay in here." He positioned his erection so it was hidden by his shirt and reached for my hand.

I took his hand and followed him downstairs. Ari was home. We found her watching television and eating dinner on the couch. Michael led me to the couch, and I sat next to Ari. He walked to the recliner on the opposite side of her and sat there.

She looked at me, then at Michael. Her expression was clearly asking what happened.

Michael answered the unstated question. "We can't have sex because Sammi's menstruating. She feels it's too intimate for where we are in our relationship right now."

Ari and I looked at each other, then at him in disbelief.

He put his hands up. "What?"

Ari responded, "That's way too much information, Mike."

He looked at her like she was acting truly silly. "Whatever, Ari."

I added, "I think the tendency to overshare may be genetic."

Ari gave me the finger and a smile. Michael didn't get the reference.

He stood up again. "I'm going to get some more food."

We watched him leave. I said, "'Hello, how are you' sounds misplaced after that opening." I shook my head.

Ari responded, "Ya think?"

I asked, "How was your day?"

She nodded her head. "It was okay. Yours?"

"I put things in place for my next project. It was productive."

Ari got up. "I want some more wine."

I followed her into the kitchen. I was hungry. I hadn't eaten since breakfast.

14

DANCING IN NEW YORK
WEDNESDAY, AUGUST, 23

MICHAEL SAID, "They're partying at the hotel, Ari, if you want to go. Dezeri and Karin asked about you."

Ari responded, "Sounds appealing, but I'm going to work tomorrow—and we're going dancing tomorrow night. Are you going?"

Michael responded, "To the hotel? Not if you guys don't want to. My things are here and checkout's automatic."

She looked at me, smirking. "Uh-huh."

I narrowed my eyes at her, then asked, "Are you going to work for the rest of the week?"

"No, I'm taking Thursday off to hang out with you guys."

I asked her, "Do you want to do anything in particular?"

She responded, "No, not that I can think of right now."

I asked Michael, "What about you?"

He responded, "I'm open. I don't care."

I said, "Okay, we'll just play it by ear then."

We stood around the kitchen island eating and talking for a while. We went back to the den and watched an episode of an old sci-fi series. Michael dosed off in the middle of it.

When it was over, I shook him. "Go to bed."

He peeked at the television and said, "Okay." He got up and walked out of the room.

Ari and I watched two more episodes, then turned in ourselves.

WHEN I WOKE UP, it was 9:30 a.m., and Michael wasn't in bed. I got up, brushed my teeth, and set off to find him. I expected to find him in the kitchen, but he wasn't there. He also wasn't in the den. I found him in the guest room.

He said, "Good morning," as I walked into the room.

"Good morning. Why are you sleeping in here?" I sat on the side of the bed.

"Not sleeping, just chilling. I was restless and didn't want to wake you."

I leaned over to give him a quick kiss on his forehead, but he moved. I ended up kissing his mouth. We let it linger for a moment. Then I sat up. He stroked my cheek, and I turned my face so I could kiss his palm. It was taking all my willpower not to fall into him. I whispered, "The pull is so strong."

He whispered back, "Yeah." Then we broke contact. He cleared his throat and repositioned himself so he was sitting with his back against the headboard. He gave me a goofy smile. "I came in here because you were snoring so loud."

I smiled back. "I wasn't."

"You were. You woke Ari up too. You can ask her."

I threw a pillow at him. He caught it and hugged it.

"Seriously, I woke up in the middle of the night. We were entwined, and I was really turned on. Given how our bodies react to each other, I couldn't relax and go back to sleep. Maybe it was because I spent the past two days pretending to be on the brink of having sex with Noelle. Maybe it was just our connection. My friend was like, 'Come on, Mike. Our girl is right here. I can feel her.'"

"I'm sorry." Again, I hoped he didn't feel I was toying with him.

"Don't be. That's not where I'm coming from."

"Did you sleep okay once you left?"

"I slept fine. I came in here because this is where I stayed when I visited the first time. I like to look out on Ari's tiny New York yard." He glanced toward the window.

"What do you want to do today?"

He said, "I need to work out. I want to take a class. What do you want to do?"

"Go to the diner and go dancing tonight. Other than that, I'm open."

"Great, I'll go to the diner and dancing with you. You come take a class with me."

"I'm not at your level, Michael."

He responded, "It doesn't matter. I'll take whatever level you're comfortable with. If there's a teacher that you like, we can take one of their classes."

"I could enjoy a class today, and I like the idea of taking a class with you. But I'm going to be awkward because I feel very intimidated. I'm not as good as the people you're used to dancing with."

"Don't worry about it. It's not a competition."

I found a shirt and some leggings I could dance in. We showered, got dressed, and went to the diner for a leisurely breakfast.

WE WENT into Manhattan to take an intermediate ballet class at noon. Michael wasn't in the classroom when I got there. I had consciously avoided seeing him in dancer mode. I didn't know if I was ready for it, especially if he wore tights. I had such a weakness for men who moved deeply. The strength. The control. I broke out of my reverie when he walked into the classroom. He was wearing straight-legged warmups and a fitted T-shirt. He was moving with an extra lift and grace he didn't employ when he wasn't dancing.

He walked over and stood in the space next to me and said, "Excuse me, is this spot taken?"

My first thought was, *Why would he ask that when it's obvious I've saved it for him?* When I glanced at him, it was clear he was playing. He liked to turn things into little games. I was ready. I answered, "I'm sorry, sir, but it is." I looked away from him dismissively.

He smiled. "By whom, may I ask?"

"Why, by my date, sir. He'll be here at any moment."

He looked around as if he were looking for someone. "Your date isn't coming, ma'am. According to the clock, this class should be starting now." He stepped into the space.

I made my eyes big and looked around. "Surely you're mistaken, sir."

He half smiled. "I'm quite certain that he's not coming, ma'am. What's more, I'm also certain that the fates mean for me to take this place."

I gasped, as if I were appalled. "That's quite an assertion, sir."

"Well, I know it's true, and I can prove it."

"How would you prove such a thing, sir?"

Michael leaned over to kiss me. Before he could make contact, the teacher walked into the room.

She cleared her throat and said, "If we're quite done with flirting, I'd like to start class."

Michael and I took our places. I was on par with most of the students in the class in terms of technique, but I lacked endurance. None of us were on par with Michael. It was clear from the moment class started that he was a dancer's dancer. He'd perfected his craft as much as a person could. He knew exactly where his center was. His technique was precise. His lines were clean. His timing was impeccable. I was happy I'd gotten to know him before I saw him dance. I would've been infatuated.

He was waiting for me when I walked out of the dressing room. I blushed. "I hope I didn't embarrass you." I avoided eye contact.

He wrapped his arms around me. "On the contrary, I think you did quite well." He kissed my hair.

I added, "Considering—"

He interrupted. "Considering that you don't do it every day. Everyone knows that to make it look effortless, you have to do it every day."

"You're an amazing dancer, Michael."

"Thank you, Sammi. I'd like for this to be something that we share."

"I'd like that too." I kissed him on his chest.

He gave me a little squeeze. "What do you want to do now?"

"Let's just wander around for a while, unless you want to go to a museum or something."

"I'm good with wandering."

"I want to get back to Ari's around six so that I can take a nap. Tonight's going to be a late night."

"Sounds like a plan."

I said, "Speaking of plans, I've been meaning to ask you why we are going back to LA on Friday."

"With all the shit that happened with Alex, I forgot to tell you a friend of mine is throwing a beach party on Saturday. I want you to come with me. The music will be unleashed."

I wanted to protest about him making plans for me without my knowledge, but he looked so excited about it. And I loved to be in the presence of great music. I said, "Sounds like a plan."

We wandered around the Village. I showed him where my dorm was while I was at NYU. We sat on benches in Washington Square Park and watched people. We window shopped. We ate an excellent early dinner at a small Greek restaurant. We lost track of time, and it was 7:30 p.m. when we left Manhattan to go back to Ari's.

———

It was 8:15 p.m. when we walked into Ari's brownstone.

Ari greeted me, saying, "You do realize that we're supposed to meet folks at nine in the city. We need to be leaving right now." She was dressed to play: skinny blue jeans, a fitted T-shirt that revealed her midriff, and a pair of strappy wedges. Her makeup was bold.

I responded, "I know. It's my fault. We'll be quick. You look good, girl."

Michael did a double take at his first sight of Ari's outfit, then smiled in approval.

I took his hand and dragged him up the stairs. "Come on. We have to hurry." I walked into my room, taking off my clothes. I closed the door and locked it once he was inside.

He just stood there, checking me out with a come hither look on his face.

I snapped my fingers. "Michael! Move! There's no time for you to stand there gawking. We need to shower and leave."

He looked back at my bedroom door and looked at me from head to toe. "Okay." He disrobed.

I went into the bathroom that was attached to my bedroom and turned on the shower. I was basically done when he stepped in. As I stepped out, I kissed him on the cheek. "Hurry."

He looked confused. "Okay."

I put on a pair of skinny blue jeans with a white stripe down the sides. I followed Ari's lead and wore a fringy suede vest that showed off my midriff too. I was dressed by the time Michael came out of the bathroom.

He checked me out. "Wow."

I smiled. "I'm glad you like what you see. Get dressed." I went back into the bathroom to put on my makeup. I went for bold, like Ari.

He stepped back into the bathroom wearing only his boxer briefs. "I should wear jeans, right?"

"Anything fun and comfortable. Did you bring your black jeans?"

"Yeah."

"Wear those with one of your designer's long T-shirts and a pair of his high-tops."

He blinked like he was surprised. Then he checked me out again and bit his lower lip. He hunched his shoulders like he'd made a decision and said, "Okay."

Ari knocked on my bedroom door. "We need to leave."

I finished with my makeup by putting on my lipstick, the same color I wore on our first date. Michael was zipping his jeans when I came out of the bathroom. They were funky beige-colored jeans, not the black ones, but they had the same cut. He kissed my neck as I walked by. I waited for him to slip on a T-shirt that was tie-dyed in light brown tones with an elaborate picture on the front of it. The T-shirt was sleeveless, and it showed off his tattoos perfectly. Just as Ari was about to knock again, I opened my bedroom door.

I said, "Did you borrow those platform sandals that I left here? I want to wear them tonight."

She turned toward her room without saying a word.

I looked back at Michael. He had a funky pair of brown Huarache sandals that basically amounted to a desert boot of woven leather in hand, and he was smiling. I reached for his hand. "I love the way those jeans hug your ass." I led him back downstairs. "Go ahead and put on your shoes so that we can be waiting on Ari when she gets down here."

He said, "Yes, ma'am," as he leaned down and kissed me.

Ari appeared at the top of the steps. "We don't have time for that now."

Michael dropped his sandals on the floor and stepped into them before Ari could get to the bottom step. "We were just passing time while waiting for you."

She shot daggers at him from her eyes and handed me my sandals.

I said, "You know that no one's getting there at nine, right?" and slipped them on.

She shot daggers at me too. Then she said, "Let's go," and quickly walked out of the door.

I locked the front door before we followed Ari to the subway. We were lucky. The train pulled up as we walked onto the platform.

After we sat down, Ari asked, "Why were you guys so late? What were you doing?"

I handed Michael a wet nap. "You need to wipe off my lipstick." I answered Ari, "We were just meandering around the Village. We lost track of time."

Michael asked me, "Did I get it?"

I responded, "Most of it." I took the wet nap from his hand. I wiped the little that he missed.

He told Ari, "We went to a dance class earlier."

Ari asked, "How was that?"

He smiled. "Nice, Sammi has skills."

I laughed. "Your brother's a master. Have you seen him dance?"

Ari said, "Not yet. He's been holding out. I was beginning to doubt his story."

Michael answered, "Our LA season starts in September; you should come out. We'll be in New York in February, I think. That's an option too."

I hadn't thought of how it would be with him touring. I guessed I traveled for shoots.

Ari said, "Well, whatever you saw today, you haven't seen Sammi bust a move with her peeps. You have no idea about her skills."

Michael said, "I think I have some idea."

Ari swatted him, "Michael!"

"Don't hit me because you have a dirty mind." He started flicking her ear. Each time she reached for his hand, he moved it out of reach quickly, then flicked her again. They became completely engrossed. The game continued until I said, "Children, stop." They settled down, and we were mostly quiet for the rest of the ride in, watching people.

WHEN WE GOT to the entrance of the pub, Andre, the security man, said, "It's been a long time. How are you?"

I answered, "I'm good. I live in LA now. How are you?"

He responded, "I'm hanging in there. It's good to see you. Have fun."

I said, "I know I will. I've been looking forward to this."

I led the way toward the booth, where I saw some of our friends. Michael took up the rear. He must've flicked Ari's ear again as we were walking in because they were playing that game again when we got to the table. I left them to it. It gave me a chance to get my hugs. And it gave the people who hadn't seen them together time to compare their features. The first person I hugged was Tommy, a close friend of ours from middle school. Then I hugged Luis, a friend of Ari's from grad school. I gave Kumiko a hug and waved at Luke, who was sitting at the back of the booth. Just as let I go of Kumiko, Lamine, a friend of mine from grad school, walked in. He snuck up to hug me from behind. We'd gone out twice, and he hadn't let it go.

Michael and Ari's game had become more aggressive. She'd started swatting him every time he flicked her ear. She was clearly irritated, and he was clearly amused. We all turned toward them. At some point, they realized we were watching and waiting patiently, so they stopped.

I started introductions by saying, "As if their behavior doesn't make it obvious, this is Michael, Ari's biological brother." I introduced Michael to everyone in turn.

Luis, who'd been eying Michael from head to toe since he first caught sight of him, whispered to me, "Oh la la."

To put Luis out of his misery before he made a move, Ari said,

"He doesn't play for your team." To everyone, she said, "He and Sammi are dating."

Michael and I exchanged a glance. I slipped my arm around his waist.

Luis said, "Go on, girl. Handle your business." Then he wrinkled his brow. "Wait, aren't you married?"

"My question exactly," Val said, walking up. She gave both Luis and me a hug.

I responded, "Greg and I are getting a divorce."

Luis said, "I'd ask why, but I follow him on Instagram. He's all over the place."

I added, "In all kinds of ways."

Everyone except Val laughed. She pursed her lips.

Ari put her arm around Luis and said, "They just opened the doors."

I said, "Let's go downstairs where the band is." I'd been looking forward to it since Monday night. Without looking back, I let go of Michael and went downstairs with Tommy on my heels. The band had already started playing and there were people at two of the other tables. The host directed me to our reserved table. I laid my jacket on the back of our booth and went straight to the dance floor and started dancing. Tommy was right there with me. When I turned back toward our booth, I saw that our crew had come downstairs too. Michael was talking to Lamine and Ari.

Tommy asked, "How long before Greg's part of our history?"

I answered, "I don't know. I hope soon."

He looked at Michael. "Ari's brother seems cool."

"He is. He's smart and quirky like she is, but he's a lot more laid-back."

"What does he do for a living?"

"He's the principal male dancer for the Torus Contemporary Ballet."

"Really? He's wearing quite a bit of black label." The question was how he was affording it.

"He also models. I think designers give him clothes to promote their brands."

"Hmmm."

I asked, "What does that mean?"

"Nothing. Just taking it in. So you're already ready to start a new relationship?"

"It just happened."

"Hmmm."

I rolled my eyes at Tommy. "What?"

"Nothing."

The band shifted into a funky cover of "Papa Was Rolling Stone." I forgot about talking to Tommy and let myself be transported by the music. Tommy and I danced together like we always did: him with his white boy two-step, me dancing around him, us with our suggestive, flirty innuendo. Luis and Kumiko joined us. The place was filling up. Several songs passed before we came up for air. I glanced toward our table and locked eyes with Michael. He was half smiling. He gave me a head-to-toe look and bit his lip. I broke from the group and walked back to our table, taking a seat next to him. He put his arm around me.

Michael said, "You look like you're having fun."

"I am. This is my favorite club. It's laid-back and easy, and everything about it from the people to the music is eclectic."

"I got you something to drink. Do you want some food?" He handed me a bottle of water and pointed to a glass of red wine. When I looked at the wine, he said, "It's a Syrah, like you like."

He was kind and thoughtful. "Thank you." I leaned over and kissed him. "I'll eat some of whatever you're having." I took a fork and helped myself to his plate. He pushed the plate closer to me and played with my shoulder absentmindedly. He was relaxed. I took a few more bites, then stood up. I said, "Are you guys going to come dance?"

Michael said, "Yeah, when I finish eating."

Ari and Lamine both said, "In a minute."

Val didn't hear me. She was staring at the dance floor, lost in thought. I was pretty sure she was thinking about her boyfriend.

Luke didn't dance.

The dance floor had gotten crowded. I had to weave through people to get to my folks. A song later, Michael joined us with Val in tow. He danced with her. I thought he was trying to pull her out of her reverie. Finally, Ari and Lamine hit the floor. Lamine danced with me, and Ari danced with Tommy.

Kumiko motioned to Luke to join us. He waved her off. She said, "He's going to be upset that I didn't spend more time sitting with him."

Lamine said, "So going from that creep, Greg, to this guy? He looks like a woman."

I punched him playfully. I looked at Michael. He was beautiful, but he wouldn't pass as a woman. His build and demeanor were much too masculine. I chuckled when I thought of how he'd respond if Lamine made that comment to his face. I looked back at Lamine. "Oh, he's all man. Trust me. And he's a really good person. You should get to know him."

"Good person. Whatever. He doesn't have a real job, Sammi. He can't take care of you. You're going to end up taking care of him." Lamine had strict ideas about the roles of men and women.

"Whatever happens, it's not your concern, Lamine."

"Are you dating him exclusively, or can I ask you out? You won't regret giving me a chance."

"We've had this conversation. You already know my answer." I wanted to point out that I lived in LA and he lived in New York, but I was sure that he'd twist that into the reason I was saying no.

"Okay, okay. One day you're gonna come to your senses."

I closed my eyes and focused on the music.

The DJ started playing as the first set ended. On the way to the green room, the singers and drummer stopped to exchange hugs and salutations. We chatted briefly about my move to LA and the woes of being artists. Then they made their way through the crowd. *If Ari and I had been male,* I thought, *they'd be people we considered friends by then, given how much time we'd spent there.*

By the second set, we weren't just dancing with each other. We were dancing with people from the crowd who had gathered as individuals, in pairs and groups. Quite a few of them were people who came all the time like I used to. It felt good. Even Val was smiling. Michael and I stayed connected by glancing at each other from time to time. I liked that being enough. He was having a great time.

About halfway through the second set, the band started playing a soulful rendition of "Pony." I let the music wash over and through me. A guy danced up and matched my rhythm. After a moment, he took ahold of my hips and stepped toward me so our bodies were in full contact: no "Hello," no, "How are you?" He just wanted to bump and grind. Of course, he was trying to force me to move to his strange rhythm. He was what Ari and I called a "grabber." I glanced at Michael. As expected, he was watching the grabber with a dead look in his eyes. I knew the situation with Alex was still in the air. So I needed to resolve things quickly.

I stepped back and removed his hands from my hips and said, "I don't want to dance that close to you, and please don't grab me like that. I don't like it."

The grabber responded, "Oh, don't be afraid. We dance well together." He stepped toward me again.

I stepped back once more and stopped his hands before they could make contact again. I looked at him with dead eyes. I'd set my boundaries; there was nothing else to say.

The grabber lingered a moment, then walked away.

I looked at Michael, mostly to make sure that he wasn't going to do anything. Michael made eye contact with me. I smiled at him, but he didn't return it. He turned his gaze back to the grabber who was moving away from me and searching out his next target. Ari was dancing with Michael. She tapped his arm and said something to him. Michael looked at her, back toward the grabber, back at me, then back at Ari. He said something to her, then started dancing again. Finally, he looked at me and smiled. Of course, my song was ending by then.

The band started a rock medley. I relaxed back into my groove. When I looked back at Michael, a woman who Ari and I had named Busty was making a move on him. We called her Busty because, though she was a beautiful woman, she exposed much more of her healthy bosom than was necessary to get attention from men. I was convinced it had the opposite effect that she wanted. Of course, I could've been wrong. I enjoyed watching him deal with her advances. It looked like he was trying to encourage her to just enjoy dancing, but she wasn't settling for that. He glanced at me and saw that I was taking pleasure from his predicament and gave me the finger.

I went back to our table when the second set ended to get some water and a snack. I stayed to enjoy watching the crowd. Michael was dancing with Val and Ari. He noticed I was back at the table and came to join me. He sat down next to me and drank what was left of my water.

He said, "If only for tonight, I'm really happy that you decided to come to New York with me."

"Me too. I love this place."

"And I get to hang with your crew. I like them."

I looked around the room at my friends. They were all having fun in their own way. "Yes. They're really good people."

He put his arm around me. I leaned into him and tilted my head up to give him a kiss. We got into it. Suddenly, he pulled away and flicked Ari on her ear again. I guessed that she flicked him while we were kissing. They were back into that game again.

Tommy sat down next to me. "Do they always act like this when they're together?"

I looked at them and thought back. "Not always. I think it may be getting worse."

Tommy said, "I admit I had my doubts when Ari said that she'd found her brother. I was concerned that whoever it was would find her wealth alluring. Seeing is believing. It's strange how much they look alike. Is that weird for you? Does it seem like you're kissing Ari when you're kissing him?" Only Tommy could come up with that. I thought he was trying to twist the situation into one of his lesbian lover fantasies.

"No, it doesn't seem like I'm kissing Ari. When I look at Michael, I don't see Ari. I'm aware of how similar they look, but that's not at the forefront of my mind when I'm interacting with him."

Tommy looked at Michael and Ari as he considered my response. "Hmmm. Well, he seems like he's genuinely into you. I've been watching him. He hasn't been scoping the room. He's been watching you."

"Thank you for letting me know, Tommy."

Val joined us. The waiter had put a carafe of water on the table. Just to push Tommy's buttons, Val poured water from the carafe into Tommy's glass, then drank it down. Tommy gave her the desired look of frustration. To me, she said, "Michael's really nice. I get why you're attracted to him. He's a lot easier to be around than Greg."

Michael had worked his charms. "Thanks, Val."

The band started the third set. Luis came over and pulled Val and Ari onto the dance floor. Tommy followed them.

I turned to Michael and said, "Excuse me, sir, will you dance with me?"

He responded, "I'm sorry, ma'am, but I have a date."

"I'm sure that your date's not coming, sir. You should dance with me."

With a straight face, he said, "Why would you say such things? I'm certain she's coming."

"Well, sir, this is the third set. The party's almost over. If she were coming, she'd be here by now. I believe the fates intend for you to dance with me."

"Really? Why?"

"Because I'm a better match for you than your date."

"How could you know such a thing?" he asked.

I answered, "I'm extremely insightful when it comes to things like this. I can prove it to you."

He asked, "How could you prove it?"

"Well, you have to have an open mind."

He was fighting back a smile. "My mind's open."

"You're sure?"

"I'm sure."

I said, "Okay" and gave him one of his sweet and present kisses. When it ended, I said, "See what I mean?"

"Somewhat. But I'm still not clear."

I kissed him again, sweetly and tenderly. "Is it clearer now?"

"Yes, it's much clearer. There's just one little cloud."

As I was leaning in to kiss Michael again, Luis reappeared. "OMG. You can do that later. Now, it's time to dance."

We let Luis lead us to the dance floor. Even though it had only been a few weeks since we last went out dancing, we were a million miles away from where we were then; I loved him. We let the music take us into a place where there was only us and the rhythm. We moved together seamlessly and effortlessly, not bumping and grinding, but in the lyrical play of giving and taking space.

I noticed Matt had made an appearance. He and Ari were dancing intimately and sharing a kiss. Michael looked at me. I answered his unspoken question. "That's Matt. He and Ari are …

how do we say … buddies. They're not exactly dating, and they're not together."

He watched Ari for a moment. I think he was trying to make sure she wasn't being taken advantage of.

I gave him more information. "He can't commit, so she ended it. He comes if ever, whenever, wherever she calls. He's her placeholder while she looks for her next guy." I looked at Matt for a second. "I'm not sure that he realizes that though."

Ari came over to us with Matt in tow.

I said, "Hey, Matt. How's it going?"

He said, "Good. You?"

I answered, "I'm great."

Ari gestured toward Michael. "Matt, this is my brother, Michael. Mike, this is Matt."

While Michael and Matt exchanged greetings, Ari said to me, "I'm leaving with Matt. I took off from work tomorrow. I'll be home by the time you wake up."

I said, "Okay, have fun."

Ari said, "See you in the morning, Mike," and walked off.

Michael stood frozen in place and stared at them as they left. I couldn't tell if he was stunned or just lost in thought.

A short while later, the third set was over, and it was time to go home. I hugged everyone and said my goodbyes. Michael and I jumped into a cab.

He asked, "You've known Tommy since middle school?"

"Yeah. Sixth grade."

"You seem really close."

"We are. We don't talk all the time, but we're always there for each other."

He asked, "Does he know what happened with Pete?"

"Before I told you, he and Ari were my only friends that knew."

He pondered for a moment. "You and Tommy remind me of Alicia and Paulo."

"Does that bother you?"

He shook his head no. "Did you ever date?"

"No. We became friends first. We got to know each other well enough to know it wouldn't work. The friendship became sacred."

"I like him." He paused. "How long has Ari been seeing Matt?"

"For about a year."

"What does he do?"

"He has a startup. He's the outdoorsy type. He's from Northern California."

He said, "She didn't invite him to come out until after midnight."

I hunched my shoulders. I resisted saying, *Yes, Michael. She's using him for sex.* Instead, as nonchalantly as I could, I said, "That's typical. It's almost 3 a.m. now. She'll be back at her place by nine." He was quiet, so I added, "She doesn't like to bring him to her place because he always wants to stay and have breakfast with her."

A few thoughts flitted across his face. I guessed he was trying to wrap his head around it because he didn't ask any more questions during the few minutes it took us to get to Ari's.

15

———

THE PAST

THURSDAY, AUGUST 24

It WAS ALMOST 4 a.m. when we got back to Ari's house. I was feeling that relaxed, calm, happy feeling I get when I dance. Michael and I kicked off our shoes and made our way up to my room.

He closed the door behind us. "It's Thursday. Can we make love now?"

I could relate. "Yes!"

He locked the door. "Do you need to do anything before we do?"

"I want to take this makeup off."

He came into the bathroom with me. We washed our hands. I took a cotton swab and started to remove my makeup.

He watched me for a moment, then asked, "Can I do that for you?"

I handed him the swab. He gently wiped every inch of my face. When he was done, he said, "That's better." He gave me a quick, passionate kiss and motioned for me to go back into my bedroom, following me.

We stopped in the middle of the room. He was still behind me. He ran his hands across my butt and let them come to rest on my hips. "I really like the way these pants look on you." He reached around me and unbuttoned and unzipped my jeans. "But you won't need them for the rest of the night." He turned me around, removing my jeans and underwear at the same time. He kissed me as he walked me back toward the bed.

When I felt the bed on the back of my legs, I sat down and braced myself with my arms slightly behind me.

Anticipating my inclination to close my legs, he stood with his feet in between mine and pushed my feet apart to open my legs. He stepped back. The whole time he was taking his pants off, he stared at my vagina. I'd never had a lover that was so direct in his observation. It made me feel exposed. He shifted his focus back to my eyes as he kneeled in front of me so our bodies were about two inches apart. He placed his hands just outside of mine on the bed. The only place we were touching was where his erection was pressing against my abdomen.

We were both turned on, and the current between us almost burned. I positioned his erection at my opening.

He hissed a silent, "Ahhh."

Then his hips pulsed forward, and he filled me with his erection. I moaned with the pleasure of it. We were both moving instinctually with strong, urgent undulations. He stopped and became completely still. I kept moving in the rhythm we'd established.

He let me continue for a moment, then said, "You have no idea how good that feels." His body quivered; then he grabbed my pelvis and said, "Stop, stop, stop. Don't move."

I obliged.

When he was no longer on the brink of having an orgasm, he put his forehead to mine and said, "What I really want is to make you come. Will you let me do that?"

I whispered, "Yes."

"You're going to need to be still. If you move, I'll come. Understand?"

I whispered, "Yes."

"Just relax and receive."

"Okay." I lifted his T-shirt up over his head and dropped it on the floor.

He opened my vest and unclasped my bra. I took them off and let them fall on the bed. He palmed my breasts with his hands. His body pulsed. He whispered, "Sammi," and became still again. When he regained control, he kissed the side of my mouth. "Lie back."

I complied.

He shifted me so my pelvis was teetering over the edge of the bed and held it so I couldn't move. Then he started a winding, undulating stroke.

I closed my eyes and relaxed completely, losing myself to the sensation. When I opened my eyes again, he locked into my gaze. He was watching my every response, taking pleasure from my pleasure. That released me. My river flowed around him. My orgasm was quiet and intense. He was still coming as I landed.

When he was grounded, he pulled me the rest of the way off the bed so we maintained our sacred connection as he sat back on his heels. Then he leaned us forward so my back was resting against the side of the bed.

I kissed the bridge of his nose and rested my head against his. After a moment, I said, "Let's get in bed."

"Okay."

I threw my vest and bra on the chair and pulled back the covers. We crawled into bed and fell asleep entwined.

I woke up because Michael was playing with my shoulder. He was only half awake himself. I don't think he was aware he was doing it.

I asked, "What are you thinking about? Are you okay?"

"Um-hum. I'm thinking of last night. I had a lot of fun."

"Which part of last night are you thinking of?"

"The dancing part. The sex was much more than fun. It was incredible."

"I can't argue with that." I peeked around him to see what time it was. It was 9 a.m. I could've stayed in bed for a few more hours, but we were going back to LA the following day. I forced myself to sit up and realized I was hungry.

He curled around me. "Don't get up. Let's spend the day in bed."

Now that was an idea. "That sounds wonderful. I'll take a raincheck on that. This is our last day in New York, and I'm starving. You need to feed me."

"Okay. I need a shower first to help me wake up." He hadn't moved at all.

"I want to go back to the diner."

"Again?"

"Yes. I have six favorite things there. I've only had three of them." I disentangled myself from him and got out of bed. "See you in the shower."

He watched me walk into the bathroom, but he still didn't move. He never joined me in the shower. When I came back into my bedroom, I saw that he'd fallen back asleep. He'd had a rough week filled with my drama and at least four unusually early mornings. Then we'd stayed out all night last night. I was glad to see him so relaxed. I got dressed quietly, then sat on the side of the bed and watched him sleep for a few minutes. He was beautiful. I couldn't resist; I kissed him on his forehead. He half puckered his lips in response. It was more a thought than an action. Otherwise, he didn't move. I picked up my computer and tiptoed out to go to the diner. I noticed Ari hadn't come home yet as I left the brownstone.

I had a leisurely breakfast, read a few articles, and started researching some ideas for future creative endeavors.

Just before 11 a.m., Michael texted me, "Where did you go?"

I texted back, "I'm at the diner. I'll come back now. I'll bring you back some food. What would you like?"

He texted, "An omelet. Loaded."

I responded, "Okay. X"

I ordered his omelet and a sandwich for Ari in case she'd come home.

He was in the kitchen pouring himself a cup of coffee when I got back to the brownstone. Ari was still not home—I smiled to myself.

As I walked into the kitchen, I said, "Good morning, sleepyhead."

He said, "I couldn't wake up earlier. I was really tired. I'm sorry."

I shook my head. "It was good to see you sleeping so peacefully. You have no reason to apologize." I gave him one of his signature kisses as I heard Ari unlocking the front door.

He smiled. "Well, if you hadn't taken advantage of me last night and made me work so hard, I may have been able to get up earlier."

I gave him a look of concern. "It sounds like you're being abused." Ari was walking down the hall toward the kitchen.

His smile broadened. "I am. And then you just got up and left me here all alone. You abandoned me."

I asked, "So I abused and abandoned you?"

"Yes."

"Is there any way you could ever forgive me?"

He looked up at the ceiling. "I don't know. That might not be wise."

I said, "Please, I'm willing to beg." I kissed him again.

He said, "See, now you're trying to confuse me so you can do it again."

Ari cleared her throat. "Enough. I'm standing here." She was looking at us like we'd gone insane.

Michael kissed me more deeply than usual for Ari's discomfort. When he peeled away from me, he said, "Oh, you've decided to come home. Good morning, Ari."

She was wearing her jeans from last night and a T-shirt that clearly belonged to Matt. It was at least three sizes too big for her. I looked at the clock on the stove and opened my mouth to comment about the time.

Before I could utter a sound, she pointed at me and said, "Don't."

I smirked and slid her the sandwich I'd bought for her.

She gave me the finger and caught it. "Thanks. I'll eat this in a little while. I want to take a quick nap." She turned and left the kitchen.

Michael took a seat at the kitchen island and opened the food I'd brought him and started eating. "Thank you."

I sat his coffee down next to him and took a seat.

He said, "It was really good to see you with your friends last night."

"Yeah, I really needed that. I'm so glad that you and Ari insisted on me coming to New York."

"That was the first time I've really gotten to see you be social with a group of people. I'd mistaken you for a loner."

I shook my head. "I'm definitely not a loner. I just haven't found my crew in LA yet."

"Why not?"

I huffed. "Dealing with Greg and losing myself in my work to avoid dealing with Greg."

"How did you meet him?"

"I met him at Pete's party before things got out of hand that night."

He grimaced. "Oh yeah, you already told me that. I'm sorry."

"It's fine, Michael."

"How did you two get together?"

"Do you really want to hear the story of me and my ex?"

He considered the question. "Honestly, I'm trying to figure out how you ended up married to someone so …" He was searching for the right words.

I offered, "… fucked up."

"Yes, but those aren't the words I'm looking for. Given what I've seen of your personality, I don't understand why you married someone who's so full of shit."

"You're sure?"

He nodded. "Uh-huh."

"Will you tell me about you and college girl?"

He responded, "Her name was Celine. Of course. But I didn't end up married to her, so you have to go first."

"Alright." I started the story post-accident. "Greg had just had his accident when I first moved out to LA. One evening, I went by the hospital to see him."

"You went to the hospital to see someone you didn't actually know?"

"You take people to meet your mom after the first date." I shrugged. "I don't know, Michael. I had a lot of alone time. It was in the news. I went on a whim. Given his celebrity, I didn't expect to make it in. I ran into Kenny. He recognized me from the party and granted me admission. Things evolved from there."

"You started dating and fell in love?"

I shook my head. "Nope. We became friends. His injuries were extensive, and he was in a lot of pain. He would do his physical therapy better when I helped him. Since I didn't know many people in LA, I'd go by the hospital most days. When he went home, I'd go by his place. While he was healing, he was a different person. He was kind and appreciative. We developed a really good rapport. We didn't start courting until a year into his recovery."

"And then you fell in love and got married?" He had finished with his food and got up to get himself more coffee.

"I came to love him, but no, I didn't fall in love with him."

"Why did you marry him, then?"

"Because I liked him, respected him, and he showered me with adoration. He made me feel like I meant the world to him. My Ferrari was a gift from Greg, a token of his love. He said that he wanted to take care of me the way that I'd taken care of him. Given how well it works in places where marriages are arranged, I figured that friendship, love, and genuine, mutual respect were a good foundation for marriage. I'd say that and culture are the reasons I married him. There's still an undercurrent in our culture that teaches girls to look for people who can provide for them. I didn't want that, but I thought that at least we could have a mutually supportive financial partnership. We got married about a year after we started dating. Things between us were really good. But ..." I paused to collect my thoughts.

He offered, "But that all ended when he got better?" He sat next to me with his arm resting on my chair and absentmindedly played with my shoulder again.

For the most part, I could be open with Michael about what'd happened between Greg and me. I didn't mention that the sense of stability between Greg and me had lulled me into a false sense of safety. I'd believed that I could trust Greg, that I could open my heart to him. I hadn't told him I'd caused his accident because I was waiting for the right time: when I got to know him, when he'd healed, when I could trust him. It weighed on me. When I finally believed I could trust him, I told him the truth, and I was prepared to face the consequences. Then I figured out he'd been cheating on me for months before I told him the truth. My trust was misplaced. Guarding my heart had been much wiser.

Michael was watching me closely.

I collected my thoughts and continued, "The moment he healed, he cheated on me. He didn't see it as cheating. He considered it his right as a man. Around the same time, they came to repossess my Ferrari because he wasn't making the payments. I was so pissed at him I charged the balance to one of his accounts and let him pay it off immediately. That's when I started paying attention to his finances. He was burning through money like tomorrow wasn't coming. I reached out to Ari, and we made a plan. Your sister is a genius. Thanks to her, he's wealthy instead of bankrupt. And just so you know, I didn't marry him for his money. I always contributed to all of our household expenses. Since I decided to leave him, I haven't used any of his money to support me. I pay my own way. That's the story of me and Greg in a nutshell."

He asked, "What about the paparazzi? I see him in the press from time to time. I don't remember ever seeing you."

"I didn't want any part of that. He was twenty-nine when the accident happened. It'd been at least three years since their last hit and two years since their last album. The press and paparazzi weren't aggressively pursuing him. When he was in the hospital, I never went near him if the press was there. When he was convalescing at home, things were quiet. That said, our marriage isn't a secret. There are photos of us as a couple out there. Since he got well and started whoring, I haven't gone out with him. He takes whoever he's fucking at the time to events. People know he's cheating."

"How long did the adoration phase last?"

"For about a year and a half."

He asked, "Do you think he loves you?"

"Yes. In his mind, there's no greater expression of caring than sharing his stuff. He committed to that and to taking care of me by marrying me. I have every*thing* I need or want, so he's fulfilled his part of our relationship as far as he's concerned. Regarding the connection you're asking about, no. Greg doesn't do 'in love.'"

"How was he about taking care of your needs?"

"You're really going there?"

"The question is on the table."

"He was seriously injured. It was a while before he could really have sex. He was okay as a lover." I paused to figure out how to say it. "You know how some people have good technique but no emotional feel?"

He nodded.

"Greg's a good technician."

He asked, "So you never felt deeply attracted to him?"

"I did for a while during the adoration phase. Like I said, I came to love him deeply, but I never fell in love with him." I let that settle for a moment.

He squinted. "So it sounds like there was no passion, no risk for you. You were playing it safe."

I felt like an open book. "Did I answer all of your questions?"

He was still processing everything I'd told him. "Yes, you did."

"Great. Now I can stop talking about Greg."

"Actually, I have one more question."

"Shoot."

"When will the divorce be final?"

"I don't know. His lawyer acknowledged that they got the papers. I haven't heard anything else from them. I'm going to check in with my lawyer next week."

He said, "I find it very strange that he hasn't tried to be with you or even spoken to you in three months, but he doesn't seem to want to end your relationship."

Michael had a way of cutting through the bullshit. I took a moment to consider how to answer that. There was no way in hell I was telling him how Greg could be that angry at me.

"The fact that he's married is the perfect excuse for him not being available."

He responded, "That's true. But you're his wife, and it's been three months." He was sensing the gaps in my story.

Hearing Michael say I was Greg's wife was sobering. I was talking to my lover, who I was in love with, about my relationship with my husband. It was a mess. How had I ended up there? And then there was the situation with Alex.

Michael stroked my cheek. "Hey. Sammi. Where are you right now?"

I shook my head. "I'm sorry. Hearing you call me Greg's wife struck a chord." I had to put this subject to rest. "Things got really bad a few months before I decided to divorce him. He became strung out and out of control. He really pissed me off with his whoring and irresponsibility. We had a really bad fight. Really bad. The kind where you end up not speaking to the person." It was slightly out of order, and there were some details missing; but everything I said was the truth.

He pulled me into his arms and kissed my forehead. "I didn't mean to upset you. I'm sorry."

I relaxed into his embrace. I loved how it felt to be held by him. "It's fine. Just, can we talk about something else?"

"What do you want to talk about?"

"Tell me the story of you and Celine."

"You really want to talk about that now?"

I responded, "I do."

He lifted his eyebrows. "Alright. But let's go sit on the couch. These stools aren't exactly comfortable."

I led him into the den, sat down on the couch sideways with my back against the armrest, and opened my arms for him to sit in front of me. He sat and leaned back so I could wrap my arms around him. "I'm listening."

He said, "There's not much to tell. We were both going to Caltech when we met. She was a senior. I was a sophomore. We were in the same English lit class. I struck up a conversation, and things progressed from there." He sounded like he was done with the story.

I chuckled and kissed the top of his head. "And?"

"And we dated for two years until she broke up with me. I told you about that." He put one of his hands on top of mine, and I played with it.

"Was she one of your fans?"

"No."

"Were you in love with her?"

"Yes."

"Did she love you?" I loved the way it was his story but I was doing most of the talking.

"Yes. She said she did, and I believed her."

"Did she satisfy your needs?"

He laughed. "Yeah. We screwed a lot."

I couldn't resist. "So sex is your only need when it comes to women."

He squinted and smirked. "She was smart. We had some things in common. We would talk … some."

"Do you ever regret that you broke up?"

"No, I don't regret that we broke up. It would've happened eventually anyway. What I thought I needed and wanted then is totally different than what I think now. Looking back, I don't think we were all that compatible."

"But your longest relationship was with her."

He hunched his shoulders. "I was twenty."

"Were you a good lover then?"

"I tried to be. You guys can be complicated."

"How did you learn?"

"Practice. One person in particular was a good teacher."

I asked, "Did you fall in love with her?"

"No. That relationship was purely physical for both of us. She was bisexual with a preference for women. I was her man pet for a while. It was great because she could relate to the challenge of making sure your woman got off and, as a woman, talk about what needed to be done to achieve that."

I asked, "Were you actively dating when we met?"

"Yes."

"Have you gone out with anyone else since we started dating?"

"Twice during the first week we were dating." He smirked. "Neither ended in a stand." He became somewhat pensive and kissed my hand. "You've changed the subject, Sammi. Complete dating history is not a conversation people who're just dating have."

"We've spent six of the last seven nights together. We aren't doing such a good job dating."

"True." He repositioned himself on his side so he could look at me. "So you think I'm a good lover?" His eyes were playful and penetrating. I always felt exposed when he looked at me.

I couldn't answer that straight. "You're okay." I bit my lip to contain my smile.

"Just okay?" He was smiling too.

"A little more than okay."

"Only a little more?"

I closed my eyes to get a respite from his gaze. I let the feeling of being with him surface. I opened my eyes to take in his gaze again.

"You've been an amazing lover to me." I wondered if my eyes betrayed all I wasn't ready to say.

"I feel the same way." A few seconds later, he looked away and laid his head on my chest with his eyes closed.

I tilted his head so I could kiss both of his eyelids in turn. I whispered, "Get up and come with me."

I took his hand and led him to my bedroom, closing and locking the door behind us. Turning to him, I lifted his shirt over his head. He knew this game, so he waited for my next move. I stepped back and took off his shorts and boxer briefs, walking around him to take in the view. "I really like what I see." His erection was growing, even though I hadn't touched him. I propped the pillows against the headboard, then motioned for him to sit with his back against them. When he had settled, I kneeled in front of him. I kissed him softly, deeply as I stroked his erection, hand over hand. He let out a hiss. I said, "It's my turn to watch you come. You relax and receive." I added French kisses to the attention that I was giving to his erection.

He moaned loudly, louder than he ever had before.

Without stopping the stroke, I said, "Shhh. You're gonna wake Ari up."

He panted, "Okay, okay. I'm quiet."

I added the kisses back in with the stroke.

For a few moments, he vocalized quietly. He moaned again at the top of his voice.

I looked at him.

He panted. "I'm quiet. I'm quiet." He was laughing. He did it again as soon as I kissed his jewel. Before I could look at him, he whispered, "I'm under control." He was laughing outright then.

I started going down on him.

His laughter subsided, and his moans were soft for a good while. He basically screamed, "Ahhh! Sammi." In a softer voice, he said, "I'm going to come. I want to come inside."

I looked at him and asked, "Why are you being so loud?"

"I don't know. It's-it's-it's really intense."

I kicked off my shorts and underwear and straddled him. I initiated a penetrating and passionate kiss by parting his lips with my tongue.

He laughed. He knew why I was doing it. He pulled back from the kiss and tugged my cotton cami up. "I want to see your body."

I finished taking off my camisole.

He took the opportunity to fondle and kiss my breasts. It felt nice. So I let him continue for a while. I kissed both of his palms, one at a time. "Relax. Receive. I'll tie you up if I have to."

He chuckled and relaxed.

I reinitiated my kiss and took him inside of me. I hissed from the pressure of him. I undulated my pelvis in a fluid motion with an urgent rhythm.

Within a few minutes, his body moved with mine reflexively. He was heading toward orgasm and pulling me with him. I pulled back from the kiss to watch his release. He moaned softly as the pulses of his orgasm ran through him. His climax tipped me into my own. He responded to my orgasm with a series of loud, aspirated moans. We were both laughing when we regained our equilibrium.

I asked, "Have you been holding out on me? Is being loud your norm?"

"No. I'm not usually loud. I'm just hypersensitive right now." He kissed my forehead. Pensively, he said, "It's just another thing that you make me do."

I really wanted to know what he was thinking, but I decided to let it go. "I think I heard Ari. Let's get dressed and see what she's up to."

We rinsed off, got dressed, and went downstairs.

When we walked into the kitchen, Ari was sitting at the island eating the sandwich I brought her and drinking a cup of coffee.

I said, "How was your nap?"

She responded, "Interrupted."

I chuckled and looked at Michael. He was looking inside the refrigerator, oblivious.

When he turned to face us again, Ari smirked and said, "I take it you two can have sex again."

He responded, "Yes, we can have sex now. Sammi's cycle ended yesterday." He said it as if it were totally normal to share details like that.

Ari and I exchanged a look and looked back at him incredulously.

He said, "What? You both know that people have sex. Ari knows that we have sex. We know that Ari had sex last night. You both know that women have cycles. I honestly don't understand what's so shocking." He returned our looks of incredulity.

Ari looked like she was trying to stop herself from saying something. Ultimately, she gave in. "Why were you being so loud?"

With one of the best impersonations of innocence I'd ever witnessed, he said, "Because Sammi was taking advantage of me. She does that when we're alone. She can be quite demanding."

Ari was clearly trying to wrap her mind around his answer.

I looked at her and said, "It's genetic. You know all of it's genetic."

She gave me the finger.

Michael asked, "Why's she flipping you off?"

I kept my gaze on Ari and answered Michael. "Because she can see that you two have more in common than she cares to admit. On that note, I need to run a few errands in the city. You two genetically related creatures could use some alone time. If you're done hanging by dinnertime, let me know."

I could see from Michael's expression my answer didn't satisfy his curiosity, but he didn't press. He asked, "How long do you need? There's a place that I'd like to take you guys for dinner."

I looked at the clock on the stove. "It's one now. I'll be done by around five."

He asked, "Where will you be?"

"Midtown."

He asked, "Can you meet us in Hell's Kitchen at five thirty?"

"I can." I kissed his chin. As I exited the kitchen, I told Ari, "You should help him with his finances." I told Michael, "It'll feel very invasive, but you should let her help you."

Ari gave me a serious evil eye.

I smiled in response. "Love you, girl. See you later." I stuck my tongue out at her as I walked out of the door.

I headed into the city. My big errand was to stop by a store to replace the earphones I'd lost. I spent the afternoon at MOMA. When I met up with them, it seemed their time had done them good. Michael took us to an authentic Italian restaurant. When we got back to Ari's place, Ari and I went straight to bed. Michael went to the den to watch TV.

16

BACK TO LA
FRIDAY, AUGUST 25

WHEN I ROLLED over the next morning, it was around 9:30 a.m. I'd heard Ari go downstairs hours ago. I found her in her study and made myself comfortable in one of the big armchairs she had in there.

I said, "I can't believe we're going back to LA today. I've had so much fun. I'm not ready to leave."

"You have at least a few days before you have to go back to work. You could stay." She closed her laptop and leaned back in her chair.

"Michael's really excited about going to that party tomorrow."

"Uh-huh."

I had no counter. I just said, "Yeah" and laughed to myself a little.

"Did Michael get any more information about what's going on with Alex?"

"I don't think so. I don't know. I haven't asked him because he gets so upset."

"You guys need to keep talking about it. You need to ask him."

Michael said, "Ask who what?"

Ari and I both jumped because we didn't hear him approaching.

Before I could object, Ari responded, "Can you give us an update on Alex?"

Michael blinked a couple of times and let out a quick exhale. He sat in the only other chair in the room. "Ummm, there isn't one, really. I've been reaching out. He's not talking to me, but he's spent time with Paulo and Alicia. He's still upset, and he hasn't opened up. The working theory is that he got high, or maybe was drugged, and did something fucked up." There was a crinkle in his brow. His temper was rising.

To deter Michael from becoming angry at Alex again, I said, "That theory makes sense to me. I have a feeling that Alex doesn't know what happened. That's why I'm such a threat." It didn't help at all.

"Yeah, well, if he'd just stayed the fuck away from Pete, none of this would be an issue. He knew better." He was seething.

We sat in silence for a few minutes. I broke it by saying, "I have less than eight hours left in New York. This has been an amazing trip. Those assholes can't have any more of my time. I'm hungry and want to go to the diner one last time. I have two favorite things that I haven't had yet, and I'm ordering both of them."

Ari responded, "Sounds good to me."

I asked her, "Don't you have to go to work today?"

"Technically, yes. I put in a few hours this morning. They'll have to survive until you guys leave for the airport because I'm hanging out with you until then."

We looked at Michael. He was still fuming.

I went over to him and sat on his lap. I kissed him on his cheek, then turned his face so I could look directly into his eyes. "Hey."

He gave me some of his attention. "Hey," I said. I could tell, mostly, he was still thinking about Alex.

"Let's start over." I kissed his lips chastely. "Good morning, beautiful."

He shook his head and exhaled. I had more of his attention. "Good morning, beautiful." He kissed me back. "How can you just switch topics and let shit go like that?"

I kissed his forehead and hugged him. "I don't know. Practice maybe. It's a practical approach. In this moment, no more information's available. You can't let the assholes make you miss out on the good things."

He leaned back from my hug, looked me in my eyes, and stroked my cheek. "You're strong and wise." A thought that he didn't express flitted across his face. He gave me one of his sweet and present kisses.

When he moaned a little, Ari said, "Hello! I'm here."

He deepened our kiss in response. I felt him smiling against my lips.

Ari threw a pillow that hit the back of his head.

He ended our kiss and, with an almost straight face, said, "Oh. Hi, Ari. Good morning."

Ari gave him the finger and said, "Let's go. I'm hungry." She started walking toward the front door.

"Me too." I got up and followed her.

WHEN WE WERE SEATED at the diner, Michael said, "I don't see how you two can eat here so often."

I responded, "That's because you aren't interacting with the menu properly. You keep ordering the same thing."

He said, "It's a diner. You order breakfast."

Ari and I exchanged a look. There was only one response to that statement. "No."

I said, "Not at this diner."

Ari said, "Yeah, everything here is really good."

I nudged Ari. "Shall we school him?"

She nodded. "I think he's earned it."

I directed him. "Close your eyes …"

Ari continued, "… then think of what you'd like to eat at the moment."

He looked at us like we were stupid. I crossed my arms to let him know I was serious. He resisted for a moment and then did as he was told.

As his eyelids met each other, Ari asked, "So what do you want?"

"My eyes were still closing." He relaxed a bit. It was clear he was taking pleasure in keeping us waiting.

I said, "It can be a category. It doesn't have to be a specific dish."

He held up his hand. "Give me a moment. I'm thinking."

Ari huffed. "We're hungry."

He opened his eyes and looked at her. He said, "I could get my usual," in a patient, soothing voice.

She huffed again. "What do you want, Mike?"

He closed his eyes again. There was the barest hint of a smile on his face. Just as Ari started to growl at him, he opened his eyes with a faraway look. A moment later, he bit his lip. As her lip quivered, he said, "You know …" He waited until she squinted at him. "… I could really enjoy spicy sausage with eggs, grits, and biscuits like we had at my mom's house."

I said, "Now look for it on the menu."

He looked at me doubtfully.

Ari said, "Do it."

He looked at her for a second and then looked at the menu. We watched his face settle into awe.

After we'd ordered, I said, "See? This place is magical."

Ari asked, "When does your next project start?

"If things go as planned, in a week. When are you coming back to LA?"

"I don't know. Soon. You guys should move here."

Michael responded, "You should move to LA."

We stayed at the diner for an hour or so. Then we walked back to Ari's brownstone to pack up and go to the airport.

As I set my bag down by the front door, Ari came out of her study with a bound document. To me, she said, "These are the financial documents for your lawyer. Give them to him on Monday. I emailed you a digital copy. And I have backups. I want to be there when you're negotiating the settlement."

Ari was intimidating when she was doing her thing. I said, "Yes, ma'am."

She looked at Michael and said, "Based on the conversation we had yesterday afternoon about your finances, I have some concrete plans on how to get you started. I need the amount that we came up with a week from today, first thing, 8 a.m. New York time."

Michael followed suit and said, "Yes, ma'am."

Ari said, "Good. I'll come out to LA in a month or so to check progress and hang out." She gave me a look to let me know she decided I was right about letting Michael into the space she reserved for family.

"Love you, girl." I hugged her.

"Love you, girl." She hugged me back.

She hugged Michael. "Hang in there. I'll see you soon."

"Yeah." He hugged her back.

With that, we left. The airport was crowded, and we made it to the plane just before they closed the doors. I got comfortable quickly, rested my head on Michael's shoulder, and fell asleep before the plane took off.

AS WE APPROACHED the exit for ground transportation, Michael was looking at me more and more intensely. I could tell he wanted to say something.

I asked, "What is it, Michael?"

"I'm so excited about the party tomorrow. I want the day to be perfect."

I knew where that was going. "Don't tell me. In order for it to be perfect, we need to spend tonight and tomorrow night together."

He lit up like a kid negotiating for a toy he really wanted. "That way we can make love in the morning as we wake up and tomorrow night after the party ends. That's the perfect way to start and end tomorrow. Then we could be apart on Sunday. And Monday even … to let the dust settle. I know that's important to you."

At the rate we were going, we might as well have moved in with each other. But his eyes … I couldn't resist him. And unlike last week, this time, he was happy and carefree. I said, "Okay. What's the plan?"

He smiled broadly and went right into it. "We'll take a car to my house so that I can pick up my car and my swimming trunks. Then we'll spend the night at your place. I'm having breakfast with my mom on Sunday this week, and the party doesn't start until two. So we can take our time in the morning. We'll have a perfect day. You're going to love it! Then you can take advantage of me tomorrow night. I'll leave your place on Sunday morning and not see you again until Tuesday."

All I could do was laugh. "Make it so."

"Yes!" He gave me the quick version of his sweet and present kiss and led us off to the taxi line.

As the car pulled into his driveway, we both received a series of text messages. Mine were from my mom and Ari. I responded to Ari first. "We're back in LA. I'll let you know how the party goes."

Michael's attention was on his phone as we walked into his house. I decided it was a good time to give my mom a quick call. I caught her up on my week, and she suggested I should move back to New York.

Michael said, "Something to drink?" from across the room.

I gave him a thumbs-up.

My mom realized I wasn't alone and almost hung up on me. She was happy I was spending time with friends in LA.

Michael handed me an energy drink with electrolytes in a sports bottle. "We gotta go. I have errands to run. I need to pick up things for tomorrow because Paulo's inept. Do you want to come with me? Or do you want me to take you home?" He walked over to his front door where, in the short time I was talking to my mom, he'd piled up a bunch of beach gear: a mat, chairs, and two umbrellas.

"I'll come with you."

He turned toward me suddenly and said, "You were talking to your mom. Good call. I need to call my mom. She'll want to speak with you to check in."

"What have you told her?"

"That you're okay. Nothing about what happened to you."

Helen had been kind to me. I wanted her to know the truth. "Okay, I'll talk to her."

"Thanks." He kissed my forehead as he called her. He started taking the beach gear out to his car. He said, "You must've been holding your phone," as he disappeared through his front door.

I drank a squirt of my energy drink and picked up the umbrellas, all that was left of the pile of beach gear, and followed him out to his car.

As I got close, I heard him saying, "… their friends. We had a lot of fun." He waited for a minute. "She's right here. Say hello to her yourself."

He handed me his phone, which buzzed with more than one incoming text or email as soon as I touched it. He kissed me while I was trying to say hello. My first attempt came out garbled. I cleared my throat and started again. "Hello."

As expected, Helen was supportive of me. I told her the one-line version of what happened that night at Pete's. I asked her about Alex. Her response made it clear she was really worried about him.

Michael took the phone and wrapped an arm around me. To his mom, he said, "Okay, that's enough. Are you okay?" He listened to her response. He made eye contact with me and said, "Don't take on the pain of possibilities that haven't been confirmed." He listened again. "I'm going to check in with Paulo in a little while. I'll see you on Sunday. Love you." He hung up the phone and searched my eyes in a way that he hadn't done since before we went to New York.

I took a deep breath and said, "Assholes away."

He half smiled and said, "Assholes away."

"What are these errands we have to run?"

"We need to get food, beverages, and ice for the beach tomorrow. And a cooler. I can't find my cooler."

"I have a cooler. I have lots of beach stuff."

"Do you have any food at your place? I want to stay in for breakfast tomorrow."

"We need to buy food for my place."

He picked up my carry-on. "Let's go."

THE FIRST PLACE we stopped was Paulo's. He jumped into the back seat of the car while Michael was still pulling into his driveway.

As he was situating himself, he said to Michael, "Come on, man. Let's go. We don't have time to waste." He leaned up between the seats, kissed me on the cheek, and said, quite sweetly, "Hi, Sammi. It's good to see you. Did you have fun in New York?"

Michael stopped the car abruptly and waited for Paulo to look at him.

Paulo looked at Michael. "What the fuck, man! Stop playing. We got to go." He looked back at me.

Michael didn't move. He just continued to look at Paulo.

Paulo said to me, "Next time you go to New York, I want to come too, whether or not Michael goes."

Michael cleared his throat.

Paulo looked at him. "What are you waiting for?"

Michael said dryly, "I'm waiting for you to sit back and put on your seatbelt like a normal person so that we can leave."

Paulo complied and huffed. "You can block all you want to, Mike. I'll still be the one she loves in the end."

"Only in your dreams, Paulo. Where to first?"

Paulo responded, "Happens every time, man. The wine store. It closes in thirty minutes."

It occurred to me Paulo could be my man on the inside regarding Alex. When we got to the wine store, I motioned to Paulo to slow down. Once Michael went inside, I asked him, "How's Alex?"

He responded awkwardly, "Better."

I dealt with it head on. "Michael told me that you and Alicia know what happened to me."

He exhaled. "I'm sorry, Sammi." It landed that the people in Michael's support system were offering compassion, not judgment.

"Thank you, Paulo. Thank you. Has Alex opened up any?"

"Not to me. Mostly, he's been talking to Alicia."

"Is Alex coming to the beach party tomorrow?"

"Yeah, as far as I know."

"Does he know that Michael's bringing me with him?"

Michael peeked out of the wine store and made a questioning gesture.

Paulo motioned for me to lead the way. "Yeah, Alex is a part of our group chat."

I said, "Thanks," and we walked into the wine store. I felt a tinge of guilt about going to the beach party with Michael and Alex's friends.

Paulo waved his hand and said, "Choose anything you want, Sammi. Mike's paying."

Michael looked at me quizzically.

"I asked Paulo about how Alex is and if he knows I'm coming to the party tomorrow."

He took my hand and kissed my cheek. "Everyone knows you're coming to the party tomorrow. It'll be fine. Paulo and Alicia talked to Alex."

I still felt guilty.

With the help of a sommelier, we chose a set of wines that were good for a picnic on the beach.

Before we could get back to the checkout counter, Paulo fixated on a fancy picnic setting. He said, "I need to know if an angel would find this pleasing. Does this set please you?"

"It's okay, but it's overpriced."

"I want to impress my date tomorrow with a beautiful setting."

"You can borrow one of mine. I have a few really nice ones."

He gave me the same look as when he found out I had more than one car. "That would be perfect." Paulo took my hand to kiss it.

Michael put his hand on top of mine so Paulo kissed his hand instead. When Paulo gave him the evil eye, he raised his eyebrows playfully.

They continued their antics throughout the trip to the grocery store. I steered them away from food choices that required cooking and kept them in line with what went with our wine selection. We made good time. We dropped Paulo off at home, agreed he'd be at my house at 11 a.m., and made it to my house by 10 p.m.

I WATCHED Michael put the drinks in the refrigerator while I folded the grocery bags. Even though this wouldn't last forever, he was definitely one of the good ones. He set a bottle of water on the kitchen island. I decided to play. I took it and went to the far side of the island. When he was done putting the other bottles of water in the refrigerator, he reached for the one he'd set aside without looking. He looked at me immediately, and the game was on. He caught me quickly and sat me up on the island and stood in front of me, with his arms on either side of me. He was all smiles. He loved to play as much as I did.

I taunted him. I opened the bottle and inclined it forward a little. "Did you want some water?"

"Yes." He took the bottle out of my hand before I could drink any. He took a big gulp. "Do you want a sip?"

"Yes, thank you. I'm parched." I drank as much of it as I could. I gave it back to him, but I couldn't look at him without bursting into laughter. So I looked everywhere else.

He squinted at me. "You just drank all of my water after I was kind enough to offer you a sip. You know that was wrong, right?" He touched my nose with his.

I still couldn't look at him. "I thought you were offering me the whole thing." It was taking all my will not to laugh.

He was trying not to smile. He was beautiful. I kissed him.

He cleared his throat. "Distraction won't work, Sammi. Admit that you drank all of my water when you shouldn't have."

Distraction. There was an approach. I looked him in his eyes and caressed his lips with my tongue.

On cue, he purred. "Okay, distraction does work, but it doesn't make it right."

I kept looking at him and touched my tongue to his. He huffed and pulled me closer. I was turning him on. I kissed him more passionately.

When I stopped to catch my breath, he said, "It was still wrong of you to drink all of my water. I could die of thirst now."

It was official. I was totally in love with this man. I hadn't felt this happy or relaxed in so long I couldn't remember. I was elated that I'd gone to New York with him. "Thank you for New York. I needed it. I had an amazing time."

"Thank you for deciding to go with me. It was pretty great."

My mind went to the night during my cycle when I wore the threadbare cotton camisole to bed. I was sending mixed signals. I should have worn a T-shirt. I didn't think it through. "I hope you don't feel that I was toying with you sexually in New York."

He raised his eyebrows and shook his head slightly.

I bit my lip as I processed how random my statement was.

"I don't. I understand and support your boundaries, Sammi." He was being patient and sincere. "I'm trusting you to let me know when and if you want it. I promise to do the same. Safety's a big part of intimacy. It's important that you know you're always safe with me."

Yep, all my wards were gone. "I am safe with you, Michael. Thank you. I was just worried because you slept in the guest room at Ari's."

"I was exceptionally horny that night. Don't tell me that never happens to you."

"That situation's a bit different from my perspective; men don't often refuse sex, but I can relate to being exceptionally horny." I put my arms around him.

A moment or so later, his jewel chimed in.

"Yeah, I'm pretty turned on too." I couldn't resist him. I let myself melt into him, and we moved together in a gentle undulation.

Skimming my ear with his teeth, he whispered, "You know what? Let's not have sex until in the morning." His erection was still growing. He couldn't be serious.

"Why?"

He pulled away a little. "Why not?" His hips were still moving, and he was almost panting.

He was taunting me. Two could play that game. "Okay, I can wait." I moved back so we were no longer touching.

He almost laughed. "Unless you want to now."

He definitely wanted it. I decided to let him beg. "No, I'm good." I got down from the island and waggled my ass as I walked to my bedroom to keep him focused.

He fell into step. "Yeah. Me too."

He was just a step behind me when I got to my bathroom. He was still really turned on. I said, "I'll take my shower first," closing the door slowly. I expected him to knock on the door to join me, but he didn't.

I showered quickly and put on a T-shirt and some underwear.

All he was wearing when I exited the bathroom were his boxer briefs and half a smile that said, *I know you want it.* He said, "My turn," then walked into the bathroom and watched me gawk as he removed the briefs. *Damn.*

I closed my eyes to commit that image to memory forever. His phone buzzed in his pocket. It had been buzzing all night. It made me think of the party. The party … I needed to make sure this wasn't an event that Greg would attend. I should've gotten more information as soon as he mentioned it. If it was a concert, I'd have to bow out. Reality shined its cold light on my Michael oasis.

I got into bed and braced myself to talk this through with him. A few minutes later, he came out of the bathroom with another pair of briefs on. As he got into bed with me, I said, "Tell me more about this party that we're going to."

"It's a party that my friend, Cam, throws every year. We meet at the beach. We play games. We dance. Since she's a DJ, the music's really good. Really, really good." His phone buzzed again. He gave it an exasperated look.

"So it's not a concert or a production."

"No, it's basically a house party at the beach." He looked at his phone and crinkled his brow.

This was a private party. That meant no Greg. *Great!* "What should I wear?"

"A swimsuit and sandals you feel comfortable swimming and dancing and playing in. You'll be by the ocean and in sand all day." His phone buzzed a few more times. "You've got to be kidding me." He looked at it for a second, then showed it to me. "I thought that ignoring these would get the point across that I'm not interested, but it doesn't seem to be working."

The first word that came to mind was, *Wow.* There were almost thirty messages from at least eight different women asking if he was coming to the party. I was sure there were others that hadn't reached out. He was a PLAYER, all caps. It was only a matter of time before this dance ended, but my game was also strong. Without missing a beat, I casually responded, "Less is usually more. If you keep ignoring them, they'll get the point."

"I didn't think that through. I didn't mean it as a move." I was surprised by how tense he sounded.

The look in his eyes stripped away all the wards I'd just repaired. I could see and feel he was being sincere. I asked heaven to help me. I could only laugh at my predicament. He was giving me nothing to guard against. "I know. I can tell."

He held out his phone like he was going to take a picture of us in bed. "Since we're only dating, I guess it wouldn't be appropriate if I sent them a picture of us."

"Correct."

"You should be more territorial."

"That's not my game."

"So you're willing to take advantage of me, but you won't

protect me?" He deleted the text conversations and put his phone on Do Not Disturb.

"Nope, I won't protect you from your fans."

He looked at me like he was considering something for a moment. Then he said, "We should go to sleep. We have a full day tomorrow."

I turned off the light, and moonlight flooded in. We cuddled, closed our eyes, and got still. Immediately, I felt the currents of our connection. His scent. His breathing. I squirmed a little and tried to will myself to sleep.

He said, "You feel that too, don't you?"

"Yeah, I do. It's nice."

"Really nice. This is what was happening to me that night at Ari's."

We wrapped ourselves around each other.

I asked, "Do you think that it's a chemical reaction? You know, just the way our pheromones interact with each other? Would we be here even if we didn't have much in common and couldn't talk?"

"No. I think that pheromones play a part, but the way we relate to each other is where the magic is. Surely, you've had an experience where the attraction was purely pheromonal."

"Yeah. You're right. That doesn't work."

"I think chemistry is a good metaphor for our connection though. There's a definite exchange of energy between us. It's not unlike two atoms sharing electrons."

As if being present and kind and gorgeous weren't enough, he was also reminding me he was intelligent. "I can see that. As a chemist, what type of atoms would you say we are?"

"Definitely carbon."

"Hmmm. The foundation of life on Earth. I like that."

"Yeah, and since we each need four valence electrons to be chemically stable, we can share, give, and take energy equally. We can truly balance each other."

"And if we play our cards right, we could one day become as beautiful and strong as a diamond."

"Exactly."

"You know, pure carbon tends to come together in lattices where four atoms share electrons." I leaned back to see how he'd react.

He half smiled. "Now you're messing up the beautiful metaphor, Sammi."

"I'm just trying to be accurate."

"You're just being the geek that you are."

"You're more of a geek than I am."

"Nope. Not by a long shot."

"Based on what?"

"Based on the fact that I know accuracy is not the objective of a metaphor. Metaphor is the foundation of poetry, a thing that true geeks don't know about. You know, broad strokes with words that paint clear pictures in your mind."

Okay, he's a genius. "That was a pretty good comeback."

"Uh-huh. I know. Besides, we're not common carbon atoms. We're the type of carbon atoms that prefer a binary covalent structure."

"I don't know about those." My wards had completely failed. He was attractive to me in every way.

"That's because you didn't major in chemistry. They're very rare."

"So given the right carbon atoms, the metaphor is perfectly accurate."

"Exactly."

"I have a question."

He laughed. "Okay."

"When was the first time that you felt the currents?" I wanted to kiss him, but I knew how that would end. My pride was still intact, and it helped me resist the urge.

"Just before the first time I kissed you."

"Leaning on your car, looking at the ocean?"

"Yeah. How about you? When did you first feel it?"

"I came to terms with it when we were kissing in your car. I felt it before then, but I'm not sure when it started." In support of my failing pride, I stopped looking at him and nuzzled into his chest.

He asked, "Hmm. When do you feel it?"

"I feel it whenever we're close. It's more intense when we're touching. You?"

"It's pretty much the same."

We bantered on like that until we dosed off.

17

THE BEACH PARTY
SATURDAY, AUGUST 26

HE KISSED me as I opened my eyes, a sweet and present kiss. His eyes were bright and happy. He'd been waiting for me to wake up. Though we were already entwined, he pulled me closer.

"Good morning, beautiful." He rested his forehead against mine.

"Good morning, beautiful. Did you sleep well?"

He stroked my cheek and gave me a quick kiss. "Yeah, like a rock. You?"

"Me too. So what's the plan?"

"That depends. Are you hungry?"

"No."

"In that case, the plan is that I take advantage of you, and then I'll make us breakfast. This time will be slow and easy. It'll involve toes and knees and smalls of backs."

"That sounds like fun."

"Yeah." Other than shifting his hand to my chin, he didn't move. He looked into my eyes.

As I returned his gaze, I felt like all my secrets were at his fingertips. He had to know I loved him. I put my palm on his cheek and slipped my fingers into his curls. He smiled, seemingly enjoying my touch. There was so much kindness and caring in his eyes.

He stayed in that moment for a good while, at least five or ten minutes. He whispered my name and hugged me. He loosened his hug just enough to undress us and crawl over me, so he was spooning me from behind. He parted my legs with one of his and leaned toward his back so I was partially on top of him. He gave me another hug. As he continued to hold me tightly with his lower arm, he bit my shoulder and skimmed the length of my sex lightly with the fingertips of his free hand, back and forth, slowly. I purred with pleasure. When my body matched the rhythm of his hand, he slipped two fingers inside of me. He withdrew them almost immediately and started a gentle circular caress of my clitoris.

An exasperated "ahhh" escaped my lips as a pulse rippled through my body. I basked in his body, his muscularity, his strength. My pelvis flexed, and I moaned as I experienced the first wave of my impending orgasm.

Michael tightened his hug and whispered, "You're a goddess, Sammi." Without modifying his caress of my clitoris, he rocked us forward so he was partially on top of me. Somehow, there was a pillow underneath my torso. He sucked on my earlobe as he slid into me.

My whole body quaked. Having him inside me was intense. It was glorious. I moaned loudly.

He undulated his pelvis twice as fast as his caresses. He moaned too as quakes rippled through his body. Even as the waves of my orgasm came more frequently, he maintained the same even pace.

The waves overtook me. I wanted to scream, but no sound came.

At the perfect time, Michael stopped caressing my clitoris. He maintained the rhythm of his stroke as I went to pieces around him. When he was sure that I was back, mostly, he strengthened his undulations. It felt great. He pulled me back into orgasm with him, and we came forcefully in silence. We lay in silence, entwined for a long time. The aftershocks lingered.

He said, "We should get up."

I responded, "I'm not sure I can see anymore."

"That was amazing. I may not be able to walk." He eased out of me.

I turned over to look at him. His eyes weren't focused. He was in the same state I was in. I kissed him softly on his lips and thought, *I love you, Michael.*

He pulled me close again and said, "Come on. I'll carry you into the shower."

We had a leisurely shower. We smiled in remembrance of what had just happened. The currents between us were palpable.

———

MICHAEL PUT ON A BEAUTIFUL, printed pair of swim trunks and a sleeveless T-shirt with big openings for the arms. I took the opportunity to enjoy the scenery. I really liked the shape of his shoulders and his tattoos. The only thing that brought me a bit of sadness was how underwhelming the swim trunks straight men wear are. He had such a nice ass, and it was totally lost in the shape of his swim trunks.

Once I was done with my ogling, I slipped on what I thought of as my warrior princess bikini outfit. The bikini and its cover-up were sturdy and sexy at the same time. The bottom part of the cover-up was a skort, with sexy splits on the side, so I could tumble and play however I wanted. When I turned around, I saw Michael was doing a little ogling of his own. I did a full turn so he could take in all angles.

"Like I said, you're a goddess." He picked up his phone and shook his head. "Paulo's called me five times in the past forty-five minutes."

I looked at my phone to see if we were running late. It was just after 10 a.m. We had close to an hour before he was due to arrive. "What does he want?"

Michael thumbed through Paulo's texts. "I'm not sure he knows." He took a deep breath. "I'll call him in a minute. Let's go downstairs. Now that I've taken advantage of you, I owe you breakfast."

Michael took out bacon, eggs, and milk to make us pancakes for breakfast. I set the dry goods and vanilla flavor on the counter for him. He set out the fruit and whipping cream. I put a cookie sheet on the stove and turned on the countertop oven to preheat it.

Michael asked, "Why don't you like my swim trunks?"

I ogled him again. "Because they hide the shape of your ass and most of your thighs."

He wrinkled his brow. "So what? You want me to wear spandex?"

This would be fun. I focused in on his crotch. "No. That would be overkill. But from a woman to a man, something less burlap sacklike and more fitted would be appreciated. So you have some idea of what you're signing up for." I looked back into his eyes. "If you know what I mean."

Michael's phone rang again. He squinted at me. "It's Paulo. Again." He answered the phone and put it on speaker. "What's going on, man? You're on speaker." He set the phone down on the kitchen island.

Paulo asked, "Is Sammi there?"

Michael said, "She is."

Paulo said, "Good morning, Sammi. Do you mind if I come over early? I'm riding with Vic, and he wants to go help set things up at the beach." It was clear he was looking forward to this day too.

Michael wrinkled his brow and looked at his phone like it had gone insane.

I made eye contact with Michael for some indication of how to respond.

Michael rolled his eyes and shrugged his shoulders.

I answered, "Sure, Paulo. Come on over."

Paulo responded, "Thank you, Sammi. See you soon."

I responded, "Okay."

Just as I was done putting enough bacon on the cookie sheet for Michael and me, the doorbell rang.

Michael covered his face with his hands and shook his head. He looked at me and said, "Unbelievable. I'll get it." He walked toward the door in the den.

I loved their banter, and I didn't want to miss any of it. I followed him and took a seat on the arm of one of the sofas as he opened the door.

Michael greeted him with, "How long have you been sitting in the driveway?"

Paulo walked right by him and shamelessly checked out my place. "We just got here. We weren't sitting in the driveway."

Vic walked in right after Paulo. To Michael, he said, "Hey, man." He nodded toward Paulo and shook his head, widening his eyes. "He started calling me at 8 a.m."

Michael asked, "Have you met this woman?"

Vic shook his head no and watched Paulo continue to case my place.

Paulo raised his eyebrows and looked at Michael. Then he looked at me and said, "Good morning, Sammi. Sorry for the intrusion."

His formal politeness flipped a switch in my brain, and automatically, I responded, "It's no intrusion. Would you two like to join us for breakfast?"

Paulo responded, "Yes! I'd really like that. I'm hungry. Thank you, Sammi."

Michael gave me a look. I guessed he hadn't intended to let them stay. He walked back into the kitchen with Paulo on his heels.

I motioned for Vic to follow Paulo and walked back over to the counter. I put the whole pack of bacon on the cookie sheet and put it in the countertop oven.

Once Paulo had checked out the kitchen, he looked at me and said, "You have a really nice place, Sammi."

"Thank you, Paulo." I motioned to the kitchen table. "You guys have a seat."

Before I could offer them something to drink, Michael said, "There's stuff to drink in the fridge. The glasses are in there." He pointed to the cabinet. "Help yourselves." He was doubling the pancake ingredients.

I put on some coffee for them and water for myself. Then I set up the griddle that went with my stove so Michael could make all the pancakes at once. I turned on the burners to heat it up.

He was just done mixing. To me, he said, "Thanks," then he looked at Paulo and said, "I thought you guys were in a hurry. How is it that you have time to eat?"

Paulo ignored him. He looked at me. "Do you mind if I choose the setting now?"

I said, "Sure, come on." I walked around the corner to my storage pantry. When I looked back, he wasn't behind me.

Before I could take a step to see what was keeping him, he bounded around the corner. "Sorry."

I motioned to my picnic sets. He chose the one with bright island colors. "Thank you."

I asked, "Is Alex still coming?"

Paulo nodded. "He said he is."

"Good. I wish he and Michael were talking."

"Don't worry. They will. This isn't their first fight."

"They've stopped talking to each other like this before?"

"Yes. Many times."

That made me feel better. "Tell me about one of them."

"Put me on the spot, why don't you? Let me think. Oh, yeah. There was the time that we were all grounded. Alex snuck out to hook up with a girl. He wore Mike's favorite shirt without his permission. It was a nice shirt. Alex messed it all up. Mike was pissed, so he told Mrs. Shelly about Alex's excursion. It took them three weeks and a physical fight to start talking again."

Michael yelled around the corner, "Hurry up. I'm about to scramble the eggs!"

I responded, "On our way!"

Paulo looked around the pantry. "Are those the coolers we're going to use?"

"Yes."

"Okay, you take the picnic basket, and I'll get the coolers."

I complied, and I also grabbed a few thermoses. He made his way back into the kitchen, gracefully carrying two big coolers. The table was set, and Vic was taking the bacon out of the oven when we walked back into the kitchen.

I set the picnic basket and the thermoses down and walked over to Michael. I held each plate as he put eggs on them. When he looked at me, I gave him my *I'm sorry for inviting them to breakfast* face.

He gave me an *I'm not upset at you* smirk.

I bit my bottom lip.

He gave me one of his signature kisses I cherished. It only lasted a few seconds, but I was transported by it. The currents crackled. Then I remembered that Paulo and Vic were in the room with us. Both were standing motionless, staring at us. It seemed they sensed our connection too.

Michael broke their trance. "What?"

Paulo and Vic looked at each other. Paulo whispered something I couldn't hear, and they shared a chuckle.

I took the plate of pancakes over to the kitchen table, mostly to clear my head.

Michael followed with two of the plates with eggs on them. To Vic and Paulo, he said, "Your eggs are on the counter." He sat down and started putting bacon and pancakes on our plates.

I took four mugs out of the cabinet. I left two of them in front of the coffee maker. I poured a cup of coffee for Michael and made some tea for myself. As we walked back over to the table, I followed Michael's lead and directed Paulo and Vic to the coffee cups. Michael had put just the right amount of food on my plate. I reciprocated by putting just the right amount of sugar and milk in his coffee. We exchanged a gaze. Then we dug in.

I only noticed that Vic and Paulo were staring at us again when Michael said, "I thought you two were starving."

Vic asked Paulo, "So who's this woman that made you start calling people at 8 a.m. this morning? What's her name?"

Paulo lit up. "Her name is Djo. She's sweet and smart and oh-so beautiful. She was born in the same village in West Africa as my great-great-great-grandmother."

Vic responded, "So she's your distant cousin."

Paulo was considering Vic's statement. "She's from the same village, not from my family."

Vic said, "Did you check? She could be your cousin, man." The corner of his mouth twitched a little.

Paulo was genuinely concerned. "I don't think she's my cousin."

Both Vic and Michael started chuckling. Michael said, "Don't worry about it, man. Even if she is a distant cousin, it's been so many generations that it doesn't matter. When did you meet her?"

"While you were in New York. We've been out a few times. You guys are going to really like her." Paulo was all misty-eyed. He was really into this woman.

Vic asked, "Have you slept with her?"

Paulo was caught up in his reverie and not really listening. He responded, "Who?"

Vic asked again, "Your cousin. Have you slept with her?"

Paulo narrowed his eyes in frustration. "She's not my cousin."

Michael chimed in, "So you have slept with her?" He and Vic laughed outright.

Paulo stuttered, "No. Yes. No. She's not my cousin."

Michael said, "Okay, man. She's not your cousin." He glanced at Vic and stifled a laugh. "Now that you two are done with breakfast, I think that we need to get the stuff that you came for packed so that you can leave and I can resume the quiet morning with my woman that you so rudely interrupted."

I was the only one who hadn't said a word in the last five minutes and the only one who still had food on my plate. Both the plate of pancakes and the plate of bacon were empty. I wasn't sure how I missed them eating everything. I focused on finishing my meal. Michael got up, walked over to the dishwasher, and put his plate, cutlery, and mug inside. He pointed at it. Vic and Paulo got up and followed his lead.

Michael said, "Hey, Sammi, are these the coolers we should use?" He pointed to the ones Paulo had brought in earlier.

I stuffed the last bite of bacon in my mouth and nodded yes. While they packed the coolers, I pureed the frozen fruit in the blender and put it in the thermoses so that we could have frozen drinks, virgin and otherwise, on the beach. It took us about twenty minutes to get everything packed into the coolers. Paulo insisted on also taking our mat, chairs, and umbrellas with him so he could put them in the perfect place. Then they were off. It wasn't quite 11 a.m.

I wrapped my arms around Michael. "What is it that you wanted to do?"

"I wasn't done basking in the after-currents of making love to you. I wanted to feed you breakfast and cuddle and kiss some more."

I took in a deep breath. It had been a month. We needed to slow down. *I* needed to slow down. I needed to get back on track. But this was his perfect day. I led him over to one of the love seats, pushed him into it, and climbed into his lap. "Cuddling and kissing it is."

He positioned us so we were reclining comfortably. "Tell me something that I don't know about you."

That caught me a little off guard. The reason Greg was angry with me flashed across my mind. I was definitely not ready to tell him about that. "This past month has had its challenges. You know things about me that most of my friends don't. Darkness aside, I really like art."

He gestured around the den. "That, I can tell."

"I wish that I was fluent in Spanish."

He chuckled. "I've noticed."

"I don't know. Ask me something."

Without missing a beat, he asked, "What's your favorite color?"

"Black. You?"

"Green. What's your favorite vegetable?"

"Collards. You?"

He tilted his head to the side. "Collards?"

"Yes. Collard greens with smoked meat. It's a Southern thing. Not a lot of that around here. What's yours?"

"I like kale. What's your favorite city to visit?"

"Barcelona."

"Why?"

"The fact that it's on the ocean and the way that it's grounded in Gaudi's art. What's yours?"

He huffed. "I expected you to say Paris. I really like São Paulo."

"Why?"

"The people. Granted, I always visit Paulo's family, but the people who live there seem so easygoing to me."

"So not Paris for you either?"

"Nope." He slouched underneath me. He leaned back and closed his eyes. Then he skimmed his bottom lip with his teeth and smiled a little. His lips were bow shaped and succulent.

I gave in to my desire to touch my lips to his. The openness of his response pulled me in. We shared a soft, sensual, playful kiss. When it resolved, I rested my forehead against his and let it rock with the sway of my world. I had no idea how to slow things down.

He asked, "How did you become a good lover? Was there someone in particular that showed you the ropes?"

"No. You guys are much easier than we are, and you're much more sensual than you realize. Mostly, I project. I touch you in ways and with the attention that I like to be touched."

A thought flickered behind his eyes. He shook his head and huffed. Then he leaned in for another kiss.

I broke it off. "Uh-uh. Out with it. What were you thinking?"

He whispered, "Nothing," and tried to resume the kiss.

I had a feeling I knew what had crossed his mind, and I wanted to hear him voice it. "You're going to have to tell me what you were thinking to get a kiss."

He looked at me and chuckled. After a deep breath, he said, "I was wondering how many lovers you've had."

I was right. "Less than you have." My tone was slightly sassy—men and their double standards.

He lifted his eyebrows. "Hey, I'd come to that conclusion myself. I didn't ask. I just said I was wondering. You demanded that I tell you what I was thinking." He was right.

"True." I resumed the kiss. When it resolved, I asked, "So how many lovers have you had?"

"That question isn't appropriate for dating. I'll answer it when we decide to be a couple." He kissed my cheek. "We should get out of here before we get carried away."

I grabbed towels and some sunblock, the only things that Paulo and Vic didn't take with them, and we left for the beach.

Quite a few people were there when we arrived. Paulo met us as we got to the edge of the parking lot. "Hey, Sammi. We're set up not far from the sand mats that they've laid out to serve as the dance floor." He pointed in that general direction. To Michael, he said, "Come help me with the coolers. Vic's helping Cam set up."

They walked off to get the coolers, and I followed Paulo's directions to our mats. Paulo had placed our mat right next to his and set up our umbrellas. The rest of their friends hadn't arrived yet. I put the towels and sunblock down and took a moment to look around. It was a wonderful day for the beach. There were a few clouds, just enough to give you respite from the sun now and then. The ocean was its perfect self. There was a nice breeze to take the edge off the heat. I sensed a presence to my right, so I turned to see who it was. It was a person I didn't know.

As we made eye contact, he said, "Hello, my name is Trevor. I have to say, you're looking quite lovely today."

I responded, "Thank you, Trevor."

He asked, "Is this your first Cam party?"

"Yes, it is."

"Well, brace yourself. It's only fire."

"So I've heard. I'm looking forward to it."

He handed me a postcard. "I'm a visual artist. I paint bodies. These are pictures of some of my work. I'm going to set up over there." He pointed to a spot not too far away. "Come by if you're so inclined. I'd really like a chance to paint your body."

The pictures on the postcard were nice. I wondered how well this worked as a pickup angle. "I like your work."

"Maybe I'll see you later then." He reached his hand toward my shoulder.

Before Trevor's hand made contact, Michael put his hand on my shoulder and came to stand next to me with his arm around me. He said, "Trev. Man. How are you doing?"

Trevor took a half step back. "Good. You?"

Michael took the postcard from my hand and gave it back to Trevor. "Never better."

Trevor looked at me and said, "It was nice meeting you. I'll see you around."

He was already walking away when I said, "Same here." I looked at Michael.

He was smirking. "That's how it's done, in case you were wondering." He kissed the side of my mouth and grabbed the cooler by the handle. "Do you have a preference for where this goes?"

I pointed to the left side of the mats. "Here, where it's easy to get to from both mats."

Michael pulled it into place and set it down.

Paulo walked up, tugging the other cooler. He maneuvered it next to the first one.

Paulo said, "Sammi, Djo will be here any minute. Do you think I should place the picnic set?"

I responded, "You can make it easier to get to, but I wouldn't set everything up. Let me help you." That earned me a big smile from Paulo.

Michael looked at him and shook his head slightly. "Vic's struggling with that speaker. I'm gonna go help him finish getting Cam set up."

Paulo and I placed the picnic set, chairs, and towels into a nice arrangement. I showed him the frozen fruit for the drinks. Paulo's phone buzzed just after we'd finished. He smiled in a daze. "She's here. This is perfect, Sammi. Thank you." He gave me a hug. "I'm gonna get her now." He bounded off like a puppy.

I looked over toward Cam's platform. It seemed like they'd finished the setup. I walked over to join them. As I got close, Michael reached for my hand. Cam raised her eyebrows a little in response.

Vic said, "Hey, Sammi." Then he looked down at himself. He was dripping with sweat. "I need a shower. I'm gonna jump in the ocean for a minute to cool off." He walked off.

Michael said, "Cam, Sammi. Sammi, Cam. Cam is Vic's cousin."

I said, "Pleased to meet you. I've heard good things."

She responded, "Likewise." She was wearing this retro one-piece swimsuit with a flame pattern. It was fun and funky and beautiful.

I said, "Your swimsuit's amazing."

She smiled. "Thank you. My sister designed and made it for me. She's studying fashion design. Fire's my motif."

I responded, "So I've heard. Just remember, safety first."

Cam looked at me like I'd missed the point completely. "That depends on how deep you want the cleansing to be."

So that was her goal. "Point taken. If cleansing is the goal, the only place for safety is the wind."

She pointed at me with both hands and said to Michael, "I like her." She looked at her phone. "It's time to get this party started." She gestured toward the dance floor. "Your assistance is requested."

Michael led me to the center of the dance floor. Cam went way back. She started her set with the sirens from the Ohio Players' song "Fire." She looped the intro and mixed in Mavis Staples singing the first line from the song "I'll Take You There." After a minute or so, she added the final layer, an echo of Rock Master Scott saying the refrain from "The Roof Is on Fire." Three minutes in, I knew this was going to be a journey. I looked at Michael with awe.

He responded, "Told you. And she's only getting started."

I caught the next downbeat and looked up at Cam. She was gone, completely lost in the music. Michael followed me in. We'd started a dialogue when it came to dancing together. The sense of newness I felt around him and his friends receded as I gave in to the music. I danced like I was with my crew. At least an hour passed before Cam let us come up for air. The dance floor was packed. I didn't remember all those people coming. We were all drenched, and I was thirsty.

I took Michael's hand. "Let's go for a quick dip and then get something to drink."

He followed me down to the ocean. We swam for a minute and then chilled at the point where the water was shoulder height for him. I put my arms around his neck so that I could relax without going under.

He asked, "So what do you think?"

"Two words come to mind: precise and fire." I looked back at the crowd on the beach. "Thank you for bringing me. I'm having a really good time."

"You're welcome. Me too."

"I have a question. Cam raised her eyebrows when you took my hand. What was that about?"

He smiled slyly. "Hmm. We have a saying. 'Bringing a date to this party is like bringing sand to the beach.'"

"So this party is all about the hook-up."

"It's mostly about the music. If you hook up, you hook up."

"Hmm. So you brought sand?"

"Yes. I really like your sand."

"I really like yours too." I thought, *Maybe I should just relax into this and enjoy it while it lasts.* I gave him another sweet and present kiss. We swayed in the ocean for a while.

As we approached our mat, I saw most of the gang—Jilly, Alicia, and Chris—had arrived. The only people I didn't see were Vic and Alex. Michael and Paulo were the only ones who'd brought dates. We said hello to everyone. I saw Vic as we were sitting down. Somehow, he was napping. So the only person missing was Alex. I pulled two bottles of water out of the cooler and offered one to Michael. They'd already settled into their banter, and Michael fell in without missing a beat.

Paulo tapped my shoulder. "Let me introduce you to Djo."

I responded, "Of course." I touched Michael's arm to get his attention.

Paulo said, "This is Djo. Djo, this is my friend Mike and his woman, Sammi."

I said, "Pleased to meet you."

Djo responded, "Yes, thank you. Same." She was a gorgeous woman. Her features were soft and rounded. Her lips were full, and she had flawless, creamy dark skin.

Alicia shoved Paulo playfully. "Did you bring any mayonnaise?"

Paulo shoved her back. "Did you look for it, or are you just intent on getting on my nerves?"

Djo seemed a little overwhelmed by the interaction.

I said, "They're a close-knit group. It can be a lot to get used to."

She responded, "They're like my brothers." She glanced at Paulo. "Paulo's very kind."

Paulo held up the mayonnaise, and Alicia snatched it from his hand, saying, "Why'd you put it at the bottom?"

Paulo said, "It wasn't at the bottom. You're just too lazy to look for yourself." He looked at Djo and took her hand.

Michael said, "I'm hungry too. It's nice to meet you, Djo. Don't take them seriously. They're just playing." He looked at me. "Sandwich?"

I responded, "I'll make drinks." I poured some soda water over ice and added some of the pureed fruit.

Alicia said, "See, that's what I'm talking about. Hook a sister up."

I complied, and we settled into eating. Jilly decided it was time for Vic to wake up and flicked cold water from the cooler on his face. Vic opened his eyes and, in a fluid motion, grabbed and threw a handful of ice at her. Djo watched with either concern or amusement. I couldn't tell. Alicia had just made me a fresh sparkling water when I noticed Alex standing about fifty yards away.

I took a big gulp and handed what was left to Michael, who was working on his second sandwich. He gave me a quizzical look.

I whispered to him, "Finish that for me. I'm going for a quick dip."

He looked at my plate, noticing there was still food on it. "We just went for a dip, and you're not done eating."

I kissed his cheek and stood up. "It's fine. I'll eat some more later. You have the rest." Before he could respond, I walked off toward the ocean.

I went in for a few minutes and sat at the edge to let the tide wet my feet. I looked back to see Alex had joined the group. It looked like he and Michael were talking. I turned to stare at the ocean and horizon, relaxing.

A male voice said, "Sammi?"

I turned to see that it was Gene, a good friend from graduate school I'd completely lost touch with. "Gene!" I stood up and gave him a bear hug. "It's so good to see you! How are you?"

"Great. How are you?"

"I'm great. Do you live here or are you just visiting?"

He responded, "I live here. Came right after grad school. You?"

"I live here too. I came about three years ago."

He looked at the crowd on the beach. "That looks like quite a party."

"It is. The DJ's amazing. I got overheated and overstimulated. I came down here to gather my thoughts and cool off."

We sat down to catch up a bit. I told him I'd gotten married and it'd failed. So I was getting a divorce and starting over with dating again. He had a long-term boyfriend, Evan, but the jury was out on whether they'd get married. We realized we knew some of the same people. Then we started talking shop. Thirty or forty minutes into our conversation, Gene looked at his watch. He was late. We exchanged numbers, and he ran off.

Alex was still with the crew, so I made my way to the dance floor. Cam was so on. I closed my eyes and let everything but the music melt away. I rode the beat for a good, long while. A tug on my arm broke my trance. It was Paulo. He and Djo were on the dance floor next to me. Paulo was holding my arm and giving the guy behind me a mean look.

The guy hadn't touched me. I could only guess he was doing something lewd. I turned to look at him. When we made eye contact, I hunched my shoulders, questioning why.

He bowed, apologized, and turned to walk away.

True to form, Michael placed himself so he was standing right in front of the guy when he completed his turn. The guy walked right into Michael, and Michael met him with a dead-eyed stare.

He looked back at me and mumbled, "Sorry, man."

I rolled my eyes at Michael and turned toward Paulo and Djo.

Michael slipped an arm around me.

I let a few beats pass, and I turned to face him. "Was that really necessary?"

"Nope. But it was fun."

I put my hands on his shoulders and stood on my toes like I was going to kiss him. He closed his eyes and parted his lips in anticipation. I barely skimmed his lips with mine and inhaled deeply to catch one of his breaths. I trailed my fingers down his arms and took his hands, kissing them, one at a time. I brushed my hands back up his arms, taking care to enjoy every inch of his finely sculpted body: his biceps, his shoulders and collarbones, his pecs, and his six-pack. He bit his lower lip and watched patiently while I did it. I let my hands come to rest in those wonderful furrows just above his hip bones.

Cam started playing salsa. I asked Michael, "Do you salsa?"

He shook his head no.

"Me either." On the next downbeat, I dipped into a salsa-like step. Michael picked it up on the three. We fell into a playful dialogue: leading and following, following and leading. A few songs later, I became aware that people had stopped dancing to watch us. Cam's groove was good, so I didn't care. We exited the floor when the salsa part of the set ended. Someone stopped Michael to talk, and I continued toward our mat. Just as I got there, Alicia stood up and announced she was going to the ladies' room.

I asked her, "Do you mind if I tag along?"

"Of course not." She hooked her arm into mine. "I think you're a good match for Mike. I like the way you two are together."

"Thank you, Alicia. It's really kind of you to say that. I'm sure that it's obvious, but I really like him. He's a good person."

"That he is."

We parted ways to use the bathroom. While we were washing our hands, I asked her, "Would you mind talking to me about Alex a little bit? I'm concerned about him, and talking to Michael doesn't work."

"Sure. What do you want to know?"

"Is he okay? How's he handling things? In general. I'm not asking for any personal details."

We started walking back.

"He's hanging in there. He's doing better than he was at first."

"I really hate that he and Michael are at odds about this."

She shook her head. "They've always been at odds when it comes to Pete. That's not your fault."

"It bothers me that Alex won't hang out with you guys when I'm around. He should've been here with you guys all day today. He should've helped Michael and Paulo get ready."

"That's on him. He's being childish, in my opinion," she replied with a scowl.

"Still, this seems like a time when he really needs you guys and good times."

"It was kind of you to give him space today."

"It looked like he and Michael were talking."

"A bit. They weren't at each other's throats."

We got back to our mats. "Thanks, Alicia."

"Anytime."

I made another soda water and fruit drink. Michael was still not back. I looked around. Two women were chatting him up. He looked like he wanted to walk away, but he was trying to be patient.

With my drink in hand, I walked over to where they were standing. I touched Michael's back so he knew it was me. I put my arm around his waist and snuck under his arm. I took a sip of my drink, then offered it to him. He smiled at me as he took it. He drank all of it down without stopping and kissed my forehead. Together, we looked back at the women.

He took advantage of the fact that they'd stopped talking long enough for him to speak. "If you'll excuse me, my date has been waiting for me to come grab a bite to eat." Before they could say anything, he led me away. "Did you just block?"

"I did."

"Thank you." He paused. "Took you long enough."

"Nature called." I looked around. "Did Alex leave?"

"He left while you were dancing by yourself. Don't take it on, Sammi. It's on him."

"Yeah, but I don't like it."

"You didn't finish eating earlier. You should be hungry."

He was right. I was hungry. I made another sandwich and watched them as I ate it. Chris was deep in conversation with a woman a few mats away. Vic was working it out on the dance floor. He was partnered with two women. Jilly was passionately kissing a guy. Alicia was still playing the field, talking to two guys. She hadn't made her choice yet. Djo and Paulo were cuddling. I liked these people. I looked at Michael. There was no logical reason for me not to let our relationship run its course. When I finished eating, I crawled into his arms and relaxed, playing with his hand while I took it all in.

At some point, I realized some people were looking at me, and there was a familiar hush in the crowd. I followed their gazes. No more than thirty yards away, Greg stood motionless, staring at me. He was standing just beyond the crowd on the boardwalk. I closed my eyes and shook my head to make sure I wasn't seeing things. Yep, he was definitely there. He looked okay. I could tell he wasn't doing his physical therapy, though, by the way he was holding his left shoulder. That shoulder had been crushed in the accident, and he'd almost lost use of his arm. It required constant, careful attention not to ache. He was never going to be whole again. My whole body tensed in anticipation of what he was going to do next.

Michael shifted behind me. "What's up?"

"Greg's here. Try not to respond. With Greg, the less you react, the better."

I could feel him tense, but otherwise, he stayed still.

When Greg was sure he had my attention, he lifted his left hand and pointed to his wedding ring with his right hand.

My temper flashed. He couldn't be serious. With all his whoring, he actually had the audacity to point at his wedding ring as if it meant something to him. My first instinct was to flip him off, but that would've only given him something to react to. So I just glared at him. Eventually, he pointed to his watch and walked away. When I was sure he was gone, I closed my eyes to let my temper settle. I leaned into Michael for comfort.

Michael asked, "Are you okay?"

"I'm fine. I'm just pissed."

"Do you want to leave?"

"No, I'm where I want to be." I tried to relax again. It didn't work. I stood up and reached out my hand. "I need to dance."

He took my hand and followed me to the dance floor. Cam was slowing things down. We swayed together. I enjoyed watching Vic break it down. I said, "Vic's a good dancer."

"Yeah. He can move. If you need to work anything out, now's the time. This is the endgame. Cam's gonna shut it down in ten or fifteen minutes."

"Okay." I liked the step that Vic was doing, so I followed him in.

Vic responded by bringing his partner closer to Michael and me so we could all dance together.

After about five or six song changes, Cam started looping in the Staples Singer's "I'll Take You There" again. People started two-stepping with a slow clap. Cam responded by scratching to the cadence. Then she started looping in the Ohio Players' sirens again. The crowd responded by chanting, "It's only fire. It's only fire. It's only fire." Cam signaled the end of the chant by slowing the sirens until they stopped. As it ended, everybody screamed.

I hugged Michael. "That was amazing."

He smiled broadly and gave me one of his wonderful kisses.

The boys helped Cam break down and pack her gear. Alicia and I divvied up what was left of the food and rinsed out the coolers. We left the beach and went to their favorite pub. It was close to midnight by the time we left for my place.

<hr>

WE PLACED the coolers so they'd dry. I also washed the thermoses and left them to dry in the sink.

I slipped my arms around Michael and rested my head on his chest. "I'm so glad that we came back from New York."

"I agree. Are you okay with Greg appearing like that?"

I chuckled. "You mean my husband." I shook my head. "At this point, I can't believe I'm married to him. Yeah, I'm okay. Greg was just doing what Greg does: showing up, making demands, and disappearing again. Are you okay with it? That was an awkward moment."

He lifted my chin so we were looking at each other. "It was fine. I knew what was going on, and you made it perfectly clear where you stood."

"Still, I'm sorry that he showed up like that, today of all days."

"And I'm sorry that my brother's choosing to act like a twelve-year-old. There's nothing we can do about either one of them. It was nice of you to give Alex space."

"Of course. I was basking in his support system. It was the least I could do."

He responded by showering my face with kisses.

I had to push him away to speak. "So what comes next?"

"First, we need to take a shower, and then you can take advantage of me. We'll make a production of it."

"Okay." I took his hand and led him to my bathroom. I turned on the shower. "What next?"

"Let me help you out of this swimsuit." He took his time and peeled it off my body. He rubbed his nose against mine when he finished.

"My turn." I took his shirt and swim trunks off.

He led me into the shower. "Let me bathe you."

"Let's bathe each other."

I put shower gel in both our hands. I puckered my lips, so he leaned down to kiss me. Without breaking the kiss, we started from the top and worked our way down. We gave a little extra attention to the sweet spots. It worked well until we got to our thighs. We bumped heads as we were trying to reach lower. We ended up giggling and cuddling. We washed our own feet and dried each other off when we got out.

I led him to my bed. I pulled back the covers and crawled in. When we were both comfortable, I asked, "How would you like me to take advantage of you?"

"I want you to go down on me, Sammi."

"Okay." I trailed the tip of my finger down his chest and around his nipples. I took a moment to roll both of his nipples between my index finger and thumb before continuing to trail my finger to his abdomen. I softly traced the furrows of his six-pack and the outline of his navel, then started making little circles in his goody trail. I was careful not to touch his growing erection as I traced its outline. I slipped my hand to his inner thigh and pulled it open. I continued my gentle circling up the center of his testicles and penis. When I reached the tip, I gently caressed it with little circles. He squirmed in pleasure. I kissed his shoulder and watched him enjoy my touch for a minute.

I repositioned myself so I was on my hands and knees above him, with my knees between his legs. I kissed his forehead, nose, lips, chin, and the space between his collarbones. Then I retraced the trail I'd made with my fingertip with my tongue. I took care to nip and caress both of his nipples. He purred in response. I continued the trail through the furrows of his six-pack. When I got to his goody trail, I tugged it gently with my teeth. He sighed and arched his back in response. I outlined his erection. I kissed both of his inner thighs. Then I retraced the circling path over his testicles and up his penis. I wrapped my hand around him and stroked him. I also kissed the top of his penis, watching him respond. I circled him with my tongue. He opened his mouth and panted. I took him to my mouth and went down on him again. He matched my rhythm with his pelvis and dropped his head back. He growled and came hard. It was sooner than I expected, so I had to struggle to swallow. When his orgasm ebbed, I crawled up to lie next to him. I wanted to ask him if he liked it, but his eyes were unfocused. He was still coming. I held him while the aftershocks rippled through his body.

He kissed me passionately when he landed. "I want to taste you, Sammi." He repositioned himself so he was propped up on one elbow between my legs. He used his free hand to open and caress me.

"Do you inspect everyone you date like this?"

He looked at me and chuckled. "You don't like it."

"It makes me feel so … exposed, vulnerable."

"Yeah. It's very intimate. No, I don't take the time to *inspect* everyone I date." He chuckled again and kept my gaze as he leaned in to kiss my clitoris.

I moaned loudly, and my whole body quaked.

After I settled into the rhythm of his kiss, he crawled up so he was positioned to come inside. He touched his nose to mine. "We've never really fucked each other, Sammi."

"Sounds like fucking means something very specific to you."

"It does. It's like scratching an itch. It's focused on having an orgasm. It lacks the exploration and a certain type of connection, intimacy that happens when you make love to someone."

"I see."

"We've always erred on the side of making love."

He was right. I lifted my head, buried my fingers in his curls, and kissed him with all my might.

He responded in kind. All at once, he pushed himself inside me.

I cried out. I was somewhat used to his size. It was how attracted to and turned on by him that I found overwhelming.

"Are you okay? Did I hurt you?"

"No. It's just … well … since this morning, everything feels so much more intense. It's like our connection amped up."

He restarted our kiss. Then he started his swivel.

I moaned and purred and gave in to the pleasure of it completely.

He said, "I want you to be on top."

He rolled over so I was straddling him. I leaned back and pulled him so he was sitting up. Then I started my own swivel. He matched my movement. He was watching my every response. He blew me a kiss. I dropped my head back, and my orgasm overtook me. I slowed down as I landed.

He kissed my collarbone. "Relax, I'm gonna come now." He leaned back until his back was on the bed. He took control of the movement of my pelvis with his hands.

I followed his instructions and gave in completely. He set an urgent, intense tempo. He was swiveling as he rocked me back and forth. His release was gentle compared to the one I'd just had.

I collapsed on top of him. I was spent.

He whispered, "Perfect."

"Yes." I couldn't move. I passed out.

I WOKE up to Michael's heartbeat. He was lying on his back, and I had wrapped myself around him with my head on his chest. He was breathing deeply, still fast asleep. I wasn't ready to get up either. It'd been a busy week, with lots of running around. I started drifting off to sleep. *His heartbeat became one of Cam's driving beats. I was on the dance floor …*

18

BREAK

SUNDAY, AUGUST 27

I woke back up when Michael reached to turn off his alarm. He sat up. I propped my head up and squinted to see him.

Michael kissed my forehead. "Don't wake up. I'm going to my mom's to hang out with her and Alex for a little while."

I grabbed his pillow and drifted off.

It was almost 11 a.m. when I woke up again. I'd slept well. I crawled out of bed and slipped on a pair of shorts. I reached for one of my T-shirts, then decided to put on one of Michael's instead.

Once I was in the kitchen, I made some tea and a bagel. I let my mind wander while I ate. It'd been a good week, and I was relaxed and calm. Though there was the divorce and the situation with Alex, I felt peaceful, hopeful.

I put the thermoses and coolers away. Paulo still had the picnic set, so I'd get it from him later. My spirits were high. It was a good time to call my mom.

She picked up on the third ring. "Hello."

"Hi, Mom. How's it going?"

"Good. I just got back from having lunch with my girls. What are you up to?"

"Not much. I slept late. I went to an amazing beach party yesterday and had a really good time."

"That's good to hear, Sammi. You're finally meeting people and having fun again."

"Yeah, I am."

"You actually sound happy."

She was right! "Yes, Mom, I am happy."

"That warms my heart, sweetheart. It's been too long. You dumped that Greg, and everything is coming up roses. He was just trouble."

"Let's stay with happy, Mom. Greg's history. There's no reason to think about him."

"You're right. Do you have plans for the rest of your day?"

"When I get done talking to you, I'm going to go through emails and start prepping for my next project in a little bit. Other than that, I don't have a plan. I had a busy week, so some chill time is good. What about you? Do you have plans?"

"Yes, I have an appointment with my recliner that'll last a few hours. I might do a load of laundry. I have to go into court tomorrow, so I'm not doing much."

"Sounds good. I'll check in with you over in the week. Love you, Mom."

"Love you too, sweetheart."

That worked out well. Maybe letting things flow with Michael was the best path forward, after all.

I went into my office and turned on my computer. There was work to be done. First, I had to get organized. I started with emails. This was going to be a fun and challenging project. I wondered if Gene had availability and if I could add him to the team.

IT WAS ALMOST 1 p.m. when I looked up. I'd made some good progress. I decided to break for tea. As I was walking to the kitchen, I glimpsed Michael's BMW pulling into my driveway. I unlocked the den door and left it open slightly for him, then continued to the kitchen. Just as I was done filling the teapot, I heard a big crash in the den. I thought, *What the hell? Did Michael trip over something?*

When I rounded the corner, I realized it wasn't Michael. It was Greg. He was intoxicated and in mid-tantrum. His shoulder was tighter than it'd been the day before. If he hadn't been high, he would've been in a lot of pain. He'd turned over the table by the door.

Greg had started having these tantrums after I'd told him I'd caused the accident in which he'd almost died. I became the focus of his anger, all of it. I felt I deserved it. At first, I tried to take it. I thought of it as my penance. When I realized he'd started cheating on me before I told him the truth, I chose to accept his cheating as penance too. Greg's abuse didn't come in the form of hitting. Mostly, he broke shit and screamed. Sometimes, he'd restrain me so he could scream in my face or express his anger by being too rough with me when he touched me and when we had sex, especially if he was high. After a few weeks of trying to hang in there to preserve our marriage, I'd realized I couldn't withstand it. I wouldn't survive. He had too much anger, and most of it had nothing to do with me. So I'd left. I really thought this shit was behind me. It was time to play "dodge Greg." Again.

He came straight for me, knocking over everything he could reach on his way. "Have you lost your fucking mind, Sammi?" He wanted to scream in my face.

I thought, *No, but, obviously, you have.* Silence worked best with Greg. I stayed quiet and focused on staying on the opposite side of the room from him.

"You do realize that we're not divorced. We're still married. You are still *my* wife." He pushed one of the love seats toward me to try and corner me.

I climbed over it and kept moving.

"I heard that you've been gallivanting around town with some guy. I didn't believe it until I saw it with my own eyes. Do you know how that makes me feel?"

I leered at him. It took all my willpower to hold my tongue.

"It's fucked up, Sammi." He threw one of my lamps. "It's really fucked up."

I wondered how high he was. I hoped he'd wear himself out soon. I tried to keep him in the den so he didn't wreck the rest of my house.

"You embarrassed me, Sammi!" He turned over another table. "Do you understand how fucked up it is for you to cheat on me, Sammi? Do you?"

He was in a full-on rage. He honestly had no sense that his sleeping around while we were together was fucked up in the least.

"You hear me talking to you! Answer me, Sammi! Answer me! Is he the reason you want a divorce? Is he?" He was screaming at the top of his lungs. He pushed the coffee table into my path.

I stopped so it didn't hit me and jumped over it. He caught up to me and pinned me against the wall. He twisted my left wrist at an uncomfortable angle. I bit my lip when he grabbed my face to force me to look at him.

"You have no reason to cheat on me. I gave you everything. All of my stuff. I take good care of you."

I tried to move, but he had me pinned well.

"Have you fucked him?" He was screaming right in my face.

I closed my eyes and tried to free my wrist. It turned the wrong way. I felt a sharp pain.

"Have you fucked him?" He slammed me against the wall.

I tried to turn my face but couldn't.

"Answer me, Sammi. You're still my wife." He leaned down to kiss me.

I bared my teeth.

He went for my neck instead and started giving me a love bite.

My avoidance strategy was clearly not working. I had to fight back. I was too pinned to move much, but my legs were free. So I kneed him. It landed on his thigh. When he reacted, I headbutted his chin and pushed him hard with my good hand. That got him off me. I grabbed an iron candleholder with my good hand and swung it at him.

He retreated and kept his distance. He understood he'd crossed the line when I'd started to fight back. He stumbled on one of the things he'd strewn across the floor.

"I'm not cheating on you, Greg. We're legally separated. We're in the process of getting a divorce. Apparently, you missed it, but *our* relationship is over. I married *you*, Greg. Not your stuff. *You*. And *you* cheated on me. *You* destroyed our bond as a couple. That's why I'm divorcing you. Do you have any idea how I felt? How embarrassed I was? *That* was fucked up. Do you hear me?" My anger was flowing freely.

Greg didn't face his abuse until I pulled back from him. He'd been so blinded by his anger he hadn't noticed the effect it was having on me. When he opened his eyes, he was genuinely hurt when he saw what he'd done to me. I used that to disarm him. "What are you doing, Greg? You promised that you'd never hurt me again! Did you mean it, or was that just more of your bullshit?"

He still had his conscience. It phased him. He held his head in his hands and looked a little confused. His rage was wearing off. I had to make him leave.

I yelled, "Get the fuck out of my house, Greg! Get the fuck out! *Now*! And sign the damned divorce papers." I raised the candle-holder so it was out his of reach, but I could get a good swing in if I needed to.

"I don't want a divorce, Sammi. We're good partners." He had really lost his mind.

"Partners? We're not a couple. We haven't been a couple since you started cheating, Greg. What the *hell* are you talking about?"

"Everything became more stable when you came into my life. We can work it out. We can get back to the place we were at before that big argument."

"It's over, Greg. It's been over. It was over before we had that argument. You didn't bother to notice. There's nothing to work out. *Sign* the *fucking* papers!"

He looked at me like what I had said made no sense.

"Leave, Greg. Just leave."

Thankfully, he got up and walked out. I quickly locked the door behind him. My den was trashed. I made my way into the kitchen to get some ice for my wrist. I put some ice on my lip too. I sat down at the kitchen island to let the adrenaline rush pass. I screamed, "Fuck!" to get it all out of my system.

I went back into my den to assess the damage. A few minutes later, I heard a knock at the door. This time, I looked carefully. It was Michael. I knew he was going to freak. After taking a deep breath, I opened the door and gave him a moment to take it in.

He was shocked. "What the …?"

"Greg came by."

He focused on me. He was pissed. "Did he hit you?"

"He pinned me. I'm okay. I fought him off."

He zeroed in on all my injuries at once.

"I bit my lip when he pinned me. I twisted my wrist, trying to get free of him. I'm pretty sure it's just sprained."

He looked at my hand and my lip and brushed my forehead with a questioning look in his eyes.

"I headbutted him to get him off me."

He accepted that explanation. Then he saw the love bite.

"He was trying to make the point that I'm still married to him."

He didn't say anything. He ran his thumb over it, seething.

"I'm okay, Michael."

He pulled me into his arms and held me, still not speaking.

I stayed still and gave him space to process.

We were standing in silence when Kenny, Greg's older brother, came through the door.

He yelled, "Sammi!"

Before I could answer Kenny, Michael was on him. They exchanged a few blows before Michael got the upper hand. It all happened lightning fast.

I screamed, "Stop! Please, stop!" I put my good arm around Michael's waist. Reluctantly, he let me pull him off Kenny. I said, "He's looking out for me, Michael."

Kenny righted himself and said, "I guess you're the one who Greg's pissed off about."

I said, "Kenny, this is Michael, Ari's twin brother. Michael, this is Kenny, Greg's brother."

Kenny looked at me. "Did you get my text? I tried to warn you that he was on his way. I knew I couldn't get here in time to head him off."

Kenny and Michael were still eyeing each other warily.

"No. I was in the kitchen. I left my phone in my office."

Kenny looked around the den. "Well, he's made another mess." He looked back at me. "Are you okay? I'm sorry that I couldn't get here sooner."

Michael was relaxing. He realized that Kenny was trying to take care of me too. He sat on the back of one of the displaced sofas.

"He sprained my wrist, but I'm fine."

Kenny looked at Michael. "I guess I should get going. Looks like my friend here has your back."

Michael stood up and extended his hand. "I apologize for

attacking you when you walked in. It's just, I walked in to this." He motioned around the den.

Kenny took his hand. "Oh, I get it. No worries, man."

Michael said, "Thanks for looking out."

Kenny started toward the door, then he turned around. "Sammi's a sister to me. Understand, I won't tolerate anyone mistreating her."

Michael took my wrist in his hand. "Does that include your brother?" His eyes were cold.

Kenny looked at my wrist. "Yes, it does. I'll be dealing with Greg later."

Michael said, "I see. I tell you what, if I mistreat her, I'll gladly let you kick my ass."

Kenny asked me, "Do you need help cleaning this up?"

I answered, "No. I'm not lifting a finger. Greg's paying for cleanup, repairs, and replacements. He'll spare no expense."

Kenny looked pensive and sad. "I don't blame you. I'm sorry about his behavior, Sammi." He turned and walked out of the door.

I looked at Michael. He was furious. His cheek was a little red, and he was working his hand like it was bothering him in the wake of his tussle with Kenny. At that moment, things became crystal clear. Michael and Greg were on a collision course to fight with each other. Greg was totally obsessed with Michael's presence in my life, which meant he'd drag his feet with the divorce. I'd broken my promise to myself about "me time." Finally, there was the mess with Alex. I needed to course correct immediately.

I took his hand and led him into the kitchen. We sat at the kitchen island, and I looked at his slightly bruised cheek. I took the hand that was bothering him.

He asked, "What's wrong, Sammi?"

I took a deep breath. I wanted him to know exactly how I felt. "I need you to know that I love you, Michael. I'm in love with you. Though I've only known you for a month, I feel deeply connected to you."

He touched my cheek with his other hand. "I'm in love with you too, Sammi. I feel the same way."

Those words touched my core. I avoided his eyes. I didn't think I could withstand them. "It's because I love you that I have to break this off. We keep ending up in situations where you feel you need to fight for me. I can't participate in destroying your peace of mind like this. If you got hurt and it affected your dance career, I couldn't take that."

I'd caught him off guard. "What?"

"You've known me for a month, and you've been in two fights because of my presence in your life. I can think of at least three times that you were so consumed with rage that you could barely contain yourself. I bet, before that, the last time you fought with someone was in high school."

"College."

"Exactly. I've added a level of chaos and anger to your life that you don't deserve. I love you. I can't let it continue." I looked at his hand. "Your body is your life, Michael. You love being a dancer. I can't risk it."

"What are you saying, Sammi?"

"I'm saying that I think that we should be just friends. Listen. I feel like you and Greg are on a collision course right now. If we continue dating, it's only a matter of time before you two end up fighting—"

He interrupted me. "Let me get this straight. So dude came into *your* house and roughed you up, and now you're breaking up with *me* so that I don't kick his ass. You know that's weird, right?"

I thought about Greg's shoulder. "His body can't withstand a beating from you, Michael. I have to try to prevent that from happening." I couldn't withstand the guilt if Greg lost use of his arm and couldn't play music or had some other complication because Michael had whipped his ass in my defense.

"Are you sure you aren't still in love with him?"

I looked him in his eyes. "I was never in love with him. I told you that. My relationship with Greg ended a while ago."

He looked at me for a minute. I had the feeling he was mistaking my guilt for love. "You're sure?"

"Absolutely."

He accepted my answer. "I don't want to be just your friend, Sammi. Two fights are not grounds to end this. Our connection is real. It's deep."

"Suppose you had broken your hand today. Then what?"

"I'd go through rehab like my boss, who broke his foot. I'd deal with it like any other injury, Sammi." He huffed. "You're right. The next time I see Greg, it's very likely that I'll kick his ass." He pecked my lips. "The next time I see Pete, I'm definitely going to kick his ass." He pecked my lips again. "I'll kick the ass of anyone who steps to you inappropriately." He pecked my lips again. "It doesn't matter whether we're dating or not. There's nothing you can do about that reality."

"You're right. I can't stop you from fighting, but I can make it much less likely."

He responded with a challenge. "Maybe."

"The fight between you and Kenny wouldn't have happened. I unlocked the door because I thought I saw you in the driveway. I didn't look carefully. I wouldn't have let Greg in."

"Maybe." He was just as stubborn as I was.

"The fact that we are dating has Greg triggered. He's raging about it. I think that seeing me in your arms was the first time that he even considered that I'm serious about divorcing him."

"That's a good thing, right?"

"Yeah, it's good that he knows that I'm serious. We still have to negotiate the divorce settlement. I want him focused on the negotiations, not me and you, so that I can get through it as quickly as possible. Right now, he's focused on you. He's decided that you're the reason that I'm leaving him."

"Seriously?"

"In his opinion, I'm cheating on him. And he can't understand why. And then there's Alex. It really bothers me when I know Alex isn't with you and your friends because I'm there. I just met you guys. He's spent years cultivating his connection with you all. I think he needs you now. He should've been at that party all day yesterday, not me. I understand that whatever's going on with Alex is not my fault, but I want to do what I can to make the situation better. You don't deserve all of this extra drama in your life, Michael. You just don't."

He responded, "I've said it before. Whether or not I want to deal with your demons is my choice. I have my own demons. Even if we were just friends, Alex and I'd still be at odds right now."

"But he'd be with you guys when you're partying, not me."

He hunched his shoulders. "Maybe." He crinkled his brow. "None of what you've mentioned has anything to do with us, Sammi—how we relate to each other. What about that? What about our connection? Doesn't that deserve consideration too?"

"You're right. Nothing that I've mentioned has anything to do with us, our connection. I've never experienced anything like it." A few tears escaped my eyes as I spoke. I took a deep breath to clear my thoughts. "It's precious to me. That's why I'm suggesting that we stop dating. I love you, Michael. I don't know what else to do. I have to try and look out for you. I need to focus on getting my divorce from Greg. I want Alex to have his support system."

"We love each other, Sammi. That matters too."

"It does. If the situation were reversed and I was getting into senseless fights because of you, tell me you wouldn't do the same thing to keep me out of harm's way. Tell me that if you saw me getting blinded with anger from situations that you could prevent me from being in, you wouldn't do what you could to stop it. You would do it because you love me." It was much too much. I kissed him tenderly.

He opened his mouth to counter. A thought flitted across his face. He couldn't say he'd respond differently.

I leaned my forehead against his. "I'm realizing that I need a little more time to figure out who I am outside of a relationship. Though I don't feel like I've been in a relationship with Greg for a long time, I don't feel like I've been out of it either. I pretty much went straight from the situation with Pete into helping Greg. I focused on him completely. Now, before I'm out of the situation with Greg, I've started dating you. I need to take a breath and build out the rest of my life out here a bit before settling into something new."

He gave me a bittersweet smile. "That makes sense to me." He ran his thumb across my cheek. "I'm willing to back off and just be your friend for a while to let you get your bearings." He kissed me on the nose. "And there's another reason that you're doing this. I'll let you tell me when you're ready." He looked at me like he was reading my deepest thoughts.

It seemed like Michael could see through all my facades. I could tell he knew the way I felt about him scared me. I could see it in his eyes. The last time I could remember loving a man so openly was when I loved my father, before he betrayed me. "I'm not asking you to wait for me, okay? I have no idea how long it's going to take for me to get a divorce from Greg. I want you to date other people and live your life."

He shook his head and closed his eyes. Then he kissed me, parting my lips gently and pouring all his feelings into the dance of our tongues. I returned the emotion, and he milked the passion I gave him.

As the kiss resolved, he hugged me tightly. "So what now? Am I supposed to just get up and walk out?"

"I don't know. I've never broken up with someone because I loved them before." I stroked his cheek. "I do love you. You feel that, right?" My tears flowed.

He kissed my forehead. "Yeah, I feel it. I love you too, Sammi."

We held on to each other in silence.

He said, "We're not ending our friendship, right? We're just agreeing not to be lovers for a while."

"Indefinitely. Yes."

"So let's ease into it. Give me today. Let me be your lover for the rest of today. Tonight, I'll go home. Tomorrow, we'll start figuring out how to be friends."

"Okay."

"Good. I don't know how I could just walk out of here right now. Can you feel my love for you?"

I dared to plunge into the depths of his eyes. "Yes, I can."

"So friends, huh? I should probably collect my things from your bedroom. I won't be going in there for a little while."

"I guess not. I'll meet you there. There are a few of your things in the dryer."

When I got to my bedroom, he'd already packed his knapsack. I handed him the clothes that were in the dryer. He put those in there too.

Mostly to choke back my tears, I said, "Well."

He responded, "Well."

We stood there, looking at each other with the currents of our connection washing over us. I reached out to touch him. He pulled me into his arms. We held each other and rocked slowly from side to side. I leaned back and looked up at him so I could see his eyes. He brushed my lips with his thumb. I kissed the corner of his mouth. With our eyes locked, we kissed each other. Each kiss grew in depth and duration. Our connection ignited, and we moved together.

I said, "Michael …" I was more open to him since we'd declared ourselves, but because we were separating, having sex felt like a step in the wrong direction.

He responded, "Today, we're still lovers." He put his forehead on mine and rubbed my nose with his. There was a tenderness in his eyes he hadn't let me see before.

The currents between us crackled, and I gave in. I pulled his T-shirt off and kissed his breastbone softly, slowly, presently. Breathing in his scent, I tried to commit it to memory. I ran my hands over his shoulders, down across his back, and around to his abdomen, noticing details about his contours, places of firmness, smoothness, softness that I hadn't before. I traced his six-pack and let my hands come to rest in those glorious furrows above his hip bones for a moment. Hugging him, I felt us softly melt into each other.

He said, "I want to see your body."

I understood then this was about truly owning our feelings. I no longer had the urge to hide from his gaze. I was ready to let him see me. As I pulled his T-shirt over my head, he unsnapped my bra. I let them fall to the floor. He unzipped my shorts. He hooked his thumbs into my undies and pulled them and the shorts down over my hips together. I wiggled to let them fall the rest of the way off.

He lifted my good hand above my head to guide me in a turn. He took me in as I revolved in front of him. He whispered, "You're beautiful, Sammi."

"My turn." I unzipped his jeans and freed him from his boxer briefs. They joined the rest of our clothes on the floor. I walked around him, admiring his glorious physique, basking in his strength and presence. I took my time and really looked at him. "So are you, Michael." I pointed to the bed. "Lie down."

He complied.

I kneeled between his legs, then positioned myself over him, being careful not to put any weight on my twisted wrist. I stared into his eyes for a few minutes. I kissed him softly as an expression of my love. I kissed his forehead and eyes and nose and cheeks and chin. The kisses were warm and slow and chaste. I brushed his lips with mine. I parted his lips with my tongue. I kissed him deeply, passionately. When it resolved, I nibbled his earlobe, then continued my trail of soft kisses down his neck and over his breastbone and abdomen.

His breathing was deep and fiery as he purred with the spark of each contact.

I kissed his jewel and his inner thighs. He moaned when I took him into my mouth. He arched his spine as I went down on him with the same tender presence of my kisses.

Just as he started to mount, he said, "Okay, stop. I'm not ready to come." He pulled me into an embrace and rolled me onto my back. "My turn." He looked into my eyes for a moment.

I opened to be seen. With my gaze locked, he kissed my lips with his, softly, chastely, rhythmically. Each kiss sent a pulse through my body. He kissed me over and over again. Our bodies were starting to move together. I moaned to release some of the energy. He kissed me passionately, tenderly, mercilessly. We were out of breath when it ended.

He whispered, "I love you, Sammi."

I whispered, "I love you too, Michael."

He skimmed my face with the back of his finger and kissed my jaw. Then he skimmed my breasts. He French-kissed each of my nipples, then pecked my breastbone and trailed kisses down toward my belly button. He looked into my eyes.

In anticipation of what he was going to say, I met his gaze and opened my legs. Letting him look at me no longer felt overwhelming. I wanted to be seen by him. I was finally ready for that intimacy.

He smiled outright, and may have even blushed a little in response to the shift in my reaction, and kissed the side of my mouth. He positioned himself so he had a good view. He caressed the length of my sex. He smiled as my body arched in response. He slipped two fingers inside and caressed my clitoris with the same motion.

I let my body respond as it would.

"You're so sensual." He repositioned himself so that his sex was touching mine. He looked into my eyes as he disappeared inside of me slowly. When we were fully connected, he kissed me passionately. He said, "I want to take this slowly so that I can enjoy every second."

"Me too."

We kept the movements much the same, him with his glorious swivel, and me letting my body move with him in that metered way I'd established. Our declaration of love expanded our ability to see and be seen. It made every interaction more present and rawer.

We made love for hours. Our releases were gentle. We kept our sacred connection and held each other for a while.

As he was drifting off to sleep, he said, "I really like to watch you come."

He was out before I could respond. I got up and took a quick shower. I knew I had to get out of my bedroom before he woke up, or there was a possibility that we'd never leave.

I WAS SITTING in the kitchen, icing my hand, when he came downstairs. He was holding his knapsack.

I said, "Did you get your T-shirt that I was wearing earlier? I can wash it first."

"Keep it." He was rubbing his hand.

"Thank you. Is your hand hurting?"

"No. It's just jammed. One of the company trainers will take care of it tomorrow. How's your wrist?"

"It hurts. Let me take you somewhere to have your hand looked at now."

"It'll be fine until tomorrow. I'm okay, Sammi." He looked at me with a half smile.

I called Dr. Maggie Lee, the healer who helped put Greg back together. I told her what had happened. She already knew some of it because Kenny had been there earlier. She told me to come to her house immediately. I was grateful for the direction. It would be wise to vacate my house.

I kissed his hand. "Come on. We're going to see Dr. Maggie. She's amazing. I've learned so much from her. She's going to take care of your hand."

"She needs to take care of you too."

"Oh, she will." I hadn't called her in a while. I was sure I'd get an earful.

He led me to his car. Other than me navigating, we rode in silence, holding hands.

When we got there, I led him to the door to her workroom, which was at the back of the house. The chimes sounded as I opened the door. I took a deep breath. Dr. Maggie's space was tranquil. It was bright and open, and there were plants in every corner. She was a healer and a martial artist from China. The scents of the herbs and oils were calming.

Michael was looking around with curiosity, and he was more at ease too.

Dr. Maggie yelled from around the corner, "Come to the kitchen, Sammi! We talk."

Michael followed me down the hall into the kitchen. She was sitting at the table in the middle of the room, sipping a cup of tea.

She motioned to the teapot and the teacups that were on the table. "Sit down and have a cup of tea."

We sat. I pulled the teacups toward us. Michael poured the tea. Dr. Maggie observed.

I introduced them. "Michael, this is Dr. Maggie. Dr. Maggie, this is Michael Shelly, Ari's brother."

I took a sip of tea. It was delicious green tea with roasted rice flavors.

Once Michael had taken a sip as well, Dr. Maggie said, "It's good that you're divorcing Greg. He's been angry for a long time, long before he met you, and his heart is closed. Let me see your wrist."

I gave her my hand.

As she was examining it, she said, "I don't understand why you let him grab you, Sammi. You stop him one time, he'll never try again."

I looked at her. Though we'd never talked about it, I believed she knew exactly why I didn't fight Greg back. I looked at Michael. His face was full of questions.

I had to put this to rest. "I'm not as skilled as you think I am, Dr. Maggie. And today, I slipped."

She glanced up at me. "Uh-huh." Then focusing back on my

wrist, she did a quick motion, and the bones of my wrist and lower arm popped loudly. All the tension that'd been building since it got torqued released. "It's fine. One of the bones slipped out of place." She pointed to one of the bags of herbs she had sitting on the table. "Use this to get rid of the swelling and bruising."

She turned to Michael and opened her hand on the table.

He gave her his hand.

For a moment, she just looked at it. Front and back. Then she started to examine his wrist. She looked up at him. "You didn't do this today."

He responded, "No. It's really weak. I need to strengthen it."

She got up to walk around the table to stand behind Michael. She supported the base of Michael's skull with one hand and traced his spine with the other. She stopped just below where his neck and shoulders met. "Your wrist isn't weak. It's fine. The problem is here and in your shoulder. Will you let me give you an adjustment?"

Michael responded, "Please."

Dr. Maggie said, "Bring the tea" and walked off toward her workroom.

We did as instructed. When we were settled in her workroom, she motioned to her table and said, "Lie down face up, Michael."

He complied.

She took his neck in her hands. "Am I correct in assessing that your wrist started bothering you a few years ago?" While he was composing his response, she adjusted his neck. Then she took his arm. "Give me the full weight of your arm. You'll like this."

Again, he complied.

She rotated his shoulder in a circular motion until it gave a satisfying pop. "Your shoulder wasn't in the right place. Sit up." She gently pulled his wrist, and it released completely.

Michael rubbed his wrist and looked at her in awe. "Wow."

"With your shoulder in the right place, you can access the strength in your wrist, no problem." To me, she said, "You keep this one. He has a strong mind and a big open heart."

In my most mature fashion, I blushed.

Michael half smiled.

She took a sip of her tea. "You smile all you like, Michael. I offer you some advice." When he looked at her, she continued, "Don't let your temper get the best of you."

Then, he was speechless too. I suppressed my smile.

She handed him the other bag of herbs that was on her kitchen table. "Use this. Sammi'll explain how. Tomorrow, all of the soreness will be gone." She took our teacups. "Now, you two need to get out of here so that I can relax." She opened her back door. As we walked through it, she said, "Call me tomorrow, Sammi."

When we were back in his car, he said, "That was incredible." He was still working his hand. "My hand has been bothering me for over a year and she just … fixed it."

"Told you." My stomach growled loudly.

"Have you eaten anything today?"

"I had tea and a bagel for breakfast. I don't really have an appetite."

"Well, I'm starving, and you still need to eat. I know the perfect place."

I slipped my hand into his.

"What was Dr. Maggie saying about you putting a stop to Greg attacking you? Are you good at martial arts?" Naturally, that caught his attention.

I kept it simple and honest. "I know a few sequences very well. In an actual confrontation, my performance would be hit or miss. Dr. Maggie's lethal though."

He glanced at me. "I see." I don't think he believed me.

I changed the subject. "Before I forget, let me tell you how to use the herbs. Boil the tea in a gallon of filtered water for an hour. You can put the tea in the fridge once it's cooled. Drink a few ounces two or three times a day for the next few days."

He chuckled and said, "Thank you, Sammi," in a singsong fashion as if we were in second grade.

I couldn't think of a response.

"You're evading the subject. I can tell." He lifted his eyebrows. "I'll let it go," he kissed my hand, "for now."

I looked away to avoid eye contact and scowled. *Sucker.*

My response made him laugh out loud. "I do love you, Sammi."

I squeezed his hand and closed my eyes to savor how that made me feel. As we pulled into the parking lot of a cute little bistro, I whispered, "I love you too, Michael."

Dinner was filled with silence and kisses that seemed stolen. We took our time. We even fed each other. After dinner, we walked in silence with our arms around each other until the sun went down.

Finally, I mustered up the strength to say, "I should go home."

"I'll take you." He squeezed my shoulder.

"No, I'll call a car. It'll be easier that way. It's probably best that we don't get too close to my house." I turned so I could really hug him.

"True." He hugged me back.

"Did I leave stuff at your house?"

"I don't know. Maybe. We'll figure it out."

I called the car. While we waited for it to come, we kissed.

The car pulled up. I said, "Remember, we're not saying goodbye to each other. We're still going to be friends."

He huffed. "Yeah. I'll check in when I'm done with work tomorrow."

"Okay." I willed myself into the car. I watched him until he disappeared from sight.

During the ride back to my house, I distracted myself by checking my phone. There was the warning text from Kenny and a thousand texts from Ari. She wanted to know about the party. There were even two calls and a text from Greg, apologizing for what he'd done.

I texted Ari, "On my way home. I'll text you when I get there." I was grateful it only took ten minutes for me to get home.

I lost it as I walked into the den. I missed him. I just wanted to crawl into bed and cover up. I went to my bedroom. The bed was still unmade from earlier. I couldn't be in there. I picked up the T-shirt he'd given me, closed the door to my room, and went down to Ari's room. I took off my clothes and slipped into his T-shirt.

19

RESET

MONDAY, AUGUST 28

I WOKE up just before the sun peeked over the horizon. I covered my head to see if I could fall back asleep. It didn't work. I had to face it, that empty feeling that came when a relationship ended. A little voice inside suggested maybe it was only temporary. That was just a great way to postpone the pain. It was better to deal with it immediately, head-on. Michael and I were done. I wondered if we could truly be friends. I feared we may have to settle for acquaintances. I tried reason. I'd only known him for a month. I was being overly dramatic. That didn't work at all. I curled up and let that wave of emotion roll through me.

When the feeling of numbness settled in, I got out of Ari's bed and went up to my bedroom. His presence was everywhere. It would be a while before I could be in there without thinking of him. Maybe I needed to move and get new furniture. At least it didn't end badly. I could hold on to the good times, free and clear.

I moved my wrist. It was sorer than it was yesterday, but it wasn't swollen. I looked in the mirror. My eyes were puffy from crying, but my lip looked pretty good. The woman gazing back at me looked stunned. I touched the mirror and told her, "You're gonna get through this. Just give yourself time."

I decided the best path forward was to wash my linen. Ultimately, I decided to wash everything except the pillowcases and his

228

towel. I wasn't ready to be without his scent. I could ease into letting him go. That would be gentler.

Once downstairs, I threw the linen in the wash, started boiling Dr. Maggie's herbs, and put on a cold eye mask. I sat with some tea and made plans for my day. Since I looked okay, I was going to call someone to help me get my den back in order today. Oh, and I needed to call my lawyer to make sure he got the financial documents that Ari had put together.

My phone chimed. My heart leaped. I wanted it to be a text from Michael. I looked at the clock. It was almost 9 a.m., so he'd be at work by now. I looked at my phone. It was Michael.

He texted, "Morning Sammi."

I texted back, "Morning Michael."

"I couldn't wait until this evening."

"I'm glad you didn't."

"What time should I call this evening? Having something concrete to look forward to would make today easier."

I had no idea how this was going to work. I couldn't imagine being able to hang up the phone. He was right, though; the day seemed lighter with that to look forward to. I responded, "Yes. I agree. Seven?"

"Good. Talk to you later."

"Yes. Talk to you later." With a few short sentences, he'd shifted my whole mood. While my spirits were higher, I decided to check in with Ari.

I texted her, "Now?"

She responded by calling me. "That party must've been amazing if I'm just hearing from you now!" She was expecting a happy story.

So I told her the happy parts: breakfast with Vic and Paulo, how Cam was the best DJ ever, and how I bumped into Gene. I dropped the gem I knew she'd find especially hopeful. "I started to believe that Michael and I should be a couple."

She picked it up immediately. "Wow! Coming from you, that's huge!"

"Don't get carried away. I didn't say that I believe it'll end well."

"Okay. But still …"

I interrupted before she could continue going on about how big a deal it was. I told her that Greg showed up and we had a stare down. I also told her about the condition of Greg's shoulder and that his appearance at the beach didn't bother Michael.

She said, "Wow. Things are really good between you and Michael. I bet Greg was shocked to see you out and about."

"Yeah, I'm sure; three months later, he expected me to be where he left me."

"He's so fucking spoiled." After a few seconds of silence, she said, "Okay. So what's going on, Sammi? You sound really sad."

I told her about Greg's tantrum and that I'd broken it off with Michael to get back on course and to keep Greg focused on the divorce. She made it clear she knew I was freaked about being in love with Michael. However, she thought that my goal to have some single time before I started a new relationship was wise.

I said, "Well, at least now he's not taking me for granted anymore."

"You should use his tantrum as leverage to get him to sign."

I huffed. "You know I can't because of the accident."

She said the words "the accident" at the same time I did.

I continued, "He and I are walking a tightrope; if I report him, he reports me. Fortunately, neither of us wants to go that route. Greg's always late to the game. The best way through is to give him time to accept that we're done."

"You're good at shepherding him. How long do you think that'll take?"

"A few weeks. My next contract starts in a week. I'll be in Vancouver for a month. He should be ready to negotiate when I get back."

"Sounds like a plan." She paused. "I still think that fate will favor you and Michael. Where are you now?"

I didn't respond to her aspiration for Michael and me. Ari was hopelessly romantic. "I'm at home."

"Is there anything that I can do?"

"No. Only time will help."

"Okay. Call me if you need me."

"Okay. Love you."

"Love you too."

I decided that some anger would help assuage my feelings of

sadness. So I went into the mess that was my den to assess the damage. It was chaos, but only one or two things were broken.

After I restored order, I curled up in my favorite chair and tried to find my way back to the peace I'd created in this space. This was my sanctuary. Greg's chaos was never supposed to touch this place. My phone buzzed. Greg was calling. I declined his call three times.

Then he started texting me. "I'm sorry, Sammi. You know I love you. Let me help clean up the mess. We can talk."

I looked at those texts for a long time. I was all talked out with Greg.

He texted again. "Please talk to me, Sammi. Please. I love you."

His bullshit made me angry. I texted back, "Sign the papers Greg." I put my phone on Do Not Disturb. I had to get out of that situation.

The doorbell rang, and I thought, *You have to be kidding me.* I held my breath as I peeked out to see who it was. It was Kenny.

I opened the door. "You're up and out early."

"Yeah. I had an eight thirty meeting. These were sitting in front of the door." He handed me a vase with two cornflowers in it and a note attached to it.

"Come in. Want some coffee or something to eat?" Without looking at the note, I knew it was from Greg. I rolled my eyes and shook my head.

Kenny said, "I take it those are from my brother."

"Yep. And he's been here too. This is my favorite vase. I left it at his estate by mistake when I moved out." I looked at the wonderful blue and innocent flowers. "We planted these in the garden. He knows they're my favorite."

Kenny looked around the den. "I came by to give you a hand, but it looks like you've already cleaned up. I'd like some coffee."

"This time wasn't so bad. It looks like he only broke two things. It was mostly a matter of putting things back where they belonged."

"If there's anything you haven't done, I'll help you with that. How's your wrist?"

"It's sore but it'll be okay." I pushed him toward the kitchen.

He grabbed a mug and looked at the coffeepot.

I smiled. "Make some coffee, then you can have some." I turned off Dr. Maggie's herbs.

He looked at me with concern. "You haven't eaten, have you?"

"Nope. I'm not hungry."

"Be polite. Eat a bite with me." He opened the fridge and took out the eggs. He kept looking.

I joined him at the fridge. "There's no bacon. You can use some of that prosciutto."

"I'm really sorry that I didn't make it here before Greg yesterday. I apologize for my brother's behavior."

"I know. Thank you, Kenny. The situation between me and Greg isn't your fault." I put a bowl on the counter for him to stir the eggs, then prepped the skillet.

"You don't deserve for him to treat you like this, Sammi." He shredded the prosciutto into the eggs. "Do you have cheese?"

"I know that." I took a deep breath and handed him the cheese.

He started cooking his omelet-like thing.

I put on the coffee, set two plates by the stove, grabbed some utensils, and took a seat at the island.

As he was plating his prosciutto scramble, he said, "I spoke to Greg about his behavior. I told him that I'll break his fingers if he pulls that shit again. He's pretty upset about that guy …"

"Michael." I tasted the scramble. It was good. Once I started eating, I found that I did have an appetite.

"Michael. He says he can't believe you're cheating on him."

I gave Kenny an incredulous scowl.

He laughed. "I know, I know, I know. It is my understanding that Greg has blown his chances with you. Correct?"

"Yes, you are correct."

"Well, he's not ready to face it. He wants to try and work it out."

I hunched my shoulders. "I can't. I can't help him. I just can't."

"I get it, Sammi. I'm not trying to talk you into staying with him. I just want you to know that you have your work cut out."

We ate silently for a few minutes. The coffeepot dinged.

Kenny motioned for me to stay seated. "So Michael seemed pretty at home here yesterday."

"And?"

"And nothing. You're entitled. He seems like a good guy. I wouldn't want to meet him alone in an alley though."

I chuckled. "He is a good guy. I met him a few weeks ago."

"A few weeks. Really? It felt like you two have been hanging longer than that."

"Nope, we haven't. I broke it off because I knew Greg would obsess over him otherwise, and I don't want the two of them to cross paths."

"Greg's already obsessing over him." He shook his head. "And my brother wouldn't fare well if they crossed paths. Did you say he's Ari's brother? I didn't know she had a brother."

"She found out about him a few months ago."

"Hmmm." His phone buzzed. "I'm being summoned. I got some food in you. Are you sure that there's nothing I can help you with regarding the den?"

I'd decided to go to my lawyer's office instead of calling. I wanted to get out of the house. "Yes, I'm sure. Give me a minute to change. I want to walk out with you."

"Okay."

As I pulled out of my driveway after Kenny, I noticed a car like Greg's on my street. I wrote it off as being paranoid. When I pulled into the parking lot at my lawyer's office, I saw the car again. This time, I caught a glimpse of him. I wasn't paranoid. Greg was following me.

GREG FOLLOWED me from my lawyer's office to the beach, to the cafe where I grabbed lunch, and back home again. I knew he was watching for Michael to show up. He was keeping his distance. So I decided to ignore him. Hopefully, he'd get tired of that approach by nightfall.

I spent the next few hours distracting myself with work, making sure that everything was set for the film shoot next week. I reached out to my friend Gene to see if he'd be interested in working on the entrepreneur series. He gave me a tentative yes. He wanted to see the treatment and check his schedule to be sure.

It was 7:10 p.m. when I looked up. I'd done a great job of distracting myself. Then I remembered I was supposed to talk to Michael at 7 p.m. and my phone was still on Do Not Disturb. Greg had called me five times and texted twenty times. I deleted his voicemails without listening to them and responded, "Sign the papers" without reading his texts. Greg called me again immediately. I declined.

I saw two missed calls from Michael. He'd texted me, "Are you okay?"

I called Michael. He answered on the second ring. "Hey."

One word and I felt all the day's tensions release. "Hey. I'm sorry I missed your call. I was focused on work. I forgot that I had my phone on Do Not Disturb."

"Is he harassing you?" If nothing else, I'd found a guardian.

"Just calling and texting. It's fine. How was your day?"

"I got through it. Actually, it was good to be at work."

I could relate. "Same here. Work was a perfect distraction today."

"How's your wrist?"

"Thanks for asking me that. You just reminded me that I need to drink some of Dr. Maggie's herbal tea. It's a little sore, but it's not swollen at all. How's your hand?" I walked into the kitchen and poured a cup of the tea.

"Fine. It's like it was never jammed. Our trainer was awed. He wants to meet her. I haven't made my tea yet."

I drank down the cup in one gulp. A "blhhggg" escaped me.

"It's that good, huh?" He was chuckling.

"You have to drink it fast before you start to taste it, but it's good for you. Seriously, if you plan to see her again, you have to take it. She'll know if you don't."

"No way. That's not possible." He paused. Then he said, "Oh yeah, I wanted to let you know that Alex is talking to me again. You can stop feeling guilty about that now."

He was making fun of me. I let it ride. "How is he? Did he tell you anything new?"

"He's a little better. He admitted to feeling guilty about what was going on that night. He wanted to keep it a secret. That's why he attacked you. He knows he owes you an apology. I know he's still hiding something, though."

"Did he tell you anything new about what happened to me?"

"He said that you had your clothes on and that Pete was territorial, so it was unlikely that anyone would dare to touch you if you were with him. This is so fucked up."

When I exhaled, I realized I'd been holding my breath. "Good. Everything's consistent with my experience. I'm glad things are better between you and Alex."

He chuckled. "Thank you, Sammi."

"Are you laughing at me?"

"Yes."

"Why?"

"Because siblings fight. It's par for the course. You never fight with Ari?"

"No."

Our conversation shifted into lighter subjects, and we bantered on like that, talking about absolutely nothing while we got ready for bed. We kept it going until we dozed off. I slept in his T-shirt in my bed. The pillows still had his scent on them. I knew I was cheating, but it was nice to feel he was close.

Both Ari and Greg called while I was talking to Michael. I ignored Greg. I let Ari know I was okay, talking to Michael, and would call her in the morning.

I woke up to my phone buzzing in my face. I didn't remember ending the conversation last night, so I must've dozed off. If the imprint of the phone was any indication, I didn't move at all. I'd slept pretty hard. It was too early in the day to start dealing with Greg, so I hoped he hadn't already started texting me. I braced myself as I looked at my phone.

20

DISTRACTION
TUESDAY, AUGUST 29

MICHAEL TEXTED ME, "Morning. How did you sleep?"

Most of the tension slipped away. I knew exactly how to get rid of the rest of it. I called him. When he picked up, I said, "I slept well. I woke up with my phone stuck to my face. Did I fall asleep on you?"

"Yes, you did." The sound of his voice was the perfect antidote to Greg.

"I'm sorry. It was good to talk to you last night. Would you be up for a rematch tonight?"

"Yes. I'd like that. Is seven still good?"

"Talk to you then."

"Okay, bye."

"Bye." He hung up.

I was ready to face my day. My phone was ringing when I got out of the shower. It was Ari. I texted her, "Call you in 5." I got dressed and went to the kitchen. I put on some water for tea, kicked back some of Dr. Maggie's concoction, and cooked some more of Kenny's prosciutto scramble. I called Ari back as I was plating it.

She answered, "How's it going, girl?"

"Okay, considering. I really miss Michael, and I really don't want to deal with Greg." I took a bite of the scramble. Kenny was on to something.

"Wow. Talking to the two of you is like the difference between night and day."

I felt a pang in my heart. "Maybe us separating isn't a big deal for him."

"Please. He's very, very sad, but he's trying not to acknowledge it. He won't talk about it at all. In contrast, you have it right out on the table. You sound better than yesterday. What gives?"

"We talked on the phone all evening until I fell asleep. Then I called him again this morning. Talking to him helps me a lot. Do you think I should encourage him to talk about it?" I massaged the furrow in my brow.

"No. Let him work through it his way. He's got a strong network of friends. He'll find a way to deal with it. What's your day look like?"

I covered my eyes with my left hand. "Encouraging Greg to sign the papers, working out, and maybe starting to pack. I'm leaving to work on that indie flick on Thursday."

"When does production start?"

"Monday. I think a change in scenery would be good for me. Any more questions or comments?"

Ari laughed. "None. You know where to find me if you need me."

"I'll talk to you later." We both hung up.

I made my tea and finished the scramble. The cornflowers that Greg left yesterday grabbed my attention. I found that color blue so satisfying. More out of curiosity than expectation, I went to the door to see if Greg had left anything else on my doorstep. There were two more cornflowers with their stems protected with a wet paper towel wrapped in plastic. There was no note this time. So this was going to be a pattern. As I returned to the kitchen, I let the flowers know I knew they were innocent and I had no intention of taking the anger I felt toward Greg out on them. I saw his note from yesterday as I added the new flowers to the vase. I was in the mood to read it at that moment.

Greg's note said, "Sweetheart, these cornflowers are from our yard. They miss you as much as I do. Please come home, Sammi. I love you with all my heart. I know we can work this out. I'll do whatever it takes. Please give us a chance. Love, Greg."

He'd had a different experience in our relationship. Though he couldn't offer the same to me, I was a safe place for him. My thoughts drifted to the first time he'd let me see his vulnerability. It was about six months after the accident. We'd struck up a friendship. Sometimes, I'd help with his physical therapy, but mostly, we just talked about things in general: news, arts, sports. I didn't notice until later, but music was a topic he was still avoiding at that time. When I'd walked into his room that day, he was completely freaked out. He was frantically trying to free himself from the supports they had strapped him in and obviously causing himself a lot of pain. His nurse and therapist were trying to calm him down and convince him he could do the exercise. I persuaded them to give me a shot at calming him down.

Once they'd left the room, I said, "Relax. Stop hurting yourself. You don't have to do anything."

He grew visibly calmer.

I waited until it seemed like he wasn't in pain anymore, then asked, "What's going on?"

"I can't do these exercises, Sammi. I can't. They're acting as if repeating the same words over and over and over again is going to change that truth." He was getting agitated again.

I reminded him, "They aren't in here right now, and they aren't asking you to do anything."

He nodded. "You're right," he said and relaxed again.

When his breathing had returned to normal, I asked, "What did they want you to do?"

He held out his injured hand and said, "They want me to touch my thumb to each of my fingers. He tried to demonstrate the movement. My fingers don't move separately anymore."

I'd faced the same problem when trying to rehabilitate dance injuries I'd experienced. I offered him a solution that had worked for me. "Touch your forefinger to your thumb on your good hand first. Then try it with the injured one. Focus more on how it feels to do the movement than actually doing the movement."

He responded with curiosity. He looked at his hands and started working back and forth through his own series of movements. After about ten minutes, he'd figured out how to initiate the movement.

He closed his eyes and crinkled his brow. A tear escaped from his eye.

I said, "You're doing a good job; what's wrong?"

He responded, "What if I can't play anymore?"

My heart sank. I realized that, not only had the accident I caused almost destroyed his body, but it might've taken the thing he loved most. I started to cry too. I said, "You'll play again."

He took my hand. "Will you help me? I didn't understand how to try until you directed me."

"Yes. I'll help you." I planned to be around at least until he was well. I was going to do everything I could to make that statement come true.

If it was just him and his therapist, he'd consistently end up pissed off and frustrated. So I participated in his exercise sessions regularly. I found that if I imitated what he was doing wrong when he got stuck, he understood quickly and corrected himself. He would work through a whole series of exercises in a session if I participated. If he got really stuck, he'd ask his therapist to leave the room and work through it with me privately. He would openly admit when he was afraid. Looking back, I realized I may be the only person he let see his fear.

After a few weeks and a great deal of improvement in the movement of his left hand, he started listening to music again and talking about it. He didn't start singing again until he could play simple chords on his guitar a few months later.

Even so, I couldn't fathom how he was processing what had happened, all the arguments and conversations we'd experienced in the past year. Was he just ignoring them like they didn't exist, or was he taking them in and deciding they had no value? I couldn't tell. What I did know was he really pissed me off. I'd use the anger to fuel my workout.

My phone rang. This time, it was Greg. I declined the call. I texted, "Sign the papers."

He texted back, "I'm not signing anything before we talk."

I wanted to throw my phone in frustration. I rode my wave of anger out of the door and to Amanda's studio.

As I was walking to the studio after I'd parked my car, I realized Greg was still following me. I was happy Amanda was the only one there as I walked into the studio.

She glanced at me, then looked again. "What's going on, Sammi?"

This time, the truth would work perfectly. "I'm so angry at Greg right now that I could probably choke him to death with my bare hands."

"What did he do?"

"I'm trying to divorce him because of all of his whoring, and he's acting like we've had a minor disagreement. It's infuriating. Do you mind if I work out for a few hours? I need to burn this energy off so that I can come up with a mature, sane response to his madness."

"Sure, but go easy on the machines."

"I will." Thankfully, she didn't hover. Two hours later, I had a lot more clarity, and I knew exactly what I was going to do. The first thing was that I had to make it so he couldn't follow me. I didn't like the feeling of him lurking nearby.

When I was done with my workout, Amanda was teaching a class. I waved to her so she knew I was much better, and I left her a note saying the same and letting her know I'd be away for the next month working.

When I got back home, I pulled my Mini Cooper into the garage. I changed my flight to leave that day instead of Thursday. I had three hours to get to the airport. I called the hotel and made arrangements for me to start my stay early. Then I packed my carry-on: three pairs of jeans, ten T-shirts, workout clothes, sneakers, and flip-flops. If I needed anything else, I'd buy it there. I decided to leave Michael's T-shirt behind. It was a good opportunity to get used to the absence of his scent in a neutral place.

I was sure Greg was sitting on my street somewhere and wanted to put some distance between us. Though it was two hours before I needed to be at the airport, I chose to leave immediately. I'd eat when I got to the terminal. My car arrived five minutes after I requested it, and I was on my way. As expected, Greg followed me to the airport. So I had the driver drop me off at a different terminal from the one I was flying out of. Since I'd already checked in, I went through the security checkpoint quickly enough that Greg didn't have time to park his car and find me. I'd lost him.

My phone buzzed. It was a text from Greg. "I'm willing to wait until you're ready to talk."

Since I knew he didn't know where I was or where I was going, I felt better about talking to him. I decided to call him.

Greg answered with, "Are you meeting up with him?" I was right. He was obsessing about Michael.

"It's not okay for you to follow me around everywhere."

"I have a right to know where you are, Sammi. You're my wife."

"First of all, you don't own me, Greg. I'm not your property, and, as a self-sustaining adult, I don't have to report to anyone. Period. Second, we're legally separated. I tell you what, keep it up. I'll call the police if I have to."

He took it down a notch. "Okay. I won't follow you anymore. Are you meeting up with him?"

I wanted to tell him it was none of his business, but while I was working out, I realized I needed to coax him to the place where he'd sign the papers. For him, it was all about territory. So I played a card that made him feel like he had some claim. "No. I'm going to work."

"Is he coming with you?"

"No. He has a job. He'll be at his job."

"Where are you going, Sammi?"

I wasn't willing to play that card. "To work. That's all you need to know."

"Will you tell me how long you'll be gone?"

I didn't mind playing that card. "A month."

He was quiet for a minute. "Talk to me, Sammi. Tell me what I need to do to fix this."

"Greg, it's over between us. It's been over for a long time."

"I know you feel that way. Just talk to me. I know I can convince you to give us a chance. If it doesn't work, we can negotiate the settlement, and I'll sign the papers." He hadn't even started to accept that we were over. It would likely take him longer than a month to give up. I was happy to be passing that time working instead of waiting. Being in a place away from him was a bonus.

Since I'd taken Michael off the table, agreeing to talk to him seemed a good next step to getting him to the place where he'd sign the papers. "Okay. I'll let you know when I'm on my way back to LA."

"I love you, Sammi."

It was going to take a lot of patience. "Goodbye, Greg." I hung up the phone.

Now I needed to let people know that I'd decided to leave early. I texted Kenny about Greg following me and my plans first. He responded supportively.

Next, I called my mom. It took a while for her to answer. "Hey, Sammi." She was out of breath.

"Are you okay?"

"Yeah, I was on the treadmill."

"I'm sorry. I didn't mean to interrupt your workout. I can call you back."

"No, no. I'm done. Now's a good time."

I asked, "What's going on with you?"

"Nothing new. What's up with you, Sammi? I'd been wanting to ask you if there's any news on the divorce."

Less was best with Sylvia. "No word from Greg's lawyer yet. It may take some time. Greg doesn't want a divorce."

"Of course he doesn't. If you have any leverage, you should use it. Let me know if there's anything I can do to help."

My mom didn't know about the accident or the abuse. She had no idea about the tightrope Greg and I were walking. I couldn't tell her because she was a judge. "I will. I was calling to let you know that I'm going up to Vancouver early. I really like the city. I'm going to hang out there for a few days before the shoot starts."

"That sounds like fun. Text me when you land."

"Okay. Love you, Mom."

"Love you, Sammi."

Ari was next. She was the converse of my mom. Full disclosure worked best with her. I texted, "Greg's been following me for the last two days. I didn't tell you because he was keeping his distance, and I didn't want you to worry. I decided to leave for Vancouver today because I got tired of it. Flying out in an hour. I'll text you when I land. I'm fine."

"Okay. Good move. I'll talk to you later. Send your flight and hotel info."

I texted the requested info to her immediately.

She responded, "Got it. Safe flight. X."

Finally, there was Michael. I really didn't want to tell him Greg was following me. Maybe just telling him that I wanted to push our call back a few hours would work. I texted him, "Hey, can we postpone the call until nine?" He called in response.

I answered, "Hey, Michael."

"What's going on?"

"Nothing. I just decided to go to Vancouver today. I want to postpone our call until I get to the hotel."

"He was doing more than texting and calling, wasn't he? Did he hurt you, Sammi?" I could tell his temper was rising because he raised his voice slightly.

"No, Michael, he didn't hurt me. He was following me, but he never came near me. I'm leaving early because I didn't want to be followed anymore. I didn't tell you because I knew you'd get upset. I'm fine, and it's in the past now."

"If you need me to tell him to back off, I will."

"Thank you, but I have to handle this alone."

"You're okay?"

"Yes. I'm fine."

"If he keeps it up, you should stop protecting his reputation and call the police. His behavior's creepy, Sammi. It's not okay." He was calming down.

"I know, I know. I'm sorry that you're even thinking about this, Michael."

"We've had that discussion. It's my choice, Sammi. I love you." His tone made it clear that he wasn't going to compromise on that point. Those words zapped my body with electricity.

"I love you too."

"Call me when you get to the hotel."

"Okay."

We hung up. I had no idea how this was supposed to work, but I didn't think that saying I love you was the most constructive approach. I boarded the plane in limbo between two facts: the truth that we loved each other and the truth that we were working, albeit grudgingly, on just being friends.

I WALKED around the area after I checked into the hotel. Being in a different place and having some distance from LA was good. I had two tasks: figuring out what to say or do to finalize my divorce from Greg and how to transition my relationship with Michael into a friendship.

It was likely I wouldn't speak to Greg again before I was on my way back to LA. I'd spent a long time thinking about my relationship with him. I didn't really have anything else to say, and there was nothing to salvage.

I was going to talk to Michael within the next hour, and I knew that there was a lot worth salvaging with him. I chose to spend my time thinking about how to be one of Michael's friends.

When 9 p.m. rolled around, I hadn't made any progress. I didn't know how to stop being in love with him. My working plan was to accept it, move on, and let time resolve it. There was just one rule: we couldn't say I love you to each other. I made myself comfortable in the middle of the bed in my hotel room.

When I called, he answered with, "You made it. How's the hotel?"

"The hotel is nice. How are you, Michael?"

"I'm okay." It was an automated response. "Are you okay?"

"For the most part, yes. I feel really sad about us. Though I know that breaking it off was the best way, I really miss us."

"Try to keep it in perspective. We're not turning our backs on each other. We still have our friendship." I saw what Ari was talking about then. I let him win.

"You're right."

He huffed.

I continued, "We have to be disciplined. We can't say I love you to each other. It's counterproductive to our goal of becoming friends."

"Is that what you really want? To let go of what we have completely?" He wasn't being flippant. I could hear his heartbreak.

I wanted him to know that my heart was broken too. "Honestly, no. But I can't see any other way. We've already talked this through. I have no idea of how long it's gonna take me to get a divorce from

Greg and get myself established. I don't want you to put your life on hold."

He huffed again.

I said, "Maybe talking to each other is not a good idea after all."

"No. It's helpful. We did agree to ease into this. You're right; saying I love you to each other makes it hard to keep track of which direction we're heading. You needing space to establish yourself makes sense to me. Everything you're saying is reasonable. I'm on board."

"Okay."

"Okay."

I tried to lighten things up. "Good, because I enjoyed talking to you last night. It made things easier."

"Yeah, for me too. Let's change the subject. When are you coming back to LA?"

"September 26. Your season's starting. You'll be traveling a lot, won't you?"

"Yes, I'll be in and out of town. We're going to New Zealand for the second and third weeks of September. I'll be back before you."

"Hmmm. Are you guys ready for the season?"

"I am. There are those who are still working on it though."

He asked me about my project, and we talked until he fell asleep.

That became our pattern for the next few weeks. We said good morning and talked until we dozed off at night. The pattern shifted to texting when he went to New Zealand because of the time difference. Time and space helped us get used to not being around each other. We talked every few days after he returned from New Zealand. We still texted most days though.

After the shoot was complete, I went home to LA. We'd shot digital, so the next big task was editing, which would take eight weeks. I was set to begin supporting the editing the following week. I'd taken the day off to regroup. I started out by sleeping in. I followed that up with a long, luxurious shower and lots of pampering. My plan for the morning was to whip up a batch of Kenny's scramble and chill for a little while.

21

———————

LUNCH WITH GREG
SATURDAY, SEPTEMBER 30

As I GOT comfortable in my favorite chair, I texted Michael. "I hope your Saturday's going well. Have good performances today." We'd become proficient in chitchat and staying well clear of our connection.

The ads for the upcoming Torus Company season were all over town. There were pictures of Michael in motion everywhere. The photographer had done a great job of capturing both his expression and his technique. The pictures were mesmerizing. It was obvious Michael was an incredible dancer, although I still hadn't seen him perform. Watching men who could really move do their thing was such a turn on for me. Seeing him dance would've probably done me in.

He responded, "Thanks. I thought you'd still be asleep. I'm on my way to get ready for today's matinee. Enjoy your chill day. Talk to you later."

My phone buzzed. It was my mother. I braced myself to withstand her interrogation as I answered. I caught her up on how I was doing and how my divorce was progressing. For all my anticipation, it only took a few minutes. She was thorough but quick.

It was the day I'd finally face Greg. I made myself a fresh cup of tea and settled into chilling before meeting him for a late lunch at a restaurant we used to frequent when things were good between us.

The first time we'd gone to the restaurant together, it was just

246

over a year into his recovery. Though I'd started going to the hospital and helping him to atone for the accident, we'd settled into a genuine, easy friendship. Dinner that night was a big deal because it was the first time he was hanging out in public after the accident. I'd gotten there first and was seated at our table when he walked in the door. I stood up to help him and saw he didn't have his crutch. He was all smiles. He'd been walking without it for a few weeks. He'd kept it from me because he'd wanted to surprise me with the finished product. Hugging wasn't a thing we did, but I hugged him then. I was so happy and relieved. He'd sent the restaurant a playlist to play while we ate. We talked about music and art, mostly music, and we giggled. That was the evening when our friendship shifted into courting. He wasn't flirtatious in our friendship, and I wasn't angling to date him; I helped him easily as a friend. So I hadn't expected that.

ON THE WAY to the restaurant, I drove through the sea of Michael ads. When I got there, Greg hadn't arrived yet. They showed me to a table in a relatively private part of the dining room. I looked out the window. There were a few ads in the kiosk across the street. It looked like Michael was going to watch me deal with Greg. They poured my tea and water the way I liked it without me asking. They served my favorite appetizers without letting me look at the menu. I chuckled to myself. Greg enjoyed making simple situations into productions.

He showed up a few minutes later with another cornflower in hand. Physically, he was an attractive man. His skin was perfect. He was a redbone. His most striking feature, his eyes, were hazel. They shifted between light brown and green with the wind. They betrayed his cunning. He had full, inviting lips and soft, kinky-curly medium brown hair with red overtones. He was six foot one, slim, and muscular. The package was nice, and he knew it.

He sat across from me. "It's good to see you, Sammi. I've missed you. Thank you for talking to me." He offered the cornflower. He was sober, and his shoulder was better.

This was going to be an adventure. There were no straight lines with this man. I buckled in for the journey. I took the flower and smelled it. "Thank you, Greg."

On cue, a waiter appeared with a small vase of water for the flower.

Greg didn't mention the pictures of Michael that were just across the street. He said, "I didn't know what you were in the mood for today, so I ordered everything I know you like."

Point taken. He knew what I liked. "Thank you." He'd done a good job. They made a killer arugula and watermelon salad. I dug in while I waited for his next play.

"First of all, I'd like to apologize for my behavior last month. To be honest, I was acting out in jealousy. It was inappropriate. I'm sorry."

I nodded a little and continued to enjoy the salad.

"It doesn't matter if you were seeing someone else. I deserved that because of the way that I treated you. I just want you to give us a chance to work it out."

They set this wonderfully spicy dish, bacon and crispy brussels sprouts, on the table. I looked at him and chose to focus on the food.

"I'm willing to do anything. Just tell me what to do. Please, Sammi. Say something."

"Our relationship's been over for a long time, Greg. All that's really left are the formalities."

"Don't say that. I brought you here today so that you could remember when things were good between us. We can find our way back to that."

"You're right; the food's delicious, and I appreciate you remembering all of the things I like. Even if we erased the past year and completely ignored all of your angry outbursts, there's no way forward for us, Greg."

"Come on, Sammi. We had more good times than bad. You have to remember that too."

I'd hoped that he'd be further along in the process.

He continued, "We had a lot of good times right here in this restaurant, Sammi. You can't tell me you don't remember how peaceful it is for us to be around each other. We've spent hours together in silence creating, laughing, making love."

I looked at him.

He took it as encouragement. "Remember planning and planting our garden? We did all of that work and then couldn't reliably tell the weeds from what we'd planted. The only things that we salvaged were the cornflowers, the carrots, and a tomato plant."

We did make a mess of that. I smiled. "We didn't save the carrots, and I'm not sure those were tomatoes."

He smiled back. "Right. Remember the time you decided to meet me in Buenos Aires? I flew directly there instead of coming home first. You packed winter clothes for us, and it was midsummer there. You actually argued with me about being able to make that work. You wore the corduroy pants for three days. You were hot as hell."

"You made fun of me the whole time. You enjoyed that." I hadn't thought about how playful and silly Greg could be in a while.

"It was funny, Sammi. I love you."

He was right. There were parts of our relationship that worked. We talked and laughed. Greg liked to surround me with things that I loved. The sex was okay. None of it was like the connection I had with Michael, but it was a workable relationship. "You're right; we had some good times. There were parts of our relationship that worked, but—"

He interrupted me. "So you'll give us a try?"

He'd surprised me by how hard he was holding on. "No, Greg. I'm done."

"Why won't you even try? Is it because of that guy?"

"No, it's not because of that guy. I've told you. Your whoring and your tantrums are deal-breakers for me. You're upset about me seeing one person. How would you feel if it was twenty—?"

He interrupted me again. "I don't understand why it's such a big deal. It's just something that men do. I'll always come home to you. I love you. You're the only one that matters. Everyone else is just entertainment." He was so forthright and earnest about it. Greg had never lied to me. When I'd confronted him about cheating on me the first time, he was genuinely surprised I'd expected it to be different. Looking back, I realized he didn't flaunt it, but he never tried to hide it either.

"I can't live like that. I just can't. It feels the same way to me as it feels to you when I'm with someone else."

"I take good care of you." He was absolutely refusing to acknowledge his actions were hurtful.

"I never wanted you to take care of me, Greg. I wholly acknowledge that your financial situation when we first got together helped me. But that's not why I married you. I always paid my share. Always. And, technically, I've been taking care of you and your money for a while now."

They brought the main course. It was rosemary roasted chicken with green beans and fingerling potatoes. I asked them to box up the remaining appetizers.

"That's true. My body is in much better shape when you take care of me. I need you. My shoulder needs you. And my financials would be in a completely different state if you weren't managing them. How will I survive without you taking care of me?"

How I *cared* for him. That was what all this love he was feeling was actually about. "We need to talk about our divorce settlement."

"The purpose of this lunch is to explore ways that we can save our marriage. I'm not ready to give up yet. Let's go to therapy."

The man was crazy, but the food was good. "You want a nineteenth century relationship, and I want a twenty-first century one. Therapy isn't going to change that."

"Maybe we could find a compromise if you'd just try."

This was his brain sober. *Unbelievable.* I tasted the chicken and asked them to box the rest. Though he was still in denial, I could tell he'd been thinking about it. I wasn't going to talk him through it today. I was on the tightrope, and I just had to stand my ground and wait him out. And there was goodness in him. We just weren't a match. I'd played along enough for that day and was ready to go. I asked them to box up whatever else he'd ordered. I said, "Thank you for lunch, Greg. The food was wonderful. Let me know when you're ready to discuss the settlement."

"We can figure this out, Sammi. I know we can."

I took a deep breath and took the cornflower out of the vase. I figured that gesture would leave him with a sense of achievement.

When I got to the front door, they handed me a huge bag of food. There was no way that I could've eaten all the food he ordered at lunch that day. I wasn't going to let it go to waste, though. I'd eat it over the next few days.

When I got in my car, I called Ari. She answered, "Any progress?"

"Does a big bag of really delicious food count?"

"What?"

I told her about lunch.

She said, "I have an idea. Next time you meet with him, why don't you propose that you get back together with him, and, going forward, both of you can sleep with whoever you like and bring them home whenever you feel like it?"

"I like it. He's not going to acknowledge the absurdity of what he's asking unless he has to consider dealing with it himself."

"Yep. If it doesn't affect him, it doesn't matter."

I chuckled. "The universe definitely has a sense of humor. There were three of the millions of Michael ads in a kiosk right outside the window of the restaurant."

"Did Greg notice?"

"He didn't seem to. But with Greg, you never know. He was probably gauging my reaction."

Ari said, "How are things with you and Michael?"

"We're still mostly texting and mostly talking about work. I think we're closer to being friends."

"Did you tell him that you were meeting with Greg today?"

"I thought about it. I think it would seem too much like I'm reporting things to him like we're still in a relationship."

Ari said, "If you two were really just friends, you would've mentioned it casually, and it wouldn't have been a big deal."

"My plan was to mention it to him casually afterward. I didn't want him to worry that Greg was going to go off. Of course, I also don't want to encourage him to wait for me."

"Are you really alright with Michael starting a relationship with someone else?"

That struck a chord. "I know that Michael and I can't be together right now. There would be no way for me to keep him and Greg from clashing. Greg would be obsessed with Michael. Michael would be guarding. Greg would drag his feet with the divorce even more than he is now. That situation wouldn't work. I have no idea how long it'll be before I'm ready to start another relationship. I want Michael to be free to live his life. If that means he starts a relationship with someone else, then so be it. I honestly don't know what else I can do. I've never ended a relationship in this way. I don't have a plan or any idea how to proceed. My only hope is that time will ease the pain. You know all of this. Do you have a better way?"

"I just think you guys should be direct about how you feel about each other."

"We are direct about how we feel about each other, Ari. I know he loves me. He knows I love him. Expressing those feelings right now is just confusing and hurtful. We've done that. We can't act on them. I don't know when we'll be able to act on them, and I don't want him to wait because if he waits and it takes too long, he'll come to resent me. That would destroy the friendship that we've built. I've thought about this deeply, Ari."

"Okay. I'm sorry for pressing."

"It's fine. I'm going to let you go. I'll talk to you later."

She said, "Okay, bye."

I hung up. She had no idea how hard the situation with Michael was for me.

<hr>

I WENT to Amanda's studio and spent a few hours on the machines. It was just after 6 p.m. when I finished.

As I walked back into the lobby, Amanda said, "Now that you're done roughing up my machines, what are you up to next?"

"I'm just gonna go home. I don't have any plans for this evening."

She squinted at me in assessment. "Hmm. Come hang out with me. I'm going to have dinner and drinks with one of my friends. You should come along." She nodded yes to lead my answer.

"You sure I wouldn't be intruding?"

She sucked her teeth. "I wouldn't have asked if that were the case."

"That sounds like fun. I'd really like that. Thank you. All I have with me are a T-shirt, jeans, and sneakers. Do I need to go home and change?"

"No. That's what I'm wearing too."

"Great. I'll follow you so that I don't have to come back for my car."

Amanda responded, "Okay, meet me at the corner."

On the way to my car, I looked around for Greg. I didn't see him anywhere. It looked like he was moving forward in that regard, at least. I met Amanda at the corner and followed her to a restaurant lounge not too far from the beach. Much to my surprise, the person we were meeting was Cam.

Amanda and I joined Cam at our table. Amanda introduced me. "Hey, girl. How's it going? I invited my friend Sammi to hang out with us this evening."

I said, "Hello, Cam. I apologize for crashing your evening."

Cam responded, "Sammi. Not at all. I remember you from the beach party. You were with Vic's friend Mike Shelly, right?"

I answered, "Yes, that's right."

Cam looked at Amanda. "Girl, this woman has moves."

I smiled. "That's really kind of you, Cam."

Cam said, "I'm not being kind. I'm telling the truth."

Amanda replied, "I'm not surprised. She's a decent classical dancer. She has a really good sense of timing."

To me, Cam noted, "I've never seen anyone handle Mike like you did." To Amanda, she said, "First of all, he brought her, hand in hand, to my beach party. She mesmerized him on the dance floor. There were moments when he was just standing there, watching her move."

Amanda responded, "Hmm, now I'm really sorry that I couldn't make it to that party; but I've seen them together, and it definitely seems like he's all in."

Cam said, "Mike's a lot of man. How does it feel for him to focus all of that on you?"

I hunched my shoulders. "Honestly, he blindsided me. Based on how he looks, I expected him to be shallow and flippant. He was anything but. Being with him was a little overwhelming at times."

Amanda said, "Why are you speaking in past tense?"

I took a deep breath. "I broke it off with Michael so I could focus Greg on giving me my divorce as quickly as possible. Greg would be completely obsessed with Michael otherwise."

Amanda hugged me. "I'm sorry, Sammi. I knew you looked

more stressed than usual, but I had no idea that it wasn't just dealing with Greg that was bothering you."

I said, "I really miss Michael. He's one of the good ones."

Amanda hugged me a little tighter.

I added, "Okay, now we need to change the subject or I'm gonna start crying. Tonight's about having fun."

Amanda let go of me.

I shook it off, then looked at Cam and said, "How did you meet her?" I gestured to Amanda.

Cam nodded toward Amanda. "I went to college with her."

I asked Cam, "How long have you been a DJ?"

She replied, "I started spinning a few months after I got out of college—"

Amanda interjected, "This woman is a hell of a musician. She has perfect pitch. She plays most instruments. And she can sing."

Cam nodded in agreement. "It's true."

I said, "I need to take a page out of your book. I love that you own your mastery completely."

Cam responded, "It's the only way, girl. You have to have humility for all the things you don't know or can't express and gratitude for the gifts. But if you don't know and own what you're offering and state it clearly every step of the way, you're going to get rolled over and taken advantage of. You don't have to be aggressive, but you do have to be firm. Me, I have worked too hard at cultivating my gifts to be under-acknowledged."

Amanda said, "Uh-huh. Holla."

We toasted to that.

I said, "Greg's brother, Kenny, would love you. He would be blown away by one of your DJ sets. I'll introduce you to him."

Cam narrowed her eyes. "Wait. The Greg that you're divorcing is Greg Albert? I saw him checking out one of the sets at my beach party."

I nodded. I gave her a moment to process it.

She said, "He's got quite a reputation. I don't have to wonder why you're divorcing him. Here's to good decisions."

We toasted again.

Cam scrunched her eyebrows. "After we're done eating and lounging, I know a perfect underground spot where we can lose ourselves in the groove. Given what you're going through, I think a little dance therapy is in order."

I smiled before saying, "That would help a lot. Thank you."

At around 10 p.m., I got a text from Michael. "I'm wiped. I did two shows today, and I have to do it again tomorrow. I'm gonna pass out. Let's talk in the morning."

I texted back, "Rest well. Talk to you in the morning."

I was glad I'd taken Amanda up on her offer. We had a wonderful evening eating, laughing, and dancing. Amanda and Cam moved from my circle of acquaintances to friends. I talked to them a few times during the week. A part of me that I hadn't experienced in LA resurfaced. It felt good, like I was coming back to me.

22

GREG'S FAMILY
SATURDAY, OCTOBER 7

MICHAEL HAD BEEN EXHAUSTED by the company season, especially on the weekends, because there were two performances each day. Our texts were mostly good mornings, good nights, and well-wishes. I was hoping I'd get a chance to talk to him on Monday when he had a day off. I missed him, but it didn't feel as heavy as it did when we first stopped dating.

In the spirit of letting him think he had the control he so desperately needed, I'd let Greg choose the time and place for our next meeting. It was 2 p.m., and I was on my way to Kenny's house to have an early dinner and talk. I really hoped he'd gotten beyond his insistence on saving our failed marriage.

On the drive over, I pondered how infuriatingly one-sided Greg's perspective was. He wanted to be in a relationship with me in which only his needs were considered and met. He felt that, in exchange for access to his stuff and all the things that I liked, he should be able to do whatever he wanted. I didn't think he saw me, Sammi the human being, at all; I thought, in his mind, I was just a possession. While it was true that he knew the things I liked, as far as I could tell, he had no genuine interest in who I was as a person. Yet, he said he loved me and wanted me in his life. How did you love or want a person you didn't see? I couldn't make sense of it.

Greg walked out to meet me as I was pulling into Kenny's driveway. "It's good to see you."

I responded, "Hello, Greg. How are you?"

His mother, Grace, and her sister, Justine, pulled into the driveway right after I did and joined us. They were pretty women with light hazel-green and brown eyes. They were both happily plump. In addition to their talents, Greg and Kenny got their looks from their mom. Greg had her eyes, her features, and her toffee skin with red overtones. Kenny had her eyes too, but his features and coloring were influenced by their father.

He smiled at me. "Mom, you've been asking about how Sammi is. Here she is. You can ask her yourself."

He'd played his cards well. He knew I loved his mother and wouldn't want to upset her. With Grace there, he knew I'd play along cordially until we were done with dinner. For the same reason, I knew I could also expect him to be well-behaved. Instead of talking about the good times we'd had, he was showing me. Clearly, he was still stuck on saving our marriage.

Grace folded me into a hug. "Sammi, sweetheart. It's good to see you. You look wonderful."

I hugged her back. I really liked Grace. She was warm, talented, and grounded. She'd welcomed me to her family with open arms. I'd missed her. "Thank you, Mama Grace. It's good to see you too."

Justine interrupted my hug with Grace. "Child. Where have you been?" She hugged me. Grace and Justine were inseparable. You couldn't know one without knowing the other.

I hugged her back. I felt guilty for not reaching out to them earlier. "Just working, Auntie Justine. It's good to see you."

She said, "Well, you're going to set up a lunch date with Grace and I before you leave. I've watched some of the films that you've worked on. I think they're very good, Sammi. I want to discuss them."

I smiled. "Okay, Auntie Justine."

Greg smiled pensively and gestured toward the front door. He opened the door for me. "Go to the den." He followed me in.

We walked through the foyer. At least a few extra people were in the house. There was lots of talking and a bit of bustle. There was a formal dining room on the left and an old-school living room on the right. The dining room table was set for six people. The foyer ended in what was essentially a big open room. The kitchen was to the left.

It was spacious, with a table for casual dining, and I saw a catering staff preparing food. The den was an expansive room with a grand piano and a few acoustic guitars in the far-right corner. Kenny had decorated his house himself, based on pictures he'd found in magazines, and he was proud of it. His colors were muted, grays and tans. The furniture was sleek. Not all of it was comfortable. The artwork matched the color palette. It wasn't personal, but it was obvious that he put some work into replicating what he'd seen.

Greg placed his hand on my lower back just before we entered the den. I glanced at him with a look that was contained in my eyes because there were people around. It was decidedly not warm. I was sure he understood I was going to karate chop his arm if he didn't move his hand.

He dared me to hit him with his eyes, but he understood my boundary. And he moved his hand.

Kenny walked up and put his arm around me. He turned me toward the wall opposite the piano. There were two signs. One said, "Happy Birthday Kenny" and the other said "Happy Birthday Sammi." My birthday was during the previous week, and Kenny's would be sometime during the next one.

Kenny looked at me and rolled his eyes. He whispered, "It was a surprise for me too. My brother's still hopeful."

I whispered back, "Your brother's insane." We both laughed.

"Happy birthday, Sammi."

"Happy birthday, Kenny. By the way, I met a person whose musicality will blow you away. I'm going to send you an email with a link to her site and her contact info. Her name is Camille Zhao."

"If you're saying that, she must be something. I look forward to it. Thanks." He gave me a squeeze and walked away.

I looked back at Grace and Justine. My mom was confident in who she was because of all she'd accomplished, how well she'd done according to the checklist of "shoulds." In contrast, these women were just comfortable in their bones. They were happy with who they were, like Dr. Maggie and Helen. Both had an MFA in music. Grace finished college after she'd divorced Greg's father. They had a center where they taught young people music.

Greg walked up to where I was standing. He cleared his throat. "This is a surprise party for my wife and my brother. Happy birthday, Sammi." He gave me a challenging look as he kissed my hand. "Happy birthday, Kenny." Kenny and I locked eyes.

We both said, "Thanks, Greg."

I had to stifle a laugh because I kept thinking the words "karate chop."

Greg misinterpreted my smile. He leaned in and said, "I know you love my family. I thought it would be good for you to spend some time with them as you consider our future."

I just looked at him. He was right, though, about how much I loved his family.

Greg continued, "The chef and her assistant have prepared a wonderful Cajun meal for us." He nodded toward his mom and aunt. "If you guys are ready, let's have dinner."

Grace sat at the head of the table. Justine sat to her right, on the side of the table. I sat to her left across from Justine, and Greg sat on my other side. Kenny sat to Justine's left, across from Greg. The sixth seat was unclaimed. I was sure that it was for Keith, Greg's father. Once we were seated, a person from the catering staff took a few pictures of us.

The food was hot, spicy, and delicious. Dinner was pretty much heads down. There wasn't a lot of talking. We looked at each other and laughed when we'd finished eating.

When the chef's assistant came in to collect the empty plates, Justine touched her arm. "Sweetheart, I'm going to need one of the cards for your restaurant. I'm planning to spend quite a bit of time there. This was some of the best jambalaya I've ever had."

The young lady said, "Of course. Thank you, ma'am," handed Justine a few business cards, and left the room with the plates.

Justine read the card. "Gregory! This restaurant is located in the French Quarter in New Orleans."

Greg put his arm across the back of my chair; he knew better than to touch me and leaned across me to smile broadly at Justine. "I know. I flew the chef and her assistant out to make this meal. You and Mom are always talking about how you wish you could have some food from home. I wanted it to be as good and authentic as possible."

I locked eyes with Kenny. He shook his head and chuckled.

Greg continued, "She made a restaurant-sized portion. So there'll be plenty left over. You should see if she'll give you the recipe before she leaves."

The assistant brought in two cakes for dessert: a green tea one for me and a chocolate one for Kenny. Greg, Grace, and Justine sang Happy Birthday and made a round of the "Happy Birthday" part. They all had such beautiful voices. We ate the cake, but they never stopped singing.

Grace led us over to the piano when we were done with the cake. She sat on the piano bench and started playing chords. I sat in a nearby chair. Greg sat next to me on the low ottoman beside the chair and leaned against the side. I held my ground and gave him a stern look. He understood the arm of the chair was his boundary. Justine sat next to Grace on the bench, and Kenny sat on a chair on the other side of the piano.

Grace said, "Justine, do you remember this song?"

She launched into a rendition of the song "Ode to Billie Joe" reminiscent of the way Nancy Wilson sang it. She took her time with it. Her notes flowed out like honey, round and full of overtones. When she was a few lines into the song, Justine picked up the acoustic bass guitar and added a bass line. She tapped out a rhythm in between the notes. Greg listened for a few lines more, then picked up one of the acoustic guitars and started playing a rhythmic guitar line with taps that added to the complexity of the rhythm. As Grace started the second verse, Kenny picked up the other acoustic guitar and rifted over the chords. It was jazzy and majestic. This was how they relaxed and played as a family. I felt a little sad it would probably be the last time I'd get to experience it. I'd miss that blessing. There was a moment of laughter when Grace finished.

Then Justine said, "I've got one for you." Grace scooted over to give Justine better access to the piano. Justine played chords for a minute to set the context. After she'd settled into a rhythmic, staccato set of chord changes, Justine sang a playfully sultry version of "Son of a Preacher Man." Grace listened and giggled. They were sharing a memory. Greg and Kenny added parts when they thought they understood Justine's approach. Within two bars, Grace shook her head and made them stop. She held her hand out for one of the acoustic guitars. Greg gave her his. Grace gestured for them to listen. First, she played the body of the guitar like a Brazilian pandeiro. It was a funky two-sided Samba based rhythm. Then she added chords that accented and countered the ones Justine played. Kenny laid down his instrument. We watched as Grace and Justine showed us how it was done.

When the song ended, Kenny said, "I'm going to come by the center so that we can talk that one through. I have some ideas about how I could explore that."

Grace said, "We can talk later, Son. You've got everyone's attention; what are you going to play now? Come strong or stay home."

Kenny laughed. "We just had an amazing meal from home. I want to play a song from home." He started to tap out a second line rhythm. Greg, Grace, and Justine added in the layers. They jammed with the rhythm for a while. As soon as Kenny sang two words, they recognized it and filled in all the parts of the song. It took me until halfway through the first verse to realize that they were playing "Hey Pocky Way" by the Meters. Kenny's voice was full of overtones, like his mother's. He sang the verses. We joined in on the chorus. After the song was done, they lingered in second line. As the energy from Kenny's song started to wane, everyone's focus turned to Greg.

He said, "I want to sing one of Sammi's favorite songs." He locked eyes with me. He sang the first few bars of "Try a Little Tenderness" by Otis Redding a cappella and then added a simple chord change underneath. When Greg sang, it was stunning. He was intrinsically musical. It flowed out of him. His voice also had all the overtones. He had an incredible amount of control. It felt like there was something else going on when he sang, something you couldn't quite put words to. Everyone just listened.

He finished the song by whispering "I love you" to me. I saw a flash of the Greg I'd come to love. He kissed my hand while I was still mesmerized. We all sat in silence for a few minutes.

I thought about when things were wonderful between us. Those were happy times. If there was a way to get back to that, would I stay? I did love hanging out with his family. I was going to miss it. I needed a few moments alone, so I excused myself.

I walked into the bathroom and closed the door behind me. I looked at myself in the mirror. I told my reflection, "He knows where all of your buttons are." I felt unhappy about where we'd ended up, but there was nothing I could do about it. I couldn't change who he was. I decided I wanted to go out on the terrace to get some fresh air. Everyone had dispersed when I walked out of the bathroom. Greg and Kenny were talking to the chef and her assistant in the kitchen. I walked out onto the terrace and saw Grace and Justine sitting on the swing talking at the far end.

I said, "I'm sorry. I didn't mean to interrupt. I didn't know that you guys were out here."

Grace responded, "You're not interrupting. Come join us."

I walked over and sat between them on the swing.

Grace took my hands in hers. "I can tell by the look in your eyes that you are done tolerating my son's whoring. I understand completely. I made the same decision when I left Keith."

My tears started flowing.

Grace continued, "I also know that you love him, Sammi. I watched you nurse him back to health. I can see it in your eyes, even now, after all of his temper tantrums."

"He was so different when we got to know each other."

Grace responded, "He came back to himself while he was recovering." She tapped Justine. "You remember how he was when he was little." She paused. "I thought my son had come to his senses. It warmed my heart so when he married you. I had high hopes. But in the end, he's his father's son. I did pretty well with Kenny, but, when they became successful, I lost Greg."

I said, "I'm sorry, Mama Grace."

Grace responded, "It makes me sad too, but I don't blame you. There's a part of Greg that knows he's messed up really badly."

Justine said, "You're leaving him, but you're not leaving us. You understand?"

Grace said, "You'll always be a daughter to me and a sister to Kenny, Sammi."

Justine added, "And you're my niece. Your mother is on the other coast. We're here for you."

They kissed me on either cheek at the same time. Having these two women mother me was deeply comforting. Being with them always made me feel at peace.

I hugged them. "Thank you."

Justine whispered, "Speak of the devil. He's lurking." In a louder voice, she said, "Stop trying to eavesdrop, Greg. Come on out here."

Grace whispered, "We'll let you two talk."

I walked over to the banister to look out into the backyard.

Greg came over and stood right beside me. "Are you okay?"

"Yeah, I am. Thank you for the song, Greg. It was beautiful. You should make an acoustic album of old love songs."

"Yeah." He was bracing for what I'd say next.

"I have a way that we could make this work."

"I'm listening."

"Basically, we resume the relationship as equals. I buy you out of half of the house. I pay half of all the expenses."

"Fine, I don't care about that."

"Okay. Going forward, we have an open relationship. Both of us can go out and sleep with whoever we want to whenever we want to."

He was silent.

I waited for a few minutes. "So?"

"You wouldn't sleep around like that, Sammi."

I inclined my head so he knew I was absolutely serious. "Do you really believe that, Greg?" I held his gaze.

It only took him a few seconds to think of Michael. His expression became wounded. "So you did fuck him. Was he the only one? How many times?"

"Do you really want details, Greg?"

"How could you, Sammi?"

"The same way you did, Greg."

"But it's different. You're a woman." He was actually serious.

"And you're a selfish, sexist, self-obsessed asshole, Greg. This is the twenty-first century. Admit it. You can't deal with it."

"It's just entertainment for me, Sammi. You're the only one I love."

"What's fair is fair."

His expression shifted to confusion.

"Admit it, Greg. You couldn't tolerate it. You don't want to be on the receiving end of that bullshit."

He closed his eyes and massaged the furrow between his brows. He whispered, "No."

"So you understand why I don't either." I waited.

He didn't look at me or say anything.

Walking away, I said, "Sign the papers."

He grabbed my arm and whispered, "Wait, wait."

I looked at the hand he had on my arm.

He held both of his hands in front of himself in a gesture of compliance. "Please, you can't leave me, Sammi."

I shrugged my shoulders and narrowed my eyes.

"You owe me."

My mind went back to the first time I saw him in the hospital after the accident. The left side of his body had been crushed. All the big bones were broken. A few of them were fractured badly enough they needed to be stabilized with metal rods. He was in so much pain.

A shiver ran up my spine. "You're right. There's no way that I can ever repay you for what I did. I put my whole life on hold to try and make it right, Greg. I did everything I could to put you back together. A part of me will always feel guilty about the accident."

Then I thought back to the tantrums that drove me away. I looked him in his eyes. "I can't take the brunt force of your anger, Greg. I tried. I tried because I felt like I deserved it. But I can't survive it, Greg. It would kill my spirit. It would kill me."

"I know, Sammi. I know. I'm working on it. I'm in therapy. Listen, I own the part that I played in ending up in Pete's car. If I hadn't been buying drugs, I wouldn't have been there. I understand why you did it, and I accept that you didn't intend for anyone to get hurt. I'm not as angry as I was, Sammi. I'm working through it."

"Not all of your anger was for me. But you aimed all of it at me."

"You're right. That's not going to happen again. I promise. Just give me a little more time. Don't leave." He swallowed. "You're the only woman I've ever known I could trust. I love you, Sammi. Please." He looked exposed and vulnerable.

I saw that tender place in him I loved, but I was done. I couldn't go back. "It's over, Greg. I just can't …"

He took my hand and kissed it. "Please."

I took a deep breath and put my hand on his heart. "There's no way forward for us. I'm sorry. I've gotta go."

I left Greg standing by the banister. The chef and her assistant were gone. Everyone else was standing in the kitchen.

I said, "It's time for me to go. I really enjoyed myself. I missed you guys."

Kenny said, "You know where we live, and you're welcome here anytime. Here's a care package to take home with you." He gave me a hug.

Grace said, "We'll walk out with you." She picked up her care package with one hand and threaded her arm through my arm. Grace, Justine, and I walked out the front door. The three of us confirmed the contact information we had for each other when we reached her car.

Keith, Greg's father, pulled into the driveway as Grace was settling into her car. Keith focused on her. The look on Keith's face made what was happening between Greg and me crystal clear. My personhood had nothing to do with it. And it was deeper than possession. It was more like I was embedded. He thought of me as an extension of himself, as if I weren't a whole person by myself. Perhaps, that was why he was so shocked that I'd decided to leave.

23

FINAL CHAPTER
WEDNESDAY, OCTOBER 11

THE FIRST THING I did when I woke up was look at my phone. Michael and I were supposed to talk the night before. I was worried about him because he didn't answer when I called or texted. He still hadn't. It was after 9 a.m.—most likely, he was up. I called him again. He still didn't answer. He was scheduled to fly to San Francisco at 1 p.m. I wished I had Paulo's number so I could call him because he would've known what was going on.

Wondering about Michael aside, I expected it to be a good day. Greg had finally accepted the reality that we were getting divorced. So things were moving forward. I'd taken the day off so I could go talk to my lawyer and meet Greg at 2 p.m. for lunch to discuss the settlement.

At 10 a.m., I decided it was time to get up and get a move on. I showered and ate.

I wanted some idea of where Greg's head was at. So I checked in with Kenny who said he was sad but accepting. I felt like I'd been running an endless marathon, and I could finally see the finish line in the distance.

My visit with Grant, my lawyer, was straightforward. In California, when you get divorced, each partner gets half. I didn't want half. My lawyer thought I was stupid, but since I was paying, he'd written riders for me to take a third of what was in the joint accounts. The properties we lived in were easily divided. He could have the house we'd shared and the house in New Orleans. I wanted the beach house, the house I lived in, and the brownstone in New York. We created a corporation around the investment properties. I'd take a third of the shares because Ari recommended the properties.

THE POP-UP COFFEE shop was less than a block away from my lawyer's office and right across from the courthouse. It was on the expansive plaza adjacent to the theater where Torus, Michael's company, performed when they were in LA. I glanced at my phone. It was almost 2 p.m. He was on his way to San Francisco.

Greg was waiting when I got there. He was sitting at a corner table in the middle of the plaza. The lunch crowd had thinned, and there was no one else sitting in that area. He was wearing jeans and a T-shirt. I could tell his hair was soaking wet because it was extra curly. He removed his shades as I sat at the table.

He looked discouraged. "Sammi."

"Hi, Greg." I had the impulse to say how are you, but it didn't feel right in that situation. We sat there and looked at each other for a moment.

He asked, "Do you want something to eat or drink?"

"I don't think I can eat right now. Some mint tea would be nice."

He got up and went to the counter.

I took out my notes. It was going to be a lot harder than I'd thought it would be. I hadn't factored in how he'd react. I expected to be dealing with his callous side, not his sensitive side. I hadn't considered how emotional I'd feel in response. I felt sadder than I'd expected. I guessed I was moving beyond all the anger I'd used to walk away. He returned with tea for both of us. He was braced and vulnerable.

I inhaled deeply and launched into it. "All I really want is to continue to be able to do my art without worrying about how I'm going to survive. I propose that I take a third of the cash in the joint accounts and a third of the shares for the LLC we created for investments. It's profitable and beneficial to both of us. So we can just leave it intact. Should the need arise for one or both of us to exit, the plan is on the table. Of the houses, I want the one that I live in, the beach house, and the brownstone in New York. Their cost is within the percentage of the money that I invested." I wasn't sure he was listening to me. He was staring off into space.

After I stopped talking, he said, "Whatever you want is fine, Sammi."

"What do you want?"

"I love you, Sammi. I don't want to end our marriage."

"I don't see a way for us to go forward, Greg. We don't want the same relationship."

He looked away. "I get that now."

"So what do you want from the settlement?"

He hunched his shoulders as he looked back at me. "I'll agree to whatever terms you set if you'll keep managing my finances."

"I can do that. But what if you get married again?"

"She'll have to deal with it." A tear escaped from his eye.

I had to fight back my own tears. He reached for my hands tentatively, and I put my hands in his.

He kissed them tenderly. "I've been completely unmoored since you left. I don't know how I'm going to survive without you."

"You're being dramatic. You were just fine before I came along."

"That was before I knew what it was like to have you in my life. It doesn't count."

"I don't know what to tell you."

"I miss you. I really miss you."

I could relate. I missed the man I'd married. I said, "There's a better match out there for you, Greg. Someone who wants to be taken care of. Someone who doesn't mind you sleeping around."

"Maybe."

I had to keep us moving. "So your only request is that I manage your finances?"

He focused on kissing my hands. "Yes."

"You don't want to look at this?" I offered him my notes.

"No. I trust you. Send the details to my lawyer."

"All that's left then is to agree to set the date."

"Then we're done?" He was looking off into the distance again.

"Yes, except for signing the papers."

He squeezed my hands and focused back on me. The Greg I married came out. "Can I have one last kiss as your husband?"

"Greg ..."

"It's just a kiss. The last one."

I looked at him.

He was completely present. "Kiss me and I'll agree to the date. You'll be rid of me forever."

I leaned in a little, and he closed the gap. His kiss was tender, respectful, and chaste. Being Greg, he had to test the boundaries. He continued to give me chaste little kisses until I said, "Greg."

He laughed and sat back far enough to look into my eyes. He rubbed his thumb across my cheek. "I love you, Sammi."

"I love you too, Greg. I'm sorry we didn't work out."

He didn't say anything and continued to rub my cheek.

"I should go." I squeezed his hand and released it to sit back.

"I'll walk with you."

I stood up and walked toward the exit of the coffee shop. He placed his hand on my lower back and walked with me. When we got to my car, we gave each other a hug and went our separate ways.

I got into my car. I sat there and breathed for a while. The only thing that was left was for us to sign the papers. My marriage to Greg was almost behind me. I didn't have to shepherd or negotiate anymore. A tension released in my core.

I looked at my phone. There was a missed call and a voice mail from Michael. He'd called while I was on my way to meet Greg. In his message, he said, "Hey. Sorry that I missed your calls last night. I got a little carried away doing shots with Alex. I left my phone at the pub. I'm taking a 5 p.m. flight to San Francisco. I want to talk to you. I should be available to talk after eight."

It was 3 p.m. Maybe I could catch him before he got on the plane to say hello. I called, but he didn't answer. He was probably in transit. I'd try again later.

I couldn't wait to tell someone how it went with Greg. Ari would be home from work, so I called her. Her phone rang six times.

I was just about to hang up when she said, "Hello."

"I was just about to hang up. If you're busy, call me later."

"My phone was buried in the sofa. I could hear it, but I couldn't find it. How did negotiations go?"

I smiled broadly. "He agreed to set the date. All that's left is to sign the papers."

"Yes! What did you ask for?"

"A third of what's in the joint accounts and the properties, like I planned."

"How did he respond?"

"He didn't care. He had two criteria."

"Which were?"

"The first criterion is that I, we, keep managing his money."

Ari huffed. "He's not stupid."

"No, Greg's definitely not stupid." I huffed to myself.

"The second?"

"He wanted me to kiss him one last time before he'd agree to set the date."

Ari growled. "He's so fucking manipulative."

"True. It's just ..."

"Just what?" She had zero tolerance for me sympathizing with Greg.

"Nothing. He was really sad about us ending it. It caught me off guard."

"Really?"

"Yeah. He was more like he was before he got well. I actually miss that version of him."

Ari asked, "You're sad about ending it?"

"No. That's not it. It's more that I'm sad that our original vision didn't work out."

"Whatever. Greg knows where all of your buttons are, Sammi. Did you talk to Mike last night?"

"No. He didn't answer when I called. He went out with his crew, got drunk, and lost his phone. He left me a voice mail this morning."

"When's the last time that you talked to him?"

"We had a short chat session last Thursday. I haven't spoken to him this week."

"How do you feel about that?" She wasn't down with me pushing aside my feelings for Michael either.

"I miss him, Ari," I confessed to placate her. "But I feel that it's good that we've gotten used to not being around each other. When's the last time you've talked to him?"

"Monday at lunchtime. Are you going to get back together with Mike now that Greg's agreed to sign the papers?"

"Greg would fixate. I have to keep him focused. Michael is off the table until the divorce papers are signed."

"And then?"

"I don't know. I need to cultivate a support system for myself out here, build out my life a little. We'll see."

"Okay." She sounded dubious.

"Okay, what?"

"You always become very responsible and practical when there are feelings that you don't want to deal with."

I bared my teeth at the phone. She knew the situation with Michael touched on my fears about relationships.

Ari took my silence as confirmation. "You know I'm right."

"How about we cross that bridge when we get to it?"

"Okay." That single word was full of sass.

"Okay." I gave it right back.

She laughed. "Like I said, you know I'm right."

I wasn't gonna win this. "Whatever. I'm gonna workout for a little while. I'll talk to you tomorrow."

She laughed again. "Bye, Sammi."

I snarled at the phone and hung up. I heard her laughing on the other end.

A workout was the perfect way to recover from anticipating dealing with Greg and worrying about Michael. I made my way to Amanda's studio. She responded more appropriately to my news. We went for a quick drink after she closed the studio. I stepped away to call Michael, but he didn't answer. They were probably having dinner. Hopefully, I'd get to talk to him soon.

I NEVER REALLY ESTABLISHED COMMUNICATION WITH Michael after he'd left for San Francisco. He responded when I texted him, but his responses were vague and disengaged. All my calls went to voice mail. I hadn't reached out in the past few days. Neither had he. I thought he'd just moved on and was trying to let me down easily. He was a good person.

He was better off without the drama I couldn't seem to escape. Ari would call bullshit if I told her that. She'd say that I was making a poor excuse to avoid how deeply he'd touched me.

24

NEXT PHASE
WEDNESDAY, OCTOBER 25

No one had ever worn down my wards like Michael did. Worn down didn't really describe what had happened. It was more like they didn't apply to him, like he was standing next to me, checking them out, from the moment I met him.

I wasn't a believer. The love thing never worked out. Well, not 99 percent of the time. I knew I'd always love him with all my heart. I was so in love with him. I believed he felt the same about me at that time. It wouldn't last though. He wouldn't be able to sustain it. I thought of what my mom went through with my father and the guy that came afterward. I thought of how my father's brothers were assholes, just like him. All of them cheated on their wives and bragged about it. I thought about how I'd let Ryan break my heart in college. I thought of all the men I'd dated since then, most recently, Pete and Greg. I thought of the men Ari had gotten serious about, most recently, Matt. I thought of Val and her list of "Robbies." I had endless examples of that truth. Men weren't made that way. They always had their foot in the door. I didn't want to withstand Michael breaking my heart. I knew I could get together with him and make some incredible memories. Still, it would only be a matter of time. I didn't want to feel that pain.

My phone broke me out of my reverie. My friend Gene from graduate school texted me, "I like it. Call me when you have time to talk."

I'd been sitting in my home office with the intention of making plans for future projects. Since I'd almost finished working on the indie flick, I was considering whether to take on some commercials or to appease my mother and take a trip home. I was leaning toward the commercials. I called him back immediately.

He picked up after a few rings. "Sammi! How's it going?"

"Even better if you decide to work on that series with me."

"I really like the premise. I have some ideas of some formats that could work. With the right writers and cast, this could be phenomenal."

"I'm hearing a yes."

"You always had good ears. Have they set any dates yet?"

"Preproduction should start in January."

He responded, "Great. I'll put that in my schedule."

I did a little victory dance. "Perfect. Let's hang out. I don't know many people in LA."

"I can fix that. I'm back in town next week. I'll call you."

"Looking forward to it. Talk to you then."

"Okay. Bye."

"Bye, Gene."

My plan to establish a network of friends was going swimmingly. I was hanging out with Amanda and Cam more often, and it looked like I was going to get Gene back into my life.

The thought of Amanda reminded me I'd planned to work out today. It was just after 1 p.m. This was a good time because there wouldn't be anyone using the machines. My phone buzzed again as I was getting ready. It was my lawyer's office.

I answered and a professional woman on the other end said, "Hello, may I speak to Ms. Harris?"

"Speaking."

"Hello. Ms. Harris, I'm calling from MJR and Associates. Mr. Roberts would like for you to know that Mr. Albert contested the settlement. Per the request by Mr. Albert's lawyer, Judge Garcia will mediate the settlement agreement and issue a final judgment in her chambers on Monday, December 4." The fact that Grant, Mr. Roberts, hadn't called me himself meant that there were no big contestations. Greg was just stalling.

I said, "Thank you! Thank you very much!" A smile came across my face. In a month and a week, my marriage to Greg would be history.

She responded, "You're welcome, Ms. Harris. Have a good day." She hung up.

I called Ari immediately. She answered, "What's up?" She was working. I could tell she was distracted.

"The final judgment for the divorce will be delivered on December 4!"

"When did you find out?"

"A few minutes ago."

"Congratulations! This means we have to celebrate. Have you told Mike?" She was coming to visit, or check on me, this weekend. I was looking forward to it.

"No. I've stopped texting him, Ari. I think he may be moving on. I don't want to bother him."

"The two of you are going to send me to an early grave. Both of you are full of shit. Tell him. You know you want to. I gotta go to a meeting. I'll talk to you later. We need to make plans to party." She hung up on me.

I had to report to Sylvia. She'd been threatening to make calls to speed up the date-setting process. She was at work. I'd be able to get away with a text.

I texted, "Good news. The final settlement date's set for December 4."

She responded with emojis: a smiling face, clapping hands, and a kiss.

AMANDA WAS TEACHING a class when I arrived at the studio. When I finished my workout, she was gone, so I couldn't tell her the news. Ari was right. The person I really wanted to tell was Michael. I drove around aimlessly for a while, contemplating whether I should bother him. Naturally, I ended up in his neighborhood. Ultimately, I gave in to what I really wanted.

I texted him, "Are you busy?"

He responded immediately, "No. I'm just chilling at home."

I asked, "Do you have plans?" I didn't want to walk into an awkward situation.

"No."

"Do you mind if I drop by?"

He took a minute to respond. "Sure," was his reply, vague and noncommittal.

I didn't care. I wanted to see him. I replied, "Good." I parked in his driveway and knocked on his front door.

He unlocked the door, but he didn't open it all the way. I had to stifle a smile. I was excited to see him and walked inside. He was standing about twelve feet away from me, and he looked pained, like he did that night in the hotel in New York. I could feel tension coming off his body. He could've pounced at any second. Something horrible must've happened. I locked the door behind myself.

I reached for him. "Michael? What's going on?"

He turned away from me, and I hesitated. Maybe it was none of my business. Then instinct took over. I loved him. I was going to try to support him if I could. I followed him to his kitchen island, where he'd taken a seat on one of the tall stools. I sat on the stool next to his. He was looking down. I couldn't see his eyes, but he pursed his lips. It seemed like he was holding his breath. I reached out tentatively. When he didn't stop me, I put my hand on his chin so I could turn his face toward mine. In the same instant, he grabbed my hand. It felt like he was going to pull it away from his face, but he didn't. He held my hand to his face instead.

Gently, I turned his face so I could see his eyes. At first, he didn't look back at me. When he did, the pain in his eyes was excruciating. He winced after a few moments. I couldn't stand to see him like that. I wished I could make whatever had hurt him go away, so I gave in to my need to nurture him. I kissed both of his eyes, one at a time. His body quivered as I did. I looked at him again with my forehead almost touching his.

"Can you tell me what's wrong?"

He whispered, "You've settled things with Greg?" The question was barely audible.

What did Greg have to do with what was going on with him? Had he been talking to Greg? I was confused. "Greg? What does—"

Before I could finish my question, he kissed my bottom lip, then my top lip. The feeling of his mouth was sweet and tender. I missed touching him, kissing him so much. I mirrored the caress of his lips. He purred softly. My whole body tingled in response. I had to fight to keep my balance. It felt like he was going to pull away, but he filled my mouth with his tongue instead. I relaxed to let him explore and reveled in the pleasure of the connection. I wanted to be filled with him. I sucked his tongue until he moaned. Then I explored his mouth. I felt his face soften and almost smile. I paused to enjoy the moment. He caressed my tongue with his, and I responded in kind. The kiss deepened. I let the world drop away. The only thing I was aware of was kissing him.

He pulled back, panting. "Can we not talk right now?"

The look on his face was harrowing. If he needed to be kissed and held at this moment, I could do that. "Of course." I didn't know where we were in terms of boundaries right then, but I wanted him to know how deeply I was there for him. I loved him.

We paused in silence for a moment. I was standing in front of him. He had his hands on the sides of my face, and I had my hands on the sides of his. He rested his forehead on mine.

I closed my eyes and kissed his nose. Nurturing him was second nature. He wrapped me in a tight embrace. I pulled his face to mine and kissed him wildly, putting my arms around him and holding him as tightly as I could. Our connection took over. I could feel his erection growing as we started to wind together. I wanted to be closer to him. He was still sitting on the island stool. So I put my leg up on top of his and pulled myself up, using his shoulders with the intention of straddling him on the chair.

He chuckled. It was a delightful sound. He mumbled, "Whoa," without interrupting our kiss. His hands slid down my back, over my ass, to my thighs. He lifted me as he stood up, and I wrapped my legs around him.

I felt him walking, but I had no idea where we were going. I knew we were in his bedroom when my legs made contact with the bed as he sat down. I straddled him, and he leaned back so I could grind my sex onto his. We stopped kissing. At first, we both let our heads hang back and enjoyed the sensation for a few minutes. I wanted to be closer. I lifted the hem of his T-shirt. He helped me pull it over his head. He'd gotten leaner since the season started. The muscles of his shoulders, arms, and abdomen were more defined than they were when we'd gone to the beach. He was beautiful, inside and out. He slipped his hands under the bottom of my dress that was pooled at my hips. He ran his hands up my body with the dress in tow. I felt him undo my bra as I finished taking the dress off. I pushed my breasts into his hands as they found their way back to the front of my body. I loved the way it felt to be touched by him. His body rippled. He wasn't tormented anymore. He was there, in the moment, with me. He trailed his fingers down my abdomen and massaged my clitoris through my underwear. Yes, I wanted to touch him too. I unzipped his shorts and pulled back his briefs. His cock was beautiful. I wanted to caress him, but he was pulling me toward an orgasm. He smiled a little. He knew he had me off-balance. I smiled back. He slipped his hand inside my underwear to intensify his touch. He sat up and circled my nipples with his tongue. I steadied myself with his shoulders as he intensified the sensation again by slipping two fingers inside of me while continuing to massage my clitoris. I came hard a few minutes later.

I felt him lay me down on his bed. He reached into the drawer of his nightstand and retrieved a condom. Reality surfaced. He'd been with someone else. He rolled on the condom and eased into me while I was pondering. Having him inside me felt so good my whole body quaked. I couldn't think about him being with someone else at that moment. He'd done nothing wrong. We weren't together. He moved his hips slowly and more tentatively than usual. He wasn't making eye contact like he usually did. His eyes were closed, and his breathing was shaky. I put my hands on his shoulders. When I tried to move with him, I realized I couldn't move at all because he had me pinned. I relaxed to feel how he was moving. He wasn't doing the "waltzy" thing he usually did, but it still felt heavenly. I felt myself mounting again. I wanted to move.

I said, "Michael—"

He kissed me passionately before I could finish the sentence and increased his pace. My abdomen clenched. He stopped kissing me as I came undone around him.

I wanted to do the same to him. "Michael—"

He interrupted me again. "Sammi, please. You promised that we wouldn't talk." I couldn't see his face, but his voice was full of anguish. I wrapped my arms around him and kissed his shoulder.

He opened his eyes. He was purring with a strange mixture of pleasure and pain as he released into orgasm. He cried out as it overtook him. I could feel he was no longer completely present. I held him tightly as he regained his equilibrium. He eased out of me and sat up to deal with the condom. His whole body was tense.

I touched his arm. "What's going on, Michael? Talk to me."

He didn't look at me. He put his hand on top of mine for a minute. Then he abruptly grabbed his shorts, walked into his bathroom, and closed the door.

I was confused. I got dressed. Then I looked around to try to get some idea of what was going with him. Only his side of the bed was unmade. So whoever he'd been with, he hadn't brought them home. Yet, if he hadn't brought them home, then there was no way that things could've gotten intense enough to elicit the strong reaction that I was seeing.

He'd mentioned Greg. Had Greg contacted him?

The bathroom door opened. He was wearing his shorts. His eyes were cold. He said, "I need you to leave now, Sammi."

I responded, "Michael! We just made love. What the fuck is going on?"

He looked at me. He was a million miles away. "Please."

The iciness in his eyes unnerved me. So this was how he was going to fuck everything up. "Fuck you too, Michael." I stormed out and slammed his front door as hard as I could.

I RODE the wave of my anger home. When it ebbed, I realized I was more concerned than angry. I wished he'd told me what was going on. I didn't even get to tell him about the date being set. It was 6 p.m., so Ari would be watching television. I called her.

She answered with, "Congratulations again, Sammi. You've done it. The Greg saga's almost done. How did it go with Michael?"

I laughed. "You should ask me if I told him before you ask how'd it go."

She huffed. "Life is short. Breath is precious. So?"

"Seriously, I went over to his house to tell him, but I never got a chance to. He's in a very strange place. I have no idea what's going on with him."

"What did he say?"

"He asked me had I settled things with Greg, but he wouldn't let me answer the question."

She responded, "That's strange."

"Right."

"Why's he asking questions about Greg?" We said it at the same time.

I continued, "It makes me wonder if Greg contacted him somehow."

"Did you ask him?"

"No, he wouldn't let me. He didn't want to talk."

"If you didn't talk, what did you do?"

"We had sex. Then he asked me to leave."

Ari squeaked, "What?" She paused. "You're going to have to slow down and tell me what happened, like I'm in first grade. I'm totally confused."

"You and me both. I texted him. He didn't refuse my request to visit him. It was clear that he was in a lot of pain the moment he opened the door. I tried to console him. I kissed his eyes, and I asked what was wrong. He asked about Greg, then kissed me before I could answer. One thing led to another, and we ended up in his bed. He was emotionally available while we were doing foreplay, but he shut down completely as soon as we started to have intercourse. He retreated into his bathroom right after he came. When he walked back into his bedroom, he asked me to leave. His expression was tormented. His eyes were cold and icy."

"That was a little more detail than a first grader would want, but we can roll with it. I don't know if I really want to know this, but did you come or was he just on the take?"

"He made me come twice. He—"

She interrupted, "Okay! You've answered the question."

"I just wanted to tell you that he has moved on. He's definitely slept with someone else."

"Did he tell you that?"

"No."

"So how do you know?"

"He used a condom. He's never done that before."

She screamed, "Way too much information! I didn't need to know that! Now it's in my brain, and I'll never be able to get it out." She took a couple of deep breaths. "What did you do after he asked you to leave?"

"I yelled at him and stormed out. I'm worried about him, but his behavior was fucked up."

"I agree. That's really strange, Sammi. I'll try to talk to him."

"Hopefully, he'll talk to you. What is it about me and men and drama?"

"In my experience, if you're in a relationship with a man, you're bound to have some drama at some point."

I inhaled. "Enough about Michael. What are we going to do to celebrate?"

"I took next Thursday and Friday off. I booked a flight that gets me there late Wednesday night."

"You're going to really enjoy hanging out with Amanda and Cam. I'm back in touch with Gene too. I invited him to work on a series with me, and he said yes."

"You've been busy building a support system."

"Yes, I have. This time has been very productive in that way. Thanks for talking me down, Ari."

"Anytime."

It was early still. I'd think about Michael for the rest of the evening if I didn't do something fun. I texted Cam and Amanda and suggested an impromptu dinner. Cam invited us to have dinner at her place and insisted on cooking so she could use up the food in her fridge before it went bad. Her taste as a decorator was eclectic. She had a talent for pulling apparently unrelated items and styles into a unified, beautiful whole. Her talent for pulling odd things together extended to her cooking. She made us a delicious meal out of a set of ingredients I would have never put together. I continued to sample long after I'd gotten full.

On the way back home, I went over my visit with Michael in my head. I got stuck on how he wouldn't let me move and how he was moving. He wasn't doing that swivel "thingy." The memory of his lesson on the difference between date sex and relationship sex came back. I remembered him saying, "This is how you fuck while dating." He was doing that same simple in and out motion he was doing today. My anger rose again. He date-fucked me and then kicked me out! I was so glad that I'd yelled at him.

25

PLAZA

THURSDAY, NOVEMBER 2

I was sitting at my kitchen island thinking about the remaining tasks for the film I would complete the following week. Ari had come in from New York after I went to sleep the night before. She was getting dressed. I knew she was going to interview me about what was going on between Michael and me first thing.

She walked into the kitchen and gave me a big hug. "I finally get to say congratulations in person. Good morning."

"Good morning. Thank you."

She searched the shelf where the coffee should've been.

"There's no coffee and no breakfast food. We have to go out for breakfast. Want some tea?"

She gave me an exasperated look. "I want to go see art and talk. Let's find a place near one of the museums." She looked at me sideways.

Before she could start her inquisition, I answered, "No, I still haven't tried to get in touch with Michael since last week. Like I've told you, it's his move."

She squinted at me. "You're still angry?"

"Yes, I am."

"I can't say I blame you." She hunched her shoulders. "I'm hungry. How close are you to being ready to leave?"

"I'm ready now." I looked at my phone. It was almost 10 a.m. Michael should be in rehearsal until 1 p.m. "Speaking of your brother, they've released photos from that shoot that he did while we were in New York. I've seen at least two billboards. And I think there's a spread in one of the fashion magazines. One of the girls at Amanda's studio had a copy."

"Do you have a copy?"

I put my hands in a prayer position and pursed my lips. "It's hidden underneath my bed. How did you know?" I rolled my eyes at her. "No, I don't have a copy of the magazine," I said as dryly as I could.

She raised one eyebrow and smirked. "I guess, technically, you don't need one."

I gave her the finger.

She smirked again. "My. Point. Exactly."

I gave her a hard look. She met my gaze and held it. Then, we were in a staring contest. I crossed my arms. She never won those.

After thirty seconds, she said, "Get your stuff together so that we can leave."

"Trying to distract me won't help you win this volley."

A giggle that she couldn't suppress made her blink. She gave me the finger.

I closed my computer. "Today, we're riding in Spencer. First stop in our celebration, the place where I got Greg to agree to the divorce. Their breakfast menu's really good."

She looked down at her outfit.

"What?"

"Just making sure I want to wear what I have on in Spencer."

"You're the silliest person I know. Let's go."

As we approached my Spider, she gave me puppy dog eyes.

I laughed and shook my head. "Okay. You can drive." I threw her the keys. "I'll show you one of the billboards."

"Oh, joy! I get to ogle my brother."

Ari pulled to the side of the street when we got in front of the billboard. It was a giant picture of Michael and Noelle. She was topless and wearing jeans with the top button undone. Her arms were conveniently hiding her breasts. He was also shirtless and wearing jeans with the top button undone. They were both soaking wet, with beads of water glistening on their skin. Michael had his hands around her forearms. They were looking into each other's eyes. Their lips were slightly parted, like they were about to kiss or had just finished kissing.

Ari said, "That's a really steamy picture. The video must be really hot."

"I get how it can be seen like that." If I couldn't read his eyes, I was sure that I'd have a pang in my heart right then.

"What do you mean?"

"It's obvious to me that he's not turned on at all. He looks irritated."

Ari looked back at the billboard. "I don't want you to expand on that statement at all." She merged back into traffic, and, together, we laughed out loud.

When we got to the plaza, I checked my phone again. It was 10:15 a.m. The coast should be clear. We bought our food. As we turned to find seats, I said, "This is where Greg agreed to end it." I looked out over the tables.

My breath caught. Michael was sitting at one of the tables with another woman. They were sitting on the same side of the table. It was obvious from the way they were talking they knew each other well. They weren't touching, but they were in each other's personal space. She was probably the person he'd slept with.

She was dazzling. She had flat black hair and medium brown skin with big green eyes and full, pouty lips. She looked like she had Persian or Moorish ancestry. She was obviously also a dancer. He'd probably started dating her.

I said, "We should go," and turned on my heel.

Ari asked, "What?" She quickly located Michael. "Oh, no you don't. You said that you were okay with him moving on. This is where the rubber meets the road."

"Let's just go."

She waved at him. "It's too late. He's already seen us." She walked toward them. I let her get far in front of me before I followed her. She took the seat across from Michael. I sat next to her, across from the woman.

Ari spoke first. "Good morning, Mike. How's it going?" She took a sip of her coffee.

Michael responded, "Good. You?" He kept his eyes on Ari.

Ari said, "I'm good." She opened her sandwich and took a bite. I looked at Ari too.

Ari looked from Michael to me, then back to him. She inhaled deeply and extended her hand to the woman. "Hi. I'm Ari, his sister, and this is my friend, Sammi." She nodded toward me.

The woman shook Ari's hand. "I'm Neva. Mike and I dance together from time to time. Nice to meet you, Ari." Neva extended her hand to me.

I played it cool. I smiled and gave her a firm handshake. "Nice to meet you, Neva."

Neva responded, "Same here."

I had a little momentum, so I kept it going. I looked at Michael and said, "Morning, Michael."

He looked at me. His eyes were distant. "Morning, Sammi."

I looked at Ari. This was her idea. I was letting her lead the charge. I couldn't eat. So I focused on sipping my tea.

Ari looked from me to Michael again. She raised her eyebrows and looked at Neva. "Are you dancing with Torus now?"

I decided that the best way to look normal was to look at whoever was talking with as much interest as I could muster.

Neva responded, "No, I've been working with the performing arts program at UCLA. Do you live here?" She pinched off a piece of the muffin sitting between her and Michael.

Ari responded, "No, I live in New York." She was eating her sandwich in stride.

I snuck a glance toward Michael before Neva responded. He was looking at me. We locked eyes. I pretended he was Greg and tried to keep my expression blank. He had that same pained, anticipatory look in his eyes from last week. I wondered what was going on with him.

Neva said, "I love New York. I need to look for a job dancing there." She ate another piece of the muffin.

Ari said, "New York is a great place for the arts. I'm not so sure it's easy on the artists."

Michael shifted in his seat. He removed his cell phone from his pocket, looked at it, and laid it face down on the table. He clasped his hands and rested his forearms on the table, with the cell phone in the middle. He closed his eyes for a few seconds and looked off into the distance. I shifted my gaze to Neva so that it didn't seem like I was staring at Michael.

Neva asked, "So you aren't in the arts?"

Ari answered, "No. I'm in finance. How long have you known my brother?"

Neva looked at Michael from the corner of her eye. He was still staring off into the distance.

She answered, "About five years, I think." Neva smiled fondly and ran her hand along his forearm and let it come to rest with her fingers between the thumb and fingers of his right hand.

My heart skipped a beat. Reality bit. The best cover I could think of was to take a sip of my tea and look at Ari. Michael moving on hurt. I didn't want him to go. I felt myself getting emotional. I couldn't give in to my feelings there, then. I had to think of something else. I looked at the table where I'd gotten Greg to agree on the settlement and divorce. That was a victory. I closed my eyes so I could focus on that completely. I sipped my tea and hoped it looked like I was really enjoying it.

I looked at Ari when I opened my eyes. Thankfully, she was taking the last bite of her sandwich. I was ready for this encounter to end. I counted to ten slowly, then finished my tea. I stood and picked up my sandwich.

I said to Ari, "We need to move on to our next destination." I forced a smile and said, "It was very nice meeting you, Neva. It was good to see you again, Michael." I looked Ari in her eyes and dared her to counter me.

Ari was clearly amused. She looked at Michael. "Is six thirty a good time for dinner?"

Michael nodded. It seemed he was happy the encounter was ending as well.

Neva said, "It was nice to meet the two of you. I hope to see you again."

I smiled again, then turned my back and walked away at a slow, measured pace. Watching Michael move on was hard, *really* hard. My eyes filled with tears.

Ari caught up with me easily. "Are you alright?"

I started walking a little faster. "I just want to get back to my car. I can't talk about what just happened out here."

She said, "Okay," and fell into step.

I slid into the passenger seat of my car. For the first time in a while, I cried about breaking up with Michael. Ari reached into the glove compartment and took out the tissues. She sat there and let me cry. The wave of emotion passed after a few minutes. I took a breath and said, "I don't want him to move on."

"I know you don't."

"I don't want him to wait either."

"That's not true. You do want him to wait. You guys need to talk to each other."

"I tried to talk to him. He wasn't willing to talk. And he date-fucked me. And threw me out."

"You went over there to tell him about the court date. You had no intention of telling him how you really feel."

"He knows that I love him. Saying that over and over when there's a big possibility that we're not getting back together is senseless."

"He doesn't know that you want him to wait for you. If you told him, I have no doubt that he'd do it."

"That feels like too much to ask. I can't do that."

She nodded in concession. "That's fair. I respect that. At least be honest with yourself and with me."

"I can do that. I think that he's better off moving on."

She huffed at me. "Why?"

"If we were together, I can't see a way for Michael not to end up colliding with Greg. I have also put him on a collision course with Pete."

She leaned in. "Bullshit, Sammi. Though Greg deserves to get his ass kicked, you'll be divorced from him in a month. So that's fast becoming history. And, if I know Mike at all, Pete has an ass-kicking in store, whether or not you're still in the picture."

I interrupted her. "It's not bullshit. First, you can't deny that Michael would end up kicking Greg's ass. I have to concede the point about Pete. There's nothing I can do to stop that from happening now."

She shook her head. "Okay. You're probably right about Mike fighting with Greg."

I added, "I wouldn't have been able to get Greg to settle if I were still dating Michael."

"I agree it makes sense to placate Greg until the divorce is finalized on December fourth. However, that's not an argument for why Mike is better off moving on. You're still evading the core of what's going on with you. Stop trying to shit me, Sammi. Are you really going to let what happened in the past derail your love life?"

I wanted to growl at her. She was going to make me admit it out loud. "When you put it that way, no." I took a deep breath. "I need time to be with myself before I settle into another relationship."

She crossed her arms. "That's also fair. Continue."

I was silent. I didn't really know how to express what I felt.

Ari waited patiently.

"The way I feel about him terrifies me. I'm not ready to take on the risk. We both know that epic love always fails. I don't want to experience that. I don't want to feel that kind of pain. I need to feel safe for a little while."

She hugged me. "Love doesn't always fail. My parents are still happily married. They've been married for thirty-two years."

"That's your one example, Ari. They're an exception, one out of a trillion."

"For all you know, you and Mike could be an exception too. You won't know if you don't try."

"I don't know if I can take it if—when—he breaks my heart."

"If he goes that route, you'll survive it. And you'll be better off for having tried. It's also possible that you could get tired of him."

"I feel like I have a reprieve. We only dated a month, and we ended things amicably. Look at how difficult it is to be around each other. Can you imagine what would happen if we broke up because of a disagreement? You'd have to choose between me and him. You don't need that. Nope."

She looked at me incredulously and almost laughed. "Things would be fine if you'd actually talk to each other."

"I can love him as a friend."

She shook her head. "Have it your way, but you should know, whether you want him to or not, he's waiting for you."

"No, he isn't. He's clearly dating Neva."

Ari laughed. "No, he's not. I won't say that he's not doing her. But if he is, it's just for kicks. I got the feeling that the same's true for her. You need to talk to him. You need to talk to each other truthfully."

"But—"

"But nothing. You weren't really looking, Sammi. You have no idea what actually happened."

"You're right. I was focused on my tea, trying to look as normal as I could."

"I know."

"So much for the celebration."

She shook her head. "Uh-uh. The day's not done."

"Well, that was where I convinced Greg to settle." My stomach growled loudly.

"Eat your breakfast. Let's go look at some art. I think it is a good idea to leave this part of town."

I realized I was starving. I had to concentrate to keep myself from swallowing the first few bites of my sandwich whole. I was finishing up when we pulled into the parking lot for the museum.

Ari looked at her phone and laughed out loud. "Mike just canceled dinner. He doesn't want to deal with what's happening between the two of you any more than you do."

I kept quiet. She was talking *at* me more than *to* me. I could hear the exasperation in her tone.

She closed her eyes and seethed for a moment. She mumbled under her breath and huffed and opened her eyes. "I should press, but I'm not going to do it. You two are adults. Well, in terms of age, anyway, and you're not going to drive me insane. It's a big waste of time and energy but have it your way." She was still talking mostly to herself.

She texted a short response back to him. She looked at me and said, "I'm having breakfast with Mike on Sunday. He's going to take me to the airport, that is, if he doesn't cancel again."

I attempted a change in mood. "So we're free to have fun until then?"

She smiled. "Exactly."

"Track? Driving would be more captivating than looking at art."

She screamed. "*Yesss!* Driving fast is good for the soul."

We spent the afternoon at the racetrack doing laps in Spencer.

SINCE ARI WAS NO LONGER GOING to dinner with Michael that evening, she joined me in my evening of relaxation and spa at home. To make it a party, I invited Cam and Amanda to join us for spa and whatever else the evening brought. It was late afternoon, and we'd just settled into my jacuzzi. The tiles were white marble, and all the fixtures were silver. The outer walls were made of tinted glass. There were blinds that could be closed when it was dark outside.

Cam looked around. "Girl, this is a lot of house. I guess being married to Greg Albert has its perks."

I looked at Ari. Talking about good fortune and privilege was always such a delicate needle to thread. I responded, "It's true that Greg lives in the lap of luxury. You should see his estate. However, I have to take a page from your book. Greg doesn't deserve the credit for me getting this house. I owe it to my own hard work and good timing, which afforded me an incredible deal, and my best friend, Ari, who found this house and helped me get it."

Cam reassessed Ari and me. "Well, I really like it. It feels so inviting and homey. You've got good taste, Ari."

Ari held up her water bottle. "True that."

They tapped water bottles.

Amanda said, "I remember you from Atlanta, Ari. I can't believe that I didn't make the association between you and Michael."

Ari said, "That's right. You went to the same dance school when you were kids. That's crazy to think about. What was he like?"

Amanda pondered the question. "Reserved. Polite. He was an alpha male, even then."

I thought of how distant he was last week when he asked me to leave.

Ari asked, "How old was he?"

Amanda responded, "Eight or nine. He was a good dancer then too."

Cam said, "The resemblance is astonishing. Does he seem like a brother to you now?"

"At times. We're still getting to know each other."

Amanda grunted. "Have you seen his new photo spread?"

Cam responded, "Oh my god! *Yes.* He's not nine anymore!"

Ari rolled her eyes. "I haven't seen the whole spread, but Sammi showed me one of the billboards this morning. It's pretty steamy."

Amanda said, "Steamy? Uh-uh, more like solar."

Cam responded, "Solar! Yes. Cause hot is too cool."

Ari inhaled deeply and shook her head.

I smiled to myself. They had no idea how Michael looked when he was solar. I wondered how he and I had ended up in such a strange place that he couldn't even talk to me. For some reason, they all looked at me at the same time.

I gestured. "What?"

Amanda answered, "You look haunted."

I responded, "It's fine. We ran into Michael this morning. He was with someone else. I'm having to deal with the reality of ending my relationship with him."

Amanda said, "Sorry, Sammi. We're being insensitive. We can change the subject."

I asked Cam, "Is there any place to dance tonight?"

Cam answered, "There are a few places."

Ari said, "I didn't think that people danced in LA."

Amanda said, "You have to know where to look. Cam's spinning tomorrow. You guys should come."

I said, "Not to put you on the spot, Cam, but I have been raving about you to Ari. I'd love it if she could hear you herself."

Cam said, "Of course. I'll put you on my list. That reminds me. Kenny Albert sent me an email. He's going to try and come tomorrow night. I have a meeting scheduled with him next week. Thanks for the introduction."

Ari asked me, "Do you think Kenny will bring Greg?"

"I'll ask him if he's told Greg. If he hasn't, I'll ask him not to. You're going to like Kenny, Cam."

Ari added, "Yeah. Kenny's a really good person. He's definitely the better brother."

Amanda said, "Hmmm, sounds like you like him. Did you ever date him?"

Ari responded, "No. There's no spark."

I said, "Which brings us back to tonight. What's the plan for tonight?"

They all looked at me again.

I said, "Listen, I'm going through challenging times. I need to dance."

We did a few more hot-cold revolutions in the spa. Then we put on jeans and T-shirts and enjoyed an evening of dinner and dancing.

***

IT WAS 9 a.m. Ari and I were sitting at my kitchen island, half asleep. We were dragging because we'd been out dancing for the past three nights. Amanda and Cam were with us the first two. They'd bailed last night. We ended up hanging with Gene instead. Ari hit it off with Cam and Amanda, just like I thought she would. I hadn't heard from Michael at all since we ran into him in the plaza. Fortunately, I hadn't had any down time since then. So I hadn't had time to dwell on thinking about him.

26

———

SAMMI GROUNDS
SUNDAY, NOVEMBER 5

ARI SAID, "I'm having so much fun. I wish I didn't have to go back today."

"It's most certainly been a good time. Why don't you stay 'til Wednesday?"

"I have too many meetings. It would take me 'til Wednesday to reschedule all of them. What are you doing next?"

"I'm in between projects. I'm finishing up production on the indie flick this week. Most likely, I'll stick to doing commercials until the series starts next January."

"Come to New York for a while."

"I'll think about it. Are you going to Atlanta for Christmas? My mom wants me to come home."

"I don't know. My parents want me to come home too."

"Maybe we should plan a destination Christmas."

"Okay, Greg. We could charter a jet to pick up everyone, go all out."

I swatted her playfully. "Funny. I'm trying to think of a way to keep Sylvia entertained so she doesn't interrogate me to death."

"She worries about you."

"I know. Given some of my choices, she has good reason."

"Are you ever going to forgive yourself for trusting Pete? He ran a good game. I thought he was a good guy too."

"I'm trying. It's hard because the consequences of that mistake seem to be ever present." I was thinking about Greg's accident. I felt that the rape was behind me.

"Have you heard from Mike?"

I shook my head. "I don't expect to."

"You guys are costing me years of my life."

"You should be happy that we're leaving each other alone then."

"Believe me, I'm getting there." Her tone was dry. She seemed pissed at both of us. "Well, I guess I should prepare to spend the morning with my brother."

"I miss you already."

"What are you going to do?"

"I need to call Sylvia. Then I'm going to crash."

"Other than spending time with Mike, crashing's my only plan too." She looked at her phone. "I'm starting to run late. I should get going."

I pouted. "Okay."

She went to her room to get her bag. Then she called a car. She said, "You can do commercials in New York."

"I know. If I'm going to stay out here in LA, I need to continue cultivating my network. I have to be here to do that."

"You're doing a good job so far. I really like Cam and Amanda. There are no words to describe Cam's skills as a DJ. Kenny was pretty blown away. I really enjoyed partying with him. It was good to see Gene too."

Her car pulled up in the driveway, and the driver tooted his horn.

"Thanks for the celebration. Love you."

"Love you too."

We hugged, and she was off.

I DECIDED to call Sylvia while I was in a good mood from Ari's visit. My phone was ringing when I picked it up. It was Greg. What could he possibly want? The quicker I started to deal with it, the quicker it would be dealt with.

I answered, "Good morning, Greg. How are you?"

"Hey, Sammi. Can we talk?"

He had a new proposal. I could feel it in my bones. I inhaled deeply. "Sure. What's up?"

"I don't want us to get divorced, Sammi. I've been thinking. Maybe I could go to therapy to stop sleeping around." He sounded sad.

He was serious about not wanting a divorce. He'd never offered this before. I felt a little sad too, but I couldn't stay married to him. "I appreciate the offer, Greg, but we both know that you don't want that. It'll just be another thing for you to be angry at me about. Ultimately, that line of action won't work out."

"I'm willing to try."

"It would just be prolonging the inevitable. Sleeping around is part of how you define who you are. I've never wanted to change who you are. I'm not going to ask that of you."

"I know, Sammi. I've worked through my anger at you. I can't blame only you. I chose to be there. I played a part too. Maybe there's a way for me to work through wanting to sleep around."

"It's not going to work. Your whoring is only one of our problems. There's the issue of your tantrums. I believe that you've forgiven me, but you're deeply angry. I can't withstand the force of it, especially when you're high."

He whispered, "Don't give up on me, Sammi."

"We don't work. We want different relationships. That truth doesn't make either of us wrong. There's someone out there who won't mind you whoring around, Greg, someone who doesn't attract your anger."

"I can't trust anyone like I can trust you." He was reaching for my buttons.

"You'll be able to trust that person. It's not me. I'm sorry."

"Please."

"Come on, Greg. Tell the truth. Do you really want to give up sleeping around? Be honest. If not with me, with yourself."

He was quiet for a moment. "No. No, I don't."

"Just keep it real. We don't want the same relationship. That's the truth. We're done."

"I miss you."

"I miss the way we started out. We'll both be fine."

He was silent.

"Okay. I should go now. Goodbye, Greg."

"I love you, Sammi. Bye."

I went into the den and crawled into my chair. I hoped Greg wouldn't keep having doubts about the divorce. I took a few deep breaths. This was the endgame. If I had to talk him down a few more times before December 4, I could do that. I just had to make it through the final judgment hearing.

I was shocked by how resistant he was to getting a divorce. Then again, I was sure he'd be equally resistant if someone was proposing to take his favorite guitar. He was clearly grieving. I knew he'd miss having the role I played filled. I wondered if he'd miss *me* at all. It'd been so long since we connected person to person. I wondered if he even remembered how it felt to be connected to me.

I was surprised by how sad I felt about divorcing Greg. I didn't expect to grieve our relationship. I sat with the feeling. I let my mind drift to some of the better moments we'd experienced before he'd started cheating and destroyed our relationship. I missed him during that time. The truth always rose. That moment when they blow it all to hell would always come.

My thoughts moved on to all of Greg's lack of presence and bull-shit. My feelings moved into fatigue and anger. I was done. One more month before this was history.

My phone rang again. This time, it was Sylvia. I let it ring two or three times while I tried to get back to the happy place I was in when Ari left.

When I was somewhat closer to that place, I answered. She surprised me by not interrogating me about the divorce. She was focused on Christmas, but, uncharacteristically, she didn't push. My mother and I had a relaxed check-in. I figured she must've also been tired.

It wasn't 10:30 a.m. yet. The only duty I had was to crash. The only thing I was wearing was an oversized T-shirt and my undies. I was perfectly dressed. I went up to my bedroom and got back in my bed. I didn't remember when it became true, but it felt like my bed again. I'd gotten used to not sleeping with Michael. I was making good progress on all fronts.

A TEXT MESSAGE pulled me out of my slumber. It seemed too early for Ari to have landed in New York. I looked at my phone and saw it was two something.

It was a text from Michael. "Are you busy? Do you have time to talk?" It was calming.

First Greg. Then Michael. I guessed it was "talk to Sammi day."

"Sure."

"Are you at home? Do you mind if I stop by?"

I thought of the coldness in his eyes when he asked me to leave. I thought of him with Neva. I thought about how Ari called me out on not being present and observing in that situation. Maybe hearing what he had to say would make things clearer. "Yes. No."

"I'm on my way. I'll see you in about ten minutes." He was probably at Helen's.

I got up and put on a pair of shorts. I brushed my teeth and put some water on my face to try to finish waking up. My feelings were all over the place, but I wanted to see him. I heard him knock on the door as I was making my way downstairs. My heart leaped as I opened it. He was wearing warmups and a long-sleeved T-shirt. He hadn't shaven in the past few days or combed his hair after he'd showered. His eyes had his regular tenderness in them. He was deeply beautiful.

We stood there and stared at each other for a minute.

I shook my head to get my thoughts flowing again. "Ummm. Hello." I motioned for him to come in. "Would you like something to drink?"

"I came by to apologize for my behavior week before last."

"I'm listening."

"I was really upset because I thought you were getting back with Greg." He sounded apprehensive.

That was straight out of left field. "You thought what? That makes no sense whatsoever! So you wouldn't let me talk to you. And then you date-fucked me and then asked me to leave." He'd struck a chord. I was tired of men and their one-sided considerations.

"Just give me a chance to explain."

So he wanted to talk. Fuck that. "You made a stupid assumption that was completely out of character for me. Then you wouldn't let me talk. Now, you want me to listen to you. No way. Now, it's your turn to be silenced."

He whispered, "Sammi—"

I didn't realize I was so angry. "Shut up, Michael. I don't want to hear what you have to say. I don't care how reasonable it is."

"But, Sammi—"

"I'm serious, Michael. Shut up."

In that second, I decided to repay him in kind. In a fluid motion, I pushed him onto the sofa in the den and climbed on top of him, straddling his legs. His eyes were wide. I'd caught him off guard. I kissed him wildly and aggressively and invaded his mouth with my tongue.

He purred and wrapped his arms around me. I pulled back from the kiss, unwrapped his arms, and put his hands on the sofa. Holding on to his forearms, I leaned into my hands. I gave him a stern look. When I thought he understood he couldn't hug me, I resumed my kiss. His erection was growing against my sex. I wound on him. I could've easily come like that. I lost myself in the sensation.

When I came back to myself, I realized he was moving with me. He wouldn't let me move before, so he couldn't either. I stopped cold and broke all contact with him. I gave him a look that let him know I was angry. I stood up. I took off my shorts and panties.

I commanded, "Give me a condom." I considered those words. We had to use a condom because he'd been with someone else. Even though I had no right, I decided I could be angry about that too.

When he gave me the condom, I got his clothing out of my way. I slipped the condom onto his jewel and stroked him twice to remind him how I served. He moaned loudly. His whole body pulsed. Before he recovered, I straddled him again and took him all the way inside. He dropped his head back and rocked his hips in response. I didn't move until he got himself back together and looked at me.

I started a simple undulation that would bring me to orgasm in a matter of minutes. I slapped his hands away when he tried to take off my shirt. I relaxed into the bliss of riding him. When I heard myself moaning, I realized he was massaging my nipples with his long, graceful fingers. It felt so good it took all the discipline I had to push his hands away. I was date-fucking him just like he'd date-fucked me. Touching me like that wasn't allowed. He responded by putting his hands on my hips.

I growled, "Stop touching me, Michael."

He put his hands back on the sofa. I closed my eyes. I felt the beginnings of my orgasm. Just as I was about to come, he started his "waltzy," swivel movement. I opened my eyes and saw he was watching my every response. He had a smile on his face. He knew exactly what he was doing. It was exquisite. My orgasm came and washed the world away before I could demand that he be still. I had to fight not to relax into him. I forced myself to retreat. I stood up, grabbed my shorts and undies, and went into the bathroom between my office and the den.

I put my shorts and undies back on and leaned against the wall to let the final waves of my orgasm wash over me and to regain my equilibrium. When I was back in my body, I walked into the den. He was dressed. *Good.* I didn't pause. I walked to my front door and opened it.

I said, "Leave, Michael."

He opened his mouth. It seemed like he wanted to object. Instead, he whispered, "Okay." His eyes were still warm as he walked out.

I closed the door behind him and locked it, plopping into my favorite chair. I'd enjoyed that. It was good to let off some steam. And to have had sex with Michael.

<hr>

MY PHONE RANG. It was Ari.

I answered, "You made it back to New York."

She responded, "I landed an hour ago. You didn't see my text?"

I looked at my phone. It was 6 p.m. "I was sleeping."

"Sounds like you're still sleeping."

My body was tingling. It was crazy how he made me feel.

"Sammi? You there?"

"Yeah. I was just thinking."

"What's going on? You sound spacey."

"Michael came by to talk."

"How did that go?"

"It didn't. I didn't let him talk. I date-fucked him back and put him out."

Ari laughed. "Of course. That makes perfect sense."

I ranted, "He said that he date-fucked me because he thought I was getting back with Greg. I don't know how he came up with an idiotic idea like that, but it really pissed me off. Greg called earlier, proposing that he go to therapy to stop cheating. Bullshit! I've had my fill of men and their bullshit."

This time, Ari was quiet.

I said, "Say something."

"Greg actually volunteered to go to therapy?"

"Yes. He's just trying to not to deal with the fact that we're done."

"Hmmm. I'm not surprised. So what did you say to Michael?"

"I told him off about making a stupid assumption and about date-fucking me. I told him to shut up because I didn't want to hear what he had to say." I was still irritated. It felt good to rant like this.

"And then you fucked him."

"I date-fucked him. Yes."

Ari was laughing. "You're seriously angry."

"I'm *sooo* angry."

"Okay. So how did Michael respond?"

"He kept trying to be all sensuous. I made him stop."

"That didn't bother him?"

"I caught him off guard, but I think he liked it. Since my intention was to get him back, the fact that he liked it makes me angry too." I had to laugh at myself. "I don't think clearly when I'm around Michael right now."

"I can't argue with that."

"I love him, and I miss him. But it's good for me to be on my own for a while."

"That makes sense to me. You two still need to talk though. You need to be completely honest."

"Okay. Did you have fun this morning? I'm sorry that my relationship with him is interfering with you getting closer to him." I thought, *If I hadn't gotten involved with Michael, they would have spent more time together during her visit.*

"It's really not. I think that Mike and I are closer than we would've been otherwise because of your relationship with him. We had a good talk. We bonded some more. I feel closer to him now than I did yesterday."

Her tone was matter of fact; she wasn't trying to protect my feelings. "I'm glad to hear it."

She yawned. "I think I'm going to take a shower and get in bed to try and sleep 'til tomorrow."

"I'm going to get some food. I haven't eaten yet today."

"Bye."

"Bye." I hung up.

I went out for a quiet dinner and looked out over the beach as the sun started setting.

MICHAEL TEXTED as I was walking back into my house: "Are you still mad at me?"

I pondered the question. I wasn't done being angry. "I am." Not all of it was directed at him.

"Can we talk?"

"Sure."

He called me in response. Before I picked up, I let it ring a few times. I answered with, "I'm listening."

"I don't think the things that we need to talk about should be discussed over the phone. I'll start the conversation now, but I want to set a time to get together and talk about this face-to-face. Okay?"

"Okay." It had been a while since I'd talked to him. I'd missed the warmth and tenderness in his voice. I basked in it.

"I'm sorry for date-fucking you, Sammi. As I mentioned earlier, I thought you were getting back together with Greg. I was freaking out."

"Why would you think I was getting back together with Greg? That makes no sense to me. Has he contacted you or something?"

"Ari hasn't told you anything?"

"That sounds ominous. Anything about what?"

"You really don't know. You haven't seen this?"

My phone buzzed. Michael had sent me a text with a link in it. I followed the link to a gossip column. There were pictures and videos from the surprise birthday party Greg threw for Kenny and me. I saw white. "You've got to be fucking kidding me! I knew there was a reason I wanted to punch him every time he touched me. I'm going to kill him!" I took a few breaths and focused back on the conversation I was having with Michael. "So this is the reason that you thought I was getting back with Greg?"

"That's where it started. I wasn't sure. I didn't really believe it until I saw you kissing him at the pop-up coffee shop on the plaza outside of the theater."

I had to laugh out loud. Greg was nothing if he wasn't manipulative. I huffed. "His ass is mine." I closed my eyes to quiet myself. "We can talk about it more when we meet. Greg threw a surprise birthday party for Kenny and me. In those pictures, he was taking advantage of the fact that I wouldn't tell him off in front of his mother. On the plaza, he asked me to kiss him one last time in exchange for him agreeing to the settlement. He was staring off into the distance. I thought he was being emotional. Now, I'm sure that he saw you. I have no doubt that the pics and videos from the birthday party were directed at you too. When I told you that he'd be obsessed with how I relate to you, this is the kind of behavior I was talking about. Why didn't you ask me?"

"Your connection to him is strange to me. You seem to care more than you should. I thought anything was possible. I wasn't ready to deal with that." He must have been sensing my guilt about the accident.

"There's no way that I'd go back to Greg. I care about him, but we don't want the same relationship."

"Does he agree with you?"

"Enough to give me a divorce. I just have to keep him focused."

Michael exhaled. "Okay."

"Is that why you were in such a strange place when I came by?"

"Yeah. I was pretty freaked out." My heart sank. I'd caused him all that anguish.

"I'm sorry, Michael. I tried to tell you. You were the first person I called after he agreed to settle."

"I know, Sammi. I'm sorry for not letting you tell me."

"For what it's worth, I was pretty freaked out when I saw you with Neva."

He laughed. "I couldn't tell. I was freaking out then too." Seemed like Ari's assessment was correct.

"This is hard for me too. I miss you. I miss us. But this is the only path that I can see forward for now. I have to deal with Greg, and I need to spend some time with me before I settle into another relationship. I want to see how it feels to be a balanced me."

"It's not easy, but I understand."

My tears started flowing. I was causing him pain he didn't deserve. "I feel that I owe you an apology. I should've never let us hook up. I didn't know …"

"Neither did I. How could we? Don't blame yourself. I was very insistent."

I smiled. "True. And I didn't resist very well."

"I can be very persuasive. We are where we are. No one's to blame."

"I didn't mean to cause you pain. I'm really sorry."

"I'm an adult, Sammi. I had free will. Every time you pushed away, I pulled closer. You know that's true." He was right. He'd done that.

"I just want you to know that I wasn't leading you on or playing games."

"I know that you love me. I can feel it. I love you too."

My heart was wide open. I closed my eyes and willed myself to stay on course. "I'm sorry that things are like they are."

"Me too."

I shook my head to try to clear it. "We aren't doing such a good job being broken up."

"True."

"Our boundaries are all off. I don't know how to set them. I don't know how to do this."

"Me either. I don't know how to be only a friend to you."

"Well, declaring our love and date-fucking each other are definitely steps in the wrong direction."

He huffed. "Yeah. I'm really, really sorry about that."

"Well, I'm not sorry for date-fucking you. You deserved it."

He chuckled. "Deserved isn't the right word. Perhaps 'you had it coming' would be better."

"It's not." We were playing again. "Listen, promise me that you'll talk to me before you make crazy assumptions."

"I promise. You have to do the same."

"I promise. I'm happy we finally talked."

"Me too. How have you been? I know I just stopped communicating. Sometimes I lose my footing when emotions get strong."

I waited a second for him to continue. He didn't. I didn't press. There were things he didn't want to share with me. I understood. "Happy about the progress I'm making with Greg. Starting to create a support system for myself. Finishing up the film. Now I'm looking at new projects. How about you?"

"Other than working myself into a freaked-out state and driving my friends crazy, I've mostly been working."

I asked, "How long are you home for?"

"I leave at six thirty in the morning. I'll be gone for two weeks."

"International or domestic?"

"Domestic. We're going to the Southeast. Are you doing any traveling?"

"I don't have anything planned."

We sat in comfortable silence for a few minutes.

I said, "So ... what now?"

"I don't know."

"I need to give Greg a piece of my mind."

"Okay, I'll call you tomorrow."

"Okay. Get some rest. Have a good flight." Talking to him had put me at ease.

"Good night, Sammi."

I forced myself to hang up. My inner compass went crazy when I was around him. I felt drawn to him like gravity. I really wanted to know how it felt to be balanced again, not pulled by one man and repulsed by the other.

I called Greg, and he picked up on the second ring. "Hey. Did you reconsider my offer?"

Greg exasperated me. In the past few months, I always felt like I wanted to hit him. I decided not to bite. "Why did you post pics of us on the internet that implied we're together?"

"Those pics aren't about just us. Not one of them is of just the two of us. Those pics are about my family and about the fact that we're investing in a historical New Orleans restaurant so that it can expand."

"You're full of shit, Greg."

"How did you find out? Did he tell you? Is that why you're upset?"

"How I found out about them is irrelevant. You could've chosen pics without me in them if it was really about your family. I see your game, Greg. Stop trying to spin."

"Fine. You're right. I was making it clear that you're my wife. I was defending my territory and trying to give us a fighting chance. I'm not sorry about that. I'm not going to apologize."

He made me want to scream, and I didn't know how to respond.

After a minute or so had passed, Greg said, "Sleep on my offer, Sammi. I love you."

I looked at the phone, said, "Bye, Greg," and hung up. I wished I could disconnect with more aggression, but it *was* a cell phone …

27

A SHOULDER
MONDAY, NOVEMBER 13

As I PULLED into my driveway, I thought back over the past week or so. It'd been good. My friend Gene needed help with one of his projects, so we got to work together again. It was a real treat. After all that drama, Michael and I found our way back to some equilibrium. As best we could, we worked on being friends. When he wasn't close enough for me to smell his pheromones, I felt quite clearheaded. We'd settled into a pattern of texting a few times a day, just to say hello, and talking every few days. We kept the conversations superficial. Greg had finally stopped talking about going to therapy.

It was only 10 a.m., and I'd finished my workout. The day had started off well. My current challenge was figuring out how to use up all the groceries I'd bought the day before. The store had a lot of things on sale, and I was hungry.

Michael texted, "Do you mind if I visit?"

I texted back, "No."

He texted, "Good 'cause I'm sitting in your driveway."

We arrived at my front door at the same time. I opened the door for him.

He looked tired. He said, "Sorry for not giving you any warning. I was driving aimlessly and found myself on your street."

I closed and locked the door behind him. "You're not supposed to be back in LA yet. Is everything alright?"

He stopped to kick off his shoes. "Yeah. I'm okay." He sounded tentative.

I walked back to my kitchen. "What's going on?"

He came with me, limping slightly. "I pulled my shoulder again."

I turned to look at him. "*Again?*"

He sat on one of the stools at my kitchen island. "Yeah, again. This is the third time."

"I'm gonna make me some breakfast. Should I make enough for you? What happened?" I leaned against the counter.

"Yes, I'd like that. I was doing a lift with my partner during a performance. She stepped on a wet spot. Her foot slipped when she jumped, so her position was rotated instead of straight. I corrected her position so we could execute the lift and tweaked my shoulder. Not too bad. It's a strain. Nothing's torn." He sounded frustrated.

"You're worried."

"Yeah, because this is the third time."

I took out eggs, cheese, and prosciutto. "If you tweaked your shoulder, why are you limping?" I put a skillet on the stove to get warm.

"Compensating. I've irritated my hamstring."

He was a dancer, which meant he'd tried to dance through the pain. "How long did you keep dancing?"

"It happened at Saturday's matinee. I finished that performance, then did the Saturday night performance and Sunday's matinee."

I put everything into a bowl and mixed it together. "You look tired."

"I am. I took the red-eye home."

"Jack benched you?" I knew he hadn't agreed to not perform willingly. I put the mixture into the skillet with a smidge of butter.

"Yeah. I want coffee. Do you want tea?"

I observed as he grabbed the cups. "Yeah. Thanks." I divided the food onto two plates and took two forks out of the drawer.

He opened my refrigerator to get the milk. "Wow, I've never seen your refrigerator so full. Are you having a party?"

"No. I got carried away when I was shopping yesterday. You can take some home if you want. I have no idea how I'm going to be able to eat all of that." I set the plates on the kitchen island. I could tell he was uncomfortable in his body and decided to take him to see Dr. Maggie. I picked up my phone and called her.

She answered on the third ring. "Morning, Sammi. Who's hurt?" I wanted to protest, but she knew me too well.

"Michael."

"Can you get him to my house within the hour?"

"Yes."

"I'll see you soon then." She hung up.

I put my phone down and started eating. I was extremely hungry.

He sat and ate beside me. When he'd chewed the first bite twice, he said, "This is good."

"Right. It's something Kenny concocted. I call it Kenny scramble. Given he didn't make it an omelet, I don't think he really knew what he was doing, but it's delicious." I concentrated on enjoying my Kenny scramble.

He asked, "So who were you talking to on the phone?"

"Oh." *It would be helpful if I told him.* "Eat up. I'm taking you to see Dr. Maggie. We have to be there within the hour."

He half smiled. "Alright."

I finished eating first. After I put my dishes in the dishwasher, I made my tea and his coffee in thermoses so we could take them with us. I turned to give him his coffee and watched him eat. We had a contented moment of silence. He made me feel playful. I took his plate to put it in the dishwasher while he was lifting his last forkful to his mouth.

He laughed in response and almost spit out the food that was in his mouth. There was no stress or frustration on his face at that moment.

I was in pheromone central. I said, "Time to go," and put some distance between us by walking toward the front door. I grabbed my car keys and my purse, opened the door, and locked it. I was driving my Mini Cooper and didn't want it to be a discussion. "Just close the door. I've already locked it."

He didn't respond.

I looked at him. His eyes were open, but he was a million miles away. He'd completely zoned out on me.

In a normal tone, I said, "Michael."

No response.

"Michael."

Still no response.

In a louder voice, I said, "Earth to Michael!"

Finally, he returned from his reverie. He looked at me like I was crazy. "What?"

"We've gotta go. Close the door behind yourself. I already locked it."

I got into my car and cranked it up.

When he saw me sitting in the car, he opened his mouth to protest. He paused to look into my eyes, nodded, and half smiled. He knew I was waiting for him to start.

I smiled too.

Once he was inside the car, he seemed surprised that he fit.

"What?" I wanted to see if I could get a complaint out of him as I pulled out of the driveway.

He put up his hands. "What? I didn't say anything."

We both laughed.

The only difference between wordplay with my friend Tommy and wordplay with Michael was the physical attraction slurred it into flirting. That had to be about his pheromones. It had to be. I wondered if there was a way to change how I responded to them. Maybe Dr. Maggie knew.

Dr. Maggie lived nearby. We arrived at her house in a few minutes. She was in her workroom, watering her plants, when we walked in. I stopped to take in all the scents and bask in her presence.

She was assessing me. "You've been doing the exercises I taught you. Very good. You look better. Stronger. How much longer?" She was asking about the divorce.

I answered, "Two weeks."

"Good." She turned her attention to Michael. "You pulled your shoulder back out of place. You've had some work done on it. Leave on your underwear. Lay on the table face up."

Michael looked at her in awe and with expectation. "Ummm, yes. Okay."

I said, "I should give you privacy." I got up to go wait in the kitchen.

Dr. Maggie said, "Sit down, Sammi. I want you to listen and observe."

I sat.

To Michael, she said, "Why didn't you stop dancing when it happened? Now your whole system is out of balance."

Michael looked intimidated. "I guess I thought I could work through it." He laid down on the table as instructed.

Dr. Maggie quipped, "The show must go on." She started by relaxing his psoas muscles. Then, with the exception of the shoulder he'd pulled, she worked her way from his skull to his toes doing muscle tests and making minor adjustments. As she walked back to the head of the table, she had him turn over, then worked on his spine and sacrum. When she was done, she said, "Sit up."

He complied.

"How does your shoulder feel?"

Michael moved his shoulder around. "Better."

She looked at the ceiling, then back at him. "Does it feel like it's in the right place? Compare it to the other one."

Michael answered without moving. "No, it's not in the right place. The bone's sitting too high. It can't bear weight."

She was pleased that he was aware of that. "Do you know how to get it back in the right place?"

He answered, "No."

She demonstrated a sequence of movements.

He mirrored her movements. The joint popped softly back into place.

"Do that as soon as you notice it's out of place. Don't let it spiral out of control."

"Okay. Thank you."

She leaned against one of her cabinets and observed him. "You only drank one of the tea packets I gave you the last time I saw you. Finish them." Without looking at me, she said, "He needs a deep tissue massage as soon as possible. I adjusted his bones, but his muscles are just going to pull them back out of place if they aren't relaxed. Start with hydrotherapy. Keep him warm. Start with his scalp. Do his forearms and hands, followed by his calves and feet. Next massage down from his neck. Work from right to left."

I said, "Someone else could probably do a much better job than I can."

To me, she said, "You'll do fine." To Michael, she said, "Go to sleep as soon as she's done. You're exhausted. I recommend you don't perform for the next three days. Let your body rest tomorrow. Get dressed." She walked across the room to take a sip of her tea.

Michael said, "I'm really happy to know how to put my shoulder back in place. This is the third time this has happened."

She responded, "Only three times. *Hmmph.* Given how much you use your arms to do lifts, that's a testament to how strong you are."

Michael asked, "What do you mean?"

She led him into a room where there was a yoga workout machine like the ones at Amanda's. She put thirty pounds on each side and motioned for him to stand in front of the machine with his back to it and his arms above his head. She put a strap on each of his hands. She said, "Pull the straps forward."

He muscled his way through the movement.

"Your arms are extensions of your torso. Use them that way." She pointed to the point a few inches below his naval. "Use your lower psoas. Start the movement from here."

He did the movement as instructed. It took much less effort.

She turned to go back into her treatment room. "See, rocket science." Her tone was dry and sarcastic. She walked straight to the door of the treatment room and looked at me. "I'm giving a class tomorrow evening at 6 p.m. I expect to see you there." She opened the door. "Out! This is my day off."

Michael said, "Thank you." He left quickly.

I lingered until he was out of earshot. "Is there anything that can be done to make a person less affected by another person's pheromones? I want to feel less attracted to Michael when I'm around him."

She looked at me like I was insane. Pointing toward my car, she responded dryly, "I'll see you tomorrow evening, Sammi."

I left as directed.

Michael said, "Thanks. I feel much better," as I got in the car. There was noticeably less tension in his body.

"You're welcome, Michael."

"How did you find her?"

"Luck. I was looking for someone to help Greg." I pulled out of her driveway.

"The luck was all Greg's. Was he grateful, or did he take it for granted?" How he felt about Greg was clearly expressed in his tone.

I thought before I answered. "All evidence supports the belief that he was very grateful for Dr. Maggie's and my efforts during the time that he was in treatment."

"Well, I'm grateful that you brought me to her. I mean that. She's incredible." He looked at me to make sure that his statement was heartfelt. "Did you tell her that I'd had my shoulder worked on?"

"No."

"It's freaky how she knows things. How could she tell that I only drank one of those tea packets? Yuck." He stuck his tongue out and made a face like he'd just tasted nail polish remover.

"I don't know. I do know that if you want her to continue to work with you, you have to drink the tea."

"Yeah. Damn. I have no choice then."

"Speaking of having no choice, I have to put you into my hot tub and give you a massage. Do you have swimming trunks with you, or do we need to stop and buy a pair?"

"I have a pair in my car. And a change of clothes. Please don't be so overjoyed about it." He was failing at not looking pleased.

I wondered if he really needed to be massaged or if Dr. Maggie thought this was funny. Regardless, I wanted to keep working with her. So there was one path forward. I glanced at him sideways and got out of the car. I said, "The hot tub's down the hall, past Ari's room."

I walked into my house and left the front door slightly ajar for Michael. I made a beeline to turn on the jacuzzi. Men rarely like steam, so I didn't turn on the steam room. I set out towels and stood in the door to my workout and spa rooms and chuckled quietly at the hilarity of my situation. When I saw him walking down the hall toward me, I started walking too. I said, "I put out towels. The hot tub's around the corner. By the time you change, it should be warm. I'll meet you in there."

I went to the den to take a few minutes to focus on remaining clearheaded while I gave Michael his massage. For the next few hours, Dr. Maggie and the fates were having their fun. I made up my mind. I could resist his pheromones. I could do this without it becoming sexual.

I marched back to the spa. He was in the hot tub, asleep. I set up the massage table in the middle of the workout room, which was full of light. Three of the walls were floor to ceiling windows with a mirrored tint. The massage table and a ladder were the only pieces of furniture. I put the table warmer and sheet onto the massage table. I set out a thick turquoise cotton throw to cover him, went back into the hot tub room, sat on the floor behind his head, and made myself comfortable.

I reminded myself to start with his scalp. I brushed my fingertips across his forehead to let him know I was there. When he stirred, I used my fingers more strongly. I massaged his forehead and worked my way down the sides of his face, over his temples and to his jaws. I massaged and gently pulled his ears from bottom to top twice.

He opened his eyes. "Wow. I didn't know I was holding so much stress in my facial muscles."

I massaged his scalp from his face to the nape of his neck. His neck muscles were tight and ropey. I had to work into them slowly so it wasn't too painful. I realized I didn't have to worry about his pheromones. This massage was going to be real work. Once his neck relaxed, I stood up and grabbed a towel.

I put the towel near him. "Dry off, put your briefs back on, and come lay down on the massage table." I turned off the hot tub.

He stepped out of the hot tub and picked up the towel. "Okay, thanks." He was testing his neck.

"Are you alright?"

"Yeah. I'm just surprised that my neck was so tight."

"You did take a red-eye last night." I walked into the workout room.

"True." He followed me as he dried off.

He went into the bathroom to change, and I set the heating pad on the massage table to low. He walked back into the workout room with his briefs on.

I held up the throw. "Lay down, face up. Let me know if you get too warm." He complied.

I put a pillow under his knees. I hoped he didn't mind talking while I worked on him to help me pass the time. I asked, "How's Alex?"

It took a minute for him to answer. "Much the same. Things aren't resolved. He's talking some. He's still hiding something, but overall, he's better."

"That's good."

I took his right forearm into my hands. I'd never looked at it with this much attention and purpose before. His muscles were long and strong at the same time. I could see and feel each one clearly. They didn't give easily when I ran my fingers over them. Dr. Maggie was right. He was holding on to quite a bit of tension. An extremely large man with large, strong hands would have been better suited to the task of massaging the tension out of Michael's body. I took a deep breath. I was going to have to pace myself to keep from being worn out.

Michael shifted. "Ari thinks that we should talk more about how we feel and what we're up to day-to-day." He was resisting; that meant I needed to lessen the pressure.

"I don't think talking about how we feel would be constructive. Our goal's to cultivate the friendship aspect of our relationship. I mean, Paulo and Alicia don't tell each other they love each other; neither do Tommy and I." After a few passes, I found an approach that worked without too much effort on my part. The trick was to slowly intensify the pressure; that way, he didn't resist.

"They do talk about how they feel. It just happens to not be about how they feel about each other because that's not a thing."

"We've been talking about how we feel about things in general. I was even trying to tell you about Greg. In fact, other than the situation with Greg, I think we were doing alright." I laid his right hand down on the table. His fingers were much more relaxed. I went to the other side of the table to work on his left forearm.

"I agree."

"I decided to give you updates after the fact. I thought it would keep you from worrying. If I'd told you beforehand, you would've known what was going on, and maybe you wouldn't have freaked out so bad."

"I did freak out pretty bad."

"I was waiting to talk to you to tell you how the birthday party went. Texting about it didn't seem right." One of the muscles in his left forearm was especially stuck. I had to hold on to it for a while.

He breathed deeply to manage the intensity. "That was when everyone was injured. I was exhausted. We were only texting then. I understand why you didn't want to text about it."

"But you needed to know. I'll text anyway from now on if something like that happens and we don't get a chance to talk."

"Knowing before I saw that column would've helped a lot. I'll do the same."

I moved to the foot of the table and realized he needed to be facedown for me to get to his calves. "Turn over."

He fulfilled my request.

I made sure he was covered up and comfortable. "I can't believe you thought I was reconciling with Greg." I ran my hand over his right calf. My hands were no match. I had to use my elbow.

"Yeah, well, I was tired and on the defensive."

"I was trying to figure out what could've happened to get you in that state. I touched you. The next thing I knew, we were having sex."

He chuckled. "Yeah, we were."

"Why did you hold me like that?" I knew the answer as soon as the question was out of my mouth.

We said it at the same time. "To manage the intensity."

He continued, "I thought you were back with Greg ... sexually. I wanted to make love to you one last time. If you were moving too, I wouldn't have been able to handle it."

I could feel his sincerity, but I needed to finish telling him how he'd pissed me off. "Then you went cold and asked me to leave."

"I'd lost it by then. I'm sorry, Sammi. I wasn't trying to be hurtful. I was freaked." He sounded remorseful.

I was glad I couldn't see his eyes. I stepped back and directed my thinking to his calf. It was tight. "I was so pissed."

"So you date-fucked me to get back at me." He was laughing.

"You liked it." I narrowed my eyes.

"I loved it." He laughed harder.

I leaned into his right calf.

"Ow!" He laughed more. "Having sex with me is not a good

way to get back at me, Sammi. I can't think of anything that you could do that I wouldn't enjoy."

I eased up. "We shouldn't be having sex with each other anyway."

"It doesn't work casually."

"True." I took a breath. "I'm not going to be able to break up the tension in your calves without causing you some discomfort. I'll be as gentle as I can. Try to relax."

"My calves are like steel cables right now. Go for it."

Steel cables was a perfect description. I had to put in a lot of effort to get them to soften up. It took all my concentration. He did a good job of relaxing through the pain. I was sweating by the time I was done with the left one.

When I stepped back to take a break, he said, "I think you made that more painful than necessary."

"I had to get back at you in a way that works."

"Seriously, that feels much better."

"Good. You've worn out my hands and arms. I'm going to work on your back and hips with my knees."

"I think you like torturing me."

"Trying to flirt with me will only make me go harder on you."

I moved the setup to the mat on the floor. He was taller and heavier than me, so it took all my strength and some engineering to massage the rest of his body into relaxation. He was dozing when I was halfway through, so I knew I was doing a good job. He was sleeping when I finished.

I grabbed his clothes and woke him up. "Get up. You can sleep in Ari's bed."

He palmed his eyes. "You massaged Greg like that?"

"Yes."

He reached out a hand. "And then he cheated on you?"

"Yes." I pulled him to his feet.

"He's an idiot." He followed me into Ari's room.

"I couldn't agree more." I put his clothes on the chair and his cell phone on the nightstand. It buzzed as soon as I set it down. He had four text messages from someone named Lana. I kept my expression neutral.

He looked at his phone and almost shook his head. "We aren't dating. It's—"

I interrupted him. "We're not together. You can do whatever you want." I felt jealous, but I couldn't ask him to wait for me.

He continued, "I want you to know that it's purely physical. I hooked up with her when I thought you'd gone back to Greg. And yes, it's purely physical for her too."

I wanted to make sure he knew I wasn't making any demands on him. I loved him too much to do that. "You're free to move on."

"It's the same with Neva. We hook up if it's convenient when we're in the same city. I've known her for six years. She sensed our connection."

I didn't know what to say. "Okay. You should get some rest." I pointed to the bed.

He climbed in. "Thanks for taking care of me, Sammi."

"You're welcome." I left the room and closed the door behind me.

I was exhausted then too. I went to my bedroom and stretched out on my bed. I was happy the experience hadn't been as sensual as I thought it would be.

My phone woke me up. It was Ari. I answered, "Hello."

She responded, "You've been asleep all this time?"

I looked at my phone. It was almost 5 p.m. "Man, I passed all the way out. I fell asleep about an hour ago."

"I called three hours ago. Why didn't you answer my text?"

I looked at my phone. There were a few texts from her asking if I thought she should go forward with a deal. I answered, "Because I was giving Michael a massage. Afterward, I was so tired, I passed out. I do think that you should go forward with the deal, by the way."

"I thought Mike was on the East Coast. How did you end up giving him a massage?"

I told her about his shoulder and the visit to Doctor Maggie.

She prompted, "And?"

"And what?"

"What else did you two do?"

"What do you mean?"

"Come on. Don't be coy. Did you have sex?"

I answered indignantly, "No. We didn't have sex."

"That's a change. You two always end up having sex when you're alone and in arm's reach. Where is he now?"

I wanted to deny it, but I couldn't. "Whatever. He's in your bed asleep."

"And where are you?"

"I'm in my bedroom."

"Well, the night's young."

"Not helpful. What do you want, Ari?"

She laughed. "Wanted to know why you didn't respond to my text and what you thought about the deal."

"Well, I've answered both of those questions. Is there anything else?"

I let her pull the details of the conversation that she was interested in from me.

"Well, you're grumpy, so I'll talk to you later." I'd irritated her by not being more talkative.

"Okay, I'll call you when I finish waking up."

I had a hunger pang. I had a refrigerator full of food that needed to be used, so I was going to cook. I'd take advantage of the fact the Michael was there and make big portions. That way, I could send some home with him.

MICHAEL WALKED into the kitchen about thirty minutes after I finished cooking pecan pies. "I've never had a massage that was that good. Thank you so much. I can't tell you how much better I feel. I was out for almost five hours."

"You're welcome. How did you sleep?"

"Hard. I don't remember putting my head on the pillow."

"You were pretty tired."

"And now I'm starving. The aromas woke me up. What did you cook?" He was looking at the stove.

"I cooked a Southern style meal this time: collards, black-eyed peas, baked sweet potatoes, potato salad, roasted chicken, corn-bread, fresh sweet tea to drink, and pecan pies for dessert. You don't know nothing about any of that."

"That's a lot of food. Enlighten me, please."

I made him a big, full plate and poured him a glass of sweet tea with lemon.

He started eating immediately, like he hadn't had food in a year. He was basically inhaling it.

I said, "It might be a good idea to chew a few times before you swallow."

He looked up from the plate and smiled with a full mouth. After he swallowed, he said, "I'm so hungry, and this food is so good. Why aren't you eating?"

"I ate a while ago."

He started eating again, more slowly this time. He didn't look up.

As he lifted the last bite from the plate, I pushed a piece of the pecan pie on a saucer in front of him and quickly snatched my hand back.

He didn't break his rhythm. He took the first bite of pie like it was on the dinner plate. He looked up again after he finished the last bite.

I asked, "Did you taste any of that?"

He smiled into a sip of tea. "I tasted all of it. In fact, I'd like seconds."

"Seriously?"

"Yeah, I'm not full yet."

"Help yourself." I motioned toward the stove. "The pies are in the oven." I rested my chin on my hands. I couldn't believe he was about to eat more.

"You cooked two chickens. If you're not having a party, what are you going to do with all this food?" He took normal full-sized serv-ings, including another piece of pie.

"I bought way too much yesterday. I don't want it to go to waste. So I'm sending three-fifths home with you. I figured you and Alex and Paulo could eat that much. I'll freeze half of what's left and eat the rest over the next few days."

"Thank you. They're out of luck. I'm not sharing with Paulo or

Alex." He returned to his seat at the kitchen island. He ate the second plate with the same intensity, but at a slower pace. He finished all of it easily.

I was awed. "Wow."

"What? I didn't eat all day. I told you I was starving. And that was an exceptionally delicious meal." He sat back and licked his lips.

I was back in pheromone central, so I had to send him home quickly. I got up to put some distance between us and took out containers to prepare for him to take home.

"I take it you're about to make me leave."

"I am. I gave you a massage, and then I cooked. Now I'm tired. I'm going to bed early. Besides, you have to go home to make and drink a dose of your Dr. Maggie tea."

"Yah." His whole body twitched. "Do you want a hand?"

"No. I want you to chill. Dr. Maggie's orders." I wanted to stay on the other side of the room from him. I packed his food quickly and gave him four-fifths. He didn't protest. When I had it all packed up, I gave him a grocery bag filled with containers.

"I guess this is my cue."

"It is."

He got up and walked to the front door. "This was a good day."

"Yes, it was."

"Thank you for taking care of me."

There was an awkward moment when both of us hesitated to touch each other. We smiled in response.

He opened the door. "Good night, Sammi."

"Good night, Michael." I closed the door behind him. I leaned against it and inhaled a few breaths of pheromone-free air to get my head straight. All in all, I thought the day went well. We talked, and we didn't flirt. We were making progress.

I put the remaining food away. I was so tired I barely made it to my bed.

The next few weeks went well in terms of my personal goals. On the friend front, Amanda and I were getting close. I spent more and more time at her studio. I'd graduated to helping Cam with some of her shows. She was trying to talk me into VJing for fun. I was also spending increasingly more time with Gene. I was even getting to know his partner, Evan.

Things were much easier between Michael and me. The shock of breaking up had subsided, and I thought we were well on our way to becoming friends. He was mostly in LA through next February. So it was easy to stay in contact, but we didn't talk every day. Since there was no extraneous drama, it was easy to keep conversation light and easy. I was fairly certain he was hooking up with people, but I was okay with it. Mostly. *Somewhat.* Well, while he wasn't serious about any of them. Hopefully, when he went there, I'd be in a different place. No matter what, he was free, and I wanted him to be happy.

I didn't have a project, so I hadn't been very busy. I split my time between planning for the series, working out, and looking for other projects.

28

DIVORCE DAY
MONDAY, DECEMBER 4

IT FELT like it had taken an eternity for the day to come. The past week seemed to crawl by. Finally, it was the day that my divorce from Greg would be complete.

Ari had insisted on being in LA so she could give me a big hug after the final judgment. She'd arrived on Friday evening. The weekend ended up being more low-key than we'd anticipated. We did a daylong hang with Cam and Amanda, which ended with another great party, the only one for the weekend, on Saturday. We had lunch with Michael and Paulo yesterday afternoon. Then we chilled. We made a toast at midnight to celebrate the day's arrival.

I asked myself how I'd ended up married to him. The day he'd proposed came to mind. I'd known him for a little over two years and had been dating him for about a year. He'd gotten into bike riding for strengthening and conditioning, so I rode with him. It was one thing we shared. On that evening, he'd successfully completed the most challenging ride he'd dared to attempt since the accident. We were both giddy with his progress. We laid down our bikes and ourselves on his front lawn.

He kissed me.

I said, "That was amazing, Greg. You're getting so strong."

"It was amazing. I feel good, really good. Thank you, Sammi." He turned to face me. "Seriously, you know I couldn't have recovered like this without you. My life is better since you've been in it. I feel like I can relax in a way that I never have in any other relationship that I've had. I can just be myself. I love you. Marry me."

I felt his words wash over me. I knew he meant it. "I love you too." I meant it. I'd come to care deeply for him. I owed him so much, much more than he knew. I felt blessed to have his love, and I loved him in a way that was manageable for me. He didn't mess with my wards. I could commit to that, to us. I responded, "I'll marry you."

We had a small private ceremony a month later. Things were great for about a year. He was much more present and available after the accident. Maybe it was the pain or the drugs or his brush with death. He was this beautiful, tender man who I loved. That person disappeared after he'd healed and took everything I liked about our relationship with him. Ultimately, being married to who he became was impossible. Thankfully, in a few hours, it would all be history.

I was wearing one of my business pantsuits for the occasion. At a glance, it looked very conservative, like something Sylvia would wear, but the cloth the suit was made from had a virtually monotone, navy blue print on it. The shirt, which had a Mandarin collar, was made of heavy white cotton. Its sleeves ended in cuffs like Western dress shirts, but there were no buttonholes. I was wearing a very plain, dark brown belt and a stylish pair of dark brown leather desert boots. I chose to keep my makeup understated. My hair was big and kinky, the only loud part of my quietly rebellious outfit.

Ari handed me a thermos full of tea as I walked into the kitchen. "That suit's going to come up missing. I love it." She was wearing jeans and a printed shirt.

I was making her wait outside the courtroom. I knew that if the judge opened the floor to opinions, she'd have plenty. I just wanted to get in and out as quickly as possible. "I know you love it. You bought two. Why do you want mine?"

"I didn't get one in navy blue. You're stunning, Sammi. We should go."

"Is Michael going to be able to hang out with you while I'm in court?"

"Yeah. They're not working out of the theater right now, but he's going to come over from the studio. We're going to meet at that coffee shop pop-up on the plaza between the courthouse and the theater."

"Good." At least she'd be entertained.

We jumped into Spencer, which, according to Ari, was "the only car for the occasion." This time, I was driving.

I exited the car in front of the courthouse. Ari jumped into the driver's seat to park it, and I took a few sips of my tea. I was too nervous to eat. I felt sad about seeing Greg. These were our last moments of being married. My sadness still surprised me because I thought I was all done grieving. Perhaps I wasn't grieving at all. Perhaps I would always be sad Greg was choosing to be that version of himself.

The decor of Judge Garcia's chambers was lighter than I'd expected. I'd imagined it dark and traditional, like my mom's. The room was big and spacious. The bookshelves were inset and loaded with books. There was a rug centered on the hardwood floor that was almost the size of the room. A big oak wood table was centered on the rug. A large, stately chair dominated the far side of the table. There were two pairs of normal-sized chairs on the near side, with a low end table between them. Two more normal-sized chairs were on the near sides of the table that were a few feet away from the big table and closer to the wall. Four more normal-sized chairs completed the seating in the room, one in each corner. There was a low end table next to each one.

My lawyer walked in a few steps behind me. He said, "Good morning, Sammi. You ready for this?"

"Good morning, Grant. Yes, I've been holding my breath."

"Well, this should only take fifteen minutes. The judge has already reviewed Greg's contestations."

"Okay."

Three more people I didn't know walked in. One of them placed folders on the judge's side of the table. The other two stood near the chairs in the corners of the judge's side of the room. Grant decided we were sitting in the chairs to the right of the low end table. He pulled the chair that was furthest from the end table out and motioned for me to sit. No one else sat, so I didn't either.

When Judge Garcia walked in, she was in a deep discussion with a man. Her poised, no-nonsense presence reminded me of my mom. I was sure that being a Latina and a judge came with its challenges. I bet she and my mom would have many stories to exchange. She acknowledged the room and took her seat. Everyone, including Grant, also sat. I heard Greg's voice, so I turned to look at the door.

Greg walked through the door, saying, "… final. I don't want a divorce." He was wearing jeans and a T-shirt, and he was high.

Kenny was on his heels. "Calm down and be reasonable, Greg." He was also wearing jeans and a T-shirt. He hadn't planned to be here but was running interference. Greg's lawyer followed them.

Greg turned to his lawyer, who looked shell-shocked, and said, "Stop this now."

Judge Garcia stopped reading her papers and looked at Greg.

Kenny noticed. He put his hands on Greg's shoulders in an effort to direct him toward one of the chairs to the left of the low end table. Greg turned and punched him in the stomach. "Don't tell me how to act. I know what I want." He turned back to his lawyer.

Kenny stumbled a few steps backward toward me before he regained his balance.

Judge Garcia was looking at him sternly, with her arms crossed.

I stepped around Kenny, thinking maybe I could calm him down. I walked over and touched his arm from behind.

Before I could say his name, he turned toward me, yelled, "Stop it, Kenny," and pushed me.

Everything went into a blur. Greg realized it was me who he'd pushed and tried and failed to catch me. I lost my balance and stumbled backward into the low end table. Michael appeared out of nowhere. I fell onto the big oak table and hit the right side of my ribs, my shoulder, and my head. Michael punched Greg in the stomach, and Greg collapsed to the floor. Michael immediately pounced on him. He was lifting his fist to punch Greg again. Kenny was moving toward them, but he hadn't gotten his breath back. And Greg wasn't fighting Michael off.

In the instant between the time I hit the floor and the pain of hitting the table washing over me, I knew I had to stop Michael from hitting Greg again. I yelled, "Michael!"

Michael looked in my direction. He looked back at Greg. He slapped him instead of punching him. "You touch her again, you answer to me." Michael took me into his arms just as the pain hit. "Are you hurt?"

I braced and waited for it to pass.

Michael asked again, "Sammi, are you okay?"

I had to pull myself together before the pain eased. "I'm fine. I hit my side and my head hard. It hurts, but I'm okay." I forced myself to sit up. I saw Ari was there too. She must've seen that Greg was high from the plaza and followed him in. She looked shocked. She was probably trying to wrap her head around how quickly Michael had pounced. She could tell I was still in a lot of pain, but she played along to keep Michael calm.

I let Michael help me into the seat that Grant specified. I sat up with as much composure as I could muster. Grant took his seat next to the end table. Michael and Ari stood behind me.

Kenny pulled Greg into the chair near the wall on the far side of the room. Greg was breathing again, but he was still stunned. Kenny put his hand on Greg's shoulder to keep him in the chair as Greg's lawyer sat down cautiously in the chair nearest Grant's on the other side of the end table.

Two sheriffs walked in and stood at the back of the room.

Clearing her throat, Judge Garcia looked at Greg. "Well, that was quite a performance, Mr. Albert." She inhaled and looked down at the folder in front of her. "So the reason that we're all here's that you contested the settlement, which makes no sense because, based on the evidence that was submitted, Ms. Harris only wants what she's earned—even though, by law, she's entitled to half of everything you're worth." She looked at me. "I take it that this is not the first time you've had to deal with this kind of behavior, Ms. Harris. I see that you're requesting three properties, one-third of what's in the joint accounts, and one-third of the shares from the LLC that you co-own. You relinquish claims on the rest of his estate, and you're not requesting support. Based on what I have witnessed today, I'm awarding you the three properties and half of what's in the joint accounts. I'm also awarding you half of the shares from the LLC."

I said, "Please, leave it at a third, Your Honor."

She paused without changing her expression. She looked at me and said, "My judgment's final." She looked at Greg. "If it weren't clear to me that one's already in place," she nodded at Michael, "I'd issue a restraining order against you. You need help, Mr. Albert." She looked at Kenny. "Get him into rehab today."

Kenny responded, "Yes, Your Honor."

Judge Garcia continued, "Please exit my chambers now."

One of the sheriffs stepped forward. Greg's lawyer got up and started walking first. Greg stood up. He looked at me, but he didn't say anything. Kenny got behind him and basically pushed him out of the chambers.

Kenny said, "I'll check in on you later, Sammi."

I responded, "Okay, thanks, Kenny."

Judge Garcia waited until they were all the way out. "You are free to stay as long as you'd like to, Ms. Harris." She got up and exited her chambers.

Grant looked at Ari. "Is there anything I can do?"

Ari responded, "No, we'll take it from here."

I said, "I'm okay, Grant. Thank you. You can go."

Grant responded, "Okay. I'll make sure you get your copy of the judgment."

My head had stopped hurting, but my shoulder was throbbing. And my ribs were killing me.

Ari asked, "Do you think you have a broken rib?"

"I don't know. It really hurts."

Michael was looking at the door. He wanted another shot at Greg.

I focused him back on me. "Can you help me stand up?"

Ari said, "We need to get you to the emergency room."

Michael said, "Call Dr. Maggie."

I wanted to speak up, but the pain was too intense.

Ari said, "Good idea."

I unlocked my phone for her, and she stepped away to make the call.

Michael said, "I'm really glad that Ari insisted on being in LA today. You'd be going through this alone otherwise."

She came back. "Dr. Maggie said to meet her at the main entrance of the hospital in ten minutes. Can you walk, Sammi?"

The pain in my shoulder had ebbed. My ribs were still killing me though. I responded, "Yeah." I pushed myself up to my feet. I made it all the way outside of the courthouse before I had to stop. "Let me rest." I reached out with my left arm for the wall.

Michael picked me up. "I'll take her in my car. It's just down the street."

Ari responded, "I'll meet you at the hospital."

<hr>

SOMEHOW, Ari arrived before we did. She was waiting with Dr. Maggie when Michael and I pulled up. They had a wheelchair. I wanted to protest but I couldn't. Getting out of the car and into the wheelchair on my own was as much as I could muster. I heard Ari and Michael talking behind me as Dr. Maggie wheeled me away.

Dr. Maggie asked, "Where did you hit when you fell?"

"I hit my head, my shoulder, and my ribs. My head feels fine. My shoulder isn't bad, but my ribs really hurt."

"I have an idea of what's going on. I'm going to send you for X-rays and then give you a treatment plan. I'll get you something for the pain."

The blouse and suit jacket were much easier to get out of than I'd anticipated. By the time they were taking me to be x-rayed, the painkiller had kicked in, and I could relax. I dosed off. A nurse woke me up to help me change out of the hospital gown they'd given me and put on a T-shirt with the hospital logo. She set a bag with my suit jacket, shirt, and belt in it on a chair near the bed where I'd been resting.

Dr. Maggie came into the room. "The painkillers have taken effect; you look better."

"Yeah. I feel better."

"Can you walk?"

"Yes."

"Come with me to my office."

I picked up the bag with my clothes and followed Dr. Maggie through the hospital to her office. Ari and Michael were already in there, waiting, when we walked in.

They looked at me as soon as I walked in the door.

I said, "I'm better. The painkillers helped a lot."

Michael stood. I took his seat.

Dr. Maggie leaned against her desk. "Well, the good news is nothing's broken or torn. You have a nasty bump on your head, but you don't have a concussion. You have a shoulder contusion that should be better in a few days. Your ribs are bruised. It'll be six weeks before they feel right again. They'll be very painful. I'll give you painkillers to manage the pain. Use ice packs for the swelling for now. I'll have herbs delivered later today or tomorrow."

I said, "Good. So I can go home now."

Dr. Maggie answered, "Yes, you can go home, but not alone. Someone needs to stay with you for the next forty-eight hours."

I questioned, "Why? I don't have a concussion."

Dr. Maggie answered, "Because your doctor says that you shouldn't be alone for the next forty-eight hours."

Ari said, "I can cancel my flight. I'll stay with her."

Michael said, "You can go back to New York. I'll stay with her. That's not a problem."

I said, "No, it's not ne—"

Dr. Maggie ignored me and Ari. "Thank you, Michael. I've called in the prescription for the painkiller. I'll see you next week, Sammi. Have a safe trip home, Ari." She walked out of her office.

Ari said, "Take her home. I'll stop by the pharmacy to pick up the painkillers and meet you at Sammi's house."

Michael said, "See you there."

All of them had ganged up on me. Nothing I had to say mattered. My only retort was to hand Ari my clothes and walk all the way to Michael's car on my own.

As he was pulling out of the parking lot, he asked, "Do you mind if I stop by my house? I need to pick up some things. It should only take me a minute."

I was still in my mood. I mumbled, "Sure." It wouldn't have mattered if I'd objected anyway.

***

I FELT SOMEONE SHAKING ME. The remnants of a heavenly dream blurred away. I opened my eyes. Michael had opened the car door and crouched down so he could look at me eye to eye. I said, "Hey. Are we home already?"

"Yes. Come inside. I bought us some food."

I was so comfortable that I really didn't want to move. I got out of the car carefully. There was no pain. All was good.

Michael closed the car door behind me, then followed closely behind me.

"I'm okay. You don't have to hover. I'm not going to fall over." The scent of the burgers hit me as I walked inside. I was starving. I hadn't eaten all day, so I headed straight for the kitchen.

Ari pointed to the seat she'd chosen for me.

I took it without hesitation. I was so glad she had everything open. I took a bite of my burger before I sat down. "I didn't realize how hungry I am."

They followed suit.

I forced myself to stop for a minute. I asked Ari, "What time's your flight?"

She sat back. "I need to leave in twenty minutes. My flight takes off at three."

Michael said, "It'll be late when you get home."

Ari responded, "I'm working from home tomorrow. My first meeting's at nine thirty." She ate a French fry. "How are you feeling?"

I had to think about it before I could respond. "Honestly? All over the place. I'm sad and pissed that today descended into more drama. We should be celebrating. Instead, the two of you are sitting here worrying about me. I don't want to be injured. I don't want you two to be worried about me. I'm happy to be legally divorced from Greg. Except for the pain in my ribs, I'm mostly okay. How do you feel?"

Ari answered, "Happy and pissed."

I asked her, "Do you think the drama will ever end?"

Ari replied, "Yes, I think this is the last of it."

I liked the sound of that. "I hope you're right."

Ari asked Michael, "How are you feeling?"

He answered rotely, "I'm okay."

Ari asked, "No residual anger? I was worried that you were going to go after Greg for a while."

Michael shook his head. "I'm fine. My temper flashed. Though I think he deserves to have his ass kicked, I worked through my anger and released it."

Before I could start feeling guilty about Michael fighting again, Ari said, "I knew that you'd stop Greg if he got out of hand. I used you. And I know that you'd have it no other way. Thank you. I love you, Mike." She reached across the island and took his hand.

"You're welcome, Ari. I love you too. Keeping errant assholes straight is what brothers are for."

They were working together. All I could do was cede. "Well, thank you for punching him really hard only once. He couldn't have taken another one."

Michael huffed. "I didn't punch him hard. I tapped him. If I'd punched him, he would've limped out of there. You're welcome. I held back for you."

Ari said, "I need to go." She looked at Michael. "I know she'll be safe with you. Her painkillers are on the counter."

Michael responded, "Okay, I'll clean this up. Go ahead."

She hugged my unhurt shoulder and went to her room to get her bag.

I finished eating while Michael cleared their places. I walked Ari to the door when her car came. "I'm glad you were here. Love you."

She responded, "Love you too."

I said, "Text me when you land."

She responded, "Will do."

I closed the door behind Ari and turned toward Michael. "What now?"

"Well, you've got a hurt right arm so you can't cook me food or give me a massage. So I don't know." He was so damned cute when he was playful.

We needed to do something that didn't involve talking, or looking at each other, or touching. "Let's watch a series." I opened the panel that hid the TV in the den.

"Alright. But I think that I should get to choose because you hit your head earlier."

I didn't look at him. I didn't give him the finger either. I just chose a sci-fi series on one of the streaming services.

"Seriously, how's your head?"

Dr. Maggie must've thought this was hilarious. I needed a

moment to get into the mindset to resist pheromone central. "Make us some popcorn. I'm going to go put on some warmups."

I was physically attracted to him before I knew him. Knowing him had strengthened it. *Nope.* Not going through with that line of thinking. My divorce hadn't been finalized for twelve hours yet. I wasn't ready to get into another net. Reality bit when I tried to use my right arm. It'd already stiffened up. The pain shut down my pheromone rush. I was actually grateful for it. I didn't need or want to go there then. I wriggled out of my suit pants and into some warmups.

When I got back downstairs, he had popcorn and tea sitting on the end table between my oversized chairs. He'd snuggled into the chair that he knew wasn't my favorite one. He had an ice pack for my ribs on the armrest of the chair that was. I noticed my phone as I was sitting down. I remembered I hadn't called my mom. She'd called me twice and texted me four times.

"I'm sorry. I need to call my mom."

"No problem. Do you need space?"

"No. I'm keeping it light and easy."

She picked up on the first ring. I told her that the divorce was final and that I'd ended up hanging out with friends. I promised I'd tell her the details in the morning. She loved it when I was being social, so she hung up without resistance.

I looked at Michael to see if he was ready to start the series.

He was in deep thought. He said, "Your mom doesn't know about the physical abuse, does she?"

He knew more about things that had happened to me than most of my oldest friends. It was crazy how he got so close, so fast. "No." I shook my head. "She's a judge. Only you, Ari, and Kenny know about that." I watched him process my response.

After a minute, he asked, "What?"

"Nothing. I'm just waiting for your next question."

"I don't have another question."

"So we can start the series?"

"Sure. Whenever you stop talking and press the button."

I smiled and pressed the button. "Thanks for the ice pack."

"You're welcome."

I put the ice pack on my ribs, pulled the throw around my shoulders to keep warm, and got comfortable. I watched the first two episodes. A text from Ari woke me up at the end of the fourth episode. The ice pack was body temperature, and I was drenched and achy. She'd made it back to New York. I texted her a kiss.

Michael was no longer in his chair. I heard him talking on the phone in the kitchen. He hung up as I was walking into the room.

I said, "You didn't have to get off the phone on my account."

"I didn't. I just ordered us pizza for dinner. How was your nap?"

"Okay. My ribs are starting to ache again. I'm going to take one of these painkillers." I popped one of them in my mouth. It stuck in my throat when I tried to swallow it, and I washed it down with water from the faucet.

Michael read the label on the bottle. "The dose is two pills."

"I know. I think one'll be enough. I don't want to take too much. I'm drenched. I'm going to take a shower. I want to wash today off. I should be done by the time the pizza arrives."

"Okay." He sounded dubious.

I went upstairs to my bathroom and got my left arm out of the T-shirt easily. When I tried to pull the T-shirt over my head, the movement caused a searing pain that floored me. I braced and waited for it to pass. It took a while, but it finally did. I tried again, more slowly. It led to pain again. I leaned back on the wall and tried to think it through. I couldn't get my left arm back into the T-shirt. I thought maybe if I pulled it over my head quickly, I could beat the pain. I tried and failed. I was waiting for the pain to ebb from that attempt when Michael knocked on my bathroom door.

"Are you okay?" When I didn't answer, he came in. I felt him take me in his arms.

When I could speak again, I said, "I can't get this T-shirt off."

He responded, "I know. I think the best approach is to cut it off. Where are your scissors?"

"In the top righthand drawer of my desk in my office."

"I'll be right back. Try not to move."

That was an order I could follow.

He was back quickly. He cut the T-shirt off me and made me take the second half of my dose of medicine. He inhaled sharply. He was looking at my side, horrified.

I looked too. He was right—it was appalling. The pain had

subsided enough that I could stand again, so I got to my feet. "I still want to take a shower." I expected him to step away.

"I'll help you."

I looked at him.

He narrowed his eyes. "I just found you on the floor. I'm not leaving you alone in here."

I wanted to protest, but he was right. I needed help. I conceded. He basically gave me a shower. He washed all except my most intimate parts. Afterward, he helped me dry off and into one of his T-shirts. There was nothing sensual about it. However, the intimacy was overwhelming. Other than Dr. Maggie, no one had seen a bruise that I'd gotten from Greg.

He asked, "Do you want to get in bed? I can bring the pizza up here."

"No. The painkiller is kicking in again. I feel better. I'll go downstairs and eat."

We went downstairs to the kitchen and ate the pizza straight out of the box. He hovered. I was too tired to make him stop.

A cell phone buzzed. I looked down out of habit. It was his. There was a text from the woman named Lana. He must've been hooking up with her regularly. It was good to know.

He wrinkled his brow as he looked at it. After a pause, he responded quickly. His phone buzzed again. He responded again. It seemed like he was changing his plans.

"If you're supposed to be somewhere, I'm fine. You can leave." I didn't want him to break his date with her because of me ... mostly.

He donned his serious, intimidating gaze and responded flatly, "I'm not leaving."

I backed off. Talking about how we felt wasn't exactly constructive to being friends.

They exchanged a few more rounds of texts. Maybe there was more of a relationship than I'd assumed. I'd set him free. I could handle it.

He was still looking at his phone when he said, "That was Lana. Like I told you, it's casual. I'd made tentative plans with her tonight."

I wanted to clarify he didn't owe me an explanation. "You're free to be with whoever you want to be with. Don't feel obligated to stay."

"I don't want to leave and I'm not." We were still on serious and intimidating.

I felt the meaning behind his words. I knew he loved me. We were teetering on the edge of a slippery slope. I concentrated on eating to make space.

Once we'd consumed the pizza, I showed him how to soak the herbs that Dr. Maggie sent. I let him put them on my ribs and shoulder, showed him how to wrap the towel around me to keep them in place, and let him tuck me in.

Dr. Maggie was right. I did need someone to stay with me. She wanted it to be Michael in case I needed someone who could support my weight.

I spent the night dozing. I couldn't get comfortable. My head was fine. My shoulder was tender but didn't bother me much. The sensitivity of my ribs was insane. I had a habit of sleeping on my right side. It hurt if I even thought about it. I couldn't sleep on my left side, either, because my right arm touched my right side. My only option was my back. The sun was coming up by the time I found the optimal position.

29

BEING THERE
TUESDAY, DECEMBER 5

I WOKE up to the sound of water. Michael was taking a shower in my bathroom. Happily. He'd left the door open. I could see him clearly. I watched as he sniffed each of my shower gels. As best I could tell, if he liked one, he used it on some part of his body, then moved on to the next one.

I wondered if he'd thought this through. Leaving the door open so that a friend could see you shower wasn't usual. Maybe he'd figured it wasn't a problem because we'd been lovers. More likely, he hadn't thought it through at all. He was just being a dancer; nudity happened.

He went through the same process of choosing a shampoo and a conditioner. He chose the conditioner that was way, way too heavy for his hair. It was obvious he liked the way it smelled and felt. His hair was going to be flat all day.

Unlike the night before, when he was helping me shower, this was sensuous. He had a beautiful body. I liked the whole thing: the way his shoulders crowned his torso, the way his tattoos high-lighted his shoulders, the way his goody trail led down from his six-pack, the furrows above his hip bones, the dimples above his ass, his ass, the way that his thighs flowed out of his torso, the shape of his calves, and the jewel. He was at ease and full of grace.

As I watched him dry off, I laughed to myself at how different the experience of him taking a shower had been for the two of us. I was laying there completely turned on, and he was having the very mundane experience of showering and getting dressed. It was quite apparent sex hadn't crossed his mind at all. He put on a sleeveless shirt with extra big holes for the arms. He wasn't far from shirtless. I closed my eyes as he left my bathroom. I needed some time to calm down and think of something else.

I decided to call my mom to fill in the details about the proceedings. She took her time answering. She was at work and in full interrogation mode. I answered every question with as much detail as I could without telling her dollar amounts. She was ecstatic that my marriage to Greg was over. She'd worried I would never leave him. She told me that, even though I didn't talk to her about it, she could feel he'd put me through a lot because she was my mother.

With Sylvia appeased and my libido calmed, I was in a good place to start the day. I sat up. Although my ribs were still incredibly sore, they were much better than when I went to bed. My shoulder was better too. I pulled on my warmups and brushed my teeth.

Michael was eating when I walked into the kitchen. He'd filled the teakettle with water for me. I turned it on. He had yogurt, fruit, and granola sitting on the island, along with an empty bowl and a spoon. I sat across from him.

I said, "Good morning. Thanks for taking care of me. Thanks for breakfast."

He assessed me. "You're welcome. You look better. How do you feel?"

"I must've looked like hell."

"You looked like you were in a hell of a lot of pain."

I looked around for my medicine. He pushed a glass of water and a napkin with two pills toward me. I opened my mouth to object as he tilted his head to the side and waited for my protest. I narrowed my eyes at him and took the pills. He half smiled.

I taunted. "What?"

"Nothing. You should eat. You shouldn't take that on an empty stomach." He smiled outright.

I filled my bowl with fruit and yogurt. "If we remain friends, one day, you're going to need another massage. Remember that."

He laughed. "I love the way you try to get back at me by doing things that I enjoy. I can take whatever pain you bring. I'll still feel incredible after you're done."

My spoon was full of yogurt. It took all my discipline not to throw it at him. What really pissed me off was that I knew he'd like that too.

"You want to throw your yogurt at me."

As meanly as I could muster, I said, "But I'm not, and that's what matters."

When I looked up, he was looking at me, and we were sliding down that slope again. I shook my head to clear it. I concentrated on eating my food. When I was done, I said, "I don't have any food in the house. We need to go grocery shopping. I'm going to change my herbs. Then we can leave." I put my bowl and spoon in the dishwasher and grabbed a fresh pack of herbs.

"Do you need help?"

"My shoulder's better. I think I can manage." What I needed was space.

I went to my workout room to change the herbs. The sink and mirror were bigger. I took a moment to examine my side. My ribs were still extremely tender, but the swelling and bruising were much better. I figured out a creative way to wrap a thin towel around me to hold the herbs in place.

He was ready and waiting in the den when I got done less than ten minutes later. I made a thermos of tea, and we left.

GROCERY SHOPPING TOOK a lot longer than it should've. We couldn't agree on what to eat for lunch or dinner. It took us so long that we ended up eating out for lunch. For dinner, we finally agreed I'd make a big salad with lots of vegetables, and he'd make chicken cutlets to slice up and eat with it.

It was close to 2 p.m. by the time that we got back to my house and put the groceries away. I picked up my laptop and settled into my favorite chair, the only place I was comfortable sitting, to check my emails and think about my project for a little while.

Michael asked, "Can I borrow your laptop after you're done? I need to do a little work myself. Jack sent me some videos he wants me to look at and comment on."

"You can use my other laptop. It's in my office, in the bookcase, on the far wall that's closest to the desk. Top shelf. Righthand side. It's silver. It's definitely dead, though, so you're going to have to plug it in before you can use it. The cord should be next to it."

"Got it."

"You can use my desk if you like. It's comfortable, and it has two nice big monitors."

"Okay. Thanks." He went into my office.

I opened my laptop. I only read three emails before my restless night caught up with me. I put my laptop on the coffee table and gave in to the urge to nap.

I woke up three hours later. Michael was still in my office. I got up to see how it was going. When I walked around the corner, there was an image of a man having kinky sex with another man and a woman on one of my monitors.

I said, "Michael, what …?"

Then I recognized the room from Pete's party. He was looking at the video with my rape on it.

I looked at the men again. Slowly, it dawned on me that the guy with the locks was Alex. I'd never seen his face because his locks were hiding it. I still couldn't, but I knew then that was Alex because of the look on Michael's face. Alex was conscious and being held down. He was being raped. The realization winded me. I shrieked, "That's Alex!"

"Yeah." His response was vacant.

I looked at the desk. He was using my older silver laptop, and I'd left the thumb drive I took from Pete's in it. I'd forgotten to put them up on the morning after I'd met Alex, and I'd forgotten that they were on the shelf with the laptop that I'd told Michael to use.

He said, "The other laptop wouldn't boot up. I tried this one because it was there. My only intention was to read my email and look at the videos that Jack sent. This video was playing when I closed the windows for Jack's videos. I didn't go snooping around your laptop. I didn't know what I was looking at, at first. I thought it was porn." He answered the question that was forming in my mind.

"You watched the whole video?"

"Yes."

I reached past him and closed the video. I pointed to the thumb drive. "I don't think they know I have that. I believe they'd kill for it."

"I agree."

I looked at him. He'd seen my rape. The only other person who'd seen it, who I'd ever intended to let see it, was Ari.

"I went into automatic when I recognized Pete. I didn't think it through. I didn't mean to invade your privacy." His eyes were glassy.

I believed that he didn't go snooping. He already knew what had happened to me. "I believe you." I shifted the focus away from myself. "Now we know what's going on with Alex."

"Yes. Now I know what he's been hiding, what he was afraid of you telling me about." He looked back at the blank monitor.

"What are you going to do about it? Are you going to tell your mom?"

He closed his eyes and shook his head. "I don't know. I can't tell mom. He has to tell her. I don't know how I'm going to tell him that I know."

He was sitting there, motionless. I'd watched that whole video a hundred times. It was shocking when you saw it for the first time.

I took his hand. "I'm sorry, Michael."

He squeezed my hand. He put his other hand on my cheek. "Me too."

I gave in to the urge to hug him.

We let the embrace linger. A moment or so later, I felt us relax. We were slipping toward that safe space in our connection.

I stepped back. "We should … ahh …"

He stepped back too. "Yeah."

I cleared my thoughts. "Ummm, let's make dinner."

He followed me into the kitchen. I took out the chicken and set it on the counter so he could see it. Then I took out the mixings for the salad, a cutting board, and a knife. He was sitting at the kitchen island with his head in his hands. He needed time for what he saw to sink in. I washed the chicken and soaked it. Then I made the salad. He hadn't moved. I rinsed off the chicken and laid it on a cutting board so I could season it.

He came up behind me and gently put his hands on my shoulders. He whispered, "Let me do that."

I stepped aside. "Okay." I set out a skillet and oil for him, then watched patiently as he went through most of my spices before he seasoned the chicken.

He was still processing. He wasn't exactly present.

It took great effort not to take him in my arms and hold him. I'd do that without thinking about it for any of my other friends. I'd do that for Tommy. But I wouldn't end up kissing Tommy. It was best to keep some space between us.

He created a great rub and sautéed the chicken. He sliced it up and laid it out on a plate. Both of us were silent: me giving him space, him lost in thought. Neither of us ate much. I cleared everything after we finished picking. I took two pills out of my medicine bottle and showed them to him before I took them. I got a smile in response.

I said, "Alex is going to be okay, Michael. Now that you know, you can support him."

"It's hard seeing him give up like that. Seeing him break."

"When you're being overpowered, sometimes retreat is your only option. You turn inward and guard your heart and wait until you can escape."

He looked at me for a long moment. "Yeah. I guess that's what he did."

"He's managed to keep his life going since that happened. He's put up a pretty good fight all by himself with no support. He's really strong. I don't think he's as broken as you think he is."

In an instant, he closed the distance between us and wrapped his arms around me. His whole body was trembling like when we had dinner at the hotel with Ari that first night in New York. I hugged him back and waited.

He released me a few minutes later and stepped back. "Thanks, Sammi." His eyes were glassy again. There were no tears. He looked calmer.

"Let's go to the den." I led him to a sofa. He sat on one end, and I sat on the other.

"Seriously, I didn't mean to pry. I'm sorry."

His eyes. I was drowning in them. "I know. You didn't find out anything about me that you didn't already know. You know what's up with Alex now. We're in a better place."

We sat for a while in a not too awkward silence, not looking at each other.

He broke the silence. "Do you want to continue watching that series?"

"I only saw the first two episodes."

"Me too." He turned on the TV and brought it up.

I leaned back on the sofa. I watched as the main character got cornered in a warehouse. *Then I was running through Greg's estate, only it looked like that house that Pete took me to. Both Pete and Greg were chasing me. There were people cheering them on. My father was running beside me, whispering about how Greg and Pete were just being men and how they'd done well for themselves. Greg was high, and Pete was trying to make me drink wine. They cornered me in a room with a balcony. I looked down off the balcony. It was one hundred stories up. I jumped but they caught me. I fought to free myself.*

I heard a familiar voice. The dream faded. I opened my eyes and sat up. "Shit. I was having a bad dream."

"Are you okay?" He sounded concerned.

"Yeah. Seeing that tape again brought some stuff to the surface, that's all." I tried to console him, but on the inside, I was still processing.

He put his arm around me. "Talk to me."

"I trusted both Greg and Pete. I trusted my father. And all of them betrayed me. I can't go through that again. I just can't." The words flowed out, raw with emotion and unedited. I looked at him to confirm I'd just said that out loud. The look on his face said I had. I looked away. He was always so close. And it wasn't like he was getting closer. It was like he'd always been close.

We were quiet again for a few minutes.

He said, "I understand."

I felt the truth of it. I'd been careful not to end up in bed with him again. I hadn't been guarding against our connection at all. It superseded the sex.

He said it again, "I understand." He kissed the top of my head and retreated to his side of the sofa. He couldn't have felt closer.

I leaned back and relaxed.

30

———

FRIENDS

WEDNESDAY, DECEMBER 6

I woke up to the sensation that my pillow was breathing. When I opened my eyes, I was looking at Michael's chest. I was lying on my back with my head resting on his left arm. He was lying on his left side with his head on my pillow. He was leaning slightly toward me, his right arm draped across me, and his hand resting on my left hip. He'd draped his right leg across my legs. He and I were both fully dressed in the clothes we'd worn the day before. He was hard and fast asleep.

Why was Michael sleeping with me?

I moved to sit up and realized my arm was tangled in his shirt. I couldn't get it out. I was trapped. I didn't want to wake him up. I shifted position and closed my eyes to see if I could drift back into sleep. I couldn't. I was wide-awake. I entertained myself by thinking about work and tried to be as still as possible.

I felt him chuckle. As dryly as he could, he said, "It would be easier if you shook me or said my name instead of trying to fidget me awake."

I matched his tone. "I wasn't fidgeting. I was being perfectly still."

"You were fidgeting. That's what woke me up."

"You woke up on your own. Why are you in my bed?"

"I think that's obvious."

"How did my arm get caught in your shirt?" I'd broken the cadence. My question was genuine.

"I don't know. It happened when you climbed into my lap last night."

"I didn't climb into your lap last night." I was keeping the distance between us after that crazy dream.

"Yes, you did."

"I didn't."

"You did."

"I'd remember it if I did."

"Not if you did it in your sleep."

"That's your story? I climbed into your lap while I was sleeping?"

"That's what happened. You started having another nightmare. I touched your shoulder, and you rolled into my lap. I thought you'd woken up, but you hadn't. I waited for a while for you to wake up. When I got tired, I brought you to bed. I couldn't get your arm out of my shirt without waking you up, so I lay down next to you. Unlike you, I was perfectly still, so you didn't wake up. You got to sleep until you were done resting."

So subconsciously, I had a different plan. I shifted the focus back to him. "None of that would've happened if you were wearing a real shirt."

"This is a real shirt."

"But it's not normal. The holes for the sleeves are way too big. Since you're so thoughtful, you should've thought of that when you put it on."

"You should've thought of it before you climbed in my lap."

"You shouldn't have touched me when I was having a bad dream."

"You shouldn't have had a bad dream."

I couldn't keep the banter going. I laughed. "That comeback didn't work. It wasn't funny."

He shifted away from me. "And we should get out of bed."

I felt it too. "True."

We sat up slowly so I wouldn't hurt my ribs. I had to concentrate to get my arm free.

He got out of bed and went mostly to the other side of the room. "How did you do that?"

I got out of bed and took a few steps toward the bathroom. "I don't know. You're the one who was awake."

Our connection crackled.

I said, "Yeah, I'm going to take a shower."

He responded, "I'll go downstairs and get breakfast started. You'll be okay?"

"Yeah, my ribs are better."

I went into the bathroom and closed the door. I looked at myself in the mirror. I was finally free of Greg … ninety-eight percent free of Greg. I was still managing his finances, but I was no longer married to him. Work was going well. I liked the people I was getting to know. I was successfully reconnecting with myself. I was finally building out my life here in LA. All was well. And then there was Michael. I was definitely not ready to open that can of worms. After all, I'd only been divorced for two days. I touched the mirror and said to myself, "You're doing alright, girl."

I took off Michael's T-shirt. The bruising on my ribs was better than yesterday. I jumped in the shower, then slipped back into what I'd worn the day before.

He turned on the stove as walked into the kitchen. He had the salad from last night sitting on the kitchen island. He'd started coffee and tea. I made his cup of coffee and my cup of tea. I set out plates and utensils and plated the salad while he cooked what looked like eggs. The silence was comforting.

He turned toward me. He'd made two very nice-looking omelets. He put them on the plates with the salads and returned the skillet to the stove. As he sat across from me, he said, "How did you sleep?"

"Like a rock. You?"

"I slept very well," he took a bite of his omelet, "until you woke me up."

We both smiled.

I took a bite of the omelet. "Is this?"

"I was trying to make that scramble thing that you made when I came by a few weeks ago. Did I mess it up?"

"No, no. You just made it look so posh that I didn't recognize it. It's delicious."

"Okay. I was worried there for a second."

He was something special. At a different time, in a different place ... "I'm sorry, Michael."

"What for?"

There was so much. "In a nutshell, for being so fucked up. I just want you to know that I'm not trying to lead you on or play with your feelings. I just can't start something new right now. I'm not ready."

"I understand, Sammi. I do."

I believed he did. "And I have no idea when or if I'll be ready."

He was listening.

I continued, "I know we have an unbelievable connection, but I don't want you to wait for me. Move on. Be happy. Maybe with someone who isn't as scarred as I am."

The way he was looking at me made me feel completely exposed. He said, "I understand."

It was time to lighten things up a bit. I reached to the middle of the island and took two painkillers from the medicine bottle. I held my hand open so he could see the pills. I put them in my mouth and washed them down with a sip of tea.

He smiled, content.

I tried another tactic. "What's on your agenda for today?"

"Not much. I plan to hang out with you and work some. I'll go home this evening. Do you have a plan?"

"I want to look at my emails and do some prep for my project. I hope this medicine doesn't make me feel too groggy today."

"How are you feeling?"

"My ribs are still really tender, but I can work around them now."

"You're moving better."

I looked at him. "Thanks for being here, Michael."

"You're welcome. You've been there for me." He smiled tenderly.

"Our boundaries are a little off at times, but I think we're doing a good job of becoming friends."

"Me too."

"Can you tell me about the pieces that you were working on yesterday while I was napping?"

"Sure. It's just one piece, and it's really just an idea."

We finished up breakfast while discussing what we were doing at work. Surprisingly, our projects had shared concepts and questions.

It was only 9:15 a.m. when we picked up our respective laptops to work. He worked at my desk. I worked in my favorite chair.

***

THE PAINKILLERS MADE ME FOGGY. I only managed to read a few emails before I drifted back to sleep. I texted Dr. Maggie that I needed a different prescription. I got up and moved around to get my energy flowing before I settled back into working. Dr. Maggie let me know that she was having a different medicine delivered.

My cell phone woke me up an hour later. It was Grace, Greg's mother, calling.

"Hi, Mama Grace. How are you? Is everything okay?"

She answered, "I'm fine, sweetheart. I'm calling to check up on you."

"I'm okay. How's Greg?"

"Gregory is fine. We got him into rehab yesterday. I spent some time with him this morning. I understand that he pushed you at the hearing on Monday and you fell. Are you okay?"

"Yes, I'm okay."

In a mostly motherly tone, she said, "Sammi."

"I bruised my ribs. They're painful right now. They'll be fine in six to eight weeks."

"I'm so sorry, sweetheart."

"It's not your fault, Mama Grace."

"Listen, I know it's short notice, but can I come by for lunch? I really want to see you and make sure that you're okay with my own eyes."

I didn't know how to say no to Grace. "Yes. Come by."

"Thank you, sweetheart. Kenny's coming with me. He wants to see you too. I'll bring lunch. You don't need to prepare anything."

"Okay."

"We'll see you at one." She hung up.

I looked at my phone. Grace was a force. I went into my office to tell Michael.

As I walked through the door, I said, "How's it going?"

He was in the middle of the room. He wasn't dancing outright, but he was clearly working through choreography in his head. "Pretty good. Your suggestions were really helpful. Jack likes your approach."

"I'm glad. Should I leave? I don't want to interrupt your flow."

"No. It's fine. I've captured this. Did you make good progress?"

"No. The medicine knocked me out. I asked Dr. Maggie for something different."

"Sounds like a good idea."

I said, "I want to continue the discussion from this morning at some point. It's interesting where dance and storytelling intercept."

"That would be nice. While I'm thinking about it, you need to put this someplace safe." He held up the thumb drive.

"Right." I took it from his hand. "Speaking of, how are you doing with knowing that Alex was raped?" I was consciously direct.

He shook his head in response. "It's still shocking. I'm working on accepting it."

I walked over to my wall safe, wondering if I should let him see this. Given what he'd seen and knew about me, the thought itself was a joke. I moved the picture aside, opened the safe, and placed the thumb drive inside. I said, "Makes sense." I put the picture back in place. "You seeing that video yesterday was intense."

"Yes. But I'm glad it happened. I needed to know what happened to Alex." He paused. "And to you."

"Yeah. What happened to Alex was much worse than what happened to me." A shiver ran up my spine. "Well, I don't know if what happened to Alex and me can ever be fully accepted or processed. I think you just decide if you're going to let it limit you and move on."

He nodded in agreement.

I continued, "Speaking of intense ... Greg's mother is on her way over here for lunch. She should be here in the next twenty minutes. She wants to check up on me."

He furrowed his brow. "Right now? Isn't it a bit soon? Shouldn't she wait until you're better?"

I shook my head. "No. It's fine. We're close enough for her to come by now. The reason Greg held that birthday dinner is because he knows how much I love his family."

He stepped back. "Should I leave?"

I laughed. "No. I'm a single adult. Boys are allowed to visit me. Stay. You'll like Mama Grace. Oh yeah, Kenny's coming too. She's bringing the food."

"Okay. I want to take a quick shower." He walked toward the stairs.

He had a point. I sniffed his T-shirt and followed him. "Do you have another T-shirt that I can borrow?"

"Yeah." He ran up the stairs two at a time.

As I cleared the top step, he tossed me a T-shirt and walked into my bedroom. He was making a beeline for my bathroom without a second thought. He started undressing as he cleared the door. He didn't look back, and he didn't close the door this time either. *Phenomenal.* I grabbed a pair of warmups and went into the guest bathroom to change. When I looked in the mirror, I realized my hair looked like I'd just gotten out of bed. I pulled it back.

I went back to the kitchen to put on water for tea and to make a fresh pot of coffee. Michael came back downstairs and sat at the kitchen island. He reeked of my shower gel, and his hair was soaking wet and full of my heavy conditioner. It was obvious he'd just showered. The effect of his efforts was going to be the exact opposite of his intentions. I laughed to myself.

He looked at me. "What?"

I couldn't stop myself from laughing. "Are you nervous?"

"No. But you have to admit that this is a strange situation."

"That's true."

Grace knocked on the front door. I went to the den, and Michael stayed in the kitchen. I opened the door, and Grace walked in and looked around. "This is nice, Sammi. Simple. Understated. Really nice."

Kenny came in behind her, carrying the bag with the food. He looked at his mother, then at me and shook his head slightly. "Hey,

Sammi." He kicked off his shoes, kissed my cheek quickly, and walked into the kitchen.

Grace leaned on the sofa to take off her shoes. "I really like the no shoes in the house rule. I have implemented it at my house too. Let me look at you. Are you okay?"

"I'm fine, Mama Grace. My ribs are tender but I'm okay."

She locked eyes with me and inhaled deeply. I could tell that she felt horrible about Greg's behavior. She gave me a warm, gentle, motherly hug. There were tears in her eyes when she stepped back. "I miss you, Sammi. I had so much hope when you guys got married."

I reached for her hand. "We don't have to end our relationship."

"I know. I know. But it's not the same."

"Come on. Let's go into the kitchen." I took her hand and led the way.

Michael was sipping coffee and watching Kenny try to take care of the food. He faced us when we walked into the kitchen.

I said, "Mama Grace, this is Michael, Ari's brother. Michael, this is Mrs. Albert, Greg's mother."

Mama Grace crinkled her brow at me. "Nice to meet you, Michael. I went back to being Grace Benoit when I divorced my sons' father fifteen years ago. Please, call me Grace."

Michael took her hand. "Nice to meet you, Grace. Can I make you a cup of tea or coffee while you get settled?"

"Tea would be nice. English breakfast, milk, one sugar. Thank you, Michael."

I watched as Kenny and Mama Grace assessed Michael from head to toe. Simultaneously, they looked at his wet hair, his attire, his bare feet, and back at his hair. They looked at the T-shirt I was wearing. It was clear that they both inferred that he'd most likely spent the night last night. Kenny's response was basically territorial. He wasn't cool with the idea of Michael hooking up with me, maybe because it was so soon, and he didn't want Michael charming his mother. It was clear Grace liked what she saw and was impressed by Michael's manners.

Kenny said, "I expected Ari to be here." It was clear from his tone what he really meant was why was Michael there.

Michael zeroed in on it, looking at him for a moment, then responding, "She had to go back to New York. Tea? Coffee?"

Kenny answered, "I'm good." He took a glass out of the cabinet and made himself some sparkling water.

Grace pulled me toward the stove. "Let's heat up the food." She stole another look at Michael and whispered, "Whew. That man is fine. I don't blame you one bit. If I were younger, you'd have some competition."

I responded, "We're just friends. How many pots do you need?"

Grace cooked when she was stressed. This situation with Greg had her really stressed. She'd brought two gigantic containers of stew.

"One. I made jambalaya and cornbread. The cornbread's still warm." She looked at Michael again. "I'd be his friend, alright."

I nudged her as I put the pot on the stove. "Grace."

She shook her head. "Child, please." She poured an enormous amount of the jambalaya into the pot.

I cut off four pieces of cornbread and put it in the middle of the island.

Michael asked, "Do we need plates or bowls?"

Grace answered, "Bowls and forks. I hope you like spicy food."

Michael responded, "I love spicy food." He set the island while Grace and I watched.

Grace whispered, "I like him."

Michael handed Grace her tea, then returned to his cup of coffee. Kenny looked less than amused.

The jambalaya was hot and ready to eat within minutes. Michael brought the bowls to the stove, and Grace filled them. They brought them back to the island, and we all dug in.

Michael ate a few bites and said, "This is delicious," without looking up or slowing down.

Grace said, "I'm glad you like it." She watched him eat for a minute, obviously pleased with his response. Kenny rolled his eyes.

I asked, "How's Greg?"

Kenny said, "He needs to grow up."

Grace added, "He's sad and remorseful."

I asked, "Did he go to rehab voluntarily?"

Kenny responded, "No. He went because the judge suggested it."

"I'm sorry for my son's behavior, Sammi. I'm sorry he pushed you," Grace said.

"I don't think he did it on purpose," I responded.

Michael interjected, "He didn't. Not this time, anyway. I saw him try to catch you."

Kenny added, "Before you punched him."

Michael corrected, "I didn't punch him. I tapped him. I winded him so that he'd calm down."

Kenny huffed. "He deserved it. He was intent on showing his ass. You could've done some real damage to him. But you didn't. Thanks for not hurting him."

"I didn't hurt him because Sammi didn't want me to. He deserved to have his ass kicked." Michael looked at Grace. "I'm sorry. I shouldn't have said that. I beg your pardon."

Grace responded, "No, you're right, Michael. He deserved a beating." She took my hand. "He pushed you by accident this time, but yesterday, he confessed to me that he'd hurt you intentionally in the past. I slapped the shit out of him. I'm sorry that I didn't do that sooner, Sammi. I was in denial. I knew he was having tantrums. I chose to believe that he was just breaking things. I'm so sorry. There's no excuse for Greg's behavior … or mine."

I responded, "It's all history now. I already forgave Greg. And I don't blame you, Mama Grace."

Grace said, "I love you, Sammi. I mean it." She looked at Michael. "You seem smarter than my son, but understand this, if you hurt her, you're going to have me to answer to."

Kenny said, "I'm second in line now. Take my word for it, you don't want a whipping from my mother."

Michael responded soulfully. "Sammi's become dear to me in a very short time. And she's my sister's best friend. Whatever happens between us, I'll always be there for her. I'm not going to hurt Sammi. If I did, you two would be third and fourth in line. I'd be first. My sister would be second. And, just so we're clear, I don't tolerate men hitting women, and I believe in consequences."

I said, "I didn't mean to destroy the mood. No one here is angry or fighting. We're having an incredible lunch. Let's get back to enjoying it."

We ate quietly for a few minutes. Michael finished his serving and looked at Grace cautiously. "Do you mind if I have another serving?"

He'd pressed the magic button to open her heart. She loved it when people loved her food. "Help yourself, Michael."

Kenny huffed.

Michael refilled his bowl with jambalaya. He ate it without looking up.

Kenny watched for a moment and said, "It's time for us to go, Mom. I need to get to the studio. I have work to do."

Grace stood up. "This is why I don't like to ride with you, Kenny. Speaking of the studio, thank you for introducing us to Camille. I really like her. She's incredibly talented."

I responded, "Yes, and she's a good person."

Grace put her and Kenny's bowls in the sink. "I agree one hundred percent." She walked over to the counter and made sure the container of jambalaya she'd opened was closed tightly. She reached into the bag that she'd brought with her and pulled out the second container.

I said, "Take that with you. One container's enough for me."

Kenny said dryly, "Everybody gets two containers. She's stressed about Greg. She made eight."

Grace hunched her shoulders. She put both containers in my refrigerator. She looked at Michael, who was back at the stove, scraping out the pot. "You may not need to freeze any of it." She gave me another hug. "Thanks for letting me see you."

Kenny hugged me too. "And taking some of that jambalaya off our hands." He walked to the front door to wait for Grace.

Grace nodded toward Michael, who was still eating, and whispered, "I like him. I think he's a good person."

I responded, "He is."

She walked over to Michael and hugged him. "It was very nice to meet you, Michael."

He hugged her back.

Grace touched his shoulders. She looked at me and bit her

bottom lip. She lifted her eyebrows and mouthed, "He's fine," as she passed me on the way to the front door.

I saw Grace and Kenny off.

Michael was leaning back on one of the kitchen island stools, looking like he was trying to remain upright, when I walked back into the kitchen. He'd cleared the table. "I think I ate too much."

I responded, "Yep," and sat down next to him.

Michael laughed. "His mom's nice. His brother's nice. How did Greg end up so screwed up?"

"I think it's the fame. He was a young teen when it happened. He's four years younger than Kenny, and he took the brunt of it. It was terrifying to him. It shaped him."

Michael pondered my response. "Blessings and curses."

"That sums it up: blessings and curses."

Michael squinted his eyes. "Can I ask how long you endured his physical abuse? Why would you do that?" How much he cared was clear.

I gave him the truth to put the question to rest. "Remember, I told you that we'd had a really bad argument?"

"Yes."

"Well, his physical abuse started after that. I put up with it for about two months. I was caught up in the idea of being committed to my marriage, and I honestly thought he'd work through it and it would end. One day, I was done. I couldn't take it anymore. So I left."

He opened his mouth to ask another question.

I had a feeling he wanted to ask what we could have argued about that would justify me tolerating abuse. I wasn't going there. Before he could make a sound, I said, "I'm not married to him anymore. All of that's history now. Can we talk about something different? I don't want to dredge all of that up. This week's been emotional enough."

He looked right into me. "Okay. Can I see the bruises? I keep thinking about how bad they were the other night."

That was a fair request. "They're much better." I lifted his T-shirt so he could see my side.

"Wow. That's much better. Thanks for letting me see it. The

image from the other night was haunting me. How's your shoulder?"

"My shoulder's only slightly sore now, and my head doesn't hurt at all. You've been an excellent caretaker. Thanks for being here. Thanks for taking care of me."

"Always."

Those words landed on my heart.

He continued, "You've got to stop diving in between men when they're fighting with each other, Sammi. This is the second time I've seen you do that. It's not wise."

"You're right. I won't do it again."

"Good."

I had to put some distance between us. "Now that you've confirmed that I'm all better, you should go home. Us cohabitating is counterproductive to the goal of being friends."

"True."

I was on edge again. *Space*. I got up and went to the sink to wash the dirty pot. "Please take that second container of jambalaya home with you. I'm going to have to freeze some of the one we ate from today to keep from wasting it."

"Yeah, I should go." He stood up and put his hands over his stomach and took a deep, deep breath.

We were both laughing as he exited the kitchen.

I was drunk on his pheromones. I had no boundaries. So I positioned myself to keep him moving toward the front door when he came back downstairs. I held out the container of jambalaya.

He took it, saying, "So just like that, you're putting me out."

With all the clarity I could muster, I said, "I am. Do you want a bag?"

He looked at the container. "No, this is good. Can I have a hug?"

I could pull that off if I held my breath. I gave him a warm hug.

He kept it short. "I'll check in later."

"Thank you."

I watched him get into his car and leave. I took an intensely deep breath to clear my head. My foot kicked something. Looking down, I found the new prescription that Dr. Maggie promised had been delivered.

I needed some fresh air and to be around some people who

weren't Michael. I texted Amanda and Cam, "Divorce celebration dinner tonight at that oceanside restaurant? 6:30. I'm paying."

I needed to come up with an explanation for my ribs. Ultimately, I decided to tell the truth about how it happened and to leave off the part about spending the last two days with Michael.

Cam responded immediately. "See you there."

I was sure Amanda was teaching a class. I'd hear from her later.

I made reservations for three, then called Ari.

She took her time picking up.

Before she could say anything, I said, "I can't believe you didn't call to check up on me."

She responded, "Like I said before I left, I knew you were in good hands. How are you? You looked like you were in terrible pain when I left."

"My ribs are insanely tender. I don't think I could move or sleep without the painkillers. But they're much, much better than they were on Monday."

"Good to hear. You sound good. When did Michael leave?"

"A few minutes ago."

"And?"

"And nothing. We're friends. We kept our hands to ourselves."

"Because that makes perfect sense. Now that you're divorced and the two of you're talking to each other like adults, you keep your hands to yourselves."

"He understands."

"I see. So what did you do?"

I couldn't tell her about the showers or us sleeping together. That would bring her too much pleasure. "Well, we were together, and, like always, shit came up. He saw the video on the thumb drive yesterday, and today, Grace and Kenny came by for a visit."

"Shit. Okay. Start with the thumb drive. You just left it lying around? How did he find it?"

"I left it plugged into my old computer the morning after meeting Alex and forgot about it. He needed a laptop to do some work. I directed him right to it."

"How did he react?"

"I'd told him what happened to me, so there were no surprises there. The rest of it was overwhelming to him though. I think he's still in shock about it. He's working through it though."

"Why would he be in shock about the rest of it?"

She'd seen that video more than once. I gave her space to figure it out herself.

"Sammi, why's Michael in shock?"

"Because of the guy with the locks."

"The guy with the locks, what … wait! Was that Alex?"

"Yes! Now Alex's reaction to me makes sense. He's been hiding the fact that he was brutally raped. He thinks that I saw him 'get emasculated.'"

"That's a lot to process." She paused for a moment. "What's Michael's plan?"

"I don't know. I don't think that he intends to tell Helen, though. I guess he's going to talk to Alex."

"Shit."

"Right."

She asked, "How are you doing with it?"

"I didn't watch the video again. I'm okay. In conjunction with the divorce and Greg pushing me, stuff came up, but it's not over-whelming."

"Good. I'll reach out to Mike."

"Okay."

Ari inhaled. "Tell me about Grace and Kenny's visit."

I recounted the meal. We laughed at the fact that Michael was so full he could barely walk when he left. We talked about our plans for the evening and said goodbye.

I took a full dose of the new painkillers Dr. Maggie sent. I took a car service to the restaurant because I didn't know how drowsy they'd make me. I told Amanda and Cam how I hurt my ribs before they could ask, and we had a relaxing evening, which was just what I needed.

31

LIFTS

MONDAY, JANUARY 8

ARI and I came up with and executed an ingenious plan for the holidays. We treated my mom and her parents to five days of Christmas at a five-star resort in Jamaica. One of my mother's best friends from college was from there. She helped to keep them busy when Ari and I didn't have spa treatments, sailing, or fine dining planned. I spent New Year's in New York with Ari. The year got off to an amazing start, laughing and dancing with old friends.

I was having a wonderful time filling out my life here in LA. There was no man-related drama. Except for the shared monthly financial statements, which came via email, Greg was out of my life. I felt much more balanced about my attraction to Michael. While my feelings for him hadn't changed, they didn't feel as urgent. I thought the reprieve fate offered us was working out. I believed this was the best, least potentially destructive path. We were doing a pretty good job of being friends. We mostly texted, not necessarily every day. We talked every few days. He was still hooking up with that woman, Lana, regularly. He insisted it wasn't serious, but I didn't know if I believed him. I wasn't ready to start hooking up or dating yet.

It was 7 a.m., and I was on my way to the studio to meet Gene to work on the production. We were leading the show as a team; I was the executive producer, and he was the head writer. Most of the preproduction work was done. The seasons would be eight episodes long. We were planning a twelve-week shoot. We'd hired the staff, but we hadn't settled on the cast yet. Today, we were setting up our workspaces.

I arrived thirty minutes early. Gene had already unpacked and was working when I walked by his office. I sat my big plastic storage bin on my desk and walked into his office.

He looked up. "I know. I know. We're not supposed to start for another half hour. I couldn't sleep."

I asked, "How's it coming?"

"Very well. The scripts for the first season are at second draft. There are places where I feel the dialogue is weak. And I have possible arcs five seasons out." Gene wasn't a perfectionist, but he liked to know where things were going and why they were going there. The cool thing was, given a new piece of information, he could pivot on a dime.

"Did you leave any work for the rest of us?"

"Yes. You need to read the most recent versions to make sure they capture your vision. I had some insights. I want to know if they make sense to you."

I put my computer on his desk and opened it. "Are the new revisions much different from the last ones?"

"Mostly no. In a few places, yes."

"I want to read them together then. We can do the next version together. It'll save time."

"Great. Did you think about casting?"

"Yes. I can see two possible cast compositions. Maybe we should wait until we're three or four episodes into this round of revisions before we make the final decision." I showed him my lists.

He laughed out loud. "This is why we work so well together. Check this out." He showed me who he was thinking about choosing. The lists were basically the same.

I got comfortable in Gene's office, and we got to work. It was like we went into a trance when we were collaborating. We had lunch delivered when lunchtime came. By 2 p.m., we'd thoroughly worked through the first episode.

I said, "Whew, I need a break. We haven't stopped for more than three minutes since we started this morning."

He leaned back and massaged his neck. "Yeah. I've been somewhat obsessed. I need a break too."

"I vote we call it a day on the condition that you don't work on this until we reconvene tomorrow morning at seven thirty?"

He hesitated.

I said, "I'll call Evan." I stood up and stretched.

"No. Don't do that. You're right. I'll take a break." He stood up too. "You have to admit, that was fun."

"Yes, it was. And efficient."

"Yep. It's good to be working together again."

"Getting shit done."

We hugged each other.

I watched him pack up his computer. He asked, "What are you about to do?"

"I have a workout scheduled at two."

"That's why you're so fit."

"That's why I'm sane." We exited the building.

As he was getting in his car, I said, "See you in the morning."

He responded, "Have a good evening, Sammi."

I sat in my car to let my brain cool off for a minute.

AMANDA GREETED me as I walked into her studio. "Hmmm. You look cheery."

"I am. I spent the morning working with Gene on the series that I'm producing."

"You really like this project."

"Yes. I'm really excited about it, especially because Gene's working on it with me."

Amanda looked at me with a silly smile on her face. "Hmmm."

"What?"

"I haven't seen you this relaxed before. I didn't realize how stressful being with Greg was for you."

"Hmmm. It wasn't all stress. It wasn't all bad. But that relationship had its share of challenges." I turned to walk into the female teacher's dressing room. "It needed to end."

I changed into my workout clothes quickly. Amanda was talking to a group of students and parents when I walked through the lobby on my way to the machine room. I felt a definite levity. I felt like myself again. I did an intentionally intense core workout to start. After an hour, I took a break to get some water.

Amanda, who should've been decked out in workout clothes and teaching a class, was wearing street clothes and playing a game on her phone at the front desk.

I asked, "Shouldn't you be teaching now? It's four."

She responded without looking up from her phone. "Nope. I ran into Mike yesterday. I convinced him that the kids would enjoy the Fundamentals of Lifts much more if he taught it instead of me."

I peeked around the corner. Sure enough, Michael was in there teaching. Ari insisted that the balance I'd been feeling regarding him was partially predicated on the lack of proximity. Suddenly, I worried that may be true. Hopefully, that was just for today. I turned to look at Amanda. "How—"

She interrupted me. "Don't worry. He'll only be teaching the course for four weeks."

I exhaled. Okay. I was going to see him four times over the next four weeks. It wasn't like we were sharing a space.

Amanda continued, "The class is on Mondays, Wednesdays, and Fridays from three forty-five to five fifteen."

"That's right in the middle of my workout."

"It's also the same time the class has always been. The time's perfect for the kids."

We both laughed at how I was making it about me.

Amanda smirked. "Uh-huh. You're over him, right?"

Although she had the perfect scenario to deny it, I knew without a doubt that she'd done it on purpose.

I retreated to the room where the machines were to stretch. Five or ten minutes into my stretching routine, I decided I'd overreacted. We'd spent over forty-eight hours alone in my house, and mostly, we were fine. We could be in the same building and be fine. My sense of equilibrium returned. I could handle proximity. I closed my eyes and focused on my breathing.

Five or ten minutes after that, Michael said, "Excuse me, Sammi. I need your help."

I opened my eyes. "Sure, what's up?"

"I need someone to help me demonstrate lifts."

"Michael, I'm not that good of a dancer."

"Believe me, you have more technique than they do. They're just kids. All you have to do is stand in first position, do a sauté, and maintain that position. I'll lift you over my head and then put you back down. You'll land gracefully in first position. Easy. Please."

He was right. I could handle that. "Okay."

He led me back into the studio. I expected to see Amanda as we walked through the lobby, but I didn't. "This is Ms. Harris. She's going to help me teach lifts."

I understood his predicament immediately. He was teaching a room full of teenagers who were all high on hormones. All the girls were giddy in his presence. I understood why he didn't want to lift one of them.

The movements required of me started off simple, like he promised. But with each movement sequence he taught, they gradually become more complex. I let my pride take over and rose to the challenge.

Just when I was sure that I'd reached my limit, he said, "Let's put all of those sequences together. Mark it with me." He taught the combined sequence without my assistance.

I made my way to the door.

Once the kids had started the movement, he caught up with me.

"Sammi. Don't leave. Okay? I'm hungry. It would be nice to catch up, and I owe you for assisting me. Let me take you to dinner."

I knew that he was doing it partly as a show. I was playing the role of shield again. I said, very nonchalantly, "Okay." I offered my hand.

He half smiled. He took my hand and kissed it. I turned and exited the room without looking back, showered, and put my street clothes back on.

Michael was surrounded by the boys when I came out of the dressing room. He was talking to them about how to strengthen their shoulders and weightlifting. The girls, and some of their mothers, were lingering on the periphery, enjoying the show.

Amanda was leaning on the front desk. She said, "See, I told you. They love it."

I said, "Yeah, they do."

She continued, "Umm-huh, all of them would be gone now if I were teaching it."

Michael looked in our direction. He said, "Listen, I have to go. I'll see you on Wednesday." He walked over to Amanda and gave her a kiss on the cheek. Then he looked at me and said, "Ready?" He walked toward the door.

Amanda said, "Hmmm. So class went well then." Her smile was full of smug satisfaction.

I gave her the evil eye.

She intensified her smugness and turned away. I walked through the door as Michael opened it.

He asked, "Do you have a preference?"

"Yes, I'd like to go back to that Mediterranean restaurant."

He huffed. "… And have dinner this time."

"Exactly. I have a question."

"Shoot."

"When did you find out that I was going to be there?" I was wondering if Michael was working with Amanda.

He answered without hesitation. "When I got there and saw you working out. Why?"

"Nothing."

"Come on. Tell me."

I felt like one of the girls. "I suspect that Amanda is trying to make sure that we cross paths. She knows that's when I work out."

He put up his hands. "I didn't know that was when you worked out. Honest."

"I know. I can tell that Amanda's working alone."

We entered the restaurant and got seated. Our waitress was there immediately to take Michael's order. I managed to get mine in too. I laughed to myself as I watched Michael settle into the booth. I was positive he hadn't noticed what'd just happened.

He said, "I have a question."

"Shoot."

"How long have you been working out on those machines?"

"Since I started college. I'm a bit obsessed."

"You're strong as hell."

"Not as strong as you."

He shook his head. "You may not have as much endurance, but

I'll argue about relative strength. I think that our mass to strength ratio's the same."

"You're such a geek."

"True. And I'm also right. Pound for pound, you're as strong as I am." Just like that, we were playing.

"I don't think so."

"So we disagree. I have another question."

I said, "Shoot."

"Would you come talk with Jack and me about telling stories through movement, basically continuing the conversation we started a month ago?"

"I thought you didn't want to tell a story with that piece."

"I don't. I want to stay just shy of telling a story but to deliver emotion as if there is a narrative."

I was becoming curious about his process. "How would you set the context for the emotions?"

"I don't know, but that's the line I want to walk."

"Hmmm. Maybe you could use repetition. I don't know." It was fun to talk about dance with him.

"Have lunch with Jack and me. Let's explore it. We both liked your ideas. It would be nice to get your feedback on the direction that we've taken."

"I'm not a choreographer, Michael."

"But you're a storyteller. Your perspective would be helpful." He was being charming.

I refused to cave completely. Working with him, watching him really dance would be a bridge too far. "Maybe."

"That's not a no. I'll take it." He smiled broadly.

Our food came. I was hungrier than I'd realized. I dug into my tabouli without looking up.

He said, "You might want to take a breath." He ordered a side of tabouli from the waitress as she walked by.

It hit me that the one I was eating was his. "This isn't my tabouli, is it?"

He shook his head slowly to imply that I should feel ashamed. "Nope. Your sandwich, that you chose, didn't come with tabouli." He was so cute when he was silly.

I smiled. "Sorry."

"Nope. Apology not accepted. You have no remorse. Uh-uh." He was still shaking his head.

"Why would you say that?"

"Oh, I don't know. Because you're smiling, Sammi." He laughed.

We ate quietly for a few minutes. The space we shared was so easy.

I took the last bite of my sandwich. "I have a question."

He responded, "Shoot."

"It's kind of serious."

"Okay."

"How's Alex?"

He pondered my question before answering. "Better actually. He's more at ease, more present, less guarded. He decided to tell Paulo. He's letting us be there for him. He's in pain, but he's working through it. I shared your philosophy about dealing with shit with him. You know, what your grandfather said about dealing with fucked-up events and how the only real question is if you'll let the action of assholes add limitations to your life. He said he found it very helpful."

"That sounds like real progress. I'm happy to hear that. I was worried."

"I know. Thanks, Sammi." He looked away for a moment. When he looked back, he said, "I have a question."

"Shoot."

"Will you be my assistant?"

The fates, with Amanda's help, were plotting against me. I shook my head no.

"Before you refuse, look at the syllabus. The difficulty level of the lifts doesn't change. We can practice before class if you're worried."

"Amanda could be your assistant."

"Please, Sammi. That way, you could run interference too."

I understood his position. Helping him earlier hadn't been so bad. My micro performance was fun. I could handle a public situation with him eleven more times. "Okay. I'll assist you. And I'll leave the studio with you. But we're not going out to dinner after every class."

He smiled broadly again. "Agreed. Thank you."

I looked at my phone. It was almost 8 p.m. We'd been hanging long enough. "I need to go. I have an early start tomorrow, and there are some things that I want to look over tonight."

He nodded. "I understand."

I stood up. "Thanks for dinner. Have a good night, Michael."

"Yeah. See you on Wednesday."

I reviewed my day as I walked to my car. Stimulating was the word that came to mind. I felt balanced, and I was having a good time. I wanted to call one of my girls to talk about it. Amanda was out because she'd instigated this situation with Michael. Cam was out because I was sure she was in on it. Ari was out too. She was on a flight to London. The evening would be a me evening. I'd spend it in my spa.

32

———

SYLVIA

FRIDAY, JANUARY 19

My mom was in town visiting me for the weekend, so I was taking the day off. I could afford to take the entire day because Gene and I had made so much progress. We finished editing our draft of the season yesterday. Gene was sending it to be punched today. We'd also agreed on the cast. Lawyers would commence negotiations with them on Monday.

As a guest, Sylvia wasn't bad. She slept in. It was 10 a.m., and she'd just gone into the guest bathroom. She was well-traveled, so she was at ease in most places. She'd been to LA enough times that there was no urgent touristy thing she wanted to do. We could simply hang out. The only things I had on my agenda were working out and assisting Michael. My only goal was not to let Sylvia and Michael cross paths. Mom and I were going to have a leisurely lunch, and then, I was going to Amanda's studio for a truncated workout. I planned to leave Michael's class fifteen minutes before it ended. That way, I could have Sylvia out of there before Michael could make it back to the lobby.

As my mom, Sylvia was much more challenging. She walked into the kitchen saying, "Sammi, I could see right into your neighbor's house from the guest bathroom. Why didn't you buy a house on a larger lot?"

"I thought you liked my house, Mom."

"I do, but for what you paid for it, you should have more land. I

369

could lean out the bathroom window and borrow the hand soap from the house next door."

"No, you couldn't, Mom. I like this area, and this is how lots are here. There are areas in Atlanta where the houses are close together."

"Yeah. But we wouldn't buy one of them."

"For whatever reason, the lots are relatively smaller out here in LA across most price brackets. I like this house."

She looked around. "It's a nice house. You should get a roommate."

"I don't want a roommate."

"You still have that car that Greg gave you?" She didn't like Spencer.

"Yes."

"You're not going to get rid of it now that you are divorced from him?"

"No, I like my car too."

"Do you have any coffee?"

"Yes, I bought the brand you like. All you have to do is turn the coffeemaker on. Everything you need's on the counter right next to the coffeemaker."

"Okay. Thank you." She walked over to the coffeemaker, turned it on, and looked at me from across the room. "Are you eating enough, Sammi? You look thin to me. You aren't depressed, are you?"

"I eat very well, Mom. I'm in the best shape I've been in since dance school. And I'm definitely not depressed. I'm happy."

She looked around the kitchen.

I looked around with her. "I'm doing very well, Mom. Everything's fine. Stop looking for things to worry about."

"Since you are single now, have you thought about getting a regular job instead of all the little projects? If you got a job with the government, you may still be able to get a pension."

"What would I do for the government?"

"You're an engineer. I'm sure that there are many things you could do for the government."

"I'm happy with my work, Mom."

"But have you thought about your future?"

"Yes. I've thought about my future."

"You have to—"

I interrupted her. "Mom, stop. I'm an adult. I know that I've made mistakes. I've handled all of them. I'm doing well. Please stop nitpicking. You're going to ruin our visit."

She poured her cup of coffee. "I know. You're right. I just worry about you. I want to make sure you're thinking things through."

"I have everything under control. Stop it. Go get dressed. The area near the restaurant where we're having lunch is nice. We can walk around some before we eat."

"Okay. Okay." She took a deep breath. "Have you eaten at this restaurant? Do you know if the food's good?"

"Mom! Stop! If you're going to keep this up, we can't hang out together. I'm serious."

"I'm sorry. I'm stopping. I'll go get dressed. I love you, Sammi." She picked up her cup of coffee and went back upstairs.

I wasn't sure I could handle another day and a half of inquisition. I was the only person she did this to. It felt like she couldn't see anything I'd accomplished. She hadn't helped me financially since I graduated from college. Dealing with her had me all wound up. I took a breath and tried to relax. I wasn't five years old. I couldn't let her pull me off-center like that.

When she came back downstairs, she was no longer scrutinizing my life. It seemed she'd taken my threat seriously. We had a nice walk and a wonderful lunch. Even so, I couldn't deny that I was happy for the reprieve when I dropped her off to spend time with her friends.

ASSISTING Michael had been much easier than I'd thought it would be. We reviewed the class plan ten minutes before class began. Though I exited the studio with him after each class, we'd only gone to dinner once more. Most days, he just walked me to my car. I'd gotten used to not reacting to how attracted I was to him. I started to believe I could love him as a friend. At least, that's what I thought.

Amanda had done a good job of making sure that she could maintain deniability in the situation. She typically disappeared around class time. She didn't bring it up when we were hanging out. Cam avoided the topic too, thus proving they were working together.

Since we saw each other every other day, Michael and I hadn't been texting and calling. We caught up before and after class. That day, however, our pre-class check-in was cut short by the father of one of the boys who had questions about how to support his son's aspiration of becoming a dancer. Michael stepped away to assist Amanda with giving him guidance.

My schedule of working out, practicing, and assisting Michael was on target until the kids had trouble understanding the last lift in class. I ended up assisting Michael fifteen minutes longer than I'd planned to. I walked out of the dressing room just in time to witness Amanda, who wasn't supposed to be there, introducing my mother to Michael.

As I got within earshot, I heard Sylvia say, "Well, you definitely have beauty in common with your sister. I think you may be prettier than she is. Tall. Simply gorgeous. How are you doing in the brains department? Are you as smart as she is?" She wielded directness like a weapon.

"Mom!"

Michael responded, "It's okay, Sammi. Thank you, Sylvia. I think I am doing alright in the brains department. I have a B.S. in Chemistry from Caltech." He was in full-on charm mode.

Amanda added, "And Mike's also an incredible dancer. If you guys don't have plans tonight, you should go see him perform." She avoided eye contact with me.

Sylvia asked, "So you dance professionally with a degree in chemistry?"

Amanda answered before he could respond, "Yes. He's the principal male dancer for Torus, one of the premier American dance companies. You should really go see him. You could go as Mike's guests." She was laying it on thick.

Amanda and I were going to have a serious talk about this. She knew I didn't want to see him dance because of my thing for guys who move deeply.

Michael responded, "Yes, of course. I'd be happy to give you comp tickets and backstage passes so that you could meet the company after the show's over." He was being all gracious and smooth.

Mom almost blushed. "Yes. We were planning dinner and a movie. I'd much rather come see you perform. What an unexpected treat. Thank you, Michael."

He responded, "The pleasure's all mine." I was surprised he didn't kiss her hand.

I didn't know if I believed he wasn't in on Amanda's little plan anymore.

"The show starts at eight. I'll leave the tickets and passes at the box office in your name, okay, Sammi?" He looked at me with a smirk on his face.

He thought that was cute. "Thank you, Michael." I made sure he understood this was going to cost him with my tone.

He looked at his phone to avoid eye contact with me. "On that note, I need to go get ready for said performance. It was very nice meeting you, Sylvia. I'll see you guys later." He gave Amanda a knowing look and walked toward the front door.

Amanda responded sweetly. "If you can get here about fifteen minutes early on Monday, I'll show you how I teach the kids how to use their cores."

He glanced over his shoulder as he walked through the door. "Okay. Thanks."

Amanda was retreating into her office when I looked back in her direction. "It was nice to see you again, Sylvia. I hope you enjoy the show tonight. Talk to you later, Sammi." She closed the door behind herself.

Before I could give in to letting myself tell Amanda off, Sylvia started in. She tugged me toward the front door. "Ari's brother is extremely handsome and charming, Sammi."

I looked back toward Amanda's office door. If Sylvia hadn't been happily dragging me out of the studio, I would've given Amanda a piece of my mind right then.

Mom continued, "It was a great coincidence that we ran into him. We can see that movie tomorrow. I'll really enjoy seeing this performance tonight. It's been months since I've been inside a theater."

I detached her hand from my arm and fell into step beside her.

"You know, I've never been backstage after a performance. That's going to be fun. I'm excited about that." She was on a roll.

And there went my swift exit. We got into my Mini Cooper.

She continued, "I'm glad that I followed my mind and brought a dressy outfit with me. We have just enough time to grab a snack, get changed, and get to the theater. We can have dinner afterward."

I responded, "Yes," to let her know I was listening.

"You know, Michael seems really nice. He's smart. He likes science and dance. You probably have a lot of things in common. I think you should date him."

"I'm not ready to date anyone right now, Mom. I've been divorced for a month."

"When you're ready, though, you should consider dating him."

I had been successful in avoiding this topic. "He's my best friend's brother."

"I don't see how that's an issue. I dated my best friend's brother when I was in college. If I'd been smart, I would've married him."

"Okay. I'll cross that bridge when I get to it. If the opportunity arises, I'll consider it then."

She patted my hand. "Good, Sammi." She was satisfied by that answer. She'd talked herself out of it, so I left it alone.

I was genuinely surprised by how excited my mom was about seeing this dance performance. She got dressed without a lot of chatter when we got back to my house. I wondered if it was dance or Michael's charm that had her so interested.

WE WERE SEATED third row center in the orchestra, perfect seats for an up-close look at the performers. I quickly came to understand how wrong I was about how well the photographer who did the Torus season posters had captured Michael's expression. Seeing him move live was a thousand times more mesmerizing than seeing photographs. Michael was a spectacular dancer. Ogling him while he was standing still was one thing. Watching his muscles ripple over his bones as he moved was quite another. Every movement was graceful, lifted, extended, and complete. He entered and exited jumps at odd angles with ease and power. The shapes he made in the air were clear, precise, and sustained. It was as if gravity, like my wards, didn't apply to him. He was as generous with his emotion and vulnerability when he was dancing on stage as he was as a lover. I couldn't take my eyes off him. The seconds when he locked eyes with me from the stage only served to intensify my experience because of our connection. In those seconds, I saw and felt so much more than the movement he was doing on stage. It was as if I could see and feel his soul.

As the final curtain closed, I also understood that all those times I'd thought I was in pheromone central, I was only in the greater metropolitan area, a distant suburb. That performance was my first actual visit to the city itself. Aside from being extremely turned on, I was in love with a whole other aspect of him. I'd been so wise to avoid this experience. All my wards were down. I needed to leave.

Sylvia was silent for the whole performance. She was mesmerized too. I thought she might've been mesmerized enough for me to get my swift exit after all. I locked arms with her and guided her toward the back of the theater.

Mom whispered, "That Michael is something. He and Ari come from good stock." She was impressed.

"He's an excellent dancer, Mom."

Halfway up the aisle, a young woman greeted us. "Sammi Harris?"

I answered, "Yes."

The young woman said, "Come with me. Mike's expecting you two backstage." She motioned for us to follow her.

My mother freed herself from my hand and fell into step behind the young woman without looking back. I watched them walk away for a few seconds before I followed. The fates were not helping me.

The young woman led us into the green room where other people were gathering and offered us refreshments. I picked up a glass of water for myself and one for my mother.

Sylva took a sip of her water. "I think some of these people are staring at you, Sammi."

Most likely, it was because they knew I'd dated Michael. I had no intention of telling Sylvia about that. I deflected. "That happens sometimes. It's because of Greg."

"Ah." She nodded and walked in the direction of the company members who were coming into the green room.

I hung back. It was fun to watch Sylvia in her element. She enjoyed meeting and interrogating people. She was entertained and having a good time.

I realized Michael was standing next to me when he said, "Hey."

I looked at him. My mouth was dry. "Hey." I could tell that sharing this performance had shifted our relationship for him too.

His mouth went slack for a second. "Umm, yeah."

I didn't know what to say either. "Yep."

He cleared his throat. "We should go."

All I could do was agree. "Yep. Watching each other move. Not constructive." That was a bridge too far.

He smiled slightly. "Now we know."

I heard Helen before I saw her. "Hey, Mikey. I ran into Jack and we got into a conversation. That was a wonderful performance." She saw me as she stepped in front of him. "Hi, Sammi. It's good to see you. I thought that was you. I could only see the back of your head from the mezzanine. I like to sit up there because you can see the whole stage. You don't have to make as many choices about what you focus on."

I responded, "It's good to see you too. And that was a wonderful performance, Michael."

I looked at Sylvia. I couldn't think of a polite way to avoid introducing our mothers to each other.

Sylvia sensed me looking at her and looked in my direction. When she saw Michael was standing next to me, she excused herself and came over to join us. "That was tremendous, Michael. Thank you so much for inviting us. This is the highlight of my trip. You're truly gifted." After seeing him execute his craft, she respected his choice of profession. Then she noticed Helen. She was in meet and greet mode. She introduced herself to Helen before anyone else could say a word. "Please excuse my rudeness. I'm Sylvia Harris. I'm Sammi's mom." She offered her hand to Helen.

Helen responded, "And I'm Helen Shelly, Michael's mom."

Sylvia said, "Very nice to meet you. I don't mean to be abrupt, but Sammi, I'm starving. I'd like to go to dinner now."

That was my out. "Okay. Thanks again, Michael. It was good to see you, Helen. I'm going to take my mom to dinner before she passes out." I looked at Michael for support.

He understood. "Okay. Thank you for coming. I'm glad you enjoyed yourself, Sylvia."

I took a step toward the door.

Helen said, "Oh, don't be silly. Michael and I have dinner plans as well. Join us, please."

Sylvia responded, "Are you sure? I don't want to intrude."

Helen answered, "The kids are close. It's not an intrusion. Come on."

Our mothers walked toward the door together without looking back.

If not for Amanda, all of this could've been avoided. I took a deep breath and massaged the bridge of my nose. The good thing was my focus had shifted away from how I felt about Michael to how to manage my mother and the situation.

There was nothing for me to do but to follow them outside. I watched Sylvia get into Helen's car. I watched Helen drive off.

I looked around for Michael. He was standing not too far behind me, squinting as he watched them round the corner.

I lifted my eyebrows at him.

He shook his head apologetically. "Yeah. I'll text you the address to the restaurant."

"Okay." I walked to my car.

Michael and I arrived at the restaurant at about the same time.

As he walked up, he said, "Listen. I didn't think this through. I shouldn't have been so insistent on you guys coming backstage." He was correct.

"True. But that ship has sailed. It's out of our control. All we can do is assess the damage."

"It might not be a bad thing."

"I'm sure that you can tell that Sylvia has no idea that I even really know you. That's for a reason. And it's not because I'm embarrassed about it."

"My mom's good with innuendo. I'm sure she's already picked up on that fact. She won't share information about our rela-tionship."

"Let's hope so. There's a lot that my mother doesn't know."

He understood what I meant.

We entered the restaurant. When we joined them at the table, they were talking about being professional women raising kids alone. Sylvia and Helen had an easy rapport. Michael and I ate and listened patiently as their conversation flowed from topic to topic. Occasionally, Michael and I got to participate. He was right about Helen being wise enough not to volunteer information. I let myself relax.

Finally, Helen yawned. "Sylvia, I'm really enjoying this conversation, but I've been up since six this morning, and I need to get home while I'm still awake enough to drive."

Sylvia responded, "I understand completely. Let me give you my contact information so that we can stay in touch." Helen handed Sylvia her phone.

Helen said, "If you don't have plans, I'm going to The Broad tomorrow. The person I was going with had to cancel. I have an extra ticket. I'd like it if you joined me."

Sylvia responded, "I'd love to. I wanted to go, but I never remember to get tickets."

Helen said, "Great. The tickets are for eleven. I'll pick you up. I'm texting you my contact info now."

Sylvia responded, "Got it." She patted my hand. "Will you give Helen your address?"

Michael responded, "I'll give it to you, Mom."

Sylvia processed that tidbit of information. Michael was oblivious he'd volunteered anything.

Sylvia seized it as an opportunity to wield her directness whip. "Helen mentioned that you two are close. You have a lot in common, and, Michael, I think you like my daughter. Why haven't you asked her out?" She aimed at Michael because she thought she could get the most out of him.

I answered for him. "I was married, Mom. You know that. I've been divorced for a month. You know that. I'm not ready to start dating again. We talked about that earlier. And you can't tell Michael who he should ask out." My tone made it clear I was fed up with her meddling.

Helen and Michael did what they could to fade into the background.

Sylvia kept on coming. "Well, I think that you two make a good match. Whenever she's ready to start dating again, you should ask her out, Michael." She looked at Helen. "Don't you agree, Helen?"

Helen shook her head. "No, Sylvia. I don't agree. I learned a long time ago not to make suggestions about who Michael dates. The kids are adults, and whatever opinions we may have, it's none of our business if or who they date."

Sylvia inhaled. "I know you're right, Helen. It's just that you've done such a good job with him. He seems like such a nice young man. It would be good for Sammi to date someone nice like him."

Helen responded, "Not your call, Sylvia."

I looked at Michael. He was beaming with pride.

Sylvia responded, "I know. I worry. I just want her to be okay."

Helen responded, "We have to let them make their mistakes and trust that they'll survive them."

Sylvia responded, "That's hard, girl." She extended her hand toward Helen.

Helen took it. "Tell me about it. We're mothers. We have to deal with it."

"True. Girls are hard. You always worry about some man taking advantage of them, especially when they're young. I can't imagine how it was to have a young Black male to worry about."

"Make that two. I have two sons. When they are not with me, there is a part of me that is always on edge, always. I have a daughter too. So I can relate to that as well."

They both inhaled and exhaled deeply and shook their heads.

Helen gave my mom's hand a quick squeeze, then stood up. "Let's get out of here. I need to make a pit stop by the ladies' room."

Sylvia stood up to follow. "Me too."

As they walked away, Michael said, "She's in good hands."

I covered my face with my hands. "I'm sorry about that. My mother tries to make all of my decisions for me. It's overwhelming." After the words left my mouth, I felt their openness and honesty. I was speaking from that intimate place where we connected.

"Don't worry about it. Maybe being friends with my mom will help." He was in that place too.

"She's taking her off my hands for a few hours tomorrow, so it already is."

"You don't tell her much, do you?"

"I can't. She's a judge. And she scrutinizes every choice and action I tell her about. She doesn't know that Pete raped me. She knows that Greg cheated on me, but not about his tantrums. Given the way she criticizes what I consider my successes, I don't know if I could take how she'd respond if she knew about the times I feel I failed." I was sharing too much.

He didn't say anything. His eyes told me everything I needed to know.

"Seeing you dance, it … I could feel … it was like I saw even more of you."

"I know. I had the same experience. I didn't expect for that to happen. Having someone watch me perform never felt like this before."

The close, quiet ease I felt with him was so much deeper than the pheromone rush. I couldn't go there. I just couldn't. I shook my head. "Michael."

"I understand. You need space. We should go home." He motioned to the waiter to bring the check.

I noticed that Sylvia and Helen were leaving the restaurant. I nodded toward them. "I guess we're supposed to pay for dinner."

He chuckled. "I guess so. You go. I'll take care of the check."

"You're sure?"

"I owe you for assisting me. Get out of here."

"Okay. Thanks, Michael." I didn't know how to process how caring he was in supporting my need not to be in a relationship. I said, "I'll talk to you soon," without looking at him. I had to get my guard back up before I got outside where my mother was.

I put on my calm, neutral face as I approached them. "It was good to see you again, Helen. Have a good night." I tugged my mother. "Come on. Let's go home."

Sylvia complied. "I'll see you tomorrow. Have a good night."

Helen responded, "Good night, you guys."

When we were in my car, Sylvia said, "I hope you don't mind that I'm going to The Broad with Helen tomorrow."

"That sounds like fun, Mom. I don't mind."

"I really like her. And Michael. She did a really good job with him."

"Yes. They're good people."

"She said you and Michael are close. You've never mentioned hanging out with him to me."

"He's one of the new friends that I've made out here in LA."

"Hmmm. I see. Well, I can tell he likes you. You should date him when you're ready."

I thought I could put this topic to rest in three volleys. "We went out on some dates, and now we're friends. It's better that way."

"I thought he was your best friend's brother."

"He's also handsome and charming."

"So you guys didn't click?"

"We get along fine, but he's soooooo handsome and charming; and there's a sea of women out here in LA. And he's my best friend's brother."

Sylvia patted my hand. "So it's best that you guys are just friends. He's really something though."

"Yes, he is."

She was quiet for a few minutes. Then she nodded. "Maybe you should give him another chance. Like I've said, not every man's like your father, Sammi."

I said sternly, "Mom."

"I know. I know. I'm stopping."

33

———

COURTING

FRIDAY, FEBRUARY 20

HELEN and my mother had been in contact consistently since the performance. It was safe to say they'd become friends. Sylvia was a fan of Michael. She let me know she liked him every time I talked to her, but she didn't suggest I should date him. Sylvia had been giving me much more space, and I knew it was because of Helen's influence. There was appreciably more ease in our relationship. Still, I knew there was a limit to what I could tell her without making her freak out and revert to her natural state. So I didn't push it. Michael was right; our mothers becoming friends wasn't a bad thing. He was lucky to have Helen. I had a deeper understanding of why he was so open with her.

This was the last day of Michael's class at Amanda's studio. We'd maintained the pattern of catching up when we saw each other in lieu of calling or texting. We hadn't talked anymore about the shift we'd felt on the night of the performance. Somehow, it didn't need to be expressed verbally. The way we interacted was quieter overall. The things we didn't say ran deeper. The way Michael related to me had changed in a way that was hard to describe. Our connection seemed to have more weight for him. It wasn't that he was more serious about it. It was like he had a different relationship to it, like he had a deeper respect for my need for space.

It was 7 a.m., and I'd just walked into work. Gene wasn't there

382

yet, so I didn't have to put my brain on right away. I went to the cafe to get a cup of tea and a croissant and chill for a moment. As I sat at one of the tables, Cory sat down next to me. He was in LA, visiting from London, to produce a limited series. He had slightly wavy, shoulder-length, dark brown hair and kind, light blue eyes. He was slim, somewhat muscular, and handsome. He went to the gym enough to stay in shape; movement wasn't his thing. He was a few inches taller than me. His style of dress was typically male: wrinkle free slacks, nice shirt, leather sneakers. He was confident, and he had loads of personality. His personality was his charm.

We'd dated for a short time when we were in grad school. He'd been circling and flirting for the past few weeks. The interaction was nice. It was light and easy and completely absent of the intensity and intimacy I'd always felt with Michael. Cory and I had gone out to lunch a few times.

"Morning, Sammi. How are you today?"

I said, "Not that bad. How are you?"

"I'd be better if I knew that you'd let me take you to dinner before I go back to London."

"When are you leaving?"

"Next week."

The last time I'd gone on a date with someone who was squarely outside of my wards was with Greg. This could be constructive. "Are you free tonight?"

"I am. Are we on then?"

"Yes."

"Great. What time?"

Gene joined us at the table. He had his laptop with him.

I responded, "How about seven?"

"That works." He stood up. "Gotta get to a meeting. I will see you this evening."

Gene watched Cory walk away. "I thought you weren't ready to start a relationship."

"I'm not starting a relationship. I'm going on a date."

Gene responded, "I see."

I couldn't help myself. I had to poke him. I looked at my phone. "You're late."

"And you're goofing off." He smiled. "I was detained."

"Sounds like fun." I could enjoy being detained.

"So. What's on the agenda for today?" He opened his laptop.

I responded, "We're getting down to the details. You can start working on scene breakdowns, and I can figure out exactly where we are with the set and costumes."

"Actually, we're going to have to pick a new female lead. Ours took another job."

These were the moments I loved working with Gene most. He liked to do pre-work just like I did, so we could be out ahead of things. Because of that, we could handle this hiccup in our stride. "Okay. I will call the casting agent and get that restarted."

We went to Gene's office and put our heads down to work. We looked up when my stomach growled. Organizing projects was tedious.

"I actually think I need a break more than I need food."

He rubbed his temples. "That may be true for me too." He looked at his phone. "I'm going to run an errand. It may take a while."

"Okay. Most likely, I'll be gone when you get back. I'll see you on Monday." I stood up and stretched. I picked up lunch from the cafe and returned to my office. I was still thinking about the same thing I had been working on that morning. I needed to change topics completely for a few minutes.

I texted Ari, "Call me when you have a moment."

My phone buzzed almost immediately.

I answered, "Hey, girl."

She said, "What's up?"

"Other than needing to hire a new female lead, not much. I just needed a break from work."

"Me too. I took a mental health day. I'm still in bed."

"Are you okay?"

"The politics at work are wearing me down."

"Things are still good with your boss?"

"My boss is great. So is his boss. The founder's son's trying to make a name for himself by exerting control. He's all power and no skill. He made a series of bad decisions and, naturally, it's everyone else's fault that things got fucked up as a result of his choices. They fired the people who executed his orders at the threat of losing their jobs."

"Your portfolios are okay?"

"Yes. My portfolios are fine. I'm not in the division that he destroyed. The problem's that they're talking about doing a massive reorg to cover his ass. I could lose the space that I have to do a good job."

If they were going to pander to ineptitude, they didn't deserve her skills anyway. "I wish that you could start your own fund."

"I don't know if I want to be a founder. I like playing with the numbers."

"You could escape to LA."

She sighed. "Unfortunately, I need to stay put for at least the next few weeks. Let's change the subject. I need distraction."

"I'm going on a date tonight."

"With Cory?"

"Yes. Light. Easy. Fun. I'm totally clear about my level of attraction toward him."

"I get it. Mike blindsided you."

"It feels good to flirt and know that it's not leading anywhere."

"I could use a change from that, but from your perspective, it makes sense."

"And I could use some male attention. It's been too long."

She grunted in agreement. "That, I can relate to. Do you think that Cory can handle a casual encounter?"

"I think so. He's going back to London next week. It would be like two ships passing."

"Have fun then."

"I will, but I'm worried about you. I want you to have fun too."

"Don't worry. Val's coming to save me. She has the whole afternoon and evening planned."

"Good. Tell her that I said hello. I think I'm going to leave work now and start my workout early. Do some extra stretching. Today's the last day of Michael's class."

"How are things between you and Mike?"

I hunched my shoulders. "Fine. The same. Quiet. You know."

"Yeah. I know. Tell him I said hello."

"Okay. Bye."

"Bye."

As I started my workout, I thought about how my life had been free of anything related to what happened at Pete's for three entire months. I smiled. It felt good to be relaxed. I used that energy and went deep into my workout. At 3:35 p.m., Amanda texted me, asking me to start Michael's class because he was running late and she couldn't make it back in time. Ballet bar was ballet bar. I felt up to the task of starting it, so I texted her back that I'd do it.

Michael walked into the classroom about thirty seconds after they did their first grand plié. He smiled broadly and kissed my hand absentmindedly. "Thanks." He looked tired.

I whispered, "Are you going to need my assistance today?"

"No. But stick around until the end of this exercise so that they can thank you."

I stepped aside and let him take control of the class.

At the end of the first exercise, Michael said, "Tell Ms. Harris thank you for helping us out."

Together they droned, "Thank you, Ms. Harris."

Michael said, "Thanks again. I'll call you later."

I played along. "Okay." I squeezed his hand and walked out.

I kept my attire casual and comfortable. I opted for cute over sexy, and I kept makeup to a minimum. I wanted it to be clear I wasn't trying too hard. In my mind, we were just hanging out. I threw on a pair of printed slacks, a cotton T-shirt, and a light, thigh-length sweater. I completed the outfit with my flat, comfortable desert boots. Cory arrived as soon as I sat my shoes by the door. He was ten minutes early.

He took me to an excellent, trendy restaurant. Conversation was fairly easy. We caught up on what'd been happening in our lives since graduate school.

Cam texted me just after we placed our orders. "You're coming to the Natural History Museum tonight, right? I'm spinning. I could use the support."

I texted back, "On a date. Maybe."

She responded, "Bring him. I'll see you there." She was trying not to take no for an answer.

I shook my head and chuckled.

Cory glanced toward my phone. "What's funny?"

"My friend Cam's a DJ. She's spinning at the Natural History Museum tonight. She's trying to make me promise to stop by."

He asked, "So there's dancing involved?" He tensed a little.

"No, I think people will just be standing around while music's playing in the background. Let's enjoy dinner first."

He visibly relaxed. "Deal."

The meal came. We relaxed into laughing about dating each other, cracking jokes, and talking shop. Other than the fact that we kept colliding with each other physically in a way that was awkward, things were going well. He'd opened the door onto my knee as we were entering the restaurant, and I'd stepped on his foot at least four times since we'd been sitting there at the table. I figured if I didn't move my feet, I could avoid kicking him. Also, if I didn't reach for anything, I wouldn't bump into his hand. By the end of the meal, we'd made a joke of the physical awkwardness and split the bill.

As he pulled out of the restaurant parking lot, he said, "You know what, I'd like to go to the museum if you're open to it. I haven't been to a dance party in a very long time."

"Like I said, this isn't going to be a dance party. This is going to be people standing around while my friend's spinning."

"Even better."

"Okay, let's go."

The space where Cam was spinning was almost full when Cory and I arrived. The set she was playing was more atmospheric than dance, but you could feel the undercurrent. She would've brought it if people had started moving.

Cory reached for my hand.

I misinterpreted the cue and moved it away because I thought it was in his way. I looked at him to apologize when I realized what'd just happened.

He took my hand, and we both laughed.

He said, "She's good."

I responded, "She's holding back. She's amazing."

Amanda walked up. "Hey, Sammi. Cam told me you were coming."

I laughed. "I told her that I'd try." I nodded toward Cory. "This is Cory Green. He's a friend of mine from grad school." I gestured toward Amanda. "Cory, this is my friend, Amanda."

Cory blossomed with personality. "It's very nice to meet you, Amanda."

Amanda looked at our entwined hands and smiled politely. "Same here, Cory." She leaned in so only I could hear. "Mike's here. He's over there." She pointed in his direction. I looked. I could see his head above the crowd.

So that was why Cam was so insistent about my coming. Amanda had claimed innocence when I confronted her about telling my mother about Michael's performance. She'd just lost all deniability. I gave her the evil eye.

Amanda blew me a kiss as she backed away. "Nice to meet you, Cory."

After that, I had to concentrate on not looking in Michael's direction.

Just as Cory and I settled into pleasant conversation, Cam mixed in samples from Rufus and Chaka Khan's song "Sweet Thing." A digitized, distorted version of Chaka singing about irrefutable attraction played in a loop on top of the ambient track she was playing.

I looked at Cam. She looked me squarely in the eye and grinned. I closed my eyes and shook my head.

Cory interpreted it as an indication that I was fond of the song. He lifted our entwined hands and spun me around.

I fell into him before I could regain my balance. I looked toward Michael unconsciously. He was looking at me. We locked eyes. I could tell he was there with someone. But I could barely see the top of her head. He wasn't serious about whoever it was. I could tell by his body language.

Cam switched the sample to the line where Chaka declares a lifetime of love. I covered my mouth and shook my head. Michael laughed.

Cam wouldn't look up from the turntable after that.

Michael was talking to the person who I couldn't see when I looked back in his direction. He looked back at me when he finished. He nodded and walked toward the door.

Cory asked, "Are you ogling someone while you're on a date with me?"

I looked at him. "Not really. Do you mind if we leave?"

"Don't take this as an indication that I don't like standing around listening to good music, but not at all."

He hadn't let go of my hand. He led me back to his car. "So what now? Are you ready to call it a night?"

"No. It's early, and I'm still having fun. Let's go have a few drinks."

"Okay."

We went to a bar not too far away. We had one drink each and talked shop.

Part of me wanted to stop the pretense and cut to the chase, but I knew that sometimes guys freak if they feel they aren't the ones leading the charge. So I waited.

He was a decent guy. An hour passed before he tried to kiss me. I let him.

He wasn't bad at kissing, but if I responded instead of following, it threw him off and he had to reset.

After a while he asked, "Are you seducing me, Sammi?"

I responded, "I am. I'm horny. You're an old friend."

He smiled. "I don't have a problem with a woman who knows what she wants."

I took that as he was open. "So let's go to your place." That way, I could leave when I was ready to.

He put money on the table and stood up. "After you."

When we got to his apartment, we resumed kissing and worked our way up to the act itself. After we put protection in place, our first few attempts to make contact were physically awkward, like at the restaurant. Luckily, we could laugh about it.

It took me a few minutes to understand his approach. He was being kind and attentive. He clearly wanted to please me. It was also clear there was a list of actions he thought would achieve that. The thing was, as best I could tell, he was changing from one movement to the next based on time. He wasn't responding to any of my physical cues. All of that said, he wasn't a bad lover—when I just relaxed and let him run his script. He turned off the script when we started fucking. I smiled because I understood he'd done what he thought he should do so he could relax into doing what he really wanted to do. He came before I did and passed out immediately.

That was my opportunity to make a graceful exit. He called me as I sank down into my favorite chair at home.

I answered, "Hello, Cory. How was your nap?"

"You didn't have to leave, Sammi."

"I know. You're the first since my divorce was finalized. I wanted some space to process."

"I understand. You're home safe and you're okay?"

"Yes and yes."

He sighed. "Good. Have a good night then. And remember, I'm here if you need me."

"There's a good chance that I'll take you up on that."

"I live to serve."

"Good night, Cory."

We hung up.

Even though I didn't have an orgasm, I'd enjoyed myself. Being touched was fun. It felt good. It still felt good. And I wanted Michael. I didn't know if anyone else would ever touch me the way he did. I feared that I'd always yearn for him. But I didn't let that destroy my postcoital zen.

34

AWARDS
FRIDAY, FEBRUARY 8

CORY WAS BACK IN LONDON. I'd hooked up with him a few times before he left. I even had an orgasm once. I could tell Michael had feelings about me hooking up with someone else—not unlike I had feelings about him hooking up with other people. I had to resist the urge to explain myself to him. We weren't in a relationship. I didn't owe him an explanation any more than he owed me one. We were both free to move on as we pleased. If I were being honest with myself, I didn't know how much moving on I'd do at this point. With Michael as part of my history, I wasn't sure anyone else could ever satisfy me. I was certain I didn't want to survive a breakup with him though. So, for the time being, I'd settle for this strange truce. In spite of myself, I'd admitted to Michael that my hook ups with Cory were purely physical for me. It helped to ease some of the awkwardness between us.

Gene and I had been auditioning actresses to replace the female lead. There were a few possibilities, but no one felt like the perfect fit yet. We had two more audition sessions scheduled for next week: one on Tuesday and another on Wednesday. Come Thursday morning, our goal was to have chosen a replacement.

It was 10 a.m., and I was still in bed. I was taking the day off because an independent film I worked on that had been released last March was nominated for a best film award by one of the organizations that supported independent films in LA. The awards ceremony was that evening. The task I was currently working on was beauty rest.

My phone rang. I looked down and saw Gene's name on the screen.

I answered, "Hello."

"Hey, Sammi. I'm calling to let you know that I won't be able to go to that awards show with you tonight." He sounded exhausted.

"What's wrong?"

"I brought Evan to the ER last night, and they admitted him. He has pneumonia."

I could tell he was sobbing. "Is he going to be okay?"

"Yes. He's getting better now. The antibiotics are helping. I'm just releasing. I was so worried."

"Can I do anything to help?"

"Do you mind bringing me my laptop? It's in my desk. Now that I'm sure he's going to be fine, I need something to distract me."

"Not at all."

"I could go get it myself, but I don't want to leave him."

"I understand. I'll be there within an hour."

"Thanks, Sammi."

I showered, dressed, and delivered Gene's computer to him. Then I stopped by Amanda's studio. She was there alone, doing paperwork.

She unlocked the door to let me in. "I thought you weren't working out today."

"I'm not. I came to see if you'd be up for lunch?"

"Sure."

"I also want to know if you'd come to the awards ceremony with me."

She crinkled her brow. "Gene bailed?"

"Evan's in the hospital. He's getting better though."

"What's wrong?"

"Pneumonia."

Amanda said, "Whew, I'm glad Evan's going to be alright."

I begged, "Come with me tonight."

"Uh-uh. I have plans tonight."

"Oh, you can postpone. I don't want to go alone because I'm pretty sure that Greg'll be there."

"Why would Greg be there?"

"He writes lots of scores. Please."

Amanda squinted. "You know. I think I have a solution for this. You can take my date." She picked up her cell phone and texted someone.

I was confused. Before I could formulate my question, my cell phone buzzed. It was Michael.

I answered, "Hello."

"I thought Gene was going with you to your ceremony."

"Evan got sick."

"I see. Amanda just kicked me to the curb. So I'm willing to go with you if you want me to."

Amanda responded into my phone, "Yes. Thank you, Mike. That would be perfect."

I looked at her incredulously. She challenged me with her eyes.

I couldn't think of anyone else. A bonus was that Greg would likely keep his distance. I could handle an evening in public with Michael. I gave in. "You need a tux."

"That's not a problem. Can you send me a picture of your dress?"

"Yep."

He responded, "That's pretty. What time do I need to pick you up?"

"Six should be fine."

"Okay. I'll be in touch." He hung up.

Amanda was beaming.

"Are you ever going to stop trying to make sure we spend time together?"

She shook her head. "Uh-uh. Nope. Let's go get some food."

I got a text from Michael. "Reached out to Maria for a tux. She's arranged hair and makeup for you. It'll be fun. Go with it. Can I pick you up at your house at one thirty?"

My first inclination was to decline. But having someone else do my hair and makeup would be fun. I looked at the time on my phone. It was noon. I texted back. "Yes. Thank you." I smiled.

Amanda said, "Admit it. You're looking forward to spending the evening with Mike."

I rolled my eyes at her. "You know that the issue isn't that I don't enjoy spending time with Michael. The reason that I'm smiling is that his modeling agency is going to do my hair and makeup."

"Ooh. So you're about to get pampered all because of me." She was beaming again. "You can buy me lunch to thank me."

"We have to rush because I need to get back to my house by one fifteen."

We went to a salad bar. Amanda was smart enough to not press me about getting back with Michael. We talked about executing a strategy for our careers instead.

I WALKED into my house running. I threw my base, concealer, and foundation powder into a makeup pouch. It wasn't likely they'd have those things to match my skin color. I also threw in my bronzer. Looking around my bathroom, I decided to bring my shampoo, conditioner, and hair gel. The last things my hair needed were suds and alcohol. I took out a garment bag for my dress, my wrap, and my shoes. The only thing I could think of that was missing was jewelry. I put earrings, a necklace, and bracelets into my purse. I put the hair products into a plastic pouch and threw it and the makeup pouch into a backpack. I was ready with five minutes to spare.

Michael knocked on the door.

I remembered underwear. I opened the door. "I forgot something. Be right back." I retrieved a set from my bedroom and threw them into the garment bag. Leaning against the couch in a relaxed posture, I said, "Ready when you are."

Michael shook his head and chuckled. "Hello, Sammi. How are you?"

Formal it was. "Very well, Michael. And you?"

He went into character. "I'm well as well." He did a graceful bow. "After you."

As we approached his car, I asked, "Should I drive …?"

He widened his eyes. "I'll bring you home."

I put my bags in the back seat. When I was settled, I said, "You're laughing at me."

He smiled. "True."

"That's wrong."

"Is it?"

I lingered in our silly, peaceful place. It was nice. I was happy he was coming with me. As he pulled into the agency parking lot, I said, "Thanks for changing your plans and for arranging this."

"It's my pleasure. You're welcome."

I picked up my bags, and we walked up to the front door of the agency. A stunning mixed-race person opened the door just as we arrived. They had toffee skin with wavy, dark hair and warm brown eyes. You could choose to assign any number of ethnicities to them. They said, "Hello, Sammi. My name's Sharlie. I'll be assisting you in your preparations this afternoon."

Sharlie reached for my garment bag with a look of confusion.

I handed it to them. "This is my dress."

Sharlie said, "Oh, yes. I heard about that." They held my garment bag out to the side with dismissive disdain. "Hang this up somewhere, please."

A young lady, who I assumed was Sharlie's assistant, caught my garment bag as they dropped it and walked away.

I looked at Michael. He had his back to me. He was pretending to look for someone. What he was actually doing was laughing. I could tell.

Sharlie pointed to my backpack. "What's all of this?"

I answered, "My foundation and my shampoo."

Sharlie took my backpack and put it on their shoulder. "I see. Well, first things first. Let me get you into a dressing room so that I can look at you."

I looked at Michael again. He said, "Go with it. Resistance is futile."

Sharlie took my arm and led me to a dressing room. They pointed to the bathroom. "Wash everything except your hair. Put on the thong, robe, and slippers that are in the bathroom. The thong will be all you're wearing under the robe, and you can leave your clothes hanging in the bathroom." They turned and walked to the other side of the room and opened a pantry that was full of products.

I whispered, "Okay." I took a quick, but thorough, shower. The shower gel was so rich it felt like lotion. It made my skin silky smooth. I was relaxing into not being in control. That caliber of pampering felt good so far. The thong was new. The robe was soft and thick and thirsty.

Sharlie was about to knock on the bathroom door when I opened it. "I was getting worried. I thought maybe you passed out in there." They pushed up the sleeve of my robe and ran their fingers along my arm. They huffed and said, "Your skin's dry and scaly. You need a body scrub and a wrap." They shook their head in frustration. "There's not enough time for that." They inspected my legs. "At least you've waxed." They handed me a bottle of lotion. "Put this all over your body. It's the best we can do."

I did as I was told. When I was done putting lotion everywhere I could reach, Sharlie said, "Okay, now take off the robe so that I can lotion your back. I need to get you to the salon."

I complied.

When the lotion had been applied, they quickly took my measurements, helped me slip back into my robe, and then escorted me across the hall into a salon. Michael was in a chair on the far side of the room. There were three people working on him: one was giving him a manicure, one was giving him a facial, and one was washing his hair. He looked completely relaxed.

I sat in the chair Sharlie pointed to, and three different people got to work on me. I had no idea I needed so much work. Ari would love this.

It was like I was on a conveyer belt. My fingernails were clipped, filed, and buffed, and my facial was applied while my hair was being washed. My facial set and toenails were done while my hair got a hot oil treatment. When the oil treatment was finished, I was taken to a bathroom to remove the facial. A series of creams were applied to my face, and I was returned to the salon where my hair was rinsed and styling began.

The manicurist asked, "Silver or gold?"

I responded, "Silver."

She chose a rich turquoise nail polish color based on that response without asking for my opinion.

After thirty minutes or so, the stylist was the only person left working on me. She said, "My name's Jasmine." She handed me a glass of water. "Drink up." She ran her fingers through my hair. "Your hair's in good shape. The products you use are good. Tonight,

I'm going to use something different. I think you'll like it. It'll make your curl pattern pop more." She gave me a wonderful scalp massage as she applied the products.

The makeup artist met me at the dryer. "Sharlie showed me your foundation. It's a good product, but it has too much yellow in it for you. I'm going to mix a custom blend that actually matches your skin tone. There'll be plenty for you to take home." Minutes later, she started to apply foundation to my face.

Sharlie walked into the room. "It's five fifteen, people. We need to get her dressed. How are we doing with time?"

Jasmine responded, "I'll be done with her hair in ten minutes."

The makeup artist responded, "I'm finishing up eyes now. All that's left after that is lipstick."

Ten minutes later, Sharlie escorted me back into the dressing room. They squealed as they closed the door. "You look incredible. I can't wait for you to put on the dress. Take off that robe so that we can tape your breasts."

I hadn't seen myself in the mirror since my makeup had been applied. I looked around the room. There were mirrors, but none pointed in my direction. To my surprise, they let me stick on the adhesive bra myself.

As soon as I was done, they said, "Step into this."

It wasn't the dress I'd brought with me. That was why Michael was laughing. That was what he meant about resistance being futile. I took a deep breath and obeyed. It was a full-length dress that fit my body and hung straight from my hips. There was a split up to the top of my thigh on each side that kept the straightness from being restrictive. It had a scoop neckline, and the straps almost slipped off my shoulders. The top of it was the same color as me. Starting just above my breasts, it faded into a rich textured abstract tapestry that reminded me of a Mark Bradford painting. The colors were turquoise, orange, ochre, tan, and black. It was stunning.

They zipped me into it and handed me a pair of high, strappy black patent leather sandals.

I put on the sandals.

Sharlie clapped and said, "Perfect." They turned one of the mirrors so I could see myself.

I hardly recognized myself. I said, "Wow," turning in the mirror to look from all angles.

Sharlie looked at their phone. "Let me get you downstairs before Maria has my ass."

Maria was waiting when we returned to the lobby. She inspected me. "Very, very nice, except the lipstick's too light. Bring me the reds."

The makeup artist presented five tubes.

Maria said, "That one." She chose a red that was two shades closer to brick than the one I had on.

The makeup artist changed my lipstick.

Maria inspected me again. "Much better. Jewelry."

Sharlie draped an Egyptian-inspired necklace on my chest that fit around my neck like a choker and covered the exposed part of my chest. They put matching earrings in my ears and a plain silver cuff on each of my arms.

Maria nodded. "Well executed, people. You're simply beautiful, Sammi."

I wanted to protest about the jewelry, but Maria turned away from me as Michael walked into the room. She inspected him. "Lose the tie. Unbutton the top button of the shirt. Replace the sneakers with flat black slippers."

Michael bit his lip and smiled at me. He was wearing a deep, dark brown tuxedo with a shawl lapel. He had on a white shirt and a vest that echoed my dress, except the pattern wasn't as small and the hues were much darker. He was dashing in a tux. You could sense his frame, but it was his grace and ease that caught your attention. He was smooth.

She pointed toward a door. "Filipe! I need pictures."

Michael took my hand. "Beautiful." He led me into a room with a high ceiling and lots of lights. When we got to the center of the room, he led me into a turn. He acted like he was going to kiss me on the lips.

I leaned away from him. He kissed my hand instead.

A man who I assumed was Filipe said, "Begin."

Michael said, "Follow my lead." We posed for a few minutes.

Filipe said, "You're done, Sammi. Mike, keep it going. Standards."

I got out of the way. I stood behind Maria and Filipe, not far from the door.

Maria was looking at a monitor. She nodded and whispered something to Filipe. She walked over to me. "Sammi, I'd like to use those photos, please. I'll use them for two purposes: to sell Michael to the designer that you guys are wearing and on my site. I'll send you paperwork on Monday. I'll pay you." Michael joined us. "Now, get out of here. Your car's waiting outside."

I pointed to the necklace. I was trying to figure out how to express my appreciation.

Maria said, "You can drop off the jewelry and clothes when you come back to get your car. Have fun." She walked out of the studio.

I inhaled and went with it. Michael and I got into the car that Maria had provided, and we were off.

I said, "Thank you. This is way more than I was asking for."

He responded, "Thanks goes to Maria. All I asked was to borrow a tux. Everything else is her vision."

"When did you find out that she'd vetoed my dress?"

"When I forwarded her your picture of it. She wanted to see it so that she could coordinate the suit."

"You didn't protest?"

He widened his eyes and shook his head. "I told her that I thought your dress was pretty. I knew that the price I had to pay for borrowing a suit from Maria was letting her dress me. From her perspective, by wearing her clothes, I'm representing her and her firm. I respect that. I didn't expect for it to extend to you. However, when she said no to your dress, the only clear path forward was to let go. I figured it would be a nice treat at the very least. You have to admit that her presentation's solid."

"Yes. She has impeccable taste. I'm wearing a work of art and a million dollars' worth of jewelry. And being pampered and dressed was a wonderful treat. I'm so grateful. I didn't need all of this."

"I know. Go with it. Enjoy it."

"I need to tip all of those people who helped me get ready."

"No, you don't. Maria pays them all very well. They love working with her because they know she respects them. She's done a good job of creating a space where everyone wins."

"Well, thank you anyway. Thank you, thank you, thank you. I'm overwhelmed with gratitude."

"She knows."

I closed my eyes to bask in the moment. I also acknowledged how the fates had created yet another encounter where I saw another aspect of Michael.

My phone buzzed. Michael had texted me four pictures. The first one was when we'd just gotten to the center of Maria's photography studio. In the picture, he was looking at me, and I was looking off to the side. The second one was when I completed the turn that he'd led me into. We were looking at each other. The third one was when he'd tried to kiss me. I was leaning away from him with a girlish grin on my face. I looked almost shy. His lips were puckered, and I could see the mischief in his eyes. The fourth one was of him kissing my hand. Again, we were looking at each other. It was obvious how much we cared about each other. Michael had created those moments on purpose. What I'd imagined as simply an elaborate dinner was taking on the same intensity as watching him perform.

I looked at him. He was feeling it too.

I asked, "You knew he was taking pictures, didn't you?"

"Yes. He wanted to capture you relaxed and in the moment."

"So you helped him stage it." Michael looked completely natural in all the pictures. It dawned on me how skilled he was as a model.

"Yes." He was secure in his ability to execute his craft.

The car let us out in front of the venue. We played the entrance game. After the photos had been taken, we went in and took our seats. I became fascinated with thinking about all the effort that had gone into creating this awards ceremony and into getting dressed for it.

Michael asked, "What are you thinking about?"

I had to collect my thoughts. My response wasn't really an answer to his question. "How we as humans pool into hierarchical groups and then create ceremonies to confirm our presence and rank in those groups. It's fascinating."

He looked around the room. "It is fascinating. I can't think of a situation for which that's not true." He was right with me.

"I mean, the extent to which we're all adorned and the importance we place on it is intriguing."

He smiled. "I agree."

"What?"

"Nothing. I'm just agreeing with you."

"No. You're laughing at me."

He shook his head. "With you."

I hit him playfully. We were back in our quiet place.

The show started. We settled in for the haul. To my surprise, my film won the best picture award. I got to make an acceptance speech and everything.

I walked right into Greg after I exited the stage.

He said, "Hello, Sammi." At first glance, he was wearing a simple black tux. When you looked more closely, the weave pattern of the fabric was beautiful.

I responded, "Hi, Greg. How are you?"

"Honestly, I miss you."

I could see that he meant it. "This is not the place, Greg." He was also trying to get me to let my guard down.

"I know. I'm sorry, Sammi. That's the most important thing I need to say. You look stunning tonight." He kissed my hand. He bowed as he backed away.

He knew exactly how to piss me off. I was tempted to throw my award at him. Instead, I closed my eyes and counted to ten. The most probable Greg-free zone was in the audience in my seat next to Michael. That was where I'd go.

WHEN THE SHOW ENDED, Michael asked, "Do you want to stay and mingle?"

I responded, "No, I want to leave now."

He looked confused.

"Greg's here. I ran into him backstage."

Michael squinted. "And?"

"And he was himself: charming and posing. I don't want to deal with his bullshit. Let's get out of here."

He looked at his phone. "Okay."

"The thing is, I believe that on some level, he does care about me. He's just so full of shit that it doesn't matter. I don't think I can be friends with him because he's so full of shit. *Aaargh!*" I shook it off. "I'm done. Thank you for your patience."

Michael chuckled. His response was comforting. It made me feel intimate with him.

We got into the car. We didn't say anything on the short ride back to Maria's agency. I basked in our quiet space.

When we arrived back at the agency, it was 10:15 p.m. People were still there though. I thought about it. They must've been doing shoots in the evenings and at night too. The person at reception was expecting us. She directed us into two adjacent dressing rooms on the second floor.

As I was about to enter the one with my things in it, I looked back at Michael, and the truth of how much I loved him winded me. He'd been such a good friend to me and the best lover I'd ever had. I was starting to think maybe "the wait and let it wane" approach wasn't the best one. If I were honest with myself, I couldn't really date anyone else. Based on my experience with Cory, Michael would always be at the forefront of my heart and mind until whatever it was between us had run its course. My will fractured with that truth. The only way to get beyond how I felt about Michael was to open to the inevitable. The quicker I gave in to him having my heart, the quicker he could break it. There was no way his feelings would last. Then I could move on.

He responded with concern. "What's up?" He put his hand on my shoulder.

I looked into his deep, kind eyes. "I no longer have the strength to push you away, Michael."

He guided me into my dressing room. When I saw the stool in the middle of the room, my focus shifted to freeing my feet from the torture of the sandals I was wearing. When my feet were free, I looked back at Michael.

He was leaning on a table not too far away. "Which means?"

"It means that you've been an incredible friend to me, and I love you. I'm in love with you, and I can't resist that truth any longer."

"So what do you want to do about it?"

I swallowed. "I want us to start dating again." All my wards had failed, and I was in free fall.

"Okay."

"But you shouldn't date me exclusively." Maybe I could protect myself a little.

He shook his head. "Is that what you really want, Sammi?" He caught my gaze.

I looked at him for a moment. I willed myself to say yes because it would make me less vulnerable, but the truth came out instead. "No."

"What do you really want?" He kept my gaze, touching my heart with his eyes.

My mouth went dry. I looked away and closed my eyes. I whispered, "I want you to be my man."

He reached out across the space between us and lifted my chin. "Hey. Look at me. I couldn't hear you. Say that again."

I opened my eyes and swallowed. Looking into his eyes, I said, "I want you to be my man."

He smiled. "Say that one more time, please."

I kept his gaze. "I want you to be my man."

"No on again, off again?"

"No."

"You'll let us be a couple and let our relationship evolve as it will?"

"Yes."

"No dating other people?"

"No."

"When you broke off our relationship, you said you were doing it to focus on getting divorced, to keep me from fighting, and to spend some time building out your life. There was another reason. What was it?" He was reading my soul. He wanted me to admit that our connection scared me.

I looked at the ceiling. I'd never admitted that to a guy I was dating or thinking about dating. I'd never let myself be that vulnerable. He was always so fucking close. He already had my heart. I'd already told him I was in love with him and I wanted us to be together. The train was well out of the station. Telling him the truth wasn't going to make it any more intense.

I looked back at him. "The way I feel about you terrifies me."

"Opening to love, relinquishing control like that is terrifying. I understand. It's like fire."

I whispered, "Yes. Like fire."

He brushed my cheek with his thumb. "I'm all in. I want us to be a couple." He pulled me into his arms. "I'm love in with you too, Sammi."

For the first time, I relaxed, truly relaxed, and let myself be held by him. And then I held him too. For the first time in a good while, I let myself take pleasure from the currents of our connection.

I wasn't sure how long we stood there, holding each other, freely experiencing our connection. And I felt his cell phone vibrate again and again and again.

At some point, I realized I was in pain and said, "Ouch."

Michael chuckled. "What's going on, Sammi?"

"This necklace is digging into me. I want to take it off."

He unfastened the necklace for me. I took off the earrings and gave those to him as well.

His cell phone buzzed again.

I said, "You must have plans. You should go."

He shook his head. "I'm right where I want to be."

My phone buzzed in my purse. We laughed.

I whispered, "Me too." I surrendered to our connection. I pulled his head down so I could kiss his forehead, really kiss it, experiencing the feel of his skin with my lips. He kissed my neck. I kissed his left eye. He kissed my left jaw. I kissed his right eye. He kissed my right jaw. I kissed his right cheek. He kissed mine. We kissed each other's left cheek. We touched our lips together and paused. He was touching all of me. I could feel all of him. I kissed his upper lip and then his bottom lip. He purred. I lost myself in his warmth, his scent, and his heartbeat.

I said, "I love you, Michael." I felt him accept it.

"I love you, Sammi." I let that all the way into me too.

I opened my eyes and saw his were also open. I said, "This is intense."

"Yes." He parted my lips with his.

We lingered in that moment for a second before we brought the tips of our tongues to touch. We melted into a sweet, playful, passionate kiss.

He ran his hand across my back, and the clasp of the dress pinched me. I yelped, "Shit. Ouch!"

He burst out laughing.

I explained, "The dress pinched me." Without thinking, I started taking it off. I managed to unzip it, but I couldn't work the clasp.

Michael reached around me and unfastened it without looking.

I didn't dwell. I got the dress off me. As it hit the floor, I realized that the pasties on my breasts were also driving me crazy. I tried to pull them off. They were so sticky that I couldn't get them started.

Michael walked away. I kept trying.

He came back and reclaimed his seat in front of me. "Let me help you." He opened a packet with a wipe in it. He rubbed the wipe on the edge of the pastie and it started to come off. He gently removed both.

It was much better to be free of them. I rested my hands on his shoulders. "You're good at that."

He looked me in the eye and smiled coyly. "Practice." Then he bit his lip and let his attention drift to my body. He skimmed my ribs where the bruises were with the back of his hand. He rested his hands on my hips.

I looked down. I was standing there in a thong. I'd unconsciously undressed in front of him. I said, "I'm sorry. I didn't mean to disrobe in front of you like that."

He caressed my nipples with his thumbs. "It's okay. I'm your man." He took one of my nipples between his teeth and teased it with his tongue.

A current ripped through my body. I loved the way it felt to be touched by him. I held on to his shoulders for support and took it in. It felt so good. I exhaled, and my insides clenched. I'd wanted him intensely. My release overtook me. I gave Michael my weight. When I landed, I was in his arms.

He chuckled. "It's good to know I wasn't the only one that you tortured."

All the screens I'd put up to shield myself from our connection faded. I clearly saw how, despite all my efforts, it had gotten stronger.

He pecked my lips. "I want to make love to you, but not here. Let's get dressed." He put me down so I was standing in front of him.

I responded, "Okay."

I wanted to touch him. I undid his belt and unzipped his pants and slipped my hand inside his briefs. I freed his jewel. I allowed myself to look at him and to feel him in a way I hadn't before when I'd been trying to keep things casual. I skimmed the length of him with my fingertip and softly teased the tip of him.

My touch was affecting him with the same intensity that his touch had affected me. He leaned back onto his arms to support himself. I wrapped my fingers around him and stroked him a few times. His hips pulsed.

I whispered, "We've never really made love either. We need a condom."

"No, we haven't."

He reached into his pocket to take out his wallet while I unbuttoned his shirt. He handed me the condom.

I sat it on the table. I hooked my thumbs into the waistband of his pants and briefs. He stood up long enough for me to take them off.

I said, "Sit farther back."

He complied.

I put the condom on him. I took off the thong I was wearing and climbed up on the table so I was straddling him. I sat on him. Our intimate places were touching each other, but he wasn't inside me. I put my forehead and nose to his. We stayed in that stillness for a moment, looking at each other. When I couldn't resist it anymore, I kissed him deeply, passionately.

Our bodies moved in sync. I needed to feel him. I lifted him slightly and let him inside. Our current took over. This time, I didn't temper how my body wanted to move.

Michael panted, "Aah. Sammi, I ..." He put his hands on my hips and reflected my movement with fierce thrusts. His waltz had evolved into a wind. It was maddening. He came explosively, almost immediately. Feeling him lose control like that was electrifying. His orgasm pulsed through my body and pulled me into orgasm with him. When that passed, we had to wait for our bodies to stop moving together before we could relax. We held on to each other for stability.

When I felt grounded again, I asked, "What were you about to say?"

He smiled. "I was trying to warn you that I had a lot of pent-up boyfriend energy to release. So I was probably going to come as soon as you touched me."

I smiled back. "Yeah."

"My ass is falling asleep."

"And my knees are hurting."

We stood up and hugged each other. I said, "Wow," at the same time he said, "Fuck."

He said, "That doesn't count as making love."

"But it wasn't exactly fucking either, was it?"

He kissed the top of my head. "I really missed you."

I squeezed him closer. "I'm sorry. I just needed space to …"

"I know. I know. I understand." He rocked me in his arms.

"I missed you too."

He whispered, "I know."

We held each other in silence for a while.

He gave me a chaste kiss on the lips. "You do realize that you just took advantage of me."

I chastely kissed him back. "No, I was just finishing what you started."

"Nope." He kissed me again, this time deeper. "I'm not the one who was undressing people."

He had me there. I had to laugh. "I was responding to you. I could tell that you had quite a bit of pent-up boyfriend energy."

He gave me a big smile. "Speaking of. Just so you don't get confused and think that it's about you, this week's going to be all about me working through my pent-up boyfriend energy."

I kissed him sweetly. "So you're going to be selfish and just focus on you. That's what you're saying?" I kissed him again, deeper.

When I released him, he smiled on my lips. "Yes, that's exactly what I'm saying."

"So you'll be taking advantage of me?"

He gave me a quick kiss. "Yes."

"I just want to point out that there's a pattern emerging here."

I kissed him deeply again, and this time, he responded in kind. Our passion rose.

He chuckled. "We should probably get dressed and get out of here before you get carried away again."

"True."

He took three steps back, slipped on his briefs and pants, and went to his dressing room.

I went into the bathroom and put some water on my neck to help me finish calming down. I freshened up my makeup a bit. As my head cleared, I hung up the dress and put the jewelry into the cases that had been provided.

There was a new outfit lying next to my clothes with a note that said, "A gift from Roberto for wearing his dress." It was a minidress and a jacket. The minidress was a more casual version of the gown that I'd worn. The jacket was a short, deep brown blazer. They matched my desert boots perfectly. I collected everything and walked into the hallway.

Michael was waiting for me in the hallway when I exited my dressing room. He was wearing a pair of deep brown jeans and a fitted shirt with an interesting texture. Michael took the gown and jewelry. I followed him downstairs to a desk where we checked it all in.

Both of our cell phones went off at the same time.

Amanda wanted to know how the evening went and when I was coming to Cam's party.

I looked at Michael. "Would you be up for dancing? I'm expected at Cam's party tonight." I smiled, feeling at home.

Michael responded, "I don't see how that's a question."

As we approached his car, Michael folded me into his arms and gave me one of his sweet and present kisses. I gave in and let the world drift away.

When he released me, the reality of the choice I'd made winded me. I had to catch my breath.

He looked concerned. "Promise me that you won't stifle our connection anymore."

"I promise. But I can't promise that there won't be times when I freak out a little. Promise that you'll be patient with me."

"I will." He kissed my knuckles. "I'm not going to betray you, Sammi. I'm in love with you."

I relaxed, leaning into him. I knew he meant it … for as long as that would last.

ABOUT THE AUTHOR

Carrie J. Evans has a few things in common with Sammi Harris, the main character in this book. Like Sammi, Carrie was born and raised in Atlanta. They both attended engineering school for college and then studied dance in New York City. Both are surrounded by accomplished women—and men—and have an eclectic group of truehearted, multiracial friends.

They are geeks who love the art of storytelling: stories about self-aware people who lean into their courage to make their worlds better. Sammi hasn't gotten into romance writing yet, but for Carrie, it's all about the exploration of intimacy, which is the main ingredient in steamy, passionate sex.

instagram.com/authorcarjevs
tiktok.com/@authorcarjevs
pinterest.com/authorcarjevs
facebook.com/authorcarjevs